A MAP FOR THE MISSING

A
MAP
for the
MISSING

———

BELINDA HUIJUAN TANG

Penguin Press
New York
2022

PENGUIN PRESS
An imprint of Penguin Random House LLC
penguinrandomhouse.com

LIBRARY OF CONGRESS CATALOGING-IN-PUBLICATION DATA
Names: Tang, Belinda Huijuan, author.
Title: A map for the missing : a novel / Belinda Huijuan Tang.
Description: New York : Penguin Press, 2022.
Identifiers: LCCN 2021041971 (print) | LCCN 2021041972 (ebook) |
ISBN 9780593300664 (hardcover) | ISBN 9780593300671 (ebook)
Subjects: LCSH: Chinese—United States—Fiction. |
Homecoming—Fiction. | Families—Fiction. | Missing persons—Fiction. |
China—History—1976-2002—Fiction. | LCGFT: Novels.
Classification: LCC PS3620.A6844 M37 2022 (print) |
LCC PS3620.A6844 (ebook) | DDC 813/.6—dc23/eng/20211206
LC record available at https://lccn.loc.gov/2021041971
LC ebook record available at https://lccn.loc.gov/2021041972

International edition ISBN 9780593492963

Printed in the United States of America
1st Printing

Designed by Amanda Dewey

For my waipo

Who, on his own,
Has ever really known who gave him life? . . .
Since you ask me, yes, they say I am his son.

—HOMER, *The Odyssey*

They don't want to create a place for themselves in history:
they want to create themselves.

—WANG ANYI,
The Song of Everlasting Sorrow

Part 1

老家

ANCESTRAL
HOME

———

One

JANUARY 1993

你爸不见了

Translated directly, the words mean *your father can't be seen.*

His mother's voice shouts again—

你爸不见了—

your Ba's gone missing.

He is in his office in the math department of the university, the echo of the phone's ring jarring against the silence of the hall tense with the purposeful air of research. This has never happened before; because of the expense of international calls, he has always been the one to make the calls that would travel the Pacific.

你在吗? she asks.

The shock of hearing her voice and of what she says has rendered him speechless. At last, he forces a sound out of his mouth.

"Yes, Ma. I'm here."

The cratered receiver pressed to his ear, he does a calculation. It is late afternoon in Palo Alto, which means that in China it is hardly even morning. In order to call him, she would have had to rise in the stillness of night and walk the fifteen li to town, leaving the frozen dirt roads of their village, going farther and farther until she reached the township's main avenue, which, even at that hour, would still be dark and quiet, the determination of women preparing their storefronts visible only through shadow. At the forlorn train station, she would have asked one of the half-asleep passengers which direction to board, and then when she reached the city, she'd have to question a stony-faced city dweller to read the signs illegible to her. Not until she reached the telecommunications building almost three hours later would she have been able to finally make the call.

At this realization, his stomach tumbles, down and down. He grasps for the cushioned arm of his desk chair, for its comfort, for its familiarity.

Her words are so frantic that he must take a moment to hold the receiver away from his ear, put it aloft in the empty air. She'd never been shaken of the belief that her voice had to be made very loud in order to travel across a phone line, much less the distance of the Pacific Ocean. The more she yells, the more he begins to fear the entire math department will hear her through his office walls. He stuffs the receiver into the thick sleeve of his sweater to muffle the sound.

Finally, he calms her enough to hear her explain. His father left home two mornings ago, she says, shuffling out of the courtyard with a plastic bag knotted in a bow over his wrist, as if planning on a day trip. He hasn't returned. She assumed he'd merely gone to a nearby village, perhaps to see a relative or an old army friend, but to believe this, she admits, she had to put aside her doubts about why he'd do such a thing. His father hadn't taken a trip out of their village in years.

He inhales deeply. He promises his mother he will come home.

———

He was startled for the second time by the pattering of knuckles against his office door, then the voice calling out, in that tentative tenor he heard so often in America, thick with its awareness of the possibility for intrusion—"Hey?"

Yitian looked up from his hands, twisted until the skin had risen to a red-and-white mottle, and was surprised to find that the light in his office was already softening with the sunset. He hadn't realized it was so late.

Steven Hsiung stood at the doorway, apprehensive, leather messenger bag dangling from his shoulder. On the corner of Yitian's desk, the phone was still dangling off its cord.

"I was about to leave, but I just wanted to pop in and ask if everything is all right? I heard your voice earlier, and I wanted to come check."

"Oh, nothing's wrong." It was obvious by their twin accents—Steven's only becoming audible at the ends of difficult words, Yitian's ever present—that the two of them could have conversed more comfortably in Chinese, but Yitian had followed the lead Steven set when they first met. Steven was an earlier arrival to their department, having come to America from Taiwan about a decade before Yitian. Speaking to their American colleagues, Steven made appropriate jokes at the appropriate times. When he pronounced Yitian's name, the syllables were filtered through Steven's attempt to make them American, and the result was strange, like dough kneaded flat and then remade in an unfamiliar shape. Yitian didn't even know Steven's Chinese name.

When Yitian saw Steven's eyes linger questioningly on the phone receiver, he scrambled to put it back on the cradle.

"My mother called—" It seemed impossible to avoid speaking

about the call now, but he wanted to describe it in the simplest, vaguest terms he could find. "I may need to go back home and help with my father."

Steven looked at him with the same weariness he'd worn the first time they'd met, and then, to Yitian's surprise, strode to the door, nudged it shut with his foot, and set his bag down. The department's practice was to keep their offices open—to foster collegiality, the chair had said gently, when he asked Yitian if he would mind not closing his—so that Yitian often had the sensation of being observed.

Steven sighed and leaned against the desk. "It always happens like this at their age—the call, and then you find out there's some sudden illness. . . ." His Chinese was less refined than Yitian expected.

"It will be fine. The chair is quite flexible with things like this, and he'll help find someone to cover your class for a few weeks, if you need to go. You don't know this yet, but we're actually quite lucky, in this department."

Steven began to tell him of his own mother, who'd suddenly been diagnosed with ovarian cancer two years previously and whom he now had to regularly travel back to Taiwan to care for. Yitian listened dully as he spoke about the hospitalizations, the home aid they'd hired, the emergency trips he had to take back to Taipei, the feeling of heaviness that weighed constantly upon him. This was the most Steven had ever spoken to him, aside from once when he and his wife invited Yitian and Mali over for dinner, an awkward affair where Yitian realized that he had little in common with Steven's elegant family from Taipei who could trace their ancestry all the way back to royalty in the Ming dynasty. Yitian had stayed quiet, only saying that he was from a village in Anhui, then allowing Mali to describe her childhood in a hutong home in Beijing, which he supposed they'd better understand. They'd all spoken English, and Steven's wife had ordered takeout that she had no qualms serving to them directly from their little paper boxes. He understood that he and Mali weren't considered important guests. At the door and saying their goodbyes, there had been insistences that they had to do it again, but no one ever followed up.

Neither then nor now had Yitian been able to tell Steven that he hadn't been back to China since leaving eight years previously, or that he hadn't returned to his own village in fifteen. He feared the questions that would come after the telling—Steven would surely have expressed confusion about why he hadn't been home in so long. He would have assumed that Yitian was a son, part of a family back in that place, *home*, with a set of duties toward his parents. This understanding of obligation as the core of one's being was their shared culture. How could Yitian explain that he'd failed in his fundamental duties to his father for fifteen years, and hadn't even spoken to him in all that time? Steven wouldn't understand.

"It'll be all right," Steven said, finishing his story. Yitian realized he'd hardly listened to a word.

"Thank you," Yitian said.

"Don't worry, okay?" Steven smiled. His eyes crinkled behind his polished glasses, ones that Yitian had seen actors wear in movies from the sixties. Yitian could see that his older colleague felt proud of the advice he'd given, the support he'd shown to a fellow countryman. The easiest thing to do was nod; how could he express that he himself didn't even know what kind of help he needed?

After Steven left, Yitian stuffed all his papers into his backpack and headed to his car. Normally he took the scenic 280 home, but today, he eschewed the long way and jostled alongside the traffic on the industrial 101 so that he could get home quickly and ask Mali about what to do next.

He was disappointed when he unlocked the door and found a message she'd left on the answering machine, saying that her boss had asked her to stay late. Mali did data entry for a real estate agent whom she referred to as Mrs. Suzanna, who lately had been training her to take on her own sales. Mrs. Suzanna had been the only one willing to employ her years ago when she had no work visa, and Mali could never refuse her requests.

He flipped open their address book, searching for someone else to whom he could speak. He couldn't call his mother; she wouldn't know to be waiting for the phone at the village office. Calling their friends, Junming and Meifang, would require that storytelling and recalling. No, the only person who wouldn't ask for explanations was Mali. He sat at the dining table, directly facing their front door, and stared at the decorative plastic ivy she'd strung over the entrance. To give the home warmth, she'd said. She always thought of things like that when he couldn't. When they'd moved into the home, looking at the neutral stucco walls, beige and sand and camel shades whose names he couldn't keep apart, he'd been pummeled suddenly by overwhelming loneliness, so strong it paralyzed him. He hadn't known whether she sensed his feeling or had the same one herself, but either way, she'd been the one to say, let's put in some pictures of our families, let's buy some leafy plants to decorate. And it had worked; the house began to feel like a home. Her suggestions always worked. He knew he wouldn't be able to make sense of what his mother had told him until he could speak about it with her.

She found him staring blankly at the doorway and immediately she came to him, dropping the thick stack of paperwork she'd lugged home with her. Only after she'd pulled out the chair across from him, leaned her elbows upon the table, and took his hands into hers did he begin to parse his mother's story.

"So what will you do?" she asked.

"I said I would go back," he said.

When he'd told his mother this, it was without conscious choice. Instinct drove him to urgency. She'd been yelling; he was a son and his father was missing.

"Will you?" He looked in her eyes and saw that she hadn't been expecting his answer.

"You don't want me to go?"

"It's not that. I just think it's not so strange, right? To leave and go on a trip. Old people forget to tell others these things, sometimes. He can't have gone so far."

He looked across the table at her face, searching for some hope that he could latch on to and steal for himself. She seemed so certain as she reassured him—but she was always so certain, he realized.

"It would be a big trip for you." She bit her lip. "And I wonder if by the time you get there, he'll already be back."

"Maybe." Mali's practicality and optimism didn't have their usual effect tonight. Over the years he'd told her so little about his father, keeping the terms vague enough that she knew about the estrangement but not its reason. She thought this was a simple matter of an old man traveling in his later years to see friends. But his father hadn't left the village in years, never breaking the outline of that circumscribed space where things were familiar to him, which protected him from the dangers he'd seen of the world outside.

"I didn't mean I don't want you to go," she said, and he could see that she felt she'd misstepped. She'd gone to see her family in Beijing twice since they'd come to America, each time with excitement and a suitcase packed full of gifts. "If you think it would help—of course you should go."

While she warmed up leftovers in the microwave, she called the airline to purchase the tickets.

"One way. What's the earliest available?" She knit her eyebrows together. "Are you sure there isn't anything sooner? It's a family emergency." A pause. "Okay. Book that." He wouldn't have been able to summon such precise English at a time like this. One hand checking the food's temperature, another twisting her finger around the cord of the receiver cradled against her ear. How was she so practiced, so calm? He was overtaken by sudden gratitude.

She hung up the phone and balanced dishes in both hands as she brought them to the table. "Tomorrow afternoon at four, there's a flight leaving from SFO. Connecting through Seoul. I booked it for you. You'll be home the next day. All good?"

He nodded. *Home.* Her words, not his.

Perhaps if Yitian and his father spoke, he would have been able to piece together a story for where his father might have gone, but he didn't know what shape his father's life might have taken in the fifteen years since they'd last seen each other.

In bed beside Mali that evening, he couldn't make himself sleep. They'd purchased an ultraplush mattress for his benefit, as he often had trouble at night, but Mali swore she could fall asleep anywhere.

Tonight the softness discomfited him. In the darkness he lay awake and tried to imagine what his father's body and face would look like after all the time that had passed. He looked into the shadows of their bedroom and tried to fill in his father's features, piece by piece. He began with the eyes. He could not imagine them ever giving up their opacity. The eyelids that drooped over them acted like a blanket for the pupils, dark as wet soil after a rainstorm. Even in Yitian's childhood, those eyes seemed to belong to a man much older. On rare occasions when his father laughed, the heavy lids made it impossible to tell if the smile reached upward.

Then the mouth, which he remembered mostly by the recoil he'd felt whenever his father opened it and the harsh words strung themselves out. Inside was the damp smell of rot, something Yitian was only able to name after leaving the village. His father never once in his entire life had brushed his teeth.

Yitian rose from bed. He craved a piece of paper upon which he could follow thoughts to their conclusions. He felt unsettled by Mali's quiet breathing and suddenly missed the noisy nights of his earlier life, when his sleep was punctuated by the rumbling sounds of others.

In his study, he clicked on the desk lamp and then extracted a single sheet of white paper from the drawer. The bulb's light cast oblong shadows on the smooth eggshell surface, upon which he began doing what he knew best—sketching out a model:

Let f(x) be the time in China (in hours),
x hours after midnight where

$$\{x : x \in \mathbb{R}, 0 \leq x < 24\}$$

then f(x) is a function defined by:

$$f : x \mapsto (x + 16)$$

*and g(y) is my father's activity at y hours in Tang Family Village,
defined partially by the following diagram:*

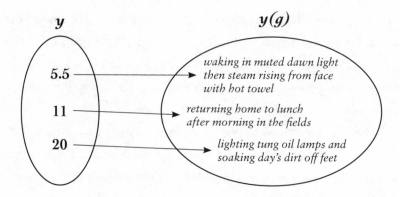

*then g(f(x)) gives my father's activity at California time x,
with the codomain of*

g(y)={set of activities my father does in Tang Family Village}

The smooth flow of his pencil stopped. He couldn't push past the mapping of the functions, which were confined to the particular space enclosed by the village's borders—two square kilometers lined on one side by the embankment and fields on the other. He couldn't make the range of the equation stretch to the artery of road that reached out of the village's northwest corner, the one that could lead a person away from the place they'd always known as home. Anyway, who knew whether these functions were still true? He hadn't allowed himself to picture his home in years. Whenever he was tempted, he told himself he needed to focus on this new life in America and all that needed to be learned here. Sad memories could only be intrusions. Still, he'd imagined his homecoming as more triumphant, his father at the scene, ready to see all Yitian had made for himself in America and how he'd finally erased the mistakes of the past.

Yitian turned off the lamp and returned to their bed just as the first lights of dawn were beginning to spread in the sky outside.

By the time Mali helped him pack the next morning, something within him had fled. He sat directly on the floor next to his suitcase while she thumbed through the items inside. When she released shirts from their hangers and asked him what he wanted to bring, he found he couldn't even guess what kinds of clothes he'd need.

"How cold does it get around this time of year, over there? Will this be enough?" she asked.

"More than enough, I think." He folded a last pair of trousers and added them in, mostly to have a feeling of contribution. The suitcase was still only half filled, full of loose room between the items inside.

"I'm going to get some stuff from my office," he said, rising.

He dislodged the stickiest, bottom drawer of his desk and extracted the only item there, a brown airmail envelope covered with stamps measuring the distance it had traveled. Sometimes, when he couldn't sleep at night, he would come to this desk, open the letter, and read it again. He would summon the past and wonder what would have happened in another version of it, if he hadn't said goodbye to Hanwen, the first woman he'd loved. He wouldn't have had that word then, *love*; that came later, when he'd come to America and picked up the language that insisted on putting names to every feeling.

Now, he flattened the letter inside the first textbook he saw. An old love pressed inside *Introduction to Topology*. It was the only thing animating the textbook. None of his students this semester had showed much interest in his class, and writing out his lecture notes was a chore bringing little reward.

"It's amazing that you can still think of work at a time like this," Mali said, when he returned to the bedroom and packed the book, lifting the other layers of soft fabric and pressing it down between them, so he knew it would be kept safe.

Two

TANG FAMILY VILLAGE, ANHUI PROVINCE

He could sense he was home before he opened his eyes. He no longer needed sight; he could tell time as he once used to, by feel and by sound—if the darkness was weakly transparent with the coming of dawn, or carts were already beginning their low roll on the road outside, if wives were calling to wake their husbands and children, then it was already past six and soon his mother would be upon him to collect manure for the fertilizer pit. Otherwise, he could stay in bed with his grandfather for a few moments longer.

He opened his eyes to the sight of the village's welcoming pine through the taxi's glass. Its branches bowed down in their familiar arc of greeting and were bare as they'd been on the day of his last departure. He could have pretended that only a day had passed.

He rolled down the window to see more clearly.

"What are you doing?" the taxi driver exclaimed. "It's freezing!"

Yitian ignored him. The sensation wasn't unpleasant and shocked him into the alertness he would need when he saw his mother again. He hadn't slept at all on the plane ride out from San Francisco, nor on the turbulent connection through South Korea and in the rocking train compartment he shared with eight others that took him from Shanghai to Anhui. At last, after crawling into the cab for the last leg of the journey—he'd justified the expense by telling himself it would have taken hours to decipher the bus system—he'd been seized by a fatigue so great that he could not even open his mouth to answer the driver's questions about why he was going so far out in the countryside. He'd fallen asleep to the sight of the construction and upcoming buildings of Hefei City and awoken to the familiar landscape of his childhood.

The sky outside was oppressively gray with winter. As the car ambled down the unpaved main road, he squinted down the narrow alleyways, trying to make out the houses he'd once known. The exteriors were of the same material, made of bricks and the mud adhering them, but under the snow blanketing roofs and the hanging icicles, the outlines of homes were much taller than they'd once been. And yet the place looked smaller than he remembered. As they passed one home on a corner, he was so surprised at the scene he glimpsed behind the half-ajar courtyard doors that he thought he was dreaming. There, in the house: a square television perched on top of a shabby dresser.

"Where do I go, boss?" the driver asked.

They'd reached the end of the road, but still Yitian had not seen the roof with cracked tiles that always told him where to turn.

"I must have missed it," he said. "Can you turn back?"

At each alley opening, he saw only layers and layers of neat eaves, all unbroken, all well kept. All the while, the meter's glaring red digits trickled up.

"Just let me out here. I'll walk," he said.

His shoes slipped against the snow as he trudged through each of the alleys. He began to wish that he had allowed Mali to pack him more clothes when she'd asked. The wind insinuated itself between the layers of fabric covering him and rendered the protection useless. He hadn't experienced cold like this in years, out there in California where there was never any real winter. Even here, a winter storm this fierce was rare and seemed to write a foreboding into his father's disappearance. He hoped that, wherever his father had gone, he was wearing his thickest clothing and had found a way to be indoors.

At last he saw it. He'd missed the turn before because there wasn't any broken roof to be found. The single-story brick and mud home of his childhood had been heightened, covered with concrete, and whitewashed. He'd walked by this house two or three times, but only now could he recognize the older structure hiding beneath. It stood apart, the kind of home villagers could walk by and point at, whispering under their breath, "Now, *those* people— *they're* rich."

The thought made him proud. It was the money he'd sent back twice a year that had built it. Even when he and Mali had first moved to America and partitioned out each week's spending down to the smallest change, he'd mailed a check to his mother. Sometimes the amount had seemed hardly worth the postage required; other times, Mali showed him how little they had for themselves and pleaded with him to keep a little more. She held out her palms, upside down, open-faced, to say, *nothing*. He hadn't known how to respond. He couldn't make sense of care as a thing that had to be compared and doled out in portions between those he loved.

He hesitated, shivering at the door with his hand on the knocker. He leaned his head close to the new wood, half expecting to hear his father's booming voice emanating from within, once again drunk too early in the day. He would step out the door, shaking off the dregs of alcohol, and tell Yitian this thing about a disappearance had all been a joke, made up because he'd finally forgiven him and wanted to lure him home. Then his mother would emerge, too, brushing her hands on her apron and apologizing for her part in the deception. They would embrace and agree that the trick had been worth the cost.

No sound came from behind the wood. He pushed upon the iron ring at last. The door yawned open.

"Is anybody home?" he called into the empty courtyard. He was surprised to hear his voice coming out in their old dialect, through no effort of his own.

His mother's body had rounded out, thickening in the middle and through the chest, bones parting and relaxing to make space for new flesh. Her head bobbed near his shoulders as she patted his arms by way of greeting, as if only the evidence of her hands upon his body could make his physical presence certain. She was shorter than he remembered, though this new image was much closer to how he always thought she should look, the firmness of her body matching the strength of her movements and speech.

"What happened to you!" was the first thing she said. "I thought you were coming days ago!"

"The flight here is long, Ma."

"Did you eat? I killed a chicken last night because I thought you would be back already. I'll warm the food up. How much did you pay for the taxi?" She rushed about the house, boiling water, taking his bag from the floor into the bedroom, each time she walked away from him returning in mere seconds with another question.

Where to begin? There was his father's disappearance, but there was also this—his mother, her solidity in front of him, for the first time in years.

He walked around the house as she boiled water for tea. The

familiar air came back to him, the scent of garlic and dust and work. The rooms were as neat as she'd always kept them. The walls were still lined with shelves of clay pickling jars, hanging knives and cutting boards, old calendars that stretched as far back as the eighties. A fraying poster in the center of the room showed mountain scenery, magically blurred, from a place they'd never go. He was struck, now, by the house's frank utility, so different from his American home that valued privacy and separation. He'd been so confused the first time he'd heard that American phrase, *living room*, because all the real parts of living, of a life—the cooking, eating, sleeping—seemed to be pushed elsewhere behind yet another wall or door. The real *living* room, though they would never have called it that, was this room, in this old home.

He sat down with his mother to drink the tea. At this table in the center of the room, he felt short against the high wooden surface. She sat stiffly on the wooden bench, refusing to allow herself to relax into the room. He realized suddenly that, for the past few days, his mother would have been living alone in this house, the first time she'd ever been alone in her life.

"Ba—" he began. Immediately her eyes welled. "Have you heard anything new?"

She shook her head. "Everyone in the village knows. They've told people in the township. I've tried to spread the word. No one has heard anything." She worried the string of her apron. "What did your father do to deserve this?"

"We'll find him." His reassurance sounded false, even to his own ears. He knew nothing about the person his father had become in these years. He didn't know how the country operated now. There wasn't anything he could do in a practical sense, and he wondered why he'd come, what he'd thought he'd be able to help with. The few hours he'd been back had already made it clear to him how much the boundaries of the place had expanded, creating more anonymity and spaces where one could become lost.

"I've been trying to make a plan. Can we go to the police first?" he asked.

"The police!"

"We could file a report. They could help us."

"Do you think that's what they do? If you went in there without a problem, you'd be sure to leave with one. You've really spent too much time in America."

"Don't you think they might be able to call other towns, at least?"

She scoffed. "What do you think they're up to in there? Making phone calls, doing work?"

"Do you have any other ideas?" When she didn't reply, he said, "I think we should go to town and file a report, if nothing else. At least they'd be able to get a record of it down. You never know. Do they still have that truck in the team office?"

"If you go around calling it that, people will laugh at you. It's the village office now."

He felt so patently aware of his unbelonging. He was about to ask her what other names were new, how else he could hide his foreignness, when he was interrupted by the sounds of footsteps in the courtyard. He jumped up from his bench. Mali had been right. It had only been a matter of time before his father would return.

"Why, it's you!" A man, diminutive and bouncy on his toes, poked his head around the doorway. He was much shorter than Yitian's father, his voice loud in the same way his father could be but with gregarious ease rather than the sternness of one who demanded to be heard.

"Oh," Yitian said. He swallowed his heartbeat and crossed his arms over his chest, hoping that no one would notice the anticipation that had animated his entire body. Moments like this were rarer now, but each one overtook him suddenly and with certainty—the way a particular man held tension in his shoulders at the gas station; driving down the highway, how a construction worker leaned against his truck and his chin cast a shadow upon the prickled skin of his neck. He'd see, in seconds, the flash of a vision of his father, hunched over a weed he picked at in the ground, how he held his limp leg when he leaned against his wall for a minute of rest. A shudder would run through Yitian's body. An accidental gesture enough to return him to an earlier time completely.

Still, this man's face was familiar. Yitian concentrated, trying to place the features he sensed underneath the aged skin.

"You remember me, don't you?"

"Don't be silly! How could he forget his Second Uncle?" his mother said.

That was it. There, obscured by wrinkles, was the mischievous face he'd once known, belonging to one of his father's only friends, if he could be called that—Second Uncle Tang. Yitian had mostly seen his features lit dimly by lamplight on evenings when Second Uncle played cards or drank with his father, their laughs boisterous throughout the home where all the other occupants tried to step around them. During the daytime, Second Uncle had always been mysteriously missing. Their nickname for him was "Idon'tknow" for the words his wife said whenever the team came looking for him.

"Someone mentioned an out-of-towner bringing a nice suitcase through the snow. I came to ask your mother if she knew anything."

His mother brought out tea and sunflower seeds for them, then settled herself on a three-legged stool by the doorway, rubbing her kneecaps. She never sat at the table when male guests came.

"I can't believe it. Our most famous villager, Tang Yitian, returning home. You must be back because of what happened with your father, right?" Second Uncle shook his head. "What a strange thing . . ."

"Do you have any ideas?" Yitian asked. "You must have seen him the most, other than Ma."

"To be honest, we hadn't seen each other as much these past few years. He'd become—" he hesitated and looked toward Yitian's mother.

"Lonely," she finished. "He liked to be alone more, now."

Of all the words she could have used, *lonely* was a strange choice. The idea of loneliness implied a need for others. His father had never even demonstrated a feeling much simpler, that of regard. He played cards and drank with Second Uncle because they were activities *he* enjoyed. If he greeted neighbors passing in the alleyway, that was only because this was their instinct in the village.

"It doesn't sound like Ba to be lonely."

"People change," Second Uncle shrugged. "Look at me—I wasted so many years of my life before! Drinking, playing cards. I could have had a different life. But *you*," he waved his hands at Yitian, "*you* always knew what to do with your life. Your father was wrong about you, you know. We can all see that now."

Yitian demurred.

"Always so humble. You bring us all to shame, Tang Yitian."

Yitian could see that his mother's back had straightened with pride.

"Your mother had an idea," Second Uncle said. "Didn't you?"

"Oh, I'm not sure about that . . ." She shook her hand and returned her gaze to her knees.

"You have an idea, Ma? I thought you said you didn't."

She flattened herself against the wall as she spoke, shy as a school-girl. "Well, I don't know. But I was thinking, the only other place your father lived outside of the village was those army barracks. He used to talk about his life there so much. Maybe he wanted to go see it again, now that he was old. See how it might have changed."

"Had he talked about going there recently?"

"Not going there, but he did tell the old stories. He was always telling them."

"I heard that place closed down now," Second Uncle said.

"It did, but the buildings are still there. Maybe he just wanted to see them."

His mother's theory suggested someone more sentimental than the father Yitian had known. Still, he had no other ideas, and at least pursuing this one would allow him the feeling of momentum, much preferable to the helplessness of sitting in this home.

"All right," he said. "We'll go to the police station and then see about visiting the barracks."

"The police?" Second Uncle said.

"*He* thinks going to the police will be helpful."

Second Uncle laughed, slapping his knees. What did they know? Yitian thought. His mother couldn't even read, and Second Uncle would always be the town drunk, whatever he might have said he'd become. The idea of wandering across the province alone, with no authority to help him, scared Yitian. He couldn't imagine going that far without first making some report, some record.

"Fine, then. We can go after lunch," his mother said. She asked Second Uncle if he would stay but he shook his head. "Second Aunt is already preparing food." He turned to Yitian and said, "You should come see her while you're here, if you find yourself with any time."

"Yes, it's been so long since you've seen her. We'll come tomorrow," Yitian's mother said.

"I'm not sure we can. It's going to be busy with Ba—" He was silenced by the hurt look on Second Uncle's face.

"Right, right, of course. You're a busy man now," Second Uncle said.

After they were sure Second Uncle had gone out of earshot, his mother snapped back at him. "How could you have been so rude? Did they teach you in America to talk to others like this?"

He'd forgotten how much they cared about good manners in this world, allowing concerns of etiquette to overwhelm urgency and logic. Even if it was true that he was only concerned for his father, he shouldn't have voiced such a thought out loud. He should have agreed to come and then never shown up—that would have been more acceptable. In America, he was sure there would be no regard toward politeness at a moment like this. Neither would his father have worried about telling a guest to leave if there was something more important to deal with. His father was direct in his speech, his own wants coming before all else. On nights when he drank too much, he simply rose and—without a second glance to any of the guests he'd invited—lay down in his bed. Sometimes he even forgot to kick off his slippers, and they dangled dangerously from his toes as he slept. Yitian's mother was the one left with the task of saying goodbye to the guests, making the situation acceptable for the version that would be later repeated as gossip around the village.

"I'm sorry, Ma. It's just that I don't know how long I can stay." He went to the sink where she was rinsing cups. He almost took her wet hand in his, the way he might comfort Mali. But his body had absorbed a heaviness now that the initial commotion had settled, the weight of their traditions that dictated one's body should be held at a distance from others. Touch couldn't be relied on for comfort.

"You don't know how long you can stay? Why not?"

"I talked to the head of my department—" He stopped himself. She wouldn't understand if he explained about needing to return to his job or the concept of limited leave. He'd lied to the chair, saying his father had just been diagnosed with a serious illness. The chair, an old man who hadn't produced any significant research in decades, had told him to take as much time as he needed.

His mother turned off the water and asked, "Is Mali's health still good?" She'd tried to make her voice casual and low, but still he could tell that this was the question she had been waiting to ask. She'd spoken the same words on the phone almost every time he called. If they had access to a truer language, he knew what she would say. Why had Mali still not given her a grandchild? Sometimes he heard Americans his age joking about how desperately their parents wanted grandchildren. He commiserated, though what they spoke of was nothing like his mother's own want, deeper and more primary. When his parents had been married this long, both Yitian and his brother were old enough to start school. Conception had seemed like a natural rhythm of the world back then, mysterious but inevitable, not the opaque and ungiving process it was now. "We're waiting until things are more stable here," he'd told his mother, when he and Mali first moved to America. When he looked at how much money they had left each month after rent and groceries and the car loan, he could not fathom how to make it stretch any further. "We'll start soon," he'd said to his mother then, as if having a child was a matter as simple as beginning one's homework. He'd been able to brush off the initial difficulties with conception as momentary bad luck, but now two years had passed and they could no longer evade their growing doubts. The referral to the fertility clinic had been stuck to their refrigerator for months, still untouched.

He pretended to be ignorant to the euphemisms behind his mother's questions. In the absence of his complicity, he knew his mother wouldn't ever say directly that she wanted a grandchild. He only ever said that Mali was doing well. This was the habit they all had, so ingrained as to be almost instinctual, to hide any information that could cause worry. Even with Mali, they avoided speaking about their difficulties together beyond the logistics of doctor's appointments. The last time they'd been hopeful, over a year ago now, he'd returned home from work one day to find her in the bathroom, sitting on the closed toilet seat, crying because her period had come. He could not remember the last time he'd seen her cry. She seemed ashamed, first burying her face in her hand and then pushing him out, closing the door so that he could only speak to her from the other side.

"It's all right. It's not that important to me that we have a child," he'd said to the door's blank face. It was true—inertia, not desire, had driven him to go to all of those doctor's appointments, a sense that having a child was the way a life would progress.

"But it is important to me." She'd opened the door and he'd seen there was anger on her face. "Can't you see that?"

"Look at me," his mother said to him now. "Once I was the strongest woman out in the fields." She held out her arm to him. "But I've gotten clumsy these last few years. A few weeks ago, my hand slipped while I was cutting grass for the furnace. Imagine! I would never have made such a mistake before."

She'd left out this story of hurting herself from their weekly phone calls. When she raised her hand, he could see a bumpy white scar running beside her etched lifeline. He was struck by how rough her palm looked. All his own callouses had long since flaked away, leaving him soft and unprotected.

"That's why it's lucky that I have a son like you, who sends me money. Otherwise, who would be here to look after me in my old age? Think about that for your own future. It's so important to have children." She sighed. "Even though our lot has been unlucky, Heaven has made up for it with you."

He didn't need to look to know she was staring at the space above the wardrobe, where the black-and-white portrait of his brother hung alongside his grandfather's, both flanked with fresh incense and offerings of apples and tangerines. She had been conscientious. His mother wouldn't call herself religious, but rather argue that it was better to respect all the sources of life and luck that one could.

In the photo, his brother hadn't yet lost the baby fat that would later reveal a strong jaw and lead others to call him handsome. By the time of his death, the skin had darkened and coarsened over his cheeks and forehead, the first layers of a toughness that would have fully hardened with a few more years and turned him into the man they'd been denied. Next to Yishou's portrait, their grandfather's picture was older and faded from exposure to sunlight. Yitian could see the learnedness written in the uneven whiskers drooping from his chin and the bright, thinking glow of his eyes. Even in the dusty tones, the man in the photo appeared ready to open his mouth and pontificate on a minor point of imperial history at any moment. The two portraits, placed side by side, were a strange sight, one that had hardly ever realized itself in the world outside. His brother and grandfather had never spoken much to one another, not out of animosity, but because of a difference in the way they moved through and thought about the world. It was Yitian who was his grandfather's favorite.

Yitian searched his mother's face. She looked like a weary visitor in her own home. There were many things she could have blamed him for, but there was no accusation written for him in her expression. He wished there was. Blame would have been easier to live with than forgiveness.

Time to eat," his mother said, lifting the lid from the steaming wok.

She glanced at an item on the shelf, one he hadn't noticed until now. Beside the jars, there was a small wooden stand-up clock, its face shiny and clear, surrounded by carved orchids blooming around the glass.

"You need a clock now, Ma? We always thought you had one inside your head." She'd used to keep time by the sun.

"I have it so I know when to wait for your call."

Of course—it was the only place she would need to go, the only instance in which time wasn't the relative and flexible concept of the village. He called her every other Sunday at eight, when it was four in the afternoon the previous day in America. She must have had one of the neighbors' children draw a diagram of what the long and short hands looked like at the correct numbers, amongst the few written symbols she could decipher.

"I bought it with some of the money you sent back."

She set down the plate of braised chicken onto the table, but he thought of something else.

"Let's eat outside." He used his chopsticks to place pieces of chicken into his bowl of rice, cradled it to his chest and with three fingers of the other hand balanced the pickled vegetables. His mother followed behind him. They stepped through the courtyard. He brushed snow off the slabs of stone around the doorsill and squatted down. All around him there was the rising smell of smoke from people cooking in their homes. How many meals had he eaten like this, sitting with Yishou? Watching the men coming home from the fields with their hoes angled over their shoulders and shouting out greetings. Soon others would come out and squat at their doorsills, too. There would be chatting but also long silences like the one he and his mother sat in now—observing, at this hour, the supremacy of the meal over all else. This, too, its own form of intimacy.

Three

OCTOBER 1977

Yitian sat on an old wooden stool in their storage shed and watched his grandfather die. He'd come to this place for months, sitting amongst the rusted tools and dried grain of the harvest, reading books as he listened to his yeye's shallow breath. They had still been able to converse in the early days of the illness, but as the months grew on, Yitian could no longer deny death's creeping maw. Many years later, in a forgotten corner of a university library, he would stumble upon an entry for liver cancer on the thin paper of a medical dictionary and find his grandfather's final days described succinctly in bullet points, but at that moment, what had happened was still a mystery. They'd called the barefoot doctor so many times that the house had smelled like bitter medicinal herb for months, but still his grandfather's eyes had yellowed like used sunlight and his skin drained gray.

Yitian reached every few minutes to rub his grandfather's cold feet underneath the padded cotton blankets. He had accidentally brushed those feet every night while sleeping on the narrow wooden pallet he and his grandfather had shared for seventeen years. His brother, Yishou, slept on a mat at the floor of their mother's bed to protect her if an intruder ever came. At night, their four atonal breaths beat different tempos, like four different songs played at the same time. Then his grandfather had become ill and they moved him to the shed, so there were only three voices left. Yitian hadn't heard one of his grandfather's stories in months. When he lay in bed alone at night, he felt as if his body were missing its most important skin.

Yitian heard the first story on a summer evening when he was six, the same year his mother cut off his childhood braid. He'd been thrashing against his grandfather's body for hours in the humid night air. It was already long past midnight when he felt his grandfather's wrinkled palms clasping his legs together to stop his fidgeting.

"Have I ever told you the story of the first Yellow Emperor?" his grandfather asked.

Yitian tapped his foot against the bamboo mat.

"It's the most important story of our people, the one you must learn!" His grandfather began to recite. "On the top of Longevity Hill, at the highest spot lightning always finds, the Yellow Emperor was born. He was the son of a farmer, from an ordinary family. In the land, there were six extraordinary beasts, plaguing their tribe . . ."

After thirty minutes, his grandfather said, "I am too old and tire easily. I must continue the story tomorrow."

Yitian hadn't noticed how much time had passed. He'd been too absorbed to move, afraid that if he so much as rustled he'd be unable to hear his grandfather's story. He'd forgotten the itchy mosquito bites, his hair sticking to his hot forehead, the warm air that felt like it would never cool. He was still wide awake and wanted to hear more. He could picture so clearly the Yellow Emperor as he devised a plan, the first in all the land, to defeat the beasts. He wanted desperately to know what happened next and whether the emperor succeeded.

"Please," he begged.

"If you go to sleep, tomorrow evening I will tell you another part of the story."

The next evening, Yitian remembered the promise. His grandfather continued, telling him of how the Yellow Emperor taught the people to build shelters and tame cattle, bringing new prosperity to the tribe.

"What happened next? Was there any more trouble?"

"I will tell you tomorrow," his grandfather said. He yawned loudly and turned to his side.

Eight days after he began, his grandfather finished the story of the Yellow Emperor. Then he began the tale of the emperor's successor, the Great Yu. A month later, they entered the Han Dynasty. This way, in three hundred and sixty-five evenings, they moved through four thousand and seventy years of history.

They kept going until his grandfather finished the five thousand years contained in the *Twenty-Four Histories*, volumes that he'd memorized as a matter of safety. It was gambling to rely on words stored on paper, his grandfather said. Books could be destroyed: a small army—sometimes Japanese, more often Chinese, your own people finding it easiest to stage a betrayal—could tear through a village, conscript the men to march farther with them, leaving the fields intact but piling all the books to be burned. Even those illiterate men knew how powerful words could be. For hundreds of years, histories and stories had burned, new ones then created and written down only to be burned again. His mind was the only place where words could truly be kept safe. He wanted to pass them down to Yitian so that they could continue to exist in the mind of another. Like water poured between cups, so the tales would remain safe for the next generation.

When he finished the country's history, his grandfather began to tell Yitian of their own. Eight hundred years ago, his distant ancestors had first come to this land by way of dry Henan. They traveled until they reached the Changjiang Delta, where they saw the soil become dark and wet. This was back when people made their own roads by walking and there were still such things as new places. They walked until they saw holly ferns giving way to leopard flowers. Coming down a hill into the valley below, they raised dust, and when the fine mist settled they put their things down and stayed. It was springtime then, and so they saw fortune in the dove trees blossoming white and the real doves flying above and the quiet tributary water trembling in the wind that had eroded for itself a road that ran through the green land. For the next twenty-three generations, the descendants of their people planted and lived by this land, sometimes as rich as the day they arrived, more often dry for long stretches, sometimes years. Still, it was their land. Had they continued walking for a few more months, they would have made it to the fertile coast, where much later the most prosperous cities in the country would announce themselves. Luck, instead, had led them here.

This was the most significant event they named in their clan history, etching this story upon steles and storing it in their ancestral temples. The stones kept the tale safe for hundreds of years, until the campaigns came, whose mission was to erase the old history and make a new one for their own use.

Yitian listened to his grandfather's cautionary stories of the dangers facing the books and felt an urgent need to save them. He wanted to leap out of bed and build a fortress to protect them. His approach became more practical as he grew older: he listened carefully to every word his grandfather spoke so that he would not miss a single one. On the long walk to school and when he worked alone in the fields, he repeated the stories to himself under his breath. He would keep the tales safe; he would not let his grandfather down. He had ample opportunity to memorize—by the time of his grandfather's illness, they'd traveled through history together four and four-fifths times over.

He'd often heard from other villagers that his grandfather did not look like a farmer. He was so thin, and folded his arms behind him and grasped his elbows in both hands as he walked, not at all like the strides, both forceful and meandering, of people on their way to work. Once, a village woman had found a padded scholar's robe deep in some forgotten corner of her home and given it to his grandfather as a joke. After he slipped his arms through the sleeves, however, he had such a look of authority that no one dared to laugh. Only Yitian privately said, "You look like you belong in the universities in Beijing!" But he was glad that his grandfather was here in their small village, even if it meant the failure of the dreams his grandfather had held in his own youth, of being a scholar in the capital. Besides, he did not think it was true that his grandfather didn't have the traits of a farmer. At night when he looked at his grandfather's body, he could see the lean of it, sinew fitting into muscle that covered bone. But after months of sickness, even those wispy tendons had dissolved into nothing.

When Yitian laid his palm on the bony chest and found it still, his first thought was how much time had passed since his grandfather's last breath. It had gone unnoticed, a common leaf falling against a full October pile. He reached out to touch his grand-father's palm, finding it already ice-cold. I have sat here, he thought, but what is the evidence of my care?

He did not call his mother or brother. Instead, he got under the blankets and lay next to his grandfather. He put his head near his grandfather's feet, as they'd always slept. His mother and brother found him like this when they came to check on him. The top blanket had been a wedding gift to his parents, years ago. His tears had made a damp spot right at the place where the character for prosperity was stitched in shiny red thread.

His mother checked his grandfather's body, while Yishou lifted Yitian up from under the covers.

"Come," Yishou said.

Yitian felt the gentle tug of his brother's hand on his wrist, then another firm hand holding up his back. He allowed himself to be pulled by his elbow and guided into the home. Yishou seated him at one of the wooden benches. Yitian sat in a daze as his brother col-lected and boiled water from the barrel. He did not realize how cold he was until the steam rose from the red bricks of the stove and warmed the room—but he couldn't have been shivering from the cold, because he'd been lying under the covers all this time. He was shocked when he felt the hot rag over his face, then Yishou's hands rubbing through the fabric at his eyes and nose to soften and dissolve the snot that had collected there.

Yishou finished washing his face and left quietly. Yitian felt grate-ful, for both the gentleness and the leaving afterward. He wanted to experience his sadness alone. Yishou hadn't cried at their grandfa-ther's death, and he would not have understood how strongly Yitian felt—no, the only person who truly understood him in his family had been his grandfather, whose stories had told Yitian of a world beyond this small one. Yitian thought of the stories with a stronger sense of resolve than any he'd felt since the very first night he'd heard them. Keeping them alive was his responsibility to his grandfather, the only thing Yitian had left of him now.

Four

All afternoon, Yitian had waited at the embankment on the highest point of the slope, watching hopefully for Hanwen down the horizon line. They usually met here Friday afternoons, but the last week was his grandfather's death. He'd missed her all the following week and wanted nothing more than to talk to her now, but sometimes in the busy season she wasn't able to leave the production team.

He looked down at the sacks of peanuts he'd brought, his excuse when his mother had asked him where he was going—"I'm going to finish my work outside," he'd said, hoping that his grandfather's recent death might allow him more room for decisions his mother would find strange. They'd observed the traditional mourning period after the death, and today his mother had given him the burlap bag of peanuts straight from harvest and said it was time to return to work.

It was sunset now, and he realized with a start how little he'd done. He began to work hurriedly, pulling at the clumps of veiny peanuts in his hand, not stopping to edge out the dirt that gathered under his fingernails or to shake off the excess loam that lingered in the crevices of the shells. Had his mother seen how he was working, she'd surely have scolded him. In his father's absence, she and his brother taught him how to work; she the one who checked over the dung he gathered every morning to make sure he'd gone far and collected enough, she who looked over the buckets he brought back from the well to see if he'd walked steady and hadn't spilled any water.

"One task at a time," she said, if he was distracted while feeding the stove's flame. "How will you get bigger things right if you can't do one small task correctly?" Or, "Look, if you hurry through a task, you'll certainly get it wrong and have to do it twice," holding up a stone she'd found in the rice he was supposed to have picked over.

Yitian pretended to assent and then quickly forgot everything she said. Her advice was useful, perhaps, for her time and world, but not for the one in which he wanted to live. Now that his grandfather was gone, the labor seemed particularly trivial against the majestic stories of Beijing and history that his grandfather imparted upon him.

He was just about to rise when he saw a shape coming toward him, dashing through the short copse of spikenards casting their late-afternoon shade. Her jacket flapped as she ran down and the scarf she'd tied around her head fell open so that her braids tumbled out across her shoulders. When she waved, her arm unfurled loosely like a kite string. It had been one of the first things he'd noticed about her, how long her limbs were, elegant and lithe like a dancer's.

He'd been waiting to see her ever since his grandfather's death, but now, as the very outline of her implied a smile, his words caught in his throat. He couldn't come up with even a single thing he could say to that smiling face.

"Yitian," Hanwen called out.

He squinted at her hand. Now that she was closer, he could see that she hadn't been waving at all. There was a small rectangular object in her palm, which she was holding up to the sky.

A transistor radio. She stopped in front of him, panting and out of breath, and held it out.

"Listen! Listen to what they're saying!" She rolled the volume dial between her fingers.

. . . the session will be held at high schools in December. Provincial committees will release the precise dates of the examination in the following weeks . . .

The radio announcer's voice was suddenly overtaken by a crackle of static, so loud that Yitian jumped back in alarm.

"What is she talking about?" he asked.

Hanwen shook the radio, but the announcer's voice didn't return.

"It was fine earlier. This thing! It never works when I need it to. Never mind." She tossed the radio into the grass. "They just announced they're reinstating the gaokao!"

A beat inside Yitian's chest thumped in recognition, but he pushed it away. He didn't dare acknowledge a hope that grand.

"How? It can't be."

"I couldn't believe it either. We were bringing in our tools when Hongxing ran in and told us to turn on the radio. It was the first announcement of the broadcast."

"Come on, you're not excited?" She nudged his leg with her toe. She took one of the burlap bags, spread it on the ground beside him, and leaned her shoulder against his. The feeling electrified him, but he tried to tamp it down. It was wrong to think in such a way about a girl so soon after his grandfather's death.

"How can you be sure it's true?" he asked. "I'll believe it when I hear it for myself." He wasn't deliberately trying to be difficult. Even if he heard the announcement himself, he wasn't sure how much he'd believe. He'd long since given up trying to understand the maneuverings of the government in faraway Beijing. New policies and new leaders, what difference would it make? The news every day was so coded that it was impossible for him to decipher what was really happening in the outside world. Chairman Mao had died, and the Gang of Four had fallen. Hua Guofeng had replaced Mao and there was a new campaign with a name that was supposed to mean something. In hardly a year, Deng was purged, then rehabilitated. Trying to predict the erratic weather was much easier than following Beijing.

"So you're saying you believe those people on the radio more than you would believe me. Is that right?" Her tone was sharp.

He looked up from the peanuts, startled. The stern expression on her face broke, her mouth stretching into a large smile that allowed peals of laughter through, joy alighting upon her crinkled eyes. Her pleasure overtook her and she threw her head back, so that a strip of pale skin revealed itself above the collar of her jacket.

It was this look of unbridled happiness that at last convinced him. Hanwen was a serious person, not given to such displays of spontaneous laughter. He'd seen her, at times, in a more consuming joy, but there always came the moment after when she would catch herself. A few months ago, on a summer evening made long and sleepless by the heat, Yishou had secretly stolen a chicken for the three of them. She'd yelped at the sight of his brother holding the chicken upside down by its feet, stuck her finger out to caress the prickled feathers of the wing, jumped back when she felt the warmth of the animal's body. But by the time they sat down to eat later, she'd been so stoic amidst the others' glee that Yishou had commented afterward, "Your girlfriend's not easily impressed, huh? Better be careful she doesn't leave you for someone else." His brother was trying to protect him from some idea of a gold-digging girl, who Yitian knew Hanwen wasn't.

"What does it mean for us?" Yitian asked her now. "When will it be?"

"I don't know. The others are trying to get more information from people they know in the city. They said on the radio that the date would be this year."

"We'll have so little time."

"If I was still in the city . . ." she said. "They're going to be studying all day back in Shanghai, I bet. They won't have any trouble getting textbooks, not like us. And how will I figure out how to study during the busy season?"

"They can't have read as much as us."

He said the words partially to convince himself. He hoped they were true. If they didn't have a chance, then who did? Whenever they met here, they talked about books. They read widely, whatever they could get their hands on. One week it had been Ibsen's *Dollhouse*, the next *The Origin of Species*. Sometimes even a mathematics textbook. Then back to fiction, Brontë or Turgenev. The Russians, most frequently. The books came to them haphazardly, cobbled together from ones she'd brought from Shanghai, his grandfather's old books, books that Yitian traded from other students when he'd attended the township's high school. He read each book first, and then passed it to her at the end of the week. She did the same the next week. They discussed the book the following Saturday. Then they began the cycle again. At times one of them dared to voice the hope that they'd one day be able to use this knowledge as students in a university, but mostly he believed that their discussions would be finite, limited to their love of the subjects themselves and the conversations here on the embankment.

"You're right," she said. She set her face, and he could see the old seriousness and determination had returned. "What's the use in complaining, anyway? We should get to work studying right away."

An abrupt horn shouting into the air caused them both to startle. He hadn't realized how late it had gotten—the evening news broadcast was about to begin. He looked down at the peanuts, on which he'd hardly made any progress. He'd surely be scolded by his mother, but what did it matter? There was an opportunity to go to college. Soon, with any luck, the world of these crops would mean little in his life.

They brushed off their clothes and walked home to the sounds of the trumpets of "The Sun Rises in the East" playing from the loudspeakers bandaged onto the trees and eaves of homes.

When they were halfway up the hill, he heard—

The Ministry of Education has announced today that there will be a trial reinstatement of the gaokao this year . . . Exact dates will be set by provincial committees . . .

He whooped aloud this time. He turned around, so quickly that he almost slipped upon the pebbled dirt and had to grab her by the shoulders. This time, she was the one surprised. She looked around to see if anyone had seen them—an instinctive gesture; surely there'd be no one else here at this time of day—and then began to laugh uproariously, uncontained, an unabashed moment of elation he rarely saw from her. "You should have seen how you looked just now!" She waved her arms wildly in imitation of his clumsiness.

"Do you finally believe me now?" she asked. He held her hand, dropping it when they began to descend back into the village. He was overjoyed at the news, even more overjoyed that it was Hanwen he'd been with when he heard it. The sterile and shiny voice of the female broadcaster continued to sound, but the words hardly registered in his ears.

"I'll let you know everything I hear," she said. "And I'll make a schedule of what we'll need to study. You'll have a lot to catch up with in math, I think."

"And you'll have nothing to catch up with at all?" The news had made him feel playful.

"No, no, that's not what I meant. You know so much more than me."

They parted in the dark, at the alleyway leading to his home. Only then did he realize he hadn't thought of his grandfather since Hanwen had come down the hill, the longest period he'd gone since the death.

I may go to college, he whispered to his grandfather, later that night after they snuffed the flames of the tung oil lamps and he lay in bed next to Yishou, who'd taken his grandfather's place beside him. *They are finally bringing back the examinations*, his mouth said against the coarse cotton revealed by the quilt's torn patches. *If only you'd made it for a few more days, you could have helped me.* Eleven years had passed since the exams had last been administered—that day's news was a miracle. He felt as if he'd been journeying on a flat plateau all his life and finally, this hope on the horizon had made the topography of his future visible. There was a crevasse in his life now: on one side were his mother and Yishou and his father and their old way of living; he and Hanwen, hope and possibility, on the other.

Five

He seemed to have entered a new season of his life; the surprises continued to come. He marveled at how, after years when the days seemed like they would never change, the events after his grandfather's death tumbled into one another with rapidity.

His father arrived home a day later. Yitian was sitting on a stool in the courtyard, still wiping sleep from his eyes, when the door suddenly swung open.

"Mother of Yishou!"

His shape caught the rays of the first dawn, so that his broad shoulders and wide back, made larger by the cardboard box strapped to it, were shadowed across the floor.

They hadn't expected him so early in the day. He wore his faded green military uniform. Yitian's mother dropped the egg she was holding, just collected from the coop, sending the still-warm yolk sliding down the courtyard floor. Yishou called *Ba!* in his own booming voice, rushing to take his father's bag onto his own back.

Yitian was so surprised that, as he rose to stand, he tripped backward against a stone in the courtyard, one he usually knew to avoid. He wanted to greet his father, but his mouth wouldn't open, his tongue sticking like sucked candy to its roof. Just a moment ago, he'd been lazily watching the sunrise and planning what subject he would study for the day in the reverie he'd entered ever since the gaokao's announcement.

His father had sent word that he would return to the village to attend the funeral for Yitian's grandfather, which had been delayed for his arrival. His mother had been busy with the funeral arrangements and hardly had time to do her usual preparations—pickling the mustard stems and cabbage his father liked, sunning and beating the blankets clean so that the bed would be fresh when he arrived. The neighbors commented that they didn't know how she was managing to plan a funeral all on her own, but Yitian never heard her complain.

After the initial commotion settled, Yitian looked more closely at his father. He was still broad shouldered, face scruffy and eyes sharp with pride, but something about his outline was changed—he appeared shorter, less imposing than Yitian remembered him to be. His father's heavy gait, which once had seemed to be making the very earth's foundation more solid with each step, now shivered upon the ground. It took some inspection before Yitian could place its source, but at last he saw that one of his father's legs bent, like a knot in a twig, behind the other.

"Did something happen, Ba?" he asked, pointing. These were the first words he said upon his father's return.

His father waved his hand dismissively and walked into the home. It was impossible not to notice the limp now, his right leg seeming to catch for the briefest of seconds on every step. Yishou rushed to his side to support him.

His father pushed him away. "I'm fine, I'm fine," he said. "Just bring my stuff in."

As he slurped noodles at the table, his father explained that his brigade had been sent to help stem a flood at a dam near the barracks after a sudden storm. A boulder had fallen on his leg while they'd been moving rocks to stop the breach, leaving a gash above his knee.

"Why didn't you write to tell us?" his mother asked.

His father waved away the steam blowing into his face from the bowl. Yitian's mother had hurried to make a bowl of noodles and eggs, a meal respectful enough for the occasion.

"Write? Do you think I have nothing better to do than write you all about every small thing that happens out there? Things like this are common, you know. I didn't think it was going to be a big deal. I just poured baijiu on it to disinfect the wound." It did work for a while, he explained. But a couple of weeks later, the pain returned in a new form. It began in his groin now, a hot sensation that radiated from his crotch outward whenever he walked.

"They couldn't stop laughing at me because I kept grabbing my balls! Everyone kept asking if my nuts were too full. *Eager to empty them?*" He laughed. "I thought maybe it was just something that happened to men when they get older." So he hadn't said anything when the pain kept him up all that evening. He wouldn't have gone to the doctor at all, if he hadn't fainted that day during morning stretches, right as the entire brigade was kicking their legs back and forth in unison. At the military hospital, the doctor told him the wound had become infected.

"They gave me antibiotics, but they said it was only the last thing they'd try. If that didn't work, they would have had to amputate the leg."

"Heaven is good to us," Yitian's mother exclaimed.

His father didn't respond. He didn't believe in the superstitions and religions of the village, as Yitian's mother did, thinking them the foolish ways of women whose minds twisted out of restlessness.

"One of the other soldiers gave me some opium to deal with the pain. I don't know where he got it from. I saw clouds forming in my vision. I couldn't even understand what the doctor was saying when he was talking to me. But when I woke up, I still had my leg. I was just thinking about what I would do when I got your letter about grandfather's death. That's why I was delayed."

"So you're staying here for good?" Yishou asked.

"They said there will be some monthly subsidy since I was injured while stationed. And then back to farming for me, I suppose." He moved his leg out from under the table and propped his heel up on the other end of the bench.

"So now you understand why I didn't write? How could I have time to even think of such a thing?"

Yitian, who sat on the bench nearest his father, recoiled at the smell of food on his breath.

His father noticed his reaction. "Have I said something that bothered my sensitive scholar son?" He laughed, swirling his bowl.

Yitian kept his gaze directed downward. He was sure his father didn't know the particular reason for his response, or he would have been teased even further. Luckily, his father didn't press the issue this time, instead occupied with asking Yishou how the harvest had been that year.

All his father's previous visits were during the New Year furloughs. Expecting those, Yitian had time to prepare himself for this arrival. He could steel himself, so that he knew not to speak whenever his father did, and to wait for his father to take the first bite of food before anyone else would be allowed to. This time, his body was more confused. He was still half stuck in the freedom with which he lived when his father was not home.

Yitian saw his father little for the first three days after he arrived home. He slept through lunch and was often out visiting neighbors during the day. At dinner, he drank a few shots of baijiu with the food. His father had developed a new habit, Yitian discovered, of massaging his hurt leg absentmindedly while he ate. He would use one hand to lift his chopsticks to his mouth, while the other kneaded circles into his thigh.

"Is it very painful, father?" Yishou asked, one night at dinner.

"The alcohol helps," his father said.

He'd always liked to drink, but this was much more than Yitian remembered. His grandfather never drank, one of the many differences between the two men. His grandfather wanted to preserve the clarity of his mind; his father enjoyed the haziness, believing it could ferry him into a more radiant version of the world.

"How have we raised you?" His grandfather's eyes were bright and sharp with meaning. Yitian felt like he had been slapped across the face. He had only been trying to be sympathetic. He hurried out of the courtyard and spent the rest of the morning wandering in the hills surrounding their village, morose and resentful.

Now, Yitian wondered if his grandfather's death would at last reveal some wellspring of emotion in his father. But still, it did not rise. His father hardly even mentioned the passing other than his dutiful words at the funeral. This was not an indication of any genuine care—Yitian knew his father would never abandon filial traditions, these being as important to his stature in the community as his ability as a farmer.

It didn't seem possible how little his father cared, although his behavior was not dissimilar to the indifference he'd always shown Yitian's grandfather, which was not even broken to show disdain. When his father was home from the barracks, the two men passed food across the table in silence, slipped next to each other in the rooms of their home without so much as an acknowledgment, even their shadows barely crossing.

Six

He decided that night to review the contents of the *Twenty-Four Histories*. Parts of it would surely be on the history section. His father and Yishou were out visiting with neighbors, drinking and playing cards, and he would have the room to himself.

He positioned the brazier under his knees and gathered two benches around him, fanning his notes out on one and placing the lamp upon the wobbly other. He stretched out his legs and sighed contentedly, thinking of the night of reading ahead of him. In his lap he cradled the bag of roasted sunflower seeds his mother had given him from her trip into town that morning. He pressed his face deeply into the bag, inhaling the rich fragrance of the roasting machine that still lingered on the shells. He planned to eat them while he studied.

When he heard his father and Yishou returning home, just as he was opening his books, Yitian could hardly believe it. He hadn't expected them back until much later, when he hoped he would already be asleep.

They were accompanied by Second Uncle and Old Seven, who greeted Yitian with a nod. Yitian wondered if he would be kicked out of the room, but his father began calling for his mother to make dinner for the guests, ignoring him entirely.

"I didn't realize that you'd be coming back to eat!" she exclaimed. She poured out all the peanuts in their home and set them on a dish on their table. As his mother rushed about preparing dishes, Yitian tried to make his body small in the corner. It was a gift to be ignored by his father now, but one he knew from experience could easily be taken away.

He began to read from his notes:

The Tang Dynasty rose to power after overthrowing the Sui . . .

Emperor Taizong went on to greatly expand the nation's borders by engaging in war with the Turks and the Tibetans . . .

Wu Zetian took over the throne to establish her own dynasty, but soon had it taken back . . .

No matter how he tried, he couldn't wholly concentrate. One part of his mind remained half alert to his father and the guests, who were now beginning to drink, his father pouring the shots and suggesting toasts.

"Not too much for me," Old Seven protested. "I'm an old man. I can't drink like I used to anymore. It would be awful for me in the morning."

Had it been anyone else, his father would have insisted, but Old Seven was a respected village elder. When Japanese armies had invaded the village during the war, it was Old Seven who'd devised the strategy to hide the villagers in the hills, so crucial to their survival that the story had now become the stuff of legend. He'd maintained the strength of his body—he was often sighted carrying full buckets of water on poles balanced across his shoulders, at which point younger villagers would run to help him and scold him for endangering his health. Yitian thought it unlikely his protests about the alcohol were true.

"Fine, then Second Uncle will take your drink," his father said. Second Uncle grabbed the shot glass eagerly. He was widely known to be a gambler and a drinker, always on the verge of having nothing, the signs of his lifestyle showing on a fatigued face that looked older than his thirty-five years.

"You know, I've actually gotten much better at drinking as I've gotten older," Yitian's father said. "We drank a lot in the army. It was so boring there—how else could we manage to entertain ourselves? We'd go months without seeing a single woman."

They looked into Yitian's corner, where his mother would usually have sat, knitting by low lamplight in the evenings. Tonight, she'd already retreated to the bedroom, promising to return for the dishes.

Yitian, frowning, quickly brought his head back down to his notes.

"You wouldn't believe how desperate some of the men were. There were days when they would have given up their whole monthly stipend just to see a woman. We'd run across a wild pig and they'd think even *she* had double eyelids!" His father laughed uproariously with the guests, even Old Seven. They were all drunk, Yitian thought.

He was hopeful when, after dinner, they settled into a silence over their cards. His father instinctively calculated a winner and loser in every situation—because every instance of life was just so black and white—and thus playing cards was one of his favorite activities. He liked this feeling of perching on the lip of luck, the oil of alcohol smoothing the edge of belief, making any outcome possible. Yitian did not think this was a trivial skill—he himself did not like to play cards, for how often he lost. Winning required an intelligence different from the kind that he and his grandfather valued. He'd never believed his father to be unintelligent, it was only that his father's thinking seemed to be diverted to a place Yitian never cared to look. His father could remember the precise pattern in which different rice formations were to be planted depending on the year's earlier weather, or predict within a few seconds the moment a rainstorm would start.

After some time, Second Uncle asked, "So you're back for good?"

"This leg," his father replied. "What could I do out there, or even in the fields? At least it's lucky I have this son."

Yitian was surprised to hear his father complimenting him in such a way. Perhaps it was the alcohol, or the guests, or the years—but something had at last expanded his father's understanding of him, as he'd long hoped for.

He looked up to see the table grinning at Yishou—of course. How could he have been so silly, to suppose even for a moment, that he was the object of his father's praise? It had always been this way. Yishou was the preferred son, powerful and useful, just as their father himself was. Yitian, on the other hand, was lanky and thin and, until very recently, too short to do much good work. Instead of contributing to the family's work points as a good son should have, he read books and recited poems as if there were money in them.

"Look at this," he said. He grabbed Yishou's bicep and lifted it up in the air with his free hand. "He's been getting adult work points since he was a teenager. He has his father's strong blood. He'll take care of me into my old age. There's nothing to worry about with him." He paused to throw peanuts into his mouth and crunched loudly down. "Not like that one."

Yitian blushed and looked back down.

"Now, now," Old Seven said.

"I want to see what he's up to, over there with his head down," his father said.

Yitian heard his father's steps toward him, the hiccuping cadence of that new gait. A half step, the *shhh* of the rolling dust across the floor, then a shuffle.

Yitian's hands were shaking. He wasn't sure why he was so afraid. It had been years since his father had last beaten him for making some clumsy mistake, and that was unlikely with guests around. Besides, he hadn't done anything wrong. Yet, now that his grandfather was gone, he felt that some raw part of him was exposed to his father's whim.

His father picked up a piece of paper from the bench beside Yitian, running his index finger under the text. His eyes focused and then unfocused upon the words. "Your characters are thin and run together, just like your grandfather's. He used to brag about how nicely he could write. Nothing like my ugly characters," he murmured.

When his father squatted down until he was at eye level, Yitian wondered how the hurt leg could handle such pressure.

"You're just like him in many ways, you know that? These words and your strengths . . . both small." He took Yitian's shoulders within his large hands and squeezed. Yitian felt his body shrinking under the pressure.

"Look at you, always studying. For what?"

Yitian was silent. His father rose to his feet, wincing.

"For what, I asked! I asked you a question."

Yitian regretted not leaving the room as soon as his father had come home. It had been an awful idea, to think he could stay in his father's presence while he was drinking.

"I'm studying for the gaokao," he murmured.

"Yes, so your brother has told me. He says you have this plan to take the gaokao, to go to college." He waved his hand, as if swatting a buzzing fly. "Let's talk reasonably, like two men. Who will pay for you to go to university?"

"The tuition is provided by the government, I've heard . . ." Yitian mumbled.

"You have an answer for everything, don't you?" His father barked out a laugh, not at all joyful this time. The sound tumbled, low and harsh, down to Yitian's ears.

His father turned to Yishou and said, "You've all given him his way too often, while I've been away. That's why he's like this. I've seen him around the house—he doesn't even do chores. Your mother and grandfather just let him read books all day while I've been gone."

"That's not true. I do help Ma." Sometimes Yitian couldn't help himself when his father spoke against him, and that was always when the beatings had come. He didn't know why he was this way; both Yishou and his grandfather had cautioned him against speaking back to his father, saying it was of no use.

From where he sat on the stool, his father's towering figure stood over him. Behind his father, he saw Yishou shaking his head, warning him not to say more.

"Time to go home," Second Uncle muttered. Second Uncle gave Old Seven a look of knowing across the table. It was not the first time Yitian had noticed how others perceived his father when he drank. It embarrassed him.

"No, no, stay," his father slurred at them. "Let's all see what the boy has to say. So you think you work enough, is that right? You think what your grandfather taught you was enough? As for me, I was smart enough to know that wouldn't work." He leaned against the wall to support himself as his voice gathered energy. "Do you know where all your grandfather's knowledge eventually got him?"

Yitian was surprised to hear Yishou's voice, interrupting from behind. "Things are changing in the world outside. It might not be that way for Yitian."

"You don't need to protect him," his father said, without looking back.

"The gaokao has been reinstated . . ." Yitian searched for words. "Do you think that's just random? There's a reason for that." He felt as he had so many times, the child that his father made him, but alongside that there was a new emotion. There was a new bravery before his father, the sense that a destiny was gathering behind him.

"What kind of good reason could there be? It's all a waste of time. All of your grandfather's studying got him nothing. When they had the campaign against the counterrevolutionaries, they came for him. Oh, everyone in the village pretends to be respectful to him, but they had no problem fingering him and letting the Party take away our land. *He, he's the one who has all the books, who used to help the nationalists. The intellectual,*" his father imitated in a high-pitched whine. "They shamed him in the village square and took away everything we had.

"Then he tried to stop me from joining the army, even though everyone else said it was the smartest thing anyone could do at the time. His head was filled with so much of the past, he could never understand what we needed to do for the future. Why do you think Yishou is so strong? Why he's lived to this age, even? Haven't you noticed, there are no other boys his age in the village? I was able to get your mother food from the barracks when she was pregnant, unlike the other villagers. Figuring things out like that is real intelligence, not whatever your grandfather has taught you."

The room was silent now. Yitian wondered if the others were thinking, too, that the words had crossed a line, even for his father. His grandfather had only been put in the ground a week ago.

"No . . ." His father shook his head. "You won't waste time by going to university. It's time you contributed something to this family."

Yitian panicked. He clasped his hands together and opened them to find they were smeared with stained ink and sweat.

"Did you hear that?" his father said. "Put your books away."

His father snatched up the notebook, held it to the lamplight. For an instant, Yitian hoped that he was only examining the cover. Then, in the next moment, he threw it across the room. The paper hit the wall with a slap.

"Useless thing."

Soon after he'd gotten into bed, Yitian felt his brother's hand on his back, patting him uncertainly. Yitian scooted away from him, pretending to be asleep. He did not want Yishou's comfort at that moment—Yishou, to whom his father never would have done such a thing.

Yitian missed his grandfather's presence in the bed. He, his father, and his grandfather were all men from the same jiapu, but Yitian couldn't find any similarity to his father. He could understand if his father felt a sense of difference from his grandfather—Yitian often had the same feeling himself with the villagers—but the hatred that consumed his father was something else entirely, extravagant in size and shameful for a son to hold. He'd imagined that he would one day ask his grandfather what had happened between their generations, but now that his grandfather was dead, he would never get the chance to unravel the cocoons that these two men had entered in private. For the rest of his life, he would only ever see glimpses of the two of them in the shapes they formed after an exit.

The next day, he heard his father shuffling through the items he and Yishou kept in the drawers of their shared wardrobe. He must have pushed aside a comb, slid their clothes toward the back, and lurched to the deepest point of the drawer to find the thin booklet whose cardboard face was pressed flat under a book.

"You won't need this anymore," his father told Yitian at breakfast. He held up the hukou booklet that Yitian would need to register for the gaokao. And then, with a wave of his hand, it disappeared into the dark breast pocket of his coat.

Seven

GAOKAO PREPARATION SCHEDULE

Hanwen had written across the top of the papers. Underneath that, the words

TEST DATE—DECEMBER XX?

They still hadn't heard when the exact date would be, so she made preparations based on the first week of the month. Against the defining edge of a ruler, she'd drawn rows for each week until the exam, then columns spanning the top for each subject. She created Yitian's copy first, then took out a fresh sheet of paper for her own. This was the gift she would leave him with. She wanted to study engineering, and he history, so the exam subjects they took would be slightly different, but there was enough in common that re-creating the schedule wasn't difficult. On his own, he would never have come up with such a plan, for he was the type of person for whom knowledge came easily and naturally, his wishes for himself matching his ability. She, instead, relied on effort and endurance to learn the subjects she loved. Hard work and judiciousness could bring a person as far as talent could, but not further. She admired people like Yitian, who had the capabilities she did not.

He was late today, which was unlike him. Usually, by the time she arrived, he was already waiting for her. She would run down the hill toward where he sat and he would gaze up shyly at her before scooting over to make space on the board he brought, so that her clothes wouldn't dirty from the embankment, often muddy from rain or frost. For the first few moments, he would be nervous, allowing her to guide the conversation until he felt comfortable again and spoke quickly and with excitement. Even though it had already been a year since they first met, he never lost that uncertainty when she first came running down toward him, as if each time he believed she stopped wanting to see him in the intervening week. It charmed her that she could assure him over and over again that nothing had changed.

She wondered if sadness at his grandfather's death had kept him today. She'd tried to comfort him, but whenever she heard herself speak, her words of reassurance felt thin and small against the expanse of his loss. She'd thought the announcement of the gaokao had excited him again, but perhaps she'd been wrong.

He was the only person whom she'd thought about as she'd made her plan to leave. She felt enormous affection for the villagers and the girls of their dormitory, nothing more. She had to remind herself that her fear wasn't on his behalf, but for the limits of the person she might be without him. She would miss him when they were apart, but he would be fine studying alone. And if her plan worked, she could write him once she returned to Shanghai. Then, with some luck, they'd be able to reunite in college.

After an hour, she gave up waiting and returned to the dormitory.

"So soon?" Pan Niannian said. Niannian was sitting in the lower bunk, knitting. "I thought you were going to spend the whole day with your boyfriend."

It was the kind of remark that the girls of their dorm would normally have stopped to laugh and gossip about, but no one turned from their studying to respond. Niannian would be disappointed, she knew. Of the four of them, Niannian was the only one who'd decided not to take the gaokao, and she seemed almost resentful that the others had. Ever since the announcement of the exam, she mocked the others for the late hours they spent studying after the day's work finished, and complained every night that their lamplight was too bright for her to sleep.

Hongxing and Wu Mei were reading at the single table they shared. Accustomed to studying under difficult circumstances, they didn't even look up. During the worst years of the Cultural Revolution, Hanwen would arrive to school in the morning to find that one of her teachers had suddenly disappeared, reassigned to education through labor without any notice. Even if the teacher was there, she'd have to strain to hear the lecture over the shouts of students in the back deliberately disrupting class, as their revolutionary teachings had taught them to do. The most important principle was not to let anything take away your concentration.

Hanwen collected her sickle from underneath the bed, where she kept her best tools, far away from the barn where there was the danger others would use and ruin them.

"I'm going out to cut some grass," she announced to the room, as lightly as she could. No one took any notice. Only when she paused by the door to fix the heel of her shoe did Hongxing look up, as if the words had just reached her.

"You're going to cut grass *now*?"

"Yes. For fuel. I wanted to do it now so that I'll have more time to study during the week." She'd prepared the excuse earlier in case anyone asked.

"You plan every part of the day around this exam. What a joke," Niannian scoffed. Hanwen ignored her and left the room.

They kept the whetstone outside the dormitory. She'd never become particularly adept at using it to sharpen tools, and she usually had to ask Niannian for help. Niannian had been in the village the longest, and in those years had mastered bringing blade to stone at the precise angle of contact that would rub the dullness away. Hanwen's motions were awkward as she scraped the blade against the stone now, but she didn't need the sickle to be as sharp as when they worked in the fields.

She walked until she was half a li behind their dormitories, where there was a small hill covered in prickly grass they cut for cooking fuel. In this season, the waist-high grass was beginning to dry, but hadn't yet coarsened to the texture of later autumn. She squatted down in the grass, so that anyone approaching would have to squint closely to notice she was there.

She'd devised the plan the week before to hurt herself with the sickle. She didn't want to injure herself permanently, only to do enough damage that it would be impossible for her to work for a few weeks. Then she'd be sent back to Shanghai to recuperate, where she could study for the exam without obligation or distraction.

She took the sickle in her hand. The splinters of the wooden handle dug into her palm. With the index finger of her free hand, she pressed lightly against the blade. She saw the skin of her finger turn white, then the bloody pucker that rose from the shallow incision. It was only the depth of a simple paper cut, but still she gasped so sharply that she dropped the tool.

She hadn't anticipated being so afraid. She'd hurt herself accidentally so many times before while using the sickle to harvest, when the blade was too dull or her chopping suddenly hit a knot in the stalks. From these accidents, she had cuts on her arms and legs, none of them ever deep enough to require more than a bandage and a few days of healing. They'd faded into brown scars that joined all the others collected upon her body from her days here, the patches like tree bark upon her shoulders where the carrying poles had rubbed against her flesh, and the glossy remnants of skin where calluses on her foot had bubbled then popped.

She picked up the sickle again, this time opening her palm against the handle. The sight of the rough calluses where her hands had once been smooth returned her resolve. She inhaled deeply. She could do this. A moment of pain, that was all she needed to exchange for the hope of her future.

She bit down on her lip.

"Hanwen! Hanwen! Are you there?"

A girl called out from below, and then came the crunching sounds of someone pushing their way through the grass up the hill.

"Hello?"

The voice shocked her, causing all the tension to escape her hand. The sickle dropped silently and powerless into the cushioning grass.

Hongxing was coming toward her. "I came to help you! I didn't want you to have to cut the grass alone!"

Hanwen pushed back the sting she felt gathering behind her eyes. If she hadn't hesitated, the wound would already have been made. Hongxing hadn't even brought her own sickle. She picked up Hanwen's and began to slash dramatically at the grass, grabbing and pulling at the tussocks as if she were a model laborer whom the Party urged others to mimic. Hongxing was the most notoriously fussy out of all the sent-down girls, known for making any excuse to avoid work. She came from a once-famous family of opera singers who'd been denounced in the earliest days of the Cultural Revolution. Hanwen had never seen her labor so enthusiastically. How had she known what Hanwen was planning? Or had she simply followed some weak instinct that sprouted from the shaky way Hanwen left the dorm? Desperation could leave a person transformed.

That night when Hanwen washed herself, there was a sliver of blood, dried to the color of rust, on the finger she'd used to touch the blade. She dragged her washcloth across it, and the blood dissolved to reveal an almost transparent cut. She pressed into the flap of skin as hard as she could. She wanted to force herself inside that sharp sting.

She could try again. She could endure more pain than that.

The next day, she rose earlier than the others and examined the tools. When she picked up the sickle, a splinter from the handle cut into her skin.

She dropped it as if burned.

She knew, then, she wouldn't be able to summon the resolve a second time. She'd ridden to the edge of her daring, a point on the horizon to which she wouldn't be able to return. How had she allowed such a brief moment of surprise to disrupt her plan? She'd been so sure that her determination was the one thing she had, what would distinguish her from those smarter and better connected. Now it, too, had fled her.

The next afternoon, Hongxing stayed behind in the fields to finish her work as the rest of the team was packing up their tools, ready to head back for the evening. Hanwen was cleaning the dirt off the ridges of her shoes when Niannian rushed into the dormitory.

"Something's happened to Hongxing," she shouted. "I think her hand slipped on her sickle. She's bleeding everywhere!"

"What?" Hanwen said blankly. She couldn't believe Hongxing had acted so quickly.

Brigade Leader Xu was there an hour later, wrapping up Hongxing in a piece of wrinkled tarp and cocooning her in burlap bags on the truck bed that would take her to the commune hospital. The evening was windy, and the blue tarp flew up and inflated like a billowy skirt around her legs, one of the fancy kind they hadn't seen since being sent down to the village.

Hongxing would be returned to Shanghai now. Anger flashed through Hanwen as she watched the truck drive off. She imagined Hongxing as a young girl, how her face would have looked when her parents were denounced in front of the neighborhood. At the thought of the embarrassment and shame distorting Hongxing's delicate features, the satisfaction of justice ran through Hanwen.

In the next moment, she was ashamed. How could she blame Hongxing? The central government's policies were always changing without warning. The gaokao could be gone again the very next year and this might be the only chance they would ever have. The announcement of the gaokao was the first time since arriving in the village that Hanwen felt the return of possibility, and she could understand the lengths a person would go to in order to preserve that sense.

In the end, she had to admit that she admired Hongxing for her bravery.

———

Hanwen had rushed to tell her mother as soon as she heard the gaokao announcement, skipping even dinner that night and spilling ink down her arm in her haste to get the words down for her world-weary mother, who returned home from work every evening with nothing to animate her life besides these letters.

The opportunity we've been waiting for has finally come! her mother replied. Hanwen asked her if she'd heard any other information, but her mother wasn't the kind to participate in the gossip of the longtangs—she heard enough, she said, while cleaning the bathrooms. Hanwen had grown up hearing the tongue of gossip exploring the alleyways, always disguised as care, vigilance, solicitude—any feeling other than the simpler truth, the euphoric rush of knowing something secret and participating in the judgment of another. Had she been in Shanghai, she would have asked down her lane whether anyone had heard a rumor about the exam date or what questions might be on the test, and someone would surely have had some information to share, passed second- or thirdhand from a relative or a friend of a friend who worked on the provincial educational committee, the kind of connections that illuminated the web of the city.

Even had she still been in Shanghai, she would not have been able to afford tutors. She knew that her family was ordinary, in both their connections and what they had suffered during the Cultural Revolution. It was exactly this ordinariness that had led her to this village— if there had been something more special about them, if they'd either been better connected or her mother had been deemed to have suffered enough, she could have avoided being sent down.

On the day she graduated from high school and received the notice she was to move to a village in Anhui Province, her mother was enraged. She spent that entire evening muttering to herself, angry at everyone and no one in particular.

"Wasting my only child's chance to get a good education! What could the peasants possibly have to teach you?" she said, sweeping the house, so angry that she didn't notice her voice had elevated above a whisper and was in danger of being overheard by the neighbors.

"Ma," Hanwen said. She motioned numbly for her mother to quiet. The news about being sent down was bad, but the punishment for her mother could also be awful if a neighbor heard and reported her.

Perhaps she'd been too late in warning her mother, or else their neighbor, Auntie Feng, a barren woman who spent her time observing and passing news on all the longtang children, had been listening with a cup to the wall, as she'd been known to. A few days later, Hanwen's homeroom teacher asked if she could stop by the next evening—for a heart-to-heart, she said. Both Hanwen and her mother knew what this would mean, the language of hearts reserved for when their loyalty to the Party was supposed to outstrip concern for their own well-being and propel them to cast rationality to the side.

Her mother devised a plan. She suggested to Teacher Ma that she come for dinner that night instead, as a token of gratitude for all the hard work she'd put into teaching Hanwen. That morning, her mother was the first person at the government grocery store, having scrimped and traded so she could buy a larger cut of pork than the paper-thin, mostly fatty pieces they were normally able to afford. As soon as she got home from work that evening, without even washing, she braised the meat, which she later set as the shiny centerpiece of their small table, on which she'd also placed sautéed loofah and egg, and a delicate Shanghai-style stir fry of potatoes, mu'er, and carrots, picked to showcase how neatly her mother could chop when there was a person to impress.

When Teacher Ma arrived, clutching her unbuttoned book bag to her chest, glasses askew and with hair sticking out in tufts from her braid, it was to the sight of Hanwen's mother harried, skin damp from the stove and still smelling of the vinegar they used as cleaning solution. Still, as soon as their guest entered, her mother was busying about, offering tea and pouring out sunflower seeds, all of which Teacher Ma refused.

"Auntie, you didn't have to do all this," she said. "I just wanted to come and talk about Tian Hanwen. Don't worry too much about all the food, just come sit, please."

Her mother obliged, but not before taking out their three nicest bowls and pairs of chopsticks and placing them out on the table.

"Please eat," her mother said, using her chopsticks to force a piece of pork onto Teacher Ma's plate. "It's our honor to host you for dinner."

Teacher Ma nibbled politely around the bone of a piece of roast pork. Hanwen had always liked her. She seemed to care. She'd stopped by their home before, much to Hanwen's fear, but when she'd expected some scolding, instead Teacher Ma had praised Hanwen's dedication and diligence. "I know it's not easy, in an environment like this," she'd said. "It shows you've raised her well, Auntie." Once, when she'd handed back an essay of Hanwen's, she'd whispered, "It's such a shame," but when Hanwen had asked her what she meant, she shook her head and said never mind.

"You must know why I've come tonight, Auntie," Teacher Ma said now. She put down her half-chewed bone and chopsticks. "It's really the best thing for Tian Hanwen to do."

Hanwen could see her mother trembling with anger, but there was a limit to what she could say aloud. She said, through clenched teeth, "All her hard work in her studies—what will that do in the country-side? You said it yourself. She's such a good student."

"She is, but . . . this is the best thing for her." Teacher Ma bit her lip, and the gesture flooded Hanwen with sadness. Teacher Ma didn't even believe in the words she said; she was no more than an actress, performing without a glamorous stage. Hanwen could better stand it if only they could tell the truth of the misfortune.

"Look," Teacher Ma continued, "if she behaves well in the countryside, is enthusiastic about her work, maybe she could get a good position there."

"As a cadre in a rural village?"

"It's a desirable position, Auntie."

"They're saying all the students are going to be sent to Anhui, is that right? That rural backwater? Look at her, she's only a young girl! Much too young to go that far, alone. A single young girl, with all those country men." Her mother shuddered.

"You should feel grateful—many students are sent all the way to Inner Mongolia. It could be much worse. She'll still be able to come home for the New Year."

"And some only get sent to the suburbs of Shanghai. Why does she have to go so far?"

"I don't know how the committee makes the decisions."

"She's my only daughter, the only child I have. My husband died years ago. . . . Doesn't that count for anything?" Her mother was practically begging now.

"It would have a couple of years ago, but now they're strict again. They need students to go down. Anyway, Auntie, your class background is poor. It won't help if she stays. She wouldn't be able to get assigned any worthwhile job when she graduates."

Hanwen's mother crossed her arms, her lips shaking with what she couldn't say aloud.

"Listen to me." For the first time, Teacher Ma looked frustrated.

She spoke in a near whisper. "You want her to be a heiren living in the city for the rest of her time here? Think about it, Auntie, how will she live! How will you feed her? She won't be able to get rations, have you thought of that? Do you want her to starve? And the neighborhood committee is really pushing this time, they're saying parents of the students who defy the order could lose their jobs, too."

"Me—"

"Ma, that's enough. Haven't you been listening to Teacher? I'll go." Teacher Ma and her mother both looked at Hanwen, surprised at the sudden interruption. Hanwen was accustomed to staying silent when adults discussed her, but her mother could not be allowed to go on. She'd been made frenzied by the news, if she wouldn't even give in at the threat to her own job.

"See, she knows," Teacher Ma said, gentle again. Hanwen's words had sucked all the air out of the room and everyone looked deflated.

"Do you think she'll ever get to come back?" her mother asked, her voice quietly resigned.

"I don't know. . . . You can't think that way. It's better to just accept things. Hoping for another outcome will only make things more difficult." Teacher Ma placed her barely used chopsticks on the plate, and then rose. "Auntie, I'm sorry. Really I am. Thank you for the meal. I can't stay any longer. I have to go visit other parents."

After she left, Hanwen and her mother stared blankly at the table piled with rich food. Hanwen had no appetite. She felt a new gravity to her impending departure. She'd seen the posters before, calling for the educated youth to go down to the countryside to help the peasants. The village scenery was rendered in beautiful tones of sun-drenched wheat, expansive blue skies that youth and villagers stood brazenly against. There was an air of the epic about them, a story that she thought she wouldn't mind being a part of. But now she realized what the new assignment would mean. She would receive a new hukou booklet with her countryside residence listed, only two characters enough to imply that she might never live in Shanghai, or with her mother, again. Perhaps she would never again stop by the bookstand outside her house on the way to school, where, for a cent, she could have her pick of the picture flip-books—she'd learned every movie plot she knew that way. Or go to the plaza at the mouth of the longtangs on a hot summer night and watch the adults eat watermelon and nudge xiangqi pieces around a board while moths flitted in the light. How she'd loved that.

Her mother cleaned up the table in quiet. It would be just like this, Hanwen thought, after she left for the countryside. Her mother would eat alone every day and then clean up in silence, so different from all the nights before when she'd made sure there wasn't a single spot of oil slickening the table before allowing Hanwen to set up her homework. "What are you looking at?" her mother said, if she ever caught Hanwen fidgeting, or even simply looking away from her textbooks. "Back to the book, unless you want to end up like me."

She hadn't had to explain any further for Hanwen to understand— her mother, the single daughter in a family of five sons, was the only one never to attend school, and she blamed their circumstances on her lack of education. "You can be an engineer—that's very stable. You'll never be without a position," her mother had said when Hanwen told her she wanted a job that allowed her to use her hands, to take things apart and look deep into their insides to understand how they worked.

These had been the conversations that had filled their house in the years ever since her father's death from tuberculosis that he'd contracted in a labor camp. That same year, her mother was denounced as a petty capitalist for the small tailoring shop she ran in the longtang and was reassigned to a position as a laborer on the neighborhood's sanitation committee. Hanwen had been seven.

After Teacher Ma's visit, they had to eat the leftovers for days. The fat of the braised pork congealed into a milky solid. When she walked down the alleyway with her mother, they passed neighbors sitting at their doors and sunning themselves in midday underneath their drying laundry. Hanwen was sure they'd all heard about the failed dinner. The thin walls between the alleyway homes were made of the flimsy material through which gossip could be threaded and sewn into a dramatic story. She looked back after they passed and saw in the beady and penetrating eyes the intimation that she and her mother would be discussed as soon as they were out of earshot. She hooked her elbow into her mother's and stared defiantly back.

So Hanwen left Shanghai for Tang Family Village on an autumn day, boarding a bus leaving from her middle school. The sky that morning was impossibly blue and cloudless, as if nature was announcing its refusal to comply with their sadness.

Her mother had been twisting her hands all morning. She checked Hanwen's bag for a fifth and final time.

"Be careful. Don't say anything political to anyone. Just keep quiet, and do your work. People will respect you," she said.

Hanwen nodded.

"Be safe, and be good."

She grasped Hanwen's arms by the shoulders.

Hanwen suddenly felt choked by all the wishes she had for her mother. "I don't want to leave you alone," she said.

"Nonsense! What's alone? You think I could ever be alone, in that alley with all the gossiping women and noisy men? I can only wish!"

Hanwen turned quickly to board the bus. She felt embarrassed to cry in front of her mother, whose voice was so stable and determined.

Not until she looked out of the window to see her mother waving furiously from the sidewalk did the dam break. All her loneliness to come seemed written into the speed of that wave.

Her seatmate leaned in front of her, trying to see her own parents in the crowd through the window, but Hanwen used her forearm to push her back. She could see her mother was trying to say something, but the loudspeakers' blasting music made it impossible to hear.

> To the countryside,
> To the borderlands,
> To the places that our motherland needs us most.

The music shouted at the children, while Hanwen tried to focus on her mother's cracked lips telling her this one last thing.

She could not decipher it before the bus pulled away. Her seatmate was yelling at her, rubbing her elbow and saying she was hurt. Hanwen turned her head away and ignored her to look back at the rows of students. Hongxing was in the seat behind her, weeping the loudest of them all. Their parents had made sure that each of their children looked their best for the occasion: girls' hair brushed into neat braids, not a single strand loose; the boys had received prickly haircuts close to the scalp. Even now Hanwen didn't dare to take off the red scarf that scratched at her neck. But she saw so many of them were crying wildly, the tear tracks like chipped varnish on the faces of pristine dolls.

The bus dropped them off at the train station. As she watched the landscape of the countryside from the muddy compartment windows, its emptiness frightened her. When night began to overtake daytime, the green fields were rendered into shadows upon which she could barely find a single glimmer of light. Occasionally, she saw a flash of bright parting the darkness, what she supposed was a farmer carrying a lamp hurrying from place to place. Even they did not want to be out there for long.

She hardly slept on the train ride away from Shanghai, and when she looked in the mirror, the reflection she saw was ashen. On the platform, she made her way through the sounds of people shouting in a country dialect she'd never heard before. She found Hongxing amidst the crowd, and though they'd never been friends in Shanghai, they gripped each other's hands as they were directed onto the bed of a truck that would take them to their final destination.

The truck they rode had last been used to transport livestock. The driver hadn't taken down the rope that had previously kept pigs corralled inside, strung across the width of the truck bed. For two hours, each time the truck drove across a rock on the road, manure lurched a centimeter closer to them from the puddles where it had collected. None of the six students gathered there spoke, but they huddled closer and closer together, so that by the end of the journey they hardly took up any space at all. It was clear now that life in the villages was nothing like that of the posters calling for the Educated Youth to Go Down to the Countryside. She would not meet a brawny farmer, nor the village girl standing beside him in the fields of golden grain that whispered as high as their waists.

An older girl greeted them at the dormitory when they arrived. As soon as they were alone, she threw her arms around Hanwen's neck.

"Oh, I'm so glad you're here! It's been so lonely here by myself." She looked like one of the village women, with her heavy padded jacket and ruddy face, but when she spoke, it was with the crisp, defined accent of a Shanghainese, cutting off words in a high, sharp pitch at their endings.

Her name was Pan Niannian. She was also from Shanghai, but had been a member of the production team for four years. She was part of the earliest group of students who'd been sent down to the village. All the others had been able to leave in the intervening years, through relatives or connections.

As she slowly unpacked her items, Hanwen examined Niannian's face. Her hair was coarse and cropped short around her chin, skin tanned darker than any of theirs. When she lifted her hands to help the girls place their items on the shelves lining the small room, Hanwen saw dirt crescent moons stuffed under her fingernails. What would Niannian's mother have said had she seen? Hanwen wondered whether if she spent enough time here, she, too, would become an unrecognizable version of herself.

She did not ever want to change in such a way.

They retired early that evening, their first in the village. The next morning, Hanwen experienced the first day of her new life. They were awoken at four thirty for breakfast, so that they could take advantage of every second of sunlight.

Part 2

上山下乡

UP TO THE MOUNTAINS, DOWN TO THE COUNTRYSIDE

Eight

1993

The place smelled of pungent manure and resembled a prison, with its squat buildings wrapped in raw, unpainted cement and the low tunnel with the guard's office they'd had to pass to enter.

"I told you there wouldn't be anyone here at this hour," Yitian's mother said. They'd checked each of the four buildings in the police station and found all the doors locked.

"This *is* the police station, right?" he asked the single other occupant, an old woman sweeping circles around the courtyard. She hadn't greeted them when they entered and now eyed him suspiciously.

"What else would it be?"

"We're here to report a missing person," he tried.

Instead of a response, she looked him up and down. He repeated himself.

"They're all napping at this hour," she grunted at last.

"When will the break end?"

She shrugged.

"Why are you looking at us like that?" Yitian's mother snapped. "Have we done anything to you?"

"Where are you two from?"

"Tang Family Village. We're from here, okay, sister? Satisfied? Or would you like me to tell you the exact directions to our house?"

"Even *him*?" The woman's eyes narrowed.

His mother stuck her hand through the loop of his arm. "He's my son." She pulled him away from the cleaning lady, muttering under her breath about people who'd never learned any manners.

The villagers hadn't been as rude as this woman, but they'd hardly offered him any more help. After Second Uncle, there'd been more visits from other neighbors, all of whom seemed to follow the same lines of questioning, as if they were actors with the same script in the movie set his home had become. His life in America, what his salary was, what his house looked like, did they have a television there, why hadn't he and Mali had a child? Then he would have to listen to each guest's recounting of their children's accomplishments, one story bleeding into the next without distinction. Each visit had brought him an uneasy feeling of pride at the way they knew him now and shame at that very feeling. As recently as a year ago, he and Mali had bought all their clothes secondhand (he'd casually mentioned this to his mother once, and she'd burst into tears, before seeming to ignore the fact entirely). He had the eerie sensation that he was being trailed by a ghost twin, one who'd had all the successes the villagers congratulated him for, whom he felt proud of but couldn't possibly be.

When he brought up his father, they shook their head in disappointment and marveled at how unlikely his disappearance was. He'd expected them to rush out and offer their help. Was this how the country had changed in these years, everyone worrying only for themselves? They were like Americans would be, each family hidden in their own cul-de-sac, willing to break its boundaries only if it demanded no inconvenience to themselves. Yitian had hoped for a response more like the time when he was a child and their neighbor Auntie Shan hadn't come home in the evening for dinner. She'd been in the early stages of dementia, a word he learned only later. He remembered how his grandfather and mother had rushed out with the other villagers to scour the area until the old woman was returned safely home.

His mother had warned him that the police station wouldn't be helpful at this time of day, but he'd insisted on going immediately. They'd already lost the day before because the village office car was out on official use. ("My ass," his mother said. "That new village chief just uses that car as if it's his own personal vehicle. He was probably off somewhere with his mistress.")

Now, he felt foolish for expecting more than this. He didn't want to admit to himself the images he'd had in his mind, of bursting urgently into the police station, rapidly explaining his emergency to the officers, all of them immediately rushing up to take his case. They'd search the surrounding villages, knocking on doors, hanging up posters bearing his father's picture and description. Faceless villagers would call in with their tips. He realized, embarrassed, that this image had come from an American series he'd seen on television years ago, which followed detectives as they searched for missing children in the early hours after a case. Watching them, he'd felt a sense of efficacy and competence, that it was only a matter of time before the children were returned to the warm beds in the homes where they belonged.

At two thirty, an officer finally arrived, stomping out the dregs of a cigarette as he mumbled an excuse about a problem elsewhere in town that he'd been dealing with. His hair stood out in tufts from the back of his head and bits of yellow crust still stuck to his eyelashes. He took them to a room whose walls were papered with notices and directives, so many that the edges overlapped. All the desks, however, were mysteriously bare. In the far corner was the only space that showed signs of life, fluffy leather sofas surrounding a coffee table covered with majiang tiles and small hills of discarded sunflower seeds.

Yitian shivered at the cold emitting from the cement walls.

"Well, so, can I help you?"

The officer gestured for them to sit down at a desk in the corner. He had the thick, mottled skin of a person who'd spent their entire life working in the sun. Even in this police station, hardly functional, he looked out of place.

"My father is missing."

"How do you mean?" The officer appeared unconcerned. He sat back in his chair, folded his hands, and cupped them under his paunch.

"He left"—Yitian still found it difficult to find the words to describe what had happened—"he left our home a week ago and still hasn't returned."

"Did you have an argument?"

In a sense, the answer was yes. But that had been so many years ago. Not the kind of heated domestic dispute that this officer probably meant.

"No," his mother picked up the silence. "We never argue."

"So you didn't argue, and he left on his own?"

The tone of the officer's voice made Yitian feel he was the stupid one. He looked expectantly at his mother, hoping she would answer again, but now she'd shrunk into the chair, her body caving convex into its back.

"No one took him?" The officer leaned forward, directing his words at Yitian's mother.

"No," she replied at last. "He just walked out."

"And he didn't say where he was going?"

She shook her head.

"She had an idea," Yitian said. "We think he might have gone to the army barracks where he used to serve. That's the only place outside this area he's ever lived."

The officer slapped his palms on the desk, causing the single sheet of paper there to shudder. "Well, this is an easy case! Go visit the army barracks. I'm sure you'll find your father, waiting for you there!"

"You wouldn't go with us? Or help contact them?"

"How would that help? That's not in our jurisdiction."

"I thought that was what the police did—"

"Look, there's no reason for us to help you, unless you have some other information you're not telling us about. From what you told me, it seems that he left of his own volition. There wasn't any violence, right? So where's the crime? Maybe he just went to see an old friend and forgot to tell you. You know, it's normal for people at his age to forget things. Why don't you go back home, wait a few days? He'll probably show up any day now."

The police officer yawned. His mother looked newly afraid. She said quietly, "Maybe the officer is right. Maybe your father did just forget to tell me he was going somewhere."

"What are you saying? Ba's memory was never bad." He turned back to the officer. "You're just not going to do anything?"

This time the officer didn't even bother to look at Yitian. He reached into his pocket and fished out a pack of cigarettes.

"If you don't want to help me, that's fine. I have a friend at the Hefei City office who I'm sure will help. I'm sure my friend would also like to know how the town governments are managing complaints from the people. I only came here first because I remembered how reliable and helpful the local police were when I was a boy." The firmness of his own tone surprised him. He felt oddly buoyed by a sense that if he could just stay busy enough, press hard enough, it would make up for all the other failures in his obligation to his father.

The officer stared defiantly at Yitian for a moment, then cursed. "Fine. Let's file a report." He extracted a form from the desk, then reached to fill an ink pen so angrily that dark liquid splattered upon his desk and hand.

"What will the report do?" Yitian asked.

"Your name?" The officer's hand hovered over the first rectangle of the form. Yitian sighed and gave it. He'd been so eager to ask for help at the station, but now he saw the form would only get filed away deep in some cabinet, never to be looked at again. He'd become just another victim of the gauntlet of bureaucracy that would give the appearance of action.

"And your national identification number?"

Yitian read the number from his hukou booklet.

"Not your hukou number. Your national identification number," the officer said.

"I don't have that. I just have my hukou booklet."

"Well, then, I can't help you." The officer threw down the pen triumphantly.

"Can't you just use the hukou booklet? Why does it matter?"

"You don't have a national identification number? What do you mean?"

The last time Yitian had lived in this country, there hadn't been any such thing.

"Just use mine, here." His mother shuffled through a rubber-banded packet of documents she'd brought.

The officer didn't reach out to take her laminated card. His eyes narrowed on Yitian.

"According to our country's 1984 Identity Card Provisional Bill, all citizens must have national identity cards. It's a crime not to have one, you know. I can have you fined."

"What do you mean, a crime?" His mother stood up. "We've come here to report a disappearance to you, to tell you that my husband is missing, and you have the balls to say that *we're* the ones who've committed a crime?"

"Aunt, please calm down." His voice, directed at Yitian, was much sterner. "All citizens must have valid identification cards. Where have you been living, anyway, that they let you get away with this since 1984?"

Yitian had been deliberately avoiding the fact that he lived in America. The only identity card he'd kept track of in the past few years was his green card, which, even now, was displayed in the clear display flap of his wallet, always ready to be shown in case he was asked. Until two years ago, he and Mali wouldn't ever have believed they'd get these documents. The Americans didn't want them to be citizens. But then came the massacre at Tiananmen. He sat with Mali in front of their small TV every evening for an entire month, wondering how the place he'd once known as a home had become a half-gray image inside a square box, translated to them through a white news anchor's voice. They squinted to see if there was anyone they knew amongst the students who had come from all over the country to participate—students who were rushing to pack train cars to the brim, sleeping in aisles and hanging out the windows to go to Beijing to be with the protesters. They gathered with other Chinese Americans and protested on the streets; even Steven Hsiung had approached him and said, "It looks like our country is finally changing." *Our.*

On the day the tanks came, Yitian held Mali's hand as she cried watching the footage. "It's so close to my home," Mali said. He said, "I would have gone, if we were still there." He had a feeling he'd escaped a fate he had no right to leave behind.

"*What a tragedy*," his American colleagues said to him. "*That the government would kill their own people, because they hate democracy so much.*" Then, the next year, the American president was on TV signing an order giving Chinese students green cards to protect them from political persecution. Yitian had thought there was something false about the reasoning that they needed protection from their own homes. *Protection* was an uncertain concept, implying both protected and protector, but Yitian couldn't discern the boundaries of either word. And yet, he couldn't deny his desire for the safety he had received. This was what he thought of as he signed the forms giving him the identity of a new country.

Now he told the officer, simply and lamely, that he'd immigrated to America.

"I see, I see. That explains everything! You should have said so earlier!"

The officer excused himself to make a phone call in the adjacent room, so excited that he forgot to close the door properly. Yitian could hear everything when he exclaimed that there was an American in the office.

"I told you not to say anything," his mother scolded.

When the officer returned, it was with the police chief, a younger, noticeably better-dressed man whose eyes had a sharpness to them, the gaze of one accustomed to judgment and evaluation, a person happy to tell others *no*.

"Officer Po has apprised me of the situation," the chief said. He spoke with a bland and implacable accent, not dissimilar to the one Yitian slowly adopted after he'd left the village. "It's rare that we have someone like *you* come here." He took great pauses between sentences to gaze meaningfully at Yitian. He ignored Yitian's mother entirely.

"So, I've been told your father is missing. I'm sure we can find him—he's an old man, right? He can't have gone so far. We'll contact all the villages."

"I can give you his description, if that helps. Here, I have a picture, too." Yitian pulled out a photograph of his father, the only one they had. The picture was black-and-white, depicting a man almost forty years younger, who'd just enlisted in the military. The expression on his face was defiant, clearly proud, as if in the middle of a retort to the photographer just a second before the shutter snapped.

"Yes, yes, that would help. Very smart, you are, from all your years abroad." The chief took the photo without a glance. "That's exactly the kind of information we need.

"It's a lot of work for us, though," the chief continued. "I'd need to send all my officers out to go look, and they wouldn't be here in the station for days. What if there's an incident in the township while they're away? You have to understand, it's a great burden to us."

"What do you mean, sir? Of course I would greatly appreciate it."

"We appreciate your . . . appreciation. But you see, appreciation isn't the only thing. Is there anything else you can offer us? To help us, in this small place. You must understand, we don't have very many resources. Not like you in *America*."

Oddly, the word put Yitian at ease. He felt a click of confirmation. He excused himself to the hallway, where he counted his money and calculated the very most he could afford. He rolled the bills into a narrow cylinder that he hoped would disguise how little there actually was. The amount was hardly a quarter of his monthly salary. What choice did he have? If he refused to pay the bribe, he'd be viewed as stingy, not even willing to part with this small sum of money in the hope of finding his father. He was sure that his mother would note that sad fact, even as she pretended to be outraged by the request. In the absence of providing actual help, climbing these mechanical steps on the ladder of obligation was the best he could do.

When he handed the bills to the police chief, Yitian expected a protest about the amount, but to his surprise, the chief simply squeezed the money and then smiled broadly—not the one of before, full of implication, but this time lit with genuine pleasure.

It was the simplicity of this guile that told Yitian he'd wasted his money. The officer was waiting to snigger, unable to believe he'd pulled this off. The money would be distributed to the others as soon as he and his mother left, and no one would ever speak of this case again, except perhaps to mention Yitian as the gullible foreigner who'd financed a few weeks of their drinking. They'd mock him, how he didn't understand any of their ways because he was *American* now, and in that mocking would be a scorn even deeper than they would show to a real white American, the anger at a fellow countryman who'd accessed a whole new world they never would.

A fterward, he and his mother walked slowly and silently through the central street. She did not even scold him about the bribe. Between them he felt an unspoken heaviness and disbelief that they'd reached a dead end so quickly.

Women came out of their shops, leaned against their brooms, and stared. Wrinkles collected in the straight lines of their mouths, determined to reveal nothing. They didn't seem to be affected by the cold at all. He was sure that somehow the entire town had heard about the arrival of an *American*. When they were children, the town was the exciting place Yitian and Yishou looked forward to visiting for weeks. The trips could only be demanded by some special occasion or errand, but when the work of their visit was done, he and his brother snuck out onto this street to stare hungrily at the shops selling fragrant food they couldn't afford. Yishou, the more charming one, could watch a shopkeeper with such open eyes that she'd take pity upon them and hand over scraps. The women hanging up wooden boards over their shops had been powerful people then, but now all the storefronts looked shabby and provincial. Even the smells of food wafting to him felt unclean rather than inviting. The only person who ignored them was a single boy leading a cow upon a rope, their two shadows creeping and announcing them long after they walked past.

It hadn't been a lie, that he had a friend in Hefei he could ask for help.

"You'll be back soon, right?" his mother asked. "You aren't going to go back to America without telling me?"

"How could I do that? I won't go back until we find out where Ba is."

"You really have a friend in Hefei?"

He said yes, but she continued to worry the hem of her shirt. He understood her disbelief. How could he, who hadn't lived in this country for years, who'd been to Hefei only a handful of times, possibly have someone who would help him there?

"I don't know why you need to go so far. Can't I go with you?" She searched for something else to stuff into the smaller bag he was bringing into the city, finally settling on a washcloth. He took the cloth and gingerly placed it on top of the textbook that he'd been careful to transfer out of his suitcase. It seemed so long ago that he'd looked at its cover in America and decided to pack it.

"This is the only person in any official position I know. Besides, what if Ba comes back and there's nobody home?"

She complained that he was surely overpaying for the taxi he'd arranged. He didn't reply; at a departure, he preferred the distance from the truth of a moment's feeling.

"I'll see you in a few days," he said.

He motioned for her to go home, but she continued to wait at the village entrance as the car pulled away. He watched her grow smaller in the side mirror. She'd never shown an inkling of this kind of doubt about his father. If she disagreed with him about something, she simply changed her mind. To Yitian, the relationship appeared less like love and more like obligation, but perhaps there wasn't a difference for a person like her. She boasted about her strength and ability to earn work points like a man alongside her undying loyalty to her husband without appearing to notice any contradiction.

Nine

The last time he'd heard from Hanwen was three years ago now, when she wrote to tell him her husband had been assigned to a posting in Hefei City. *Can you believe it?* he'd read. *I don't know how this happened. He has no linkages to this city or Anhui at all, so it is a surprise to be here, of all places. I thought of you when he told me. I thought I'd never return or be so close to this place again.*

It was the first time she'd written in years. He didn't know how she'd gotten his address at the graduate student office of his university, where the letter arrived unexpectedly on a dull winter afternoon when he was just about to lock up and go home. Mali had called earlier with the news that Mrs. Suzanna was giving her a raise, and she wanted to celebrate. He planned to buy her flowers.

He'd been flipping through his mail when suddenly her name jumped out at him, scrawled on a brown airmail envelope. He double-checked to make sure he hadn't imagined it. He'd never seen her write in English before, and the sloping letters on the front of the envelope were messier than he would have expected from her.

After that, he'd hoped—guiltily, but still a hope, he had to admit—for more letters. He wrote to her when his office changed so that she'd have his new address. She would surely be reminded often of the village of their shared memories now that she was living nearby. He wondered if she would go with her husband on his official trips to visit villages around Hefei. Perhaps, rounding a corner of a road, she'd glimpse a hill that reminded her of the small embankment where they used to read together, and she'd rush home, excited to write him a letter about what she'd seen and how it made her think of him.

Whenever he picked up his office mail, he scanned each envelope carefully for the loping handwriting, but nothing came from her. Once in a while, he considered writing to her at that address on the envelope, but then he thought of Mali. He stashed the envelope into a drawer in his office, where Mali never went.

Now, he didn't even know if Hanwen still lived in Hefei. Local government officials could be reassigned without notice, casualties of machinations higher above, and it was possible that she hadn't bothered to tell him.

The only hint he had was a newspaper clipping from a year-old edition of *Sing Tao Daily*, one of the few Chinese newspapers they could get in America. The sighting had taken him completely by shock: a Sunday afternoon, he and Mali just returned home from the 99 Ranch Market. He was always tired after the grocery store trips, didn't know how he'd once lived in a country that assaulted his senses as the crowds in the store and the briny smells of the fresh fish tanks did. So he'd been relaxing into the loveseat, ready to doze as he went through the paper, when he flipped the page and was shocked to see her husband's name in the text captioning a picture. Deng Xiaoping had made a state visit to Anhui, and the newspaper printed a photo of him visiting a brick factory in the suburbs. Everyone was out of focus in the picture except for Deng, who was shaking the hand of a factory employee. The person labeled her husband was the farthest back. Yitian squinted at the photo to ascertain more about him, but the man's hunched shoulders made him seem determined to blend into the background.

She'd written her husband's name in the letter she sent him, but the feeling then was softened by distance, a kind of dull recognition that time could leave a person so changed. That was nothing like looking at the man's face in the newspaper picture and his disbelief at the thought that this man had ever kissed Hanwen. Yitian's hand had slipped around the handle of the teacup and when he looked down he saw the liquid had spilled onto the carpet, creating a stain that spread then darkened the floor to the color of wet earth.

After they made it some distance out of the village, Yitian extracted the textbook from his bag, opened the front cover, and handed it to the driver.

"This is where I'm going," he said.

The driver squinted uncertainly at the address. "Don't all you people who live over there have your own drivers?"

Yitian wondered if she had become one of the rich women he'd seen in the gossip columns of newspapers, being driven everywhere with a tiny designer purse wedged in the crook of her arm. If that was the case, would they still share any common language?

"Do you do business, boss?" the driver crushed his cigarette and sat up straighter in the seat.

Yitian ignored him. He didn't remember the country like this when he left, so obsessed with status and money and finding their notions of self within the material. Back then, all anyone talked about were ideals for the country's future.

They drove for an hour, out of the village and then into Hefei, until the taxi left him off at a gated complex bordering a small, man-made lake. Yitian eyed the guard standing to the left of the gates and tried to form a plan. Perhaps if he went straight through the gate as if he belonged here, the guard wouldn't say anything to him. The man was old and diminutive, the shoulder marks of his uniform drooping down his arms, and didn't look like he could hurt Yitian.

"Who are you? What is your business here?" The guard's voice barked, before Yitian even had a chance to get close to the gate.

He was startled by the voice. The particular guttural tones and bend in the words identified it immediately as an accent from his village. He'd imagined putonghua would be more useful in this wealthy setting, but now he purposefully switched to his voice's older form.

"I'm here to see Tian Hanwen. She lives here, right?"

If the guard also recognized Yitian's accent, he didn't show any sign. He went into the guard's office and came back out flipping a register. "She hasn't told us to expect any visitors today."

So she did live in one of those homes beyond the gate. The realization arrived in him like a punch in the gut. It had been somehow easy to make the journey to this address when he didn't really believe she'd be here. This place had only been like any other dot on a map, anonymous and distant, a house that he could walk into and find the rooms entirely empty.

"She didn't know that I was coming," he told the guard.

"Then go back home and tell her to come wait for you at the gate. She has to come here and get you herself."

"I don't have her phone number, and I'm only in town for a few days—" Yitian stopped. He sounded even more suspicious than before. "You're from Tang Family Village, aren't you?"

"So what if I am?"

"I am, too! We're laoxiang."

"I've never seen you there before," the guard said.

"Well, I've never seen you there, either."

"My family moved away when I was very young. But I go back there every year to see my aunts and uncles during the New Year. So I would have seen you there, if you were really from Tang Family Village."

"How would I be able to speak like this if I was lying?"

The guard appeared to consider this. There were minuscule differences between the accents of their village and surrounding ones, created and solidified over hundreds of years. Even Baijia Village or Five Groves people didn't sound the same as those from Tang Family Village. How remarkable, Yitian sometimes thought, that now he lived in a country where people couldn't even hear the difference between Chinese and Korean.

"Fine, then you're from Tang Family Village. What do you want here?"

"I told you earlier. I'm here to see Tian Hanwen."

The guard gazed over Yitian's shoulder, where there were lines of neatly pruned bushes. Yitian understood the strategy immediately—the guard would pretend that Yitian was not there, until he had no choice but to concede to the reality of the situation and leave.

He felt hopeless as he peered through the dense shrubbery beyond the gate. He couldn't see any glimpse of houses within, which suggested that they were low and spread out, so unlike the block apartment buildings that filled the rest of the city. He was so close to her now. He could scale this gate and run away from the guard, and then sprint across the gravel path. He could run until he found her house and knocked on the door, and her smile of recognition as she answered would render the guard irrelevant.

He was sure the desperation was thick in his voice as he said, "Sir, please, I'm not trying to do anything bad. I'm from your village. My name is Tang Yitian."

"How do you know Tang Yitian?" The guard's eyes snapped into focus on Yitian's face. "*You're* Tang Yitian? No way. *No way.*"

Yitian took out his hukou booklet to show the guard, who suddenly broke into a grin. He grasped Yitian's hand, brought his whole body close, and then patted his back.

"Well, why didn't you say so earlier? My mother was always talking about you. So smart and going to America. Isn't it strange we've met in this place now? Imagine!"

The guard was laughing, suddenly eager to go through the ritual of naming all the mutual places and people they knew.

"So you know where my mother and father live, right?" Yitian said. "How could I try to trick you?"

"Yes, and I suppose . . . if I was questioned, if anything went wrong, I'd be able to tell them to go to your house and find you, isn't that right?"

"Exactly. You know where I live if anything happens. Just tell Tian Hanwen that Tang Yitian is here to see her and needs her help. We're old friends. She'll recognize my name."

The guard took his keys out and locked the gate, telling Yitian he'd be back soon. After a few steps he turned back. "Nothing inappropriate between you and Mrs. Tian, right? Nothing that would get me in trouble with her husband, right?"

"No, no, of course not."

Yitian picked the leaves off a bush until he heard the sound of footsteps and conversation from the other side of the gate. There were two voices now: the guard's, and a woman's answering him.

He inhaled deeply.

"Sir? Tang Yitian, sir? I've brought her," the guard announced from the other side of the door. It unlocked with a click, and slowly fell open on its hinges.

Yitian's head snapped up, but the person who came through the gate looked like nothing more than a young village girl. She must be hardly eighteen, he thought.

"I think there's been some mistake," he said.

The girl looked nervously at the guard, then back at Yitian. "He told me you were waiting out here. Have I done something wrong? Mrs. Wang told me to come get you."

Ten

"You *must* try this tea if you ever go to Yunnan," she said, popping the lid off a small tin and passing it to him.

Yitian, who'd been examining her appearance while she was occupied preparing tea, was startled by the sweet scent of chrysanthemum.

"Sure. I'll keep that in mind," he said lamely. He didn't know how to tell her that he couldn't imagine himself ever traveling to Yunnan, that he wasn't whatever kind of person she'd become, who took vacations to exotic destinations with her family and had a mind for such activities of leisure.

When she'd greeted him at the door, he'd been so struck by the difference in her appearance that he found it difficult to speak. As a teenager, her beauty was the kind that crept up after months of knowing her, a new feature of her face revealing itself each time they met. Now, it had become striking and purposeful, features chiseled and focusing themselves into a face that demanded admiration. Her hair had been cut short and permed into an elegant pouf that curled in around her long neck. Powder blurred her skin and her eyes were lined to make them appear deeper set than before. A wide pink skirt flounced and billowed around her calves, so glamorous that he wondered if she'd quickly changed while the ayi had gone to get him, or if she always dressed so elegantly, even in her own home. Mali had a penchant for soft, practical clothes, which she sleepily pulled out of her closet in the mornings without much consideration.

She'd led him to a table, sturdy and shined, in an alcove off the living room. The duplex was gigantic by Chinese standards. When he was young, he'd thought to have money meant to be a city person in a block apartment, a home crammed with objects the measure of one's wealth. Then, in America, he'd found that rich people liked to live in stand-alone homes far out of town. *That sounds so beautiful and idyllic*, colleagues said, when he told them about where he'd grown up. He was sure they were making fun of him somehow.

Her home now defied what he knew of both countries. In the living room they'd walked through, huge heads of jade lettuces and bok choy ornamented the side tables, chandeliers dangled, the ceiling was crimped with molding imitating the Europeans. He felt as alien as he had when the dean of his department had invited him to a party at his hillside home, an uncomfortable evening that Yitian had spent feeling acutely aware of his body—how his fingers sweated on the stem of a wineglass, which hand to hold the knife in and which the fork—while Mali chattered freely, unencumbered by her accent, which made him wince every time she spoke. She'd left the evening with promises to attend an aerobics class with the dean's wife.

Just as Mali had melted into that space at whim, so Hanwen appeared utterly at ease here.

"It's hard to believe you live in a place like this," he said.

"But you're American. You must see things like this all the time," she said. Her long fingers moved deftly with tongs to pick up teacups, just warmed with hot water. He felt himself sized up by her words.

"That's not what my life in America is like," he said. "Everyone thinks that I live some fancy existence over there. I've been a graduate student all these years, close to broke." Even had he wanted to pretend with her, he couldn't. She knew too much of him and would have easily been able to see through the lie.

She put down the teacups and, for the first time since he'd arrived, looked at him, really *looked* at him. He could see a blaze of her old determination to make herself understood as she said, "I wonder if you've been away too long. You can't see how we would see you. Our amazement at you."

"Maybe that's true. I'm too selfish in all my judgments."

"That's not what I meant," she said, and her eyes were adrift again. She handed him a cup of tea. "Never mind. It's a surprise that you're here. I wondered if you would look me up on your trips back, but I always thought you'd be too busy, what with all your obligations to your family."

"Actually"—he swallowed—"it's my first time back in Anhui."

"The very first? In how long?"

The number *fifteen* arrived heavy in his mouth. He had kept the count, but only now, seeing her face and the youth of her features, did the years not seem to add up.

"American life must be keeping you busy, then," she said. "So, you've been in graduate school."

When he mentioned that he'd studied math, she interrupted. "Wasn't that your least favorite subject? Or am I remembering wrong?"

"They forced me to take math classes in college," he explained, as if to a stranger. How could she forget helping him to learn those formulas on that hilltop when they'd first met? "And it wasn't so bad as I thought it would be. Actually, I turned out to be quite good at it, I suppose."

"I'm not surprised. Things have always come easily to you. I always knew you'd make something of yourself."

She didn't smile as she complimented him, and her words had the recited quality of a rote politeness.

"Do you have children?" she asked.

"No."

"That's good. Better to keep your own time, at least for now. And what does your wife do?"

He realized with shame that he hadn't wanted to talk about Mali.

"Real estate."

"Oh, that sounds like a good job. If it's anything like here, real estate is a lucrative industry. All of the rich people here got their money from developments." She said *rich people* as if she was not one of them. He was sure that the image in her mind was of someone touring luxury high-rises or sprawling villas, so different from the small condos that Mali and Mrs. Suzanna sold to young families.

"Do you work?" he asked.

"No. I don't need to." The declaration came from her easily.

He glanced down at the dark wood of the table, swirling his tea. He couldn't believe that they'd arrived at a silence so quickly. For years, he'd imagined the moment of seeing her again, but had never considered the possibility that they'd have so little to say.

She called the ayi in to bring more water. The teapot was still almost entirely full, their tiny, delicate cups capable of holding little volume at all.

"She seems very young," he said, not for any particular reason other than that being the first thought to cross his mind.

"She's twenty. Older than we were when we were working in the fields."

"Would you wish that on someone else, though?" he asked. "I thought we had left that period of history behind."

She glanced upward at the ceiling before speaking so softly he wasn't sure if he imagined the hesitancy in her voice.

"I think they were my happiest years."

"Mine, too," he said. At last, she'd acknowledged the time they spent together hadn't already been replaced in her mind by all the glamorous memories that must have come in her life after.

He wasn't sure if he meant the words, but it was too late—she was already smiling, her first real smile of the afternoon. "Really? Remember how you used to complain about how sore you were from the work?"

"I only said that to make you feel better."

"*Me?*" She raised her arms above her head and mimed someone hitting their own foot with a hoe, then gasping in surprise.

The closed line of her lipstick broke into laughter, then he was joining her, and suddenly the tension between them had evaporated. Their laughs were loud and consuming, shaking through his limbs and relaxing them, so that when the ayi returned with a filled thermos, she looked alarmed at how quickly the mood had shifted.

Hanwen waited for her to leave, but even the silence felt different now—loose and full of possibility. "You're right, though," she said. "It was very tiring. Thank you for reminding me. Being in the city and away for so long, I seem to have only remembered the good parts."

"It's the same for me." He took a sip of tea and the liquid warmed him. He felt relaxed and honest. "I remember only how beautiful the countryside was, not any of the worms in our stomachs or how plainly we used to eat. But even when I do remember those things, it doesn't seem so bad anymore."

"I know what you mean—it's like a nice kind of suffering, isn't it?"

He nodded. "And even if I only remember it one way, what does it matter? Things are changing so quickly. Hefei looks nothing like it did fifteen years ago. Even my village—the changes aren't as big there yet, but I had this feeling when I was back there, that everything was on the cusp of being different forever. Like I might accidentally look away and then when I turn back, everything will be gone. But I couldn't tell whether it was the same, or whether it was just me who'd changed."

"Tell me what else you notice. I can't tell, because it seems to happen right under my nose."

She looked eagerly at him. Everything he could think of seemed somehow trite, an observation that could just as easily be read in an encyclopedia article about China. He paused, then tried, "When I first arrived in America, what I thought about most was how lonely the country was. People were always in their cars or in their houses, separated from everyone else. No one really walks in the streets there or knows the people who live around them. And when everyone is in their homes, there's this deep silence all around. You can't hear anyone else at all. It's not like in the village. It feels like there's not a single person in the world other than yourself.

"Once, when I first learned to drive, there was this time I was stopped at a traffic light. I was so nervous driving back then. I always thought I was going to mess something up. My hands were sweating on the steering wheel. I looked over just to have something to do. And there was this woman in the car next to me sobbing. She was so young and beautiful, I wondered why she would be crying alone. Maybe one of her parents had died, or she'd broken up with her boyfriend. But she couldn't see me at all. Then I heard everyone honking behind me, because the light was green."

He glanced up to see if she was still listening. He was afraid the story would not make sense, but her lips were pressed together in concentration.

"I couldn't stop thinking about that for a long time afterward. I thought I'd probably seen one of the saddest moments of her life, but we were so separate. I thought, something like that would never happen in my village. People never cried alone like that. Someone would always hear you and come to you.

"But then when I was finally back in the village a couple of days ago, I wondered if that was true anymore. There were houses locked up, and from the dust on the knockers you could see no one had been inside them for a very long time. People are going to the cities to live and work, and they aren't going to come back to live in those houses ever again. The only ones left are like my mother, who wouldn't know how to survive in a big city. I thought, I could go into any one of those empty houses and cry like that woman, and no one would notice.

"I have to remind myself that there are reasons we wanted to leave so badly back then. Don't you think?" he paused. "What happened to Yishou would never happen now."

Her shoulders twitched. He imagined that she'd wanted to reach out her hands to him. "No, it wouldn't," she said at last.

"We know the names for everything now," he said. His brother's name, which he hadn't said in so long, still hung heavy between his lips. He never spoke of Yishou with Mali.

"I never knew what to say to comfort you. I always wished I'd had better words. Then when I got back to Shanghai, I realized I didn't need to say anything to you at all. That nothing would have helped."

He felt the warmth of her words, but also a prick of disappointment, of the implication that she'd felt her own griefs in those years, which he didn't know and which had made her the person in front of him.

"You did the best—"

"Ma, Ma!" A young boy's voice rang through the hallway, interrupting him. Then a small figure dashed into the room.

The boy was only about as tall as the table, on which he almost bumped his head as he rushed in. He was followed immediately by an older woman, stooped at the waist, grabbing his arm. "I told you, your Ma is busy with a guest!"

"I wanted to show Ma," he yelled. He shoved at them a piece of paper blanketed in slashes of red and green crayon. "Look, it's a rainbow!"

"Come on now," the old woman said, grabbing the boy's hand. But her gaze lingered on Yitian and she didn't move to leave the room.

"Ma, this is Tang Yitian. An old friend from my sent-down days. Yitian, this is my mother and my son."

"I've heard about you, many years ago," he said to her mother, and immediately regretted it. Her mother's eyebrows raised as she said, "Oh, really?"

"Ma," Hanwen said quickly, "could you bring Yuanyuan back to his room?"

"Come on, let's go," her mother said. To Hanwen, she said, "Don't forget, you need to leave for dinner soon. Nice to meet you." She looked Yitian up and down before she left.

When he looked back at Hanwen, the openness had gone. She was checking her watch. "My mother is right. I do have to go to a dinner soon."

Did he imagine a hint of regret in her voice, the implication that she'd prefer to stay here and talk with him?

"How long will you be in town?" she asked. "Maybe we can see one another again?"

"Yes—actually, I came here because I wanted to ask your help with something."

"Ah, so you have a favor to ask?" Her eyebrows lifted up, and he hurried to say, "Not like that—"

"I was joking," she said, but her eyes didn't have their earlier mirth.

"Something happened in my family." He paused. For the past half hour, the lingering dread in his chest had gone, so occupied was he with the surprise of seeing her again. But now it returned suddenly, roaring and even more painful than before, as if angry he'd forgotten for even a moment. "I mean, my father has gone missing. For eight days now. He left and no one has any idea of where he went."

She asked him a series of questions: Eight days? What have they discovered? Hadn't they made any progress by now? Had he gone to another official to ask for help? Her questioning was rapid and demanding, but he felt reassured. He was reminded of how she'd approached each book they read so rigorously and methodically. Each time they met she brought an organized notebook, containing all the copied passages that she thought were important. Beside her, he'd felt sloppy, but always safe in her hands.

He told her about his visit to the police station.

"So many small town officials are like that now," she said. "They ask for a bribe to do even the simplest thing. Most of them wouldn't dare try that with a foreigner, though. This man must have been especially daring. People are always coming to my husband to ask things from him, too."

"I'm sorry. I wouldn't ask unless—"

"No, no, that's not what I meant. Of course, I'll ask him to help. He can talk to the police chief for the city. They'll put out an alert to all the townships in this area. Do you have a picture and a description of him? If he's still here in Anhui, we'll find him."

Yitian's fingers lingered on the picture of his father. Even though the young man in that photo was so impossibly young, almost incredible to name as his father, this photo was the only physical evidence of his face.

As if she could feel his panic, she said softly, "I'll ask them to copy it and give it back to you, all right?"

When he mentioned he was thinking about going to the barracks to check, she said, "You don't need to do that. You'll have no idea of who to talk to if you go. I'll get my husband to contact the people over there."

He was relieved that he hadn't had to ask, that he'd said the problem and she intuited what he needed. Her utter sureness in the world, of how she could work in it, was a quality she hadn't had before, one he'd never developed himself. He felt a glimpse of that old tenderness again, but in the next moment, she was rising, saying she really did have to leave now. She couldn't keep her husband waiting at dinner any longer.

Over his protests, she called a car for him and instructed him to stay in Hefei while they waited for news from her husband.

"Here's my phone number. I'll be in touch as soon as I hear anything. I'll have the driver take you to a hotel we know," she said to him at the door.

"Oh, I already have a hotel. Don't worry."

Eyeing him with his old duffle bag hanging off his shoulder, she didn't seem to believe him, but he insisted. If he went to the hotel she suggested, then she would offer to pay for the stay, and by the rules of propriety they would have to engage in a protracted battle over the bill. It wasn't the kind of polite, phony argument he wanted for their reunion.

When the car approached, without thinking, he stepped toward her for a hug, only realizing what he'd done wrong when he felt the absence of her arms around him. Her body stiffened, and he let go quickly.

"I'm sorry."

The gesture had felt so natural to him, the one that would have marked a moment like this in America, but he could see how uncomfortable he'd made her. It was as close as he had ever held her. She stepped away from him, wobbly on the pointed tips of her shoes.

"Bye, then," he said, and ducked his head into the car.

He regretted asking the driver to take him to any cheap hotel. The instinct he had in America, to always save as much money as possible, had taken over, though he could have afforded much better here. His room had the strong odor of mildew and vinegar, and in front of his bed there was a long, wood-colored stain on the carpet, which he had to shuffle sideways to avoid. Despite the fact that he had barely slept since his arrival, he couldn't fall asleep. The blankets on the hotel bed had a slick quality to them, as if coated in a thin layer of plastic film, making them cling to his skin.

He gave up sliding around the comforter and went to the lobby.

"You want to make an international call?" the clerk asked. "You do know how expensive that will be, right? You'll have to pay up front."

She fumbled with the phone, checked the connection, and shuffled to find a phone card from inside a disorganized drawer of old hotel trinkets.

Then, miraculously, her voice came through the line.

"Hello?" Mali spoke groggily, slow, unlike her. He checked the clock on the cracking lobby wall and counted backward.

"Sorry. I forgot to check the time before I called."

"No, I should be awake anyway. How are things over there? Any news?"

He told her about the neighbors in the village and the unhelpful police department, then, "I met with an old friend today who works in the city. They said they'll help me contact some officials, to check the train records and see if my father has been there. They'll talk to the central police station, too, and send out a notice," he said. The pronoun he used—她—sounded the same for both men and women, its gender only distinguishable in written form. He knew what Mali would hear, and what she would guess instinctively. A city official, an old friend of his—a man.

"I didn't know you knew anyone who worked in Hefei," she said.

"They're an old friend. I haven't spoken to them in years."

"After all this time, I still keep finding out new things about you, Tang Yitian." He heard the smile in her voice. "Well, I feel hopeful, then. I expect I'll hear good news from you, any day now."

Yitian felt suddenly exhausted by the brightness of her, that he could not breathe in the small space around it. Even in America, she'd flung open the door of her life so widely that he was only able to squeeze himself around its sharp edges. When they first arrived, she'd jumped into learning English, making a whole group of friends in the community college where she took night classes. Her ease made him afraid to voice the deep loneliness that he'd felt for much of those first few years, the sense he held that, even as his English improved, there would always be some boundary in the transmission of meaning that he never would be able to cross. When they were at the store, and the clerk made a joke they couldn't understand, he wanted her to meet his eyes and to let their secret language pass through them, not bluntly ask the clerk what the joke meant. Her reactions to the unexpected were nothing like his own feelings of frustration, ones that quickly calcified into loneliness. If she sensed his reticence, she pushed against stating it out loud, until all he was left with was the small house of his sadness that he could only enter into alone.

And yet, her relentless ability to adapt to the new of America was what had kept him going all these years. Though he'd been the one who brought them to America, it was she who'd built the foundation of their life once they'd arrived. Of all the Chinese immigrants they knew, he and Mali were the only ones who had American friends, all because she'd been unafraid to introduce herself to their neighbors even when those greetings made up most of her English vocabulary.

He imagined her in bed by herself now, curled phone cord wrapped around her finger and letting the receiver fall over her face, so close to her mouth that her voice arrived muffled. Sometimes, it was harder to hear people when they were so close. Hanwen hadn't been like that at all. Even now, he couldn't help but wonder what it would have been like to close the distance between them. If he'd pulled his chair closer to the table and allowed his knees to touch hers underneath.

He cleared his throat. "How are things over there?" he asked.

"I didn't sleep well last night," she said. "I think I might be coming down with something." So that was why she was still in bed, which was unlike her. She'd usually be up by this time, already making him breakfast and talking excitedly about what she had to do at work that day. "I'm just not used to sleeping without you next to me."

"Same," he said mechanically. In the eight years of their marriage, he'd only slept without her a handful of times, when he had to attend academic conferences. He'd spent those evenings in hotel rooms nicer than any he would have paid for on his own, feeling lost in the wide expanses of pillows and fluffy comforters that were piled on his body. But he'd felt none of her absence when he laid sleepless moments ago; obligation, rather than need, had driven him to call her.

They spoke rapidly about the water bill before he said he had to go. Whenever they called people abroad, they talked like this to save money, so quickly that, to an eavesdropper, it would have sounded like there was an emergency. Usually this saddened him, but today he was relieved. He'd shared with her some of the day's news, but other parts were still beyond what he knew how to say.

Eleven

Hanwen waited until his car was out of sight before she unclasped her hands. She'd hid them behind her back so he wouldn't see her shaking. She was sure she'd successfully masked her reaction at seeing him, until that last embrace. When he'd remarked upon her home, she'd thought recklessly for a moment of meeting his eyes hard, and blurting out: *Can't you see I would give up all of this for your life, in an instant? Can't you see that you are living the life I wanted?* She'd wanted to shake him when he described his American life in those deprecating terms. He never understood how much he had, then or now.

She was hardly back inside the house when her mother was upon her and the questions began.

"Who was that?"

Hanwen had noticed her face, hovering at the edge of their front window, as she'd said goodbye to Yitian. She wondered if her mother had seen the hug.

"No one. Just an old friend. I told you."

"Where does he work now?"

"He lives in America."

"America?" Her mother's voice was sharp and inquisitory, a way that she hadn't been with Hanwen in years. She never voiced any opinions on Hanwen's marriage, and at the first sign of a disagreement between Hanwen and Guifan, she retreated to another room. She couldn't have been more different than how she'd been when Hanwen was young, when she'd wanted to know every corner of Hanwen's life to make sure nothing deviated from the direction she wanted it to take.

"Miss, the car's outside. You're going to be late," Ayi came to say. Hanwen checked her watch. She should have left twenty minutes ago for the restaurant the host had chosen in a small forest complex on the outskirts of town.

"Ma, I don't have time to talk about this right now," she said. "I'm already running behind."

"Let me help you get your things ready, then," her mother said.

"No, it'll only slow me down. Don't stay up waiting for us tonight, okay? We might be out late."

She left her mother in the living room, clutching her hands. Her mother was at a loss for what to do when she couldn't help around the house. Two weeks ago, she'd slipped while giving Yuanyuan a bath. Ayi had found her, sprawled prone on the floor of the bathroom, her toes dipping in the puddling water from the showerhead that had begun spraying freezing water. Since then, Hanwen had forbade her to do any household tasks, but she often still caught her mother pacing around the house, rearranging items that she'd only just nudged into place hours earlier. Hanwen encouraged her to watch television—other elderly women adored the soap operas—but her mother refused to even turn on the new color set they'd purchased for her room, saying it would rot her brain.

When she dialed Guifan's office, his young secretary answered.

"It's me," Hanwen said. "Can you give Guifan a message? I'm going to be a little late to dinner, Yuanyuan threw a tantrum—"

"Oh, Mrs. Wang," the secretary interrupted. "You better tell him yourself. He's just about to leave."

Guifan's voice, urgent and impatient, came on the line before she could object.

"Hello? Hanwen? What is it? Shouldn't you have left already?"

"Yuanyuan was being difficult. I'm going to be a little late."

"How will it look when you arrive so late? They asked specifically to have you there."

"And why did they ask that?"

She realized with a start how accusatory they both sounded, rare for them. Confrontation and blame were not in either of their personalities, and this was one of the reasons she liked him. He was more interested in peace than in his own pride, a quality she thought rare in men.

Guifan's exhalation was staticky and loud over the receiver. He would be slouched in the leather chair behind his office desk now, his eyes closed and his hand rubbing at his temples, resenting even this thirty-minute delay in the orderliness he preferred.

His voice was calmer when he spoke again. "All right, I'll tell them you're running late. Just hurry."

At the softness of his voice, her anger faded. She went upstairs to their bedroom, wanting to check her makeup in the mirror one last time. When the guard had come with news of Yitian's arrival, she'd briefly debated wiping off her lipstick. She'd wondered if it announced too much for a meeting she'd hoped to treat casually, but now she felt secretly pleased as she examined her reflection. She'd caught glimpses of him watching her, and in this way they had been like mirrors, refracting upon one another. She guessed his wife was the type of practical woman who didn't wear makeup. She hoped that her appearance might have surprised him, in the way his face surprised her when she opened the door. She'd expected someone thin and wiry, whose head might be bent slightly at the neck as he looked down upon his worn shoes. Hands shoved into his pockets, hair overgrown, falling over his eyes. This was how she always used to find him. Walking up to him, there was the impression that a part of him was not of this world, and only when other people entered his direct line of vision did he materialize completely. Instead, there'd been that alert man at the door. His back straight, eyes wholly absorbed in the world around him, taking it all in and utterly a part of it.

When he said he hadn't visited in years, her stomach—privately, guiltily—had done a small backflip. She'd been sure that he came back often and had decided never to contact her. Whenever she thought of the single letter she sent him, she felt awash with shame. What business had she, contacting someone who had no thought of her?

She was overwhelmed by desire to tell someone about Yitian's appearance. She imagined returning to the dorm room in Tang Family Village, collapsing breathlessly upon her bunk, and saying, "You won't believe who came to visit me today!" But she didn't have any friends to see in this city where her husband had been assigned, which was caught in a bland space between the provincial culture it was trying to shed and the opulence of the more prosperous cities it aspired to be. At first, she'd tried going for afternoon tea at the homes of other cadres' wives. In their homes vast and adorned with rosewood furniture, they talked about their children and gossiped about other officials' mistresses. She was sure the other women called her standoffish, now, at the parties she didn't attend. She didn't know how she would otherwise make friends. Errands that might force her into the city were all handled by others: her driver picked up and dropped off Yuanyuan at school; their ayi or her mother went to the market each morning for groceries. At times she felt the loneliness so overwhelming it became like a physical shadow pressing upon her. She'd sleep in the middle of the day to avoid the feeling, and dreamed of walking through her longtang as the mothers called their children in for dinner through the iron grates of their windows. Or she'd be weeding in the rice paddies, the water still chilly in the early spring as it lapped against her calves.

Only when she hurried into the car minutes later did Hanwen realize her mother had never mentioned the hug, and this was how she knew with certainty that the gesture had not been insignificant.

In the car driving out of the city, she told the driver not to rush. She wanted to delay the arrival at the dinner for as long as she could.

About a month ago, while Yuanyuan had been at school and her mother was out on her morning walk around the complex, there'd been a knock on the front door, which almost never happened. She was just looking up when Ayi was already running to answer.

Two strangers stepped into her house, one of them so short he could meet her gaze exactly. He was dressed in a crisp, Western-style taupe suit, the other man much taller and wearing a plain white undershirt with holes in the sleeves that pulled up around his large and ropy arms. If she hadn't been so surprised, the sight of these two men together would've struck her as comical.

They walked into the home without being invited, gazes directed firmly at some point above her. The man in the suit picked a spot on the couch with the air of someone who owned the place. The taller man stood stoically in the corner, wedged between two cabinets, watching.

"Are you here to see my husband, Wang Guifan?" she said. This seemed the most likely explanation. "He's never home during the day. Perhaps you should try his office instead."

"No, actually. We chose this time when your husband wouldn't be home. We wanted to speak to you specifically."

The suited man took his time before saying, "My surname is Qian. We're colleagues of your husband's."

They looked around the room, appearing disinterested in her, eyes pausing at various points: the bookshelf, the china cabinet, the picture of her father displayed on the wall above an offering of fruit. Perhaps they'd come to scope out her furniture before robbing her. Ever since working at the restaurant, she'd felt a pang of fear whenever she was alone with men she didn't know, and these were the kinds of men—powerful, who didn't ask permission—who put her on edge.

Mr. Qian commented briefly on the weather, colder than usual at this time of year, before saying, "We've been working on a project with your husband. A new shopping complex, the International Prosperity Center. Has he told you about it?"

She shook her head.

"Does your husband often tell you about his work?" He raised his eyebrows in suggestion. She sensed he wanted her to pick up some meaning behind his words, but she couldn't guess what. Again she said no.

"Well, we can understand that, can't we?" He turned toward his companion. "Yes, Mr. Pan agrees with me. Your husband knows the job of a good housewife isn't to know too much about her husband's work. You stay home, take care of things here. You don't need to get involved with things that don't concern you." She didn't sense a need for response. His speech was quiet and efficient, unlike all the men in power for whom she'd always felt disdain, ones she'd met at dinners and receptions and who never let the slightest drop of self-awareness or sense of discretion tinge their boasts.

He rose slowly from the couch and took a porcelain vase from the bookshelf. His long fingers stretched around the neck looked as if he could contract his hands at any moment.

"You've arranged your home beautifully. You two have a son, right?"

He returned the vase to the shelf. Her chest, which she hadn't noticed was tightened, unspooled. She gave a barely perceptible nod.

"Yes, your husband has spoken about him, too. I'd love to meet him sometime. Is he home?"

"No. He's at school."

"I'm sure you two will raise a fine child. Your husband is so different from other city officials. Just last week, I met someone who was at—where was it, the Ministry of Water and Electricity?— bragging about all the children he had with mistresses in the countryside. It's no wonder the ordinary people see things like that and get angry with their government." He shook his head, as if expecting her to bemoan the state of the country with him.

She sensed this might be an opening. "Mr. Qian, I'm sorry to be so abrupt. I'm afraid I have another appointment now."

"Of course, of course!" He jumped up. "I'm sorry to keep going on. You must be very busy. We'll get going now."

She exhaled with relief. The visit had been strange, yes, but she couldn't discern any particular threat. She'd ask Guifan about the men that evening.

"Oh, I seem to have forgotten something," Mr. Qian said, just as they were about to depart. She'd gone outside, still in her slippers, to see them off.

He reached into his pocket and produced a tiny velvet box. He flipped open the top to reveal a pair of carved rose studs, each the size of a pinky nail, pressed into a soft pillow.

"Made of ivory," he said. He held the jewelry box out, letting it linger in midair.

"I can't take that. You're much too polite."

"No, I insist." He hadn't retracted his hand.

She closed her hand on the box and right then he leaned in and said, "I wanted to say this earlier, but I wasn't sure if I should even mention it." She could smell stale cigarettes on his breath. Her heart was racing. "Your husband is in a position to help us with the International Prosperity Center. You know, we have great plans for this city. Look at how beautiful it's getting. You wouldn't want your husband to get in the way of that, right?" Coming even closer, he added, "You have a beautiful home and family. Tell your husband not to do anything that would jeopardize what you've obtained."

Then he backed away and was talking with the same airy voice again. "Don't worry. You can ask your husband about what I mean later." He smiled broadly at her and handed her a business card before departing.

She had to put her hand on the wall to steady herself after they left.

Ayi, who'd come to clean up the teacups, startled. "Miss, what's wrong?"

Hanwen shook her head and almost fell forward onto the couch in her rush to sit down. The lightness was lifting her body away from herself once again. Dark spots trickled into her vision, like an ink spill blotting out her safe home.

She gulped greedily at the hot liquid Ayi brought to her, still with her eyes closed. *They're gone, they're gone,* she said to herself. *There isn't any danger.* Slowly, she could feel weight returning to her head, allowing it to become a more solid thing again. She opened her eyes.

"I'm fine," she said, and when Ayi still appeared to be worried, she repeated herself. Hanwen hadn't experienced one of these spells in over a year, not since before this new young woman had begun working for them. The episodes had been more frequent when Hanwen was younger, but year by year, the sources of stress that would cause a spell had grown fewer. Her life was bounded and protected by the walls around the complex, the others who went out and interacted with the world for her. Now these two men had breached the barrier. But for what? Mr. Qian's words were shrouded in code, but she was sure of two things—the men had threatened to hurt her family, and it had something to do with Guifan.

That night, she told Guifan about the visit. He'd been looking over a packet of papers at the desk by their bedside, but his eyes shot up when she mentioned the International Prosperity Center.

"They came here?"

"They came straight to the door. I don't know how they got past the guards."

"How did they know where we lived?"

"Maybe you should answer that."

His eyes, behind his glasses, were large in disbelief.

Her own courage was faltering but she willed herself to press on. She didn't want to know about the problem at the same time she saw that she had to. She inhaled and said, "I never ask you about anything you do at work, but they came to speak directly to me and threatened Yuanyuan. I won't be angry with you, but you have to tell me."

She could tell he was relieved when he confessed. She wondered how long he'd kept the story bottled inside.

What he told her about was a large scheme, the kind sometimes described on the news, accompanied by grainy footage of policemen pushing a crowd of handcuffed men, exactly the type of thing in which she never imagined Guifan would be involved.

Mr. Qian worked for the Li Corporation, a national real estate development company. She'd heard of the firm—they had the tallest buildings in many large cities across the country. He'd first approached the mayor, who'd taken some money from them in the past. They had even grander ambitions for a new shopping complex. The proposed site was in the economic development zone under Guifan's authority. He would need to approve the demolition of a maze of old alleyway houses for the project to continue.

He'd balked at forcing people out of their old homes to build a new structure that there weren't enough businesses in town to fill. He thought it would be obvious they were completing the project at the behest of the corporation's interests and there would be backlash to follow. The mayor first tried to cajole him, telling him how much they each stood to make if Guifan did this one small favor. But then, after a few months of Guifan's refusals, the mayor began to imply he'd find an excuse to report him to the central disciplinary committee, on grounds of corruption.

"A few months?" Hanwen interrupted. "This has been going for that long? Why didn't you tell me sooner?"

"I was—I was afraid." Guifan hung his head. "I didn't know how to tell you, and I didn't want you to be worried."

"Well, *should* we be worried? Could he really report you like that? You haven't done anything wrong," Hanwen said.

Guifan sighed before continuing. "All these gifts. It doesn't matter that every official has things like this, or that what we've received is nothing compared to everyone else. If he wanted to find an excuse, it wouldn't be difficult."

Of course, she'd wondered about the gifts early on. Businessmen or constituents who wanted to give Guifan a token of thanks for a small ask—fast-tracking a restaurant permit or getting someone's child into the city's best high school. Inconsequential favors. Red-ribboned bottles of maotai, rubber-banded bundles of foreign currency, once even a calligraphy scroll from the late Qing dynasty. Hanwen didn't like to look at the gifts, which made her feel like a foreigner in her own life. She knew none of these could have come from Guifan's salary, which was laughably low, part of the Party's public commitment that the leaders should live like common people. Everyone accepted that there would be perks that made up for the low pay, like the subsidized housing and their drivers. She'd asked him only once about them, early on. "It's nothing. I won't ever let it get out of hand," he said. She'd decided to believe him. The country was awash with money, anyone could see that. Imported cars whizzed and stirred up dust from the construction sites springing up all around town. Investors came to erect new office buildings and apartment complexes, created shiny pamphlets to sell the city on the place it could become.

She'd been wrong to listen to Guifan, she saw. She'd underestimated the size of the troubles that could come from the gifts and put too much faith in Guifan to handle them.

"So what have you done?" she asked Guifan now.

"I've been hoping they'd back off. That the mayor would give up."

"Hoping? That's it?"

"What else would you have liked me to do?"

"Your hoping didn't work. Now they've come to our house."

If the government decided to make an example of an official, the punishment could be ruthless. Stripped of Party membership and their position, certainly. A long jail term. It was uncommon, but at worst they would find out about the crime on the nightly news broadcast: *executed by gunshot for corruption*, the news anchor would inform them, her voice cold and neutral. The decision on punishment happened in some room where men in power met, through some calculus she would never understand.

She couldn't believe that Guifan had subjected their lives to such an arbitrary whim and was now acting so helplessly before it. She'd sacrificed the whole other life she'd wanted for the safety of this one, so that her mother, and now her son, could have the stability she'd never had. If what she'd collected could be taken away so easily, then for what had she made those choices?

For the next few weeks, passing by any person smoking on the street, she was made dizzy by the reminder of Mr. Qian, standing so close to her that she could smell his breath. She began writing a desperate letter to Yitian. *I know it's been a long time since we last spoke, but I wonder if I could ask for your advice on something*, she started. But what would he think, hearing about how far her life had strayed from the person she'd once been? She ripped the letter to shreds and tossed the remnants.

After that, there'd been weeks of a silent holding pattern. She'd thought that perhaps Guifan was right, that hope was enough to make the men disappear. But then, on the eve of Yitian's arrival, Guifan had announced wearily to her one morning, "The CEO of the Li Corporation is coming to town next week, and he wants to invite us to dinner."

Twelve

She could tell that Guifan was already drunk by the time a demure waitress led her to the private dining room. To anyone else, he would have looked exactly the same as always. He had the type of unremarkable features that inspired confidence in others and in Hanwen, which she thought was the reason for his quick ascent within the Party. You looked at that angular face, the suggestion of economy and concern in the wrinkles that had slowly formed on his broad forehead, and thought immediately that he was a practical person you could trust, who wouldn't reveal your secrets. And in fact, he never did. Even when she'd first met him thirteen years ago, he gave off the considered expression of a person much older than he was. But tonight, when she entered the room, his jaw was already slightly slack, his gaze occasionally blurring out of focus before snapping into the room again, resisting the alcohol's pull upon his attention. At moments, his eyes seemed to catch on the glittering chandelier that loomed above the room.

She wished that, for once, he didn't have to be so stoic and composed. She could see her husband through others' eyes, as someone trying to prove his drinking abilities to the table. If he could just pretend to be a more outlandish drunk, they'd stop forcing shots upon him. But such guile was not in his personality.

"Welcome, welcome!" Li Tuan bellowed at her from across the wide circumference of the table. "We've been waiting for you all night." She recognized him from the newspapers as the president of the Li Corporation. She'd seen his face in the tabloid section, when there'd been a recent rumor that he was having an affair with a young European movie star.

A single open seat to the right of Li Tuan had clearly been left for her. Guifan was seated closer to the door, at a position of lower honor. The dining room was beautiful, she had to admit. Behind Li Tuan, a misty watercolor of mountains and lakes spanned an entire wall. The table and cabinets appeared to be of delicately carved rosewood.

Li Tuan introduced the other members of the table, skipping over Mr. Qian. She nodded at the introductions and said, "Very pleased to make your acquaintance," though she already recognized them all. For the past month, she'd read all she could find about the corporation in old newspapers, hoping that somewhere she would stumble upon some detail of the company's imminent collapse. Instead, all the articles described its developments in cities all around China and speculated that it was certainly poised for even greater growth in the years to come, one of the country's prime jewels.

Li Tuan addressed the table. "I've only been to Hefei once before, when I was a very young child. It felt like some country backwater back then. I wasn't sure why they wanted to build in this city at first, but now that I'm here, I can understand. There's so much open land around here. So much potential for development."

Hanwen began, "Yes, it's already different from when we first—"

"That's what you need to do, if you're smart. Identify the places that are *up and coming*, not play catch-up with places that are already prosperous. . . ." He began pontificating on the particularities of the Li Corporation's strategy.

Hanwen sat back in her seat. She bristled at how he'd interrupted her without even a gaze in her direction. She should have expected it, she knew, but it had been years since she'd been given the seat next to the host, not since before she'd been pregnant with Yuanyuan. It was considered the placement of third-highest respect at the table, but the position was false. The young women picked to sit here were expected to entertain and listen to the host's comments throughout the night. They couldn't speak unless directly asked by the host. The person in the lowest position, opposite the host, could at least jump up to refill water. At least there was some choice in that.

"Vice Mayor Wang's wife knows this place well, actually. She was sent down to a village near here," Mr. Qian said.

"Oh, is that right?" Li Tuan said. Still, he did not look at her.

"Yes, that's true. It was a small place—"

"The sent-down campaigns!" Li Tuan interrupted. "What a time that was. Can you believe we all lived through it? Myself, I was sent down to a state-run farm in Heilongjiang. I still have nightmares about the cold there. . . ."

"Actually, it was very different where I was sent down," she found herself saying, to Li Tuan's description of the farm. How had she used to stand it, sitting here for hours, watching men drink and speak? "We only had a few of us together in our village, not like you up north, with hundreds of sent-down youth. We had to befriend the villagers, and I became close with some of them. We couldn't just stay amongst ourselves. Not like you all."

A few of the others around the table glanced at her and nodded, as if to acknowledge a child of whom they were proud. Guifan was the only person who looked at her sharply. She knew she'd violated the expectations of her position, but she couldn't bring herself to care. Yitian's visit had sharpened some long dormant edge inside her into an insistent point.

"So many different experiences!" Li Tuan agreed heartily.

Guifan hurried to stand and raise a cup in Li Tuan's direction. "It's an honor to have you visiting our city."

Li Tuan downed a shot with him. "We're in a very defining moment right now, you all know. In a couple of decades, maybe even less, our country will be the greatest in the world, second to no one, not even the Americans. City officials like you have the power to shape the direction of the nation. You could make Hefei City look like a totally different place in just a few years."

"Shouldn't that be up to you, Mr. Li?" she said.

Li Tuan looked over at her. She realized immediately she'd gone too far. With his face this close to her, she could see how astute his eyes were. She'd been deceived by his gregariousness. He hadn't become as powerful as he was through some accident. She saw a steely distance in his gaze, belonging to a man who could evaluate a situation and act the role of whatever person it demanded of him.

His eyebrows raised softly, almost imperceptibly, in minute judgment. "Your wife is very beautiful," he said, turning to Guifan.

He didn't turn back to her for the rest of the night as the men began to drink in real earnest, going around the table and offering shots in his honor. She hoped that he would drink so much he wouldn't remember what she'd said. Around the fourth shot she counted, the mayor entered—rushing on his way to another engagement, he said—and raised a quick glass to the table. "Vice Mayor Wang will take good care of you," the mayor said, pointing to Guifan, who winced while taking his shot. Yitian would never find himself in such a situation, she thought. Nothing like this would ever dirty his pristine scholarly life.

There'd been a time when she'd attended many of these dinners with Guifan, her eyes agape at the dishes of exotic animals weighing down tables ever more gilded and plush. At some point, all this had ceased to impress her, when every dish tasted the same and she could no longer see the rooms she entered anew. One night a man had vomited right onto her lap, and since then she'd told Guifan to make some excuse for her absence at each invitation. When she'd been a girl, all their ideals had been about sacrificing for the country and Party, any talk of money enough to kill one's reputation like a poison. But now the demonstrations of wealth were everywhere. She couldn't wrap her head around it.

When they finally rose, piles of food remained on the table, many dishes still completely untouched. The drink had been the focus of the night, and the men had ordered much more food than they needed, just to prove they could.

When she'd first moved into this home, she'd found its size unwieldy, always requiring her to shout to be heard from another room. She'd call and call her mother and Yuanyuan but receive no response. She'd imagined the names, then her entire voice, being absorbed into the house and going nowhere, all her words taken and never returned to her. Now she felt grateful for the distance and thick walls, which could provide barriers from her mother overhearing them.

"Why didn't you just ask them to stop?"

Guifan, his cheek pressed against the toilet of their bathroom, didn't respond.

"You could have just pretended you were drunk," she said. She'd never seen him like this before and it was easier to question how he'd stumbled than to think about her own mistakes at the dinner. Leaning against the countertop, she looked at his figure, kneeling and dry heaving, and couldn't believe she'd staked her entire life upon him. The sounds from his mouth were unnatural and vulgar. She, her mother, and her son all depended on this person huddling on the cold floor like a wounded animal.

She wrapped her arms around his back, holding him up as he vomited. When they'd been dating and he'd held her like this, she'd felt a surge in her heart, a feeling she thought must have been love. She'd felt safe beside him, and what was the greatest gift someone could give another, if not safety? Now she didn't feel like she was touching her husband; she felt more like she might when Yuanyuan was sick and cried and she had to hold him until he fell asleep.

"What will you do?" she asked.

He took so long to respond that she thought he might have fallen asleep.

"I don't know."

"You have to *do* something." If it were not for how pathetic he looked, sweat-soaked and fatigued, she would have shaken him. Yes, the situation was difficult, but it required action.

"If I do this one thing, it will just lead to more."

"But if you don't do anything now, we'll have no future to consider at all," she said. He was deft at thinking through all the possibilities and consequences, but when it came to taking decisive action in the present, he was of no use.

"Look at the mayor. He became involved, and now every time they need help, they go to him."

"What's the alternative?"

"What the mayor does—it's not a way to live."

"Neither is this," she said.

They sat in silence. They'd talked their way into a dead end, or at least that must have been what Guifan thought it was. He was grasping on to some old ideal of the country and his role as an official, but nothing was so pure. She'd made the compromises she'd been forced to.

"Look, I'm thinking about it," he said wearily. Empty words. He appeared on the verge of sleep and his eyes remained closed as he laid his forehead against the cold tile. Frustrated, she rose from the floor. Nothing would come from continuing to press him. She left the bathroom light on, so that he would immediately know where he was when he woke up alone.

Instead of getting into her own bed, she went to Yuanyuan's bedroom. She'd done this often in the past month, ever since the visit from Mr. Qian. She knew it was strange, that she went to her own child for comfort. Yuanyuan never woke; rather, she liked sleeping by him for the reminder that he represented, of something that she'd created and raised through her own effort.

When she lifted the blanket and hunched her shoulders to fit in the small space next to him, he stirred but didn't wake. He looked so concentrated in his sleep, and she wondered what he might be dreaming of with that slight furrow in his brow.

She was brushing his hair when she noticed a shuffling shadow in the doorway.

"Who's there?"

A face pushed through the crack of the door. She squinted. It was her mother.

"You scared me, Ma." For a sudden and absurd moment, she'd believed that the men had already come and found her after her improper behavior at dinner.

"I didn't mean to. I just thought I heard something earlier."

"Nothing's wrong. Go back to sleep."

Her mother's face floated, hazy like a reflection in the darkness. She hesitated and seemed about to leave. "It's not good to keep coming in here to sleep, you know. You should stay with your husband."

"He had too much to drink tonight. It was hard to sleep next to him."

"Is something wrong? Guifan never drinks like that." Now her mother pushed the door open and entered the room. Hanwen had no choice but to flatten herself to make room for her mother to perch on the edge of the bed. "This doesn't have to do with your friend who came to visit you today, does it?"

"No, Ma, that was just a coincidence—" Hanwen began, but her mother cut her off.

"You know you can't just look at others when there's the smallest difficulty in a marriage."

"Okay." Hanwen rolled over so that her face was pressed right into Yuanyuan's neck. "I'm tired." She didn't want to be lectured, but her mother was already taking off in a stern cadence.

"You know, when I was young and just married to your father, if we ever had a disagreement, I would get so angry. I would imagine the easiest thing—going back to my life without him. It's normal to think like that, when you're young."

"That's not what this is about, Ma." Hanwen sat up. She resented the implication that she was still a child who needed her mother's guidance to stay on the proper route of her life. Hadn't she already so precisely arrived at exactly what was desired of her?

"Well, then tell me what it's about." Her mother suddenly grasped her hand. "I can help. Let your ma help."

Hanwen wanted to believe that her mother—or someone else, anyone else—could help. "Guifan—" Hanwen started, but then she saw her mother's eyes, glowing white and opened wide. There wasn't anything for her there, only more worry. "Never mind. I really need to go to bed, Ma. It's been a long night." She lay back down.

"Okay, okay," her mother said. Her expression was crestfallen. She rose slowly. "Just think about what I said." Almost as an afterthought, she added, "And if your husband is in trouble, you should help him however you can."

Hanwen startled. Uttered in the dark by her mother's shadow, the words seemed particularly weighted.

"What are you saying, Ma?" Hanwen wondered how many other times her mother had hovered around the doorways at night.

"That's all I meant. Good night," her mother said.

The bed felt vast after the departure of her mother's weight, but Hanwen stayed pressed against Yuanyuan. She felt around Yuanyuan's chest until she found the low heartbeat. She'd only felt panicked like this a few times since her marriage, and all of them had to do with Yuanyuan. The first time they'd gone to the morning market together, she'd turned for a second to pick a bag of string beans, and when she looked back, Yuanyuan was gone. She'd run through the narrow alleys and asked frantically at each stand, finally finding him squatting by a pancake maker, watching, mesmerized, as the merchant used a spatula to wrangle the batter into crisp rounds. Sometimes she still had nightmares about that singular moment, of turning around from the vegetable stand, murmuring to Yuanyuan, the sudden drop of her stomach when she found the space empty. It was that same sense of fear that Mr. Qian and now her mother had evoked, this plunging terror at the potential of loss.

She woke late the next morning, sunlight already streaming in the room, falling on her in slats from the window and warming her. Yuanyuan was gone, but she'd kept her body nestled into a small corner of the wall. Ayi must have already quietly taken him to school without her, and her mother was likely out on her morning walk. She went to the bathroom to check on Guifan, but the floor was bare.

She dialed his office and was surprised when he answered with a voice brisk and businesslike, holding no trace of the previous night. She imagined him waking sometime before dawn, shaking off the dregs of the alcohol like a dog shook off water, slipping into his ironed clothes, and stepping back into the world as the polished man she knew.

"You're all right?"

"Yes, yes, of course."

"Guifan, the thing. From last night. Have you decided?"

"I'm still thinking about it."

There were distant sounds of papers rustling. She felt so far away from him now and wanted to reach out, through the telephone, to force him closer. Last evening on the bathroom floor, she'd at least had a sense of shared desperation between them. Now all the passages in his mind felt closed off. She had no idea of whether or not he would be able to force himself into a choice, but she was sure of one thing—whatever he decided, she would live the consequences.

"Hanwen? I'm fine. Is there anything else? I need to get back to work."

She hadn't realized how long she'd gone silent for. "I need a favor," she said. She wondered if the request would surprise him. She rarely asked him for help, even when he mentioned the perks usually accorded to people in his position—preferential school enrollment and investment opportunities, all of which felt extraneous to her. In this life, they already had all that they needed. It would be unlucky to ask for even more.

"What's that?" he asked.

"An old friend of mine is in town. His father went missing around here. He needs the police to help."

"Sure. Just tell the secretary what you need." She heard relief in his voice. It was a simple favor, one he could understand and have control over.

Without a goodbye, he transferred the call back.

Half an hour later, the police chief himself called her. He'd already transmitted the message to all the police bureaus, he said, and would be sending a subordinate to reprimand the township where they'd refused to help Yitian.

When the police chief promised he would be in touch with the first news, which he assured her would be soon, she marveled at how easy it had been to get help. The previous day, Yitian had been in her house, lost, with no other options besides her. Despite all his intelligence and where he'd ended up in life, he'd reached dead ends everywhere. And she'd been able to do all this with just a simple phone call. She might have felt helpless before Guifan, but at least she could help Yitian. Her decisions around her life had indeed led her somewhere, even if not to the place she'd expected.

Thirteen

1975

Yitian had gone to the hill on the west side of the village that day, in pursuit of quiet. Studying inside his home was always difficult, but that day particularly so. Both times he sat down to read, his mother called him away, first to unearth potatoes from their plot, then to crush soybeans on the grindstone. He complained to Yishou, who only laughed at him. When both of them weren't looking, Yitian grabbed his books and ran in the direction of the hill. He would surely face some punishment for this later, but the few hours of quiet were worth whatever was to come.

The hill was his favorite spot in the village. From this vantage point, he could make out the small arteries running through and the scattered dots of people moving along the dirt roads. Some ran quickly; some dragged their feet, as he would. The village had more legibility from up above. He could see the path that led to the world beyond and could imagine himself walking out there, leaving this small one behind.

He leaned against an abandoned well at the center of the hilltop and propped his book upon his knees. The only thing bothering him now was the crumbling bricks of the old well digging into his back. It would be perfect up here, he thought, if only there were a desk. He was just thinking of ways he might be able to smuggle a board up and hide it when a sound disturbed his thoughts.

He listened closely and decided the noise had been a trick of the wind. Then he heard something again. This time, he could not deny the "Hello?" carried through the gust, coming from an unfamiliar female voice.

He looked up and saw a figure pushing through the wild grass of the hilltop, coming toward him. As quickly as he could, he closed the cover of his book and tried to hide it behind his back. He didn't want to be teased by another villager for how much time he spent reading.

A girl emerged completely from the grass and stood in front of him. She was long limbed and held her arms loosely, without the purpose of one accustomed to the body as a functional object. To his surprise, he didn't recognize her—he thought he knew everyone from his village, if not well, then at least by sight. Perhaps she had come from a neighboring village, although it would have been a very long trek to get to the hill. There *was* something about her that didn't look quite like she belonged around here. Perhaps it was that her nose, narrow and distinguished, seemed incongruent with her ruddy cheeks and drab padded cotton clothes, the same as all the villagers wore. And yet, she walked toward him confidently, as if she'd been up here many times before.

"Hello," she said. "I didn't expect to find someone else here."

He was struck immediately by her accent, which had a thin, precise quality to it, each syllable neatly chopped off at the end, where he would have rolled it into the next.

"Were you reading?" She gestured at the well.

He glanced back. In his rush to stuff the book away, he'd done a poor job of hiding it, and the cover was clearly jutting out from behind his back. He opened and closed his mouth several times, unsure of what to say. I must look like a dumb donkey, he thought.

"I've never seen you before," the girl said, squinting at his face, as if his features would become suddenly familiar to her. "Are you from one of those villages over there?" She pointed down the other direction of the hill.

"I'm from this side. Tang Family Village."

"That's right next to my production team. Are you sure? I've never seen you there before."

"I go to school in the township most of the time. But I haven't seen you before, either."

"I see. Well, I'm one of the sent-down youth."

That explained why she'd asked him immediately about his book. Now that he could see her up close, she clearly didn't look like any of the village women. He didn't know any of the sent-down youth personally, but he knew they were all from educated families in Shanghai and that his learning and interest in books were probably meager compared to the real educations they had. He was sure that if he ever spoke to them about his studies, they would expose him for his true ignorance, and so he avoided them if he could.

"So you're in high school?" she asked.

"Yes. I'm finishing this year."

"You look young to be about to graduate." She examined his face, but not in an unkind way, he thought. "How old are you, anyway?"

"Oh, the same as me," she said when he told her.

"I started school late," he explained.

There was a long pause as they both looked at each other. She seemed to be waiting for him to say something else, but he was sure he'd already used up every interesting thing he had.

"I was actually just about to leave. My mother needs me to help her with some chores." He was eager for this unexpected encounter to end. He was noticing with every moment how pretty he found the girl, and growing more and more nervous.

He rose and brushed the dirt off his legs. "It was nice to meet you."

"Wait," she said, just as he was about to sprint down the hill in relief.

"You forgot this." She held his book in her hand. Her grip lingered on the cover when he reached out to take it from her, and he felt a little tug between them.

She looked down at the title. "I've read this novel before, many years ago. It's all right. I thought the author's depiction of the father was unrealistic."

He nodded. Moments previously, he'd thought the book was one of the best he'd ever read.

"If you like to read, I have some books I can lend you," she said.

"Oh, please don't bother yourself with that," he said. He had to stifle the surge of excitement he felt at her offer. It was so difficult for them to get books here, and he could only imagine what an educated person from Shanghai might have.

"It wouldn't be a bother. No one else is reading them."

"Really, don't worry about it." He worried he wouldn't have access to this sanctuary alone any longer. "I keep some books here. Just for myself. Please don't tell anyone," he added.

"I won't. Are you sure you won't stay? You looked like you were in the middle of something. I hope I didn't interrupt you." The expression on her face was curious, but he didn't return her smile. He put the book back into a crack between the broken tiles of the well and then ran all the way back down the hill, no longer afraid of the scolding from his mother. Chores suddenly seemed preferable and harmless—they were completely decipherable, at least, unlike that girl.

A fter that he avoided the hilltop, though there were many more afternoons when he desperately craved quiet. The memory of meeting her bothered him so much that he could hardly even think about their encounter without a prickly sensation crawling up his body.

It didn't matter that he didn't go to the hill again, because the very next week he saw her with the women in the calabash vines, snipping gourds from their spiky stems. He turned away from their direction, hoping not to meet her gaze. Then he saw her again, two days later, squatting and weeding in the rice paddies. Yitian wasn't superstitious like his mother, but it seemed a trick of God.

His classroom was separated down the middle into boys' and girls' sides, and he would have had no idea of how to speak with her, even if he'd wanted to. Sometimes her face would come to him at night when he was trying to fall asleep, making his entire body feel hot at the thought. He wondered again what books she would have given him if he'd allowed her to. He'd met other girls whom he thought pretty before, many of them, in fact, at the high school he'd attended in the township. "Don't even think about it, little brother." Yishou smacked his head. "Those girls would call us country bumpkins." And he'd been right—it wasn't until those years of high school that Yitian became aware of the fact, really *known*, that he possessed a body and a face. His old clothes and pimples and gangliness became solid in the world through the ways others looked at him. And so he tried to fold himself into the smallest, least noticeable shape possible.

But the girl on the hillside hadn't made him feel that way at all.

Her curiosity had made him curious, too. He wanted, despite himself, to know how he looked through her eyes.

The final exams for his last year in high school were approaching. Even though the grades had no meaning—there would be nowhere to go after he graduated—he wanted to do his best. Those days and in that heat, studying in his home was almost impossible. One afternoon, he was so frustrated that he did a quick calculation. It was the second week of June. Her production team was at its busiest this time of year, during the small window of time when they would harvest rice before the next planting would have to begin. He decided to risk a visit.

After he'd gone to the hilltop a few more times without seeing her, he relaxed. Math was his weakest subject, and so it was especially important that he could concentrate completely. The problems weren't hard when he put his mind to them, but he didn't understand why he had to commit the formulas to memory when, for the rest of his life, he would be able to reference them in a book. The process wasn't at all like remembering the stories from history and the ones his grandfather told him, which had so much art and logic in the way they built upon one another.

One day, he'd been studying for an hour when he heard the approaching footsteps coming up the hill. Though he knew what the sound meant this time, he still panicked.

Sure enough, there she came, just moments later, her arms pushing a path through the prickly wild grass. "Oh, it's you again. I was wondering when I would see you," she said. She didn't look surprised at all. He noted that her face was actually a bit different than he remembered, her eyes more almond-shaped than how he'd pictured her at night.

"What are you doing today? Still reading?" She sat down right beside him and glanced over his shoulder at his notes. "Oh, trigonometry?"

"I have a final exam next week," he explained lamely.

"You're studying the sum to product formulas?"

Before he could cover up his notes, she pointed at a line of his writing and said, "Sine a plus sine b, hmm, let me see." She looked up to the sky, thinking, then recited, "Sine of angle one plus sine of angle two is equivalent to two times sine of the sum of the angles divided by two, all multiplied by cosine of the sum of the angles divided by two." She checked the paper and her face fell. "Oh, it's cosine of the difference of the two angles. How could I forget?"

"How did you know that?" He was amazed.

"I really like math. But I'm not as good as I used to be. I never would have made such a mistake before."

"But how? Do you take math classes here?" That didn't make sense. The sent-down youth didn't go to school.

"I brought some of my old textbooks from Shanghai here. I review them sometimes, just in case I might need to know some fact in the future, but I don't have very much time anymore, because we're so busy. I'm forgetting a lot of stuff I used to know easily."

"You were close."

"I can help test you, if you want. I might have forgotten some of the formulas, but it won't matter if you give me the sheet to look at."

She stretched out her hand and he passed her the paper. At least if she tested him, he wouldn't have to really *talk* to her at all; he would only be reciting formulas.

They went through every line. He winced whenever she corrected him, glad that she was too occupied scanning the paper to notice.

"Have you always come up here so often?" he asked, when they finished. "I never used to see you when I came up."

"No, actually, I've been coming up to read your books."

She looked embarrassed as she said this, and he had a thought he found almost impossible to believe. Had she been coming up here in hopes of seeing him?

"I hope you don't mind. You only told me not to tell anyone, but I figured if I only read them myself, it would be all right. . . ."

"You can read them. No one else in the village cares about them."

He didn't know what else to say to her. He made an excuse that his mother was waiting for him at home, so he could rush down the hill himself without having to walk together with her. If anyone he knew spotted them, he would surely have been teased endlessly.

Even before he began to run, his heart was already pounding through his chest. Instead of the formulas he was supposed to be memorizing, he thought of her the entire way home. She'd been reading *his* books! It occurred to him then, what he could have said, an idea so obvious that he couldn't believe he hadn't thought of it earlier. Why hadn't he simply asked her what she thought of the books?

When the results of the math final exam were posted, he'd scored top in his class. This was new to him, and a surprise even to his teacher. He was near the top of every subject, but never math.

"Hard work pays off," his grandfather said, when Yitian told his family.

"Too bad there's no prize for scoring the highest," said Yishou.

"Learning is a great reward, all of its own," his grandfather replied.

Yitian looked for her in the fields all that week, trying to guess by the shape of the faraway bodies which one might be hers. It was difficult to tell, because the sent-down youth were working in an area that was three tracts away from him, but finally he distinguished someone wearing a wide-brimmed hat against the hot summer sun who seemed to match her height and figure.

She was so surprised when he approached that she leaned on her hoe, off balance, and nearly fell over.

"Be careful!" he said. He instinctively touched her elbow. Even though he'd only grazed her through her clothing, he snatched back his hand. He looked around to see if anyone had seen. His fingers felt like they'd been burned.

"I wanted to give this to you," he said. He pulled out his math textbook from the waistband of his pants, bending the softcover back and forth to soften the crease that had formed there. "To thank you. I placed first in my class. I don't need the book anymore, so I thought you might want it."

She looked shocked. "I know it's old and used," he stuttered, "but it's hard to come by textbooks here, so I thought it would be okay to give to you. It's fine if you don't want it, though—"

"No, I'm very glad to have it. This is very kind of you." She took the book from him.

A group of the other sent-down girls was approaching them. He'd never talked to so many girls at one time, much less ones who all came from the city. He panicked.

"All right, then I have to go now," he managed, kicking up clouds of dirt as he ran away.

Fourteen

She next approached him in the same way on the first unbearably hot day of the year. Passing the river, he'd stopped to dip his shirt into the water, whose depths the sun had not yet warmed. He'd been enjoying the feeling of the cool water lapping at his hands when she caught him off guard.

"I have a book for you. I thought you might like it," she said.

He glanced around them to make sure no one else had seen, before saying, "I'm sorry, I can't take this gift." It was acceptable that he'd given her something, because she'd helped him study. He'd done nothing for her, however, and a gift from her would have meant something else entirely.

He expected her to leave, but instead she put the book at his feet before walking away. Unsure of what to do and afraid a passerby might question him about it, he hurriedly stuffed the book into the waistband of his pants.

He did not have a chance to get back to it until that evening as everyone was preparing for bed. He snuck into his bedroom and took the book out to examine the cover under lamplight. He peered at the title: *Wuthering Heights* by Emily Brontë. Though he'd heard of this book before, he'd never read it.

When he heard his brother's footsteps, he wedged the book under the pallet so Yishou would not see. It stayed there for four days, until, one afternoon, he could not stand waiting any longer. He devoured the story of Heathcliff's wild spirit. He'd never read anything like the tale before, and he flipped through the diaphanous pages of their doomed love so quickly that he had to tell himself to slow down for fear of ripping their edges. After he finished, he couldn't understand why she'd chosen this book instead of any other. Was she trying to tell him something through the romance that was depicted? It was so turbulent, so doomed. And yet it seemed to express a longing that he wouldn't have been able to force into the frame of words. He sensed there was something she wanted to say to him.

In later years, he'd see even more starkly how much she'd pushed herself past her own comfort to give him that first book. She wasn't so completely bold; she, too, experienced fear. "Why did you do it?" he asked once, and she replied, a mystery even to her own self, "Sometimes I feel seized to do what I'm afraid of."

They continued to exchange books like this, passing them gently through their hands like baby calves, just born. He never became less nervous and didn't say much to her each time he gave her a new book. The most he would do was make a remark about the weather or ask how the fieldwork had been that day.

He learned about her through guessing at the small signs that she left in between the pages. Often, he discovered places where the words had been made transparent by oil spots. So she liked to read while she ate. He found this charming—her ability to be so engrossed in reading that even other forms of sustenance became superfluous.

He wanted nothing more than to meet her and talk alone, but it was also the thought that scared him most. He worked in a different part of the fields than the sent-down youth, so they didn't ever come into close contact. Now that it was autumn, the young villagers sometimes went to the dormitories of the sent-down youth to make popcorn in the little kernel popper they'd procured and that held them all fascinated, but he never went with them.

Then one day, when she gave him a book, he opened the front cover to see, written in pencil in handwriting that he would later come to know intimately:

Meet me at the hilltop this Sunday,
at the same time we met before.

He arrived there before she did and sat against the abandoned well. That morning, he'd scrubbed his face with his washcloth so vigorously that Yishou had noticed and asked what the special occasion was. There were parts of his neck that were, even now, red and raw. He kept imagining scenarios in which she and the other sent-down girls had set him up as part of an elaborate joke. A country boy with so many pimples on his face, trying to go after one of *us*!

Time seemed to be moving much more slowly than ever before as he waited. He listened closely to hear the sounds of her approach.

She finally came, with her hair flying everywhere in the wind.

"Sorry to be late," she said, sitting an arm's distance in front of him. "I got caught up picking these." She unrolled the pouch she'd made of the hem of her blouse, sending handfuls of chestnuts rolling onto the ground.

"We never could get chestnuts this fresh in the city. I couldn't help myself when I saw them on my way up. Come, help me crack them open. It'll be easier to bring them back down that way."

To help her, he dropped the book he carried. Nikolai Gogol's *The Overcoat*, the last book she'd given him.

"Did you know, I almost burned this book?" she said.

"Why?" He couldn't believe she could be so callous or violent with a book.

"Because the Soviets were supposed to be our enemies. There were campaigns to burn books all the time. The Red Guards called a meeting and they were going to make a huge bonfire. We were supposed to bring all of our bourgeois Russian books to burn. I collected all the ones I could find, but my mother prevented me from going. She told me it was stupid of me to burn them."

He took the chestnut she was struggling with from her and hit it against the decaying bricks of the abandoned well. The spiky green shell cracked open easily and he passed the chestnut inside to her.

"So your mother also loves books?"

"It's not that, exactly. I never understood why she cared so much about them until I came here. She never read anything herself. I think I've figured it out now. It's that she thought keeping the books was my way to live a stable life."

"What does that mean?" He'd never heard this word, *stable*, used the way she had, to describe a life.

"She thought that if I read all those books, I could go to college. Then I could get a job in a technical field, and I'd be protected from the campaigns forever."

"Do you think that's true, what your mother said?" He broke chestnuts while they spoke, finding that they were a good excuse not to look at her.

"Well, I'm not sure we'll ever have the chance to go to college, anyway. But"—she hesitated, causing him to look up at her—"I do like the idea of safety, I think."

There was something uncertain on her face, the first time he'd seen her unsure with her words.

The sudden silence made him uncomfortable. He scrambled to find something to say, eyes landing on the crumbling well. "Do you know why no one ever comes up here? Look at that monastery." He pointed west from the hilltop to a small compound of eaved buildings in a state of dilapidation. "There used to be monks living there. Apparently, one of the monks went crazy trying to learn chan, and one day he came up here in a fit and threw himself into the well. So everyone avoids this place now. They think it's bad luck."

"Except for you."

"I don't believe in luck."

"Why is that?"

"History is the domain of diligence and knowledge, not luck." This was something his grandfather said. "You must hate living here," he said suddenly.

"What do you mean?"

"I can only imagine what it's like to live here, after Shanghai. No books, no one interesting to talk to. . . ."

"Oh, I see. Some days I do feel like that. It seems like I'll die if I have to eat another meal made with that awful cottonseed oil. Other times, I think I can understand life here better, in some way. Sometimes life in the city is so"—she shook her head and squinted her eyes, deciding on a word—"complicated."

"How?" He did not understand the words she used to describe lives. First *stable*, now *complicated*.

"The political meetings they had all the time. First someone is an old revolutionary, the next day they're a capitalist roader. At least, here and now, things are a bit quieter. I just tell myself, I'm not here forever. It's just a break from my real life in Shanghai."

"What do you miss most about Shanghai?"

"I miss . . ." She started, then stopped. "It's not a specific thing, rather—I miss the feeling that there's a greater life waiting for me. When you live in the city, you believe you can become something, something even more than who your parents had been. My mother told me I could become an engineer. There's no possibility like that here. When I look at the villagers, they seem to have always been the same," she paused abruptly. "I'm sorry. I didn't mean to offend you."

"You didn't offend me." She'd given words to the feeling he had whenever he looked at his father or Yishou.

"These things make me sad to talk about." She tilted her head up to the wind, then turned back to him and asked, "Will you tell me another story? No one has told me any of the legends of this place."

"They're silly. You wouldn't like them. All animals and magic . . ."

"No, please!"

So he repeated a story he heard from his grandfather, one all the villagers knew, about Bao the Fifth Elder, who had been so smart he passed the old imperial exams and went to Beijing to be a confidant of the emperor. When he finished, she asked for another one, so he recited the legend of the island in the middle of Lake Chao, which was said to be formed from the sad teardrop of a mother who'd lost her daughter.

They went on like this until they'd finished peeling all the chestnuts. This time, though he was still afraid, he did not make up an excuse to leave early, and they walked slowly down the hill together. Before they parted, she told him her name was Tian Hanwen. He immediately heard the culture in the characters, a name unlike any he'd ever heard in the village. Even his grandfather, who'd given both Yitian and Yishou their names, would never have come up with something so elegant.

Questions about her life in Shanghai became his favorite ones to ask. He'd never been nearly that far—the biggest place he'd ever gone was Hefei City, but even that was a marginal point on the map compared to Shanghai.

"I've heard there are salons where people discuss literature all the time. Is that true?" he asked once, and she'd laughed.

"Professors and older scholars might do that. Not normal people like us." Then, as if she'd seen the disappointment on his face, she hurried to say, "But if we go to college, we could go to places like that. Anyway, there are other things. I could see the tall buildings on Nanjing Road from my house. Oh, and the department store where we used to go play at night, it was so big and empty. We'd hide in the basement until the guard found us. . . . I'll take you there!"

He was embarrassed by how little he knew; after she described the city to him, he could see how he'd fashioned an image of Shanghai out of childish fantasy. But he felt grateful, too, for the new practicality her stories gave him, which weighed his dreams with solidity.

He saw Shanghai and the big cities as appendices to the stories his grandfather told him, continuations of the glorious past into the present. A place like Shanghai was where history continued to be written onward, unlike his village, where history seemed to have stopped, and in recent years, even regressed to a less literate past.

After each story she told about Shanghai, he went home and repeated her words to himself as he washed and prepared for bed. He pictured once again the glamorous cinemas with movies from all over the world and the library in her neighborhood where translations of foreign novels were slowly being allowed back. Visiting all these places with her. He wanted to memorize every detail of life there, in case his imagination was the only place where he'd ever be able to experience it.

He longed to kiss her, as the protagonist did in *The Heart of a Young Girl*, the tattered book, banned and hand copied, that all the boys had secretly passed around in the ninth grade. He wondered if her lips would feel supple against his, like the book described.

He approached Yishou for advice. He waited until one late afternoon when they were alone taking down blankets from the laundry line.

"Do you ever kiss your girlfriend?" Yitian asked quietly. He knew his older brother had a courtship with a girl in Han Village, whom he sometimes walked five li on weekends to go see.

"Why do you ask?" Yishou laughed loudly. He'd made no effort to follow Yitian in speaking softly.

"Oh, nothing—" Yitian blushed.

"Do you have a girlfriend?" Yishou's grin spread wider on his face. "Is she very beautiful?"

"No, that's not what I mean. Never mind." He regretted asking his brother. Yishou had many skills, but being sensitive wasn't one of them.

"Well, if you *did*, what you would do is this." He lunged toward Yitian, bringing his face mere inches away, then yelped. Yitian was so shocked that he dropped the clean blanket he was holding onto the dirt.

His brother was laughing uproariously. "Come on, it's not so hard! Even all the animals do it without worrying so much. Just look at them if you need help."

When he met with Hanwen that Sunday, her very outline seemed charged and changed. He tried to be as carefree as Yishou would be as he sat down and closed the space next to her.

"You seem distracted," she said.

"Do young people like us date in Shanghai?" he asked.

"What a sudden question!" she laughed. When she saw that he was serious, she said, "I've heard some stories from older girls. They said it all was very secretive. If a couple went to the movie theater, they had to buy tickets separately. And they waited until after the movie had started and always sat in the back, near the end of the row, so that no one could look over and see them."

His heart pounded with the thought of what would happen after the lights had gone out in those theaters. He looked at her face, golden with the soft, late daylight of autumn, and leaned toward her. But when he brought his face close to hers, she turned away. She placed her hands on the ground behind her, so that her body was tilted away from him, and said, "Please don't."

"Is everything okay?"

After a while, she said, "When I was a kid, I saw so many women, our neighbors, accused in the large-character posters. They called them immoral and loose. They were screamed at, lost their jobs. Someone my mother knew even committed suicide."

"It's not like that anymore."

She shook her head. "Please understand."

He felt rebuked, and they sat in silence. He was afraid to look at her again. He'd tried on a role for which he was the wrong actor. He wasn't like one of those handsome men in the Western novels they'd read together. His earliest worries, that there was no way she could be attracted to his tu face, had turned out to be right, after all.

"Why did you talk to me on the hill that day?" he asked.

"What do you mean?"

"That first time you saw me up here. You could have just turned around and gone back down. Why did you keep talking to me?"

He looked back up at her. She was using a twig to pick a hole in the dirt. "Something about the way you were sitting there that first day reading, looking so engrossed. I could tell that you were someone I would want to talk to. Someone I would like."

"But you have all those girls in your dormitory who read and went to school in Shanghai. You could have just talked to them."

"It's not the same. We talk about books and our lives, but it's not the same as with you. I could tell how much you cared. They aren't like that. I'm not even like that."

"You are," he said.

She shook her head.

She'd seemed so confident the first day on the hill. Now a string hummed in his chest at the sudden recognition of himself in her.

After some time had passed, she said, "I do like you, you know that?" Her voice trembled slightly. She reached out to interlace her fingers with his. When she squeezed his fingers and buried the knot of them in the grass, he felt relieved. He was surprised to find he believed her words, fully and completely. Wasn't it true, that love grew in ways beyond what he'd ever read or understood from a book? It could come from something as small as what she'd just described, or the way a person squinted thoughtfully toward the sun before she answered your questions. That was all it took, a moment enough to lodge in your mind and replay itself over and over, affecting your days forever after.

Fifteen

NOVEMBER 1977

After his father hid the hukou booklet, Yitian felt a darkness smothering his body. A door to the future had suddenly closed and left the room of his life in shadow. His grandfather was dead. He couldn't see anything new that would come in his lifetime.

He found the act of lifting himself out of bed to be physically impossible, his body losing all the vigor that he hadn't realized had once animated it. His mother pitied him and did not scold him as harshly as he was sure she otherwise would have. His father showed no such lenience. Whenever he caught Yitian dawdling around the home, he began berating him. Only his mother's intervention stopped the shouting.

That Sunday, Yitian didn't meet Hanwen. He avoided her in the fields. Once, he saw her shape approaching him and he hurriedly announced to Yishou that he was going to use the bathroom. He did not want to see what her face might look like when he told her his father had taken his hukou booklet. He was not the person he'd made himself out to be, a scholar just like her. She would take the gaokao and go on to college, but he'd remain a farmer, just as everyone in his family had always been. They'd say goodbye soon, anyway, when she left for that life; he was only making the departure easier.

When Yishou asked him if he wanted to go to town that weekend, he was in the courtyard, laying out radishes to dry, a task so easy that he was sure his mother's assignment had been deliberate.

"Come on, little brother," Yishou said. "You need some distraction. Town will be fun. You can check out the stores while I get the grains."

"I don't want to go."

"Why not? You can't just sit here all day, looking sad."

Why can't I? he wanted to respond, but this sounded whiny, even to him. Instead, he told his brother, "There's no point. Besides, it's too cold."

"There might be a surprise for you if you come," his brother said, but Yitian was even more irritated by the childishness.

"Suit yourself," Yishou said. "You'd want to come if you knew what kind of surprise this was." He packed up his knapsack and left.

Yitian felt both annoyed at and envious at how simpleminded Yishou was. Only one character differed between their two names, but Yishou was the kind of person for whom all unhappiness was only temporary, easily cured by buying a youtiao in town. His thoughts seemed to end with life's facts, a quality that made him an excellent farmer. Their mother speculated that the difference was because of the years that separated their births. Yishou was born during the worst of the Great Leap Forward famine years, while

Yitian's birth came two years later, as conditions, though still bad, had improved tremendously.

"How can he forget that? He was born in a time when we had no mind for anything except for food. Not like you, spending all your time thinking. We were all so hungry back then," she said. "His body will remember, even if the mind forgets."

He heard the footsteps of Yishou's return late that evening, after everyone else had gone to bed. Yitian pretended to be asleep and waited for Yishou to flop himself onto the pallet and the snoring that usually began immediately.

"Wake up," Yishou said, shaking his shoulder. His voice was urgent in Yitian's ear. Yitian wondered if his brother was drunk from his trip.

"Wake up, Yitian. I have something to show you."

Reluctantly, Yitian sat up. His brother stood next to the pallet, fumbling with the lining of his coat. When he finally untangled the object from the cotton padding, he whistled quietly in celebration.

"Here," he said, handing the object to Yitian.

It was a small and thin piece of paper. Yitian rose and went to the window, so that the blue cast of the moonlight illuminated the thin text to make the print visible.

"Oh my god—" Yitian caught himself and lowered his voice. It was a permit to take the gaokao. "How did you even get this?"

"I took the hukou from Ba's coat and registered you while I was in town today."

"And Ba didn't notice?"

"I took it when he was napping yesterday afternoon. It's not like he's checking for it every second."

Yitian rubbed the paper between his thumb and index fingers. A solid thing. Somehow, the permit showed almost no signs of creases or wear. Yishou had protected it well.

"Didn't I tell you to stop sulking and come to town with me?"

Yitian was speechless. His brother had performed a miracle.

"Take a look. Is it right?" Yishou asked anxiously.

Yitian peered at the words in the moonlight again. There they all were, stamped officially with a red seal. Name, age, gender. He tilted the paper to reveal different parts of the permit, and, as he did, noticed one mistake. His brother had registered him for the mathematics and sciences exam, rather than the one for literature and history. Yitian wondered how Yishou could possibly have made such an error. The characters were completely different and impossible to confuse with one another.

"The exam type—" He stopped himself. Yishou's expression was so expectant, his smile glowing so hugely in the dark.

"Something wrong?"

"No, nothing." Yishou would surely be embarrassed if he brought up the mistake. He struggled with writing and reading, and had probably accidentally misread the form. Yitian took one last look at the paper before he placed it under his pillow. Clipped onto the document was his official photograph. Where had Yishou even gotten that? What his brother had done for him was not a simple, spontaneous matter—the trip would have required deliberate planning and sidestepping of their father for days.

"Thank you," Yitian said.

Even in the darkness, he could tell Yishou was relieved. "What are you thanking me for? I'm your brother. It's just what I'm supposed to do. Now, make sure you hide that paper somewhere good. Don't just leave it out."

"Do you really think I'd be so stupid?" Yitian slapped his older brother's head.

Yishou climbed into bed. Yitian expected him to fall asleep immediately, but instead he yawned, turning onto his back, and said, "Why do you want to leave so badly, anyway?"

"Life feels so limited here," Yitian said. When he realized the implications of what he'd said, he hurried to add, "Not limited. I meant—it's not about here. I just want to experience other places, too. Don't you?"

"Visiting is enough for me."

Yishou turned onto his side and fell asleep, but Yitian felt even more awake than before. He propped himself up to watch Yishou's silhouette, his chest moving up and down in sleep, and wanted, suddenly, to embrace his brother. He felt ashamed that earlier that day he'd thought Yishou stupid. He'd forgotten how his brother cared about his studying. Once, when Yitian was eleven and Yishou thirteen, there had been a torrential rainstorm. When the rain finally ended after three days, half a meter of muddy water remained in the schoolhouse and all the books were destroyed. The other students hadn't cared much. The teacher, who only lazily scanned the material each day before class was about to begin, was also apathetic. Yitian, however, relied on the textbooks for information on math and physics, which his grandfather knew little about and he needed to learn on his own.

Yishou had suggested they go to Five Groves Township, which housed the only library in the area. Yitian objected that the library wouldn't lend to anyone their age.

"Fine, then we'll just steal them." Yishou grinned. "That's more fun, anyway."

They'd lied to their mother. She wrapped bowls of rice in handkerchiefs for the trip, which would take an entire day.

At the library building, they hid behind one wall and watched people go in and out. The only person who looked over the books was an old man seated at a rickety wooden chair by the front door. In one hand he gripped a ring of keys loosely, while in the other he held a cane upon which he rested his chin. When the guard showed the sure droop of someone asleep, they entered quietly.

Yitian was immediately distracted by the shelves and shelves of books inside, piled up to the ceiling, titles he'd never heard the names of.

"Hurry and get what you need," Yishou said, but then they heard the creak of someone entering.

Though they weren't technically doing anything wrong, the sudden appearance startled them both. Yishou grabbed Yitian's hand and ran out the back door. Behind the building there was a tall wall that separated the library from the alleyway. Yishou made a foothold for Yitian to climb. Yitian reached the top of the wall and then jumped quickly down. He'd nearly reached the main road beyond when he heard his brother scream. When he looked back, he saw Yishou lying on the ground below the wall, one of his knees crumpled under him, the other jutting out in a strange acute angle from his kneecap.

When Yitian apologized days later, Yishou grinned and said, "It's not your fault. It was my idea. Anyway, now I don't have to go to class." There was no talk of him returning to school after he recovered. He dropped out, having finished only the eighth grade.

Later, this was the way that Yitian would remember Yishou—the crooked smile on that easygoing face that everything seemed to roll off, until the day it didn't.

Yishou began to work full time in the fields, just as all the adult men did. At the time when Yitian studied, his older brother looked over his shoulder and tried to read his writing. He read some characters correctly, but frequently he was wrong, mistaking one radical for the other and ending up with another word entirely.

At moments, Yitian caught a glimpse of his older brother far away in the fields, his outline flashing in the dusty glimmer of a horizon line as he brought his hoe down to break up a clump of dirt. Yitian would imagine he saw Yishou's eyebrows furrowing or a tightness in the body that indicated some concern, but when he walked closer to Yishou, he found what he'd seen had only been an illusion of the shimmering heat. His brother's face remained as open and unmarked as ever.

How rude he'd been to Yishou, to everyone. His pain had made him small minded. He would never allow himself to be like that again, he decided. He would never forget all the people who'd sacrificed to help him.

The next morning his body felt more awake than it had in weeks. As he dressed and splashed water onto his face, his mother looked up, surprised at the quickness of his movement.

"Even if you don't take the exam, there are things to look forward to in life, see?" she said. He nodded and smiled.

He looked out for Hanwen's figure in the fields that day, waiting to approach her when she was alone.

"I'm very behind in studying. You must have made so much progress without me," he said quietly. "There aren't many days left until the exam, and I definitely need your help."

Her brow furrowed in an expression he'd never seen her wear before, which he was sure was the beginning of an anger unfurling.

"Where have you been?"

"I'm sorry for not coming. Can we study together this Sunday? In our old place?"

"Yitian, I waited for you. I didn't have any news of you at all. You didn't even come talk to me."

"I know. I'm sorry."

She looked at him, wanting an explanation, but he didn't say anything more. He regretted that she'd been hurt, but he didn't see what else he could have done. If he'd told her about his father, what good would have come?

Around them they could hear the sounds of others returning to work. The break was ending.

"Yitian?" She took a last look at him, shook her head, then walked away.

But she was there that Sunday. He'd gone just in case. She came down the embankment, later than usual, and he looked at her apprehensively. He waited for her to say something sharp, but instead she reached into her knapsack and pulled out a folded piece of paper. It was the study plan she'd made for them.

"Here's where I am," she said, pointing to a date far ahead of where she said he was. "You'll have to catch up to me."

She sat down next to him and took out her notebooks without another word.

They continued to meet until the days became too cold, after which they moved to an old barn next to her dorm, where they stored old tools and pesticide during the slack season. They shared an old desk with a wobbly leg that Yitian had found and carried home from the local primary school. They kept the door of the barn open so they wouldn't be accused of doing anything inappropriate. Gusts blew in often. By the time he left each day he could barely feel his hands, made cracked and swollen by the cold. The fingers he interlaced into hers were spotted with crushed ink, and when he looked at them, he thought they belonged to someone else.

They largely worked without talking, her head bent over a Chinese textbook while he moved his lips silently to memorize the formulas for the area and circumference of different shapes. Then they would trade and she would double-check that she'd remembered the relationships between parts of a triangle while he would go over lists of proverbs. The turning of pages and pens scratching sounded sharply against the deadening winter air. At intervals, he snuck a glance over at her, her lower lip caught between her teeth as she flipped between one page to another, and a gentle trust lapped over him. He wondered if she did the same when he wasn't looking.

As winter approached, sometimes a sudden gust of wind blew through the barn door and sent their papers flying everywhere, and they shouted and ran after them, afraid their careful notes would be lost into the wind outside. They laughed loudly, collapsing after they'd saved the notes. Then he looked over at her and wanted to postpone the date of the test forever. He could already feel the pang of loss of this moment, when hope had appeared and grown on its own, uncurtained yet by its resolution.

Sixteen

DECEMBER 1977

A patch of his knee was soaked, a casualty of the rain that had fallen ceaselessly since that morning, the kind so steady in rhythm that the patter had already begun to lodge in Yitian's mind. He pulled at the tarp, trying to steal more for himself, but was met almost immediately by the twin motion from the passenger next to him and the ensuing tightening of the slick fabric. At least his knapsack, with his notebook and pens, was safely tucked underneath.

When he looked over, his neighbor pushed his kneecap against Yitian's. The boy had already been on the truck bed, its sole occupant, when Yitian and Yishou boarded at the township. When Yishou, jovial as they set out, asked where he was from, he'd haughtily replied, "Well, I'm *from* Shanghai, but I was sent down to Bi Shan Village. I guess you guys are locals?" Yishou had glared at him for the rest of the ride.

By the time they arrived in Hefei, the truck bed was squeezed so tightly that he could hardly move his limbs.

"How dare you! I'll report you!" a girl's voice screamed from the other corner.

"I didn't mean to do that, I swear! He pushed me into you." A boy.

"*Shame* on you, using this opportunity to try to touch young ladies."

When they got into town, the truck slowed to a crawl. The main thoroughfare of the city was packed with other cars, filled with students coming in from all directions. None could move. The driver shifted into park.

Yitian looked out the window to see other students squeezed into the beds of trucks and tractors and tricycles. They exposed their own bodies to the rain in order to protect their possessions. Still, the wet students smiled and waved at the other vehicles, honking their horns as they passed. Yitian had the sensation of watching a movie in which they were all participants, of congratulating each other for being actors, together, on such a big stage.

Townspeople had set up food stands under umbrellas along the sidewalk. The smell of steamed buns, roasted yams, and coal burning was only slightly dampened by the rain. Vendors ran up to them and waved the items up to the students who held their faces out from the truck beds. "Student! Student! A bun? Only five cents for two. Made of the freshest pork, I can promise you. You must eat protein if you want to do well on the exam."

"Bark of the Banyan tree! This is what Dong Zhongshu took himself when he sat for the imperial exams." An old lady held up a pockmarked brown substance, which looked to Yitian like a piece of mildewed parchment.

He bought the pork buns but refused the banyan bark.

"You think you have money to buy *pork*?" Yishou smacked his head.

That morning, the two of them had caught a truck out of the township near Tang Family Village. They'd devised an elaborate lie to tell their father about why they'd be gone for three days, saying that Yishou wanted to visit a distant uncle of theirs who lived in a village about fifty li away. He hinted aggressively, though did not say outright, that there was a girl in the village who he wanted to see again, whom he'd met once at a market day in a nearby township. He'd take Yitian with him, not only for safety on the journey but also so that Yitian could make observations about the girl and report back to their mother and father.

Yishou had come up with the story. Yitian thought the tale was convoluted, and their father should have known Yishou already had a girl, but, unable to come up with anything better himself, he sat silently in the other room as his brother recited.

"It's the off-season anyway, Ba, there's nothing much for us to do here," Yishou said. Yitian waited for his father to object to the idea of an off-season, but he only grunted and reminisced about the uncle in question.

"See, didn't I tell you that there would be no problem with Ba? I understand him more than you, don't I?" Yishou said to Yitian afterward.

Yitian smiled. He had to agree.

He fidgeted now at the slow crawl of the vehicle.

"We don't have time for this," he muttered under his breath. He wanted to do some last-minute studying that evening, but that wouldn't be possible if they didn't find a place where they could rest for the night soon. He was so nervous that Yishou had earlier gone to the other side of the truck bed, saying Yitian was too annoying to sit by.

Yitian called up to the driver, "Let us out here, please! We'll walk."

"Don't be silly," Yishou said. "You have no idea of where we even are! We can't just get out here."

Indeed, as Yitian looked out the window, he was struck by how little he knew about this city. He had no landmarks by which to navigate. Each time he'd visited a new place before, the streets had at least been partially negotiated for him by someone who knew more, usually his brother or grandfather.

The driver abruptly called to everyone that it was time to get off the truck. "Engine is making noise," he grumbled. "Can't go any farther."

They were stopped, not even on a corner, but in the middle of the street. Though the other students complained at the driver's announcement, they seemed to proceed with purpose toward destinations as soon as they got off. By the time Yitian and Yishou climbed down, half of the passengers had already turned a corner and disappeared. Yishou grabbed one of the few remaining students by the arm and asked, "Excuse me, brother—where are you all staying?"

The other boy looked annoyed. This was not their village, Yitian thought; Yishou should not have a grabbed a stranger like that.

"My parents found a relative's house for me to stay at."

Yitian asked, more politely, a few other students milling around. Besides one boy who said he was staying at a hotel—a luxury so unlikely that Yishou openly scoffed—everyone else had some person they knew in the city, arranged by their parents. Finally, after the last of the other students had left, Yitian and Yishou jogged to the overhang of a building across the street. All of Yitian's previous attention to the tarp became wasted in moments, and their clothes sagged heavily down their bodies.

"Look, let's just ask a shopkeeper if we can stay on their floor for a couple of nights. We'll offer them some of the money we brought for food," Yishou said.

A loud knock from the shop's window startled them. A middle-aged woman opened the door a crack and shooed them away.

"You can't stand here in front of my shop. Come on, go!"

Every shop they passed was the same. Some proprietors they asked laughed at them for even believing staying overnight was a possibility. All their things wet, they were just beginning to discuss sleeping on the floor of the bus terminal when an old lady approached them.

"Are you boys looking for somewhere to stay? I have a room in my house."

They studied the old woman, who looked up to them from barely chest level. Her back was stooped in a knot, shaped almost like the handle of a cane. Eyeing her, with baskets of dried fava beans hooked into the crooks of her arms, it was hard to imagine her posing any danger.

"I've been watching you two boys walk all up and down the street looking for a place. I've decided to take you in. One kuai a night, for the both of you. Reasonable rate, yes? This old lady is not trying to take advantage of you."

Later, when they'd brought their things up to her home and were drinking hot water around the table in her sitting room, they found out why she'd approached them. Their gaits reminded her of her own son's, she said. The mood between them was jovial after they discovered she was also originally from the cluster of villages populated by people surnamed Tang.

"You two are brothers, aren't you?" she asked.

"How did you know? People say we don't look alike."

"Ha, because they aren't as experienced as me. Look, even though you're broader than him and have a more handsome face"—she pointed at Yishou, causing Yitian to wince—"you two have the exact same posture. And your noses, see how they both widen at the tip?

"My son would have been the same age as you two when he died. He was in the army." She took out a photograph that had been flattened under a clay pickling jar and handed it to them. Yitian peered at the photo of the officer in a pressed green suit—though the photograph was in black-and-white, he registered its color, along with the gold buttons, and the star on the center of the cap that would certainly have been red—the same that his father wore in the picture from when he enlisted.

"He hated it so much," the woman continued. "Being out there, with all those men and away from their families. My son wanted to be a scholar, but the timing was never right for his life. The wars . . . and all this chaos . . ." she waved her arms in the air vaguely, afraid to say more.

"One day I received a letter. I had to ask someone to come read it for me, but even before that, I knew it had some kind of bad news. I could just feel it. They said my son was missing in action in Korea. After a while, when they couldn't find the body, they said he was dead.

"But I never believed them. There was no body. Can you believe that? They didn't even give his mother his body back. Who knows what happened? I imagined for years he might have snuck out to Taiwan and started a new life there, reading all the time, just as he'd wanted. I thought maybe he'd look how you did, walking along the streets."

They were all silent now. The water, untouched, had gone cold.

"This old lady is so annoying, isn't she?" She sprang up and began collecting the cups. "Bothering you young people with all these stories of my son, while you have your own things to worry about."

They protested when she offered to make them dinner, but she insisted.

"Nonsense! I'm just boiling some noodles!"

As Yitian watched the old woman work at the stove, he was overcome with loneliness. He thought of her son, trudging in that crisp suit of the picture, made wrinkled after all the days he spent in its unwashed folds. The image of her son gradually morphed, becoming Yitian's father, walking along with his battalion, lonely in the evenings as he lay on his bedroll. Yitian had never thought about whether his father marched with vigor alongside the other soldiers, or if instead he, too, harbored some secret hope. He wondered how he would have lived himself if he'd been conscripted into the army, had he been born in a time when his choices were even fewer. He was quiet as they ate dinner, saddened at the thought of all the individual dots, obscured by uniforms, forced into places that they hadn't decided for themselves.

After dinner, the old woman went to bed, and Yitian pulled out his notes to study. He'd debated whether to try to get some early rest the last night before the exam, but in the end he couldn't help himself.

"Will you test me?" he asked Yishou. He wished Hanwen was there instead. She was also testing in the city, but she'd left separately and was staying with the other sent-down youth. They'd made plans to meet up after the exam finished.

Yishou took the paper reluctantly and pointed to a line of characters in Yitian's scribbled cursive. "How do you read things like this all day? I can barely make out the words."

"It's just because you don't study them. If you did, you'd be able to read them without any problem."

"No, that can't be it. I used to try, but the characters would just flip and swim at my eyes." Yishou was so unabashed about how little he knew. Yitian guessed that, even now, his brother probably only recognized as many characters as a primary school student. He read slowly, "What era of Chairman Mao's thinking does the fifth volume of *Selected Works of Mao Zedong* come from? And what is the foundational philosophy of the fifth volume?"

These political questions had always given Yitian trouble. All throughout school, he'd never paid much attention during their mandatory politics classes, but he wouldn't pass the gaokao without finally taking in the material. In the previous few weeks, he'd read, really truly read, *The Communist Manifesto* and all of Mao's writing for the first time. He'd found the books as inscrutable as ever, and resigned himself to simply memorizing the important parts.

"Is this really what you spend your time trying to learn?" Yishou mimicked the military cadence of Mao: "*The masses! The army! The cadres are the three pillars!*" He didn't even finish the recitation before he burst out in laughter.

Their family had gone through too much hardship to take the Party's claims to righteousness very seriously. Yitian had been raised on tales of how the Party had caused thousands of deaths in their villages during the Great Famine years. Not even his father, serving in the country's army, believed the boastful words. When the Chairman's death was announced over the loudspeakers, his mother had closed the door of their home so they could whoop secretly. They took down the poster of Chairman Mao, which every family had to hang in their home, and secretly burned it that night in their courtyard, along with the vegetable peels. "Chairman Mao is dead! Chairman Mao is dead!" they chanted in whispers, and the words took on a new, hopeful meaning. When their team leader visited the next day,

Yitian forced himself into crying by poking his pencil so forcefully into his leg that the lead snapped in half.

For the rest of the night, Yishou murmured questions in a slow and unsteady cadence, and Yitian responded rapidly with an answer he'd memorized down to the last word. They continued until ten o'clock, and then both climbed into the pallet their host had made for them on the floor. Yitian and Yishou lay head to toe in hopes of sleeping better, but Yitian's nerves were too poor. He kept waking at half-hour intervals, sure it was already daytime and he'd accidentally missed the exam. He finally gave up on sleeping right before dawn and dressed for the day. The old woman had made them a breakfast of porridge, but he found that, upon lifting the bowl, he could hardly stomach more than a few sips.

The line to enter the exam room rose and dipped with students of all ages, from sent-down youth to young farmers like Yishou and old men like his grandfather. The site was a repurposed gymnasium of a city high school. Everyone seemed to be in various states of panic. They shoved buns into their mouths, kneaded hot-water bottles in their hands against the cold of the gymnasium, and muttered their notes under their breath. Yitian reached into his pocket and fingered the two pens to make sure the ink hadn't frozen. The previous night, he'd slept with the inkwell pressed to his chest to keep it warm.

Farther up in line, he recognized one of his teachers. Yitian went to meet him, ignoring the annoyed protests of the other students he passed.

"I didn't sleep all night," Teacher Li said. His short figure—when he'd taught Yitian in middle school, many of the students were already taller than him—was slouched over his crossed arms.

"I hardly slept either," Yitian said.

"It can't be good for us." He lifted a fingernail to his mouth and chewed the surface. Yitian swatted his hand away. Teacher Li's fingernails were so destroyed by his biting and the cold that there were bits of dried blood around the ashen cuticles.

"I can't help it," Teacher Li said. His eyes were completely bloodshot and ringed with plum-colored circles. His face, normally plump, appeared sallow and thinner. Yitian's teacher had been waiting for the opportunity much longer than he had. He was twenty-seven, and his parents had treated the local cadres to dinner year after year in hopes of currying favor for the college recommendation system. Their efforts hadn't ever worked. His parents were giving him this last chance: if he could not get into college this year, they would force him to find a wife and start his married life in the village. Yitian felt sympathetic to him; of all his teachers in middle school, Teacher Li was the only one who'd been any good.

They were allowed into the gymnasium one by one. The room was stuffed so fully with desks that Yitian could only navigate the aisles by positioning his body sideways. It would have been easy to cheat by looking at nearby desks, if he'd wanted to. In later years, he would learn that there were indeed some who'd cheated that day, the well-off children of cadres who arranged for them to have answer sheets swapped or be generously graded. He could understand why they might be driven to such means—he'd read in the newspaper that there would be six million students taking the gaokao and only two hundred thousand spots in the universities, odds so narrow he hardly dared to calculate them.

Then suddenly the proctor was scratching his long beard and reading the instructions of the exam . . . he was passing out the booklets and scolding students who tried to turn them over before time began . . . he was checking his watch and chalking the finish time on the board.

Teacher Li reached across the tiny gap of space between their desks and tapped on Yitian's.

"Here we go," he mouthed.

Yitian saw students near him rubbing their hands together and vaguely registered that the air must have been cold, but he didn't notice any feeling in his own fingers, which had gone numb. He shook them furiously and then lifted the pen to ink his name on the first line in the booklet:

唐一田

The name written there—dark, permanent, his.

Now they were opening the first page of the test booklet. He heard students around him ripping through the thin paper in eagerness, but he lifted his own gently and creased the surface with soft pressure.

Thirty seconds . . . begin . . . the proctor's voice faded in.

Yitian flipped to the long answers first. He and Hanwen had discussed this strategy of skipping to the questions with the most point value before returning to the rest. The wrong answer on just one of these could ruin his chances of passing the test at all.

A feeling of immense relief spread its hand across his heart as he read the prompt.

In his 1921 work, "My Old Home," Lu Xun wrote, "Hope cannot be said to exist, nor can it be said not to exist. It is just like roads across the Earth. For actually the Earth had no roads to begin with, but when many pass one way, a road is made." Please comment.

He pressed his pen deeply into the surface of the paper and began to write.

Seventeen

He packed his things languidly on the exam's final day. Now that they'd finished, the desks around the room had all been pushed out of their neat lines. Everyone else had already left the room, but he wanted to revel in these last few moments. To his surprise, the next three exam sessions had gone as well as the first. He was even able to quickly answer all of the questions on the mathematics exam, which had worried him most. All the time he'd spent with Hanwen, memorizing formulas according to the schedule she'd created for them, had paid off in the end.

Other students hadn't fared so well. Thirty minutes into the math exam on the second day, Teacher Li had darted up from his seat and started cursing.

"You must stay in your seat, boy!" the proctor said, alarmed.

Teacher Li had sat back down, but soon after there had been the sound of a pen tip ripping through paper, sharp amidst the steady rhythm of softly scratching ink coming from the other desks. Yitian found Teacher Li crying outside of the classroom afterward.

"My hand cramped in the middle of the test and I couldn't write anything."

He held his hand cradled to his chest as gently as a swaddled infant. Yitian patted him on the back and tried to reassure him, but Teacher Li's seat was empty in the afternoon session of the exam. The next morning, a different student had been given the desk. On the second day, the exam room was noticeably emptier, and the air had taken on a tone more serious than the simple excitement of the first day.

Before leaving, Yitian paused for a moment at the window, where a layer of condensation had formed from the heat of all the bodies cramped into a single room. The afternoon sun was just receding, darkening the room and splaying acute shadows from the window frame onto his hand. He wiped away a spot in the fog so that he could see outside. The rest of the students were gathered there on the basketball court, tearing up their notes in celebration, completely oblivious to the cold. After they threw all the remnants up into the air, they danced along the pieces of paper as if they were confetti.

The scene amused them, but he did not want to destroy the notes he'd made. He pressed his thumbnail into another foggy spot of the window and wrote

唐一田

Pink light streamed through the transparency he'd created, glowing through his name. 一田, a single field, the name his grandfather had picked for him. That was all he needed, the smallest gift from Heaven capable of sustaining life.

Here in this room, he might have begun a life for himself much bigger than a single field. His name would fade quickly when the fog melted, but it seemed significant in that moment, like the signing of some document, his scholar's name in scribbled cursive making claim on his own beautiful text.

G od was watching for us," Hanwen said to him.

"Perhaps it was God, or our own hard work."

"I worked hard," she laughed. "You just stole the smart things I said and wrote them down on your exam paper."

She could have said anything in that moment and he wouldn't have minded. They'd gone out with Yishou and some other students to a nearby food stall after the exam, and he was already tipsy from the homemade grain alcohol that Yishou had bought for them.

He knew going out to eat was reckless. It would be difficult for him to explain to his mother the spending when he'd supposedly only been away in his uncle's village. But what did it matter? They'd finished the exam! None of the students who thought they'd done poorly had come out with them to eat, so the atmosphere was loud and celebratory. Each time the proprietress brought over a dish, she sucked her teeth in annoyance at how loud they were, but Yitian didn't care. When he thought no one else was looking, he took Hanwen's hand underneath the table and rubbed his own over her fingers. He stopped at the knotted mass that'd formed over the top knuckle on her ring finger, forged from the pressure of the pen.

"It's your mark of success," he announced.

He licked his own index finger and brought the damp pad onto her callous, rubbing the rough surface to soften the dense layer of skin formed there. He would not have dared before to do something like this in public, but the days of the exam had brought him new confidence. Somehow, all of his previous concerns about propriety felt trivial after they left the village. He hoped that, in a university in the city, they would no longer have to treat their relationship as something to hide. This was one, amongst many others, aspect of the Communist ideology that he did not understand. Mao said that women held up half the sky, but to display your love for a woman publicly was considered inappropriate. They were taught in school that relationships were a waste of the time that they could have otherwise dedicated to the Revolution.

"I saw that," Yishou said.

Yitian looked up, surprised. He'd thought his brother was too engrossed in crunching on his youtiao to pay any attention to them.

"You two were completely made for each other, you know that? No one else would put up with my brother's weird obsession with stuff like this." Yishou pointed to Yitian's stack of notes, which he'd brought with him to eat. He and Hanwen had given up comparing their answers on the test when Yishou's teasing had made it impossible to concentrate any longer. "But you're exactly the same as him!" Yishou pointed at Hanwen with his chopstick and laughed.

"Can you be more polite to her, please?" Yitian said, patting Yishou's arm down.

"Who are you now, my mother? Because you've taken the college entrance exam?"

Yitian could not help but be annoyed, though he knew his brother didn't mean to be rude or malicious. Yitian immediately thought of his father at this moment. Both he and Yishou were two men from the countryside who lacked manners, who liked to drink because there was little other entertainment in their lives. Yitian recalled his brother on the night before the exam, the awkward, ugly rhythm with which he'd read the questions. Yitian did not want to talk to him at this moment; he wanted to be with Hanwen. He turned away from Yishou, who was so drunk that he probably wouldn't even notice.

Part 3

旱季

DRY
SEASON

———

Eighteen

1993

They kept their telephone under a white doily on a side table in the living room, and Hanwen found herself, over the next day, walking toward it often, lifting the white lace and placing her hand on the receiver, already sure she felt the half shudder of the vibration that came before a ring. She imagined that she would pick up the receiver to the sound of Yitian's voice. Or it would be the voice of someone from the police chief's office, which would offer an excuse to call Yitian. But then when the clanging sound of the phone's bell did peal into the air of the home, she was seized by terror, sure she would say *Wei?* and there would be the sharp exhalation of breath before Mr. Qian spoke.

"Do you want to go to the zoo this afternoon?" she asked Yuanyuan after Ayi brought him home from school. She'd stayed at home all day and the air of the home was suffocating, as she'd felt it constantly since the dinner that night. Inside the house, there was nothing to do but wait.

The question was enough for Yuanyuan to shout and bounce

around the living room, pretending to be a rabbit like the ones he hoped to see. He'd been asking to go to the zoo ever since they'd read a picture book about tigers a year ago, but she'd been there before. Guifan had taken her, when he'd first been assigned to the city. "I know it's not Shanghai or that famous a city, but there are things to do here, too. It's a big step up for me," he said. And she'd nodded and smiled, replied, "You don't have to explain," even though she was depressed looking at the tall cement walls around the poor, kept animals, because he'd made an effort, and that was already much more than what most men in his position would do.

She called Yitian's hotel.

"You've heard something?" he asked, right after the greetings, his voice eager and urgent. It was a sensible question, and yet she was disappointed. She'd hoped that some excitement at their reunion would have flooded over his fear for his father, she realized.

"Not yet."

"Oh."

"But I'll let you know as soon as I hear anything. Do you want to see some of Hefei while you're here? I'm taking Yuanyuan to the zoo."

"The zoo?"

She could hear the hesitation in his voice, so she hurried to say, "If you're free. I know you're probably busy seeing other people in Hefei—"

"I don't have anyone else to see. Okay. The zoo."

They made arrangements to meet at the front entrance in half an hour. She hurried Ayi to dress Yuanyuan, their only chance of going without her mother to slip out before she woke from her afternoon nap. Then Hanwen would be able to say they'd been in a rush and didn't want to disturb her, that she had seemed more tired after her fall and they'd wanted to let her have the rest she deserved.

When they paid twice to enter, once at the ticketing stand at the park gates and again for the zoo inside the park, he looked over at her.

"This isn't a scam, right?" She could hear, in the tone of his voice, the strain to make a joke, but the smile didn't quite reach his eyes. She noticed how much more tired he looked, though only a day had passed. The circles under his eyes collected like liquid in tiny balloons and his gaze had the dull quality of someone who'd slept fitfully.

"My mother has made me afraid that everyone is trying to scam me."

"They are. I hope that you aren't telling everyone you're from America?"

"I haven't become that stupid yet."

"No scam here. As long as you stay with me, you won't get into any trouble." A small thrill ran through her, that she was able to offer this protection to him.

"Ma says not to say *stupid*," Yuanyuan shouted at him.

"Okay, okay, I won't," Yitian said, putting his hands up in surrender. He laughed and this time his eyes crinkled at their corners.

"Yuanyuan. Don't yell at Uncle, okay?" She tried to sound appropriately stern, but she was pleased by how casually her son acted, as if his mother had a whole rotation of friends with whom he was often invited to go on outings.

Inside the zoo, a light drizzle began and he had no umbrella, so they both huddled under the one she'd brought. The park was near empty because of the weather, the only other visitors a handful of grandparents with their small children, speaking in dampened tones. They walked slowly. She could feel the rigidity in his body, how carefully he moved so that they wouldn't accidentally touch. But then, rounding a corner, his side collided into hers.

"Sorry!" he exclaimed.

"It's all right," she laughed.

They walked, still not touching, but somehow a barrier had been broken between them. When they bumped into each other next, they were slower to disentangle.

Yuanyuan ran up in front of them, unafraid of the rain, leaping from exhibit to exhibit. She gave up on calling to him to fix the hood of his raincoat.

"Imagine what we would have been like if we'd seen these animals when we were young," she said, passing an exhibit of macaques, who were huddling, disgruntled, under the overhang to stay dry. He stepped out from under the umbrella and waved his hands around his head, trying to get their attention. He chuckled when the monkey's eyes narrowed at him, and her heart swelled. His curiosity, his playfulness— she felt she could have been watching him when he was eighteen again.

"It would have been the most amazing thing I'd seen in my entire life," he said.

She nodded. "When I see how Yuanyuan reacts to things, I'm reminded to be amazed."

"Everything looks smaller than it used to be," he said. "Do you remember how big Hefei seemed when we came here for the exam? I remember Yishou saying to me, *I feel like I could turn around just once and lose my sense of direction here.* And I felt the same. I was so scared of getting lost. Even now, with all this construction, the city doesn't seem nearly as big. But I don't think anything has changed. I've just seen more, and my eyes have gotten bigger."

The tone of his voice saddened her and she felt a pang of loss on his behalf, for the boy that had been left behind.

They stopped with Yuanyuan, who was clinging on to the gate in front of an exhibit of red-crowned cranes. "These are the most famous animals here," she said. They watched the two lithe white birds, which would only be an unremarkable white and black if not for the splashes of red feathers upon their heads. The first time she'd ever seen one, she'd thought the tuft was blood.

The two birds stalked around their compound, necks oscillating as they pecked at the wet ground.

"Why aren't they scared of the rain?" Yuanyuan asked.

"I don't know," she said.

A crane dipped its beak into the hump of its back.

"It's because of their feathers," Yitian said. "They're designed so that the rain just sheds off. And they insulate their bodies. These birds are so large that they don't have to be scared, and the rain doesn't affect them much."

Yuanyuan nodded his head vigorously as if he'd understood every word.

"How did you know that?" she asked him.

"I read it somewhere."

They walked on. His answer was exactly the type she'd expected him to give, from a person who'd accumulated knowledge over the years in areas far and wide. Life with him would likely involve a patchwork of such collected facts, she thought.

Outside the zoo entrance they passed a man selling tanghulu.

"Ma! Can I have one?"

The vendor looked up hopefully from under his umbrella. "Made out of fresh hawthorn!"

"They sell these here now!" Yitian exclaimed. "I've only ever seen them in Beijing."

"The kids like them." She gestured at Yuanyuan.

"We'll take three," Yitian said. He turned to her. "I never got to eat them in Beijing. I walked past them and stared and thought how good they looked with all the syrup dripping off them. But I didn't have any money to spend. I thought they were probably the most delicious treats in the world."

They all huddled under the umbrella. Yitian wedged the handle into his armpit and distributed the skewers. When he bit into the first shiny haw, his eyes bulged and widened.

"That was the sweetest thing I've ever tasted," he said. She nibbled at the edges of a haw and blanched. The taste was pure sugar.

"Right?" he said to her.

They gave all three of the skewers to Yuanyuan, theirs both half bitten, the clear crust of syrup shattered by their teeth into crystalline shards.

In any other time, she would have been a responsible parent, concerned about giving her son so much sugar before dinner, but she felt suddenly carefree. Delight was something to be indulged. She was happy, seeing Yitian's joy at the simple candy, which she'd passed so many times on the street without a thought to try.

They watched Yuanyuan jump on a slide carved out of a stone elephant while Yitian held the remaining skewer so her son could play freely. She realized that the weight on her chest had lifted. She wondered at how the day had transformed itself, how this was possible when she was with him. In the morning when she'd called he was hesitant and she was full of fear. And now this. Days with Guifan began with an expectation that was met by the end. She hadn't minded that until now. Liked it, in fact. But their type of flat life could leave a person trapped.

"You'll get wet," she shouted to Yuanyuan, who was preparing to go down the slide. Normally she would have run to stop him, but even this she didn't worry over today. She did not want to break the moment: she and Yitian sharing an umbrella in the drizzle, the peaceful patter of the rain upon the plastic playground, the park silent as if it had emptied out just for them.

When Mr. Qian called again that night, she could feel it in the buzzing in her fingers when she picked up the receiver, different from when Guifan had called earlier that evening to say he'd be home late.

"It was nice to meet your family at dinner," he said.

"My husband isn't home." She didn't want to endure the pleasantries any longer, when it was so clear to her what they were threatening and what was at stake.

"Excuse me?" His voice remained polite.

"I had dinner with you, as you requested. The rest of this matter is my husband's, not mine," she said.

"You can't be that naive, can you? You're from Shanghai. The women there are known to be shrewd. Don't act like a child." His voice remained polite, but still she almost gasped. She had the sensation that there was nothing she could do to pierce his act, that he and Li Tuan were utterly protected in that world. They could enact any violence and Mr. Qian would continue speaking in that pristine voice.

"Anyway," he went on. "I just called to check in and see if you enjoyed the dinner. Li Tuan said he liked meeting you. He said you seemed like a rational woman who'd surely help her husband make the right decision. I'll be in touch again soon."

She didn't hang up the phone after the empty dial tone had taken over, loud and droning in her ear. Black dots began to float across her vision. She clenched her jaw and closed her eyes, trying to return to the feeling of earlier that day. Yitian's shoulder grazing her. She tried to feel the solidity of his body against hers, what the safety of being pressed together might allow her.

She hung up the phone, but the remnants of the sound had already crawled into her ear. What could she do, so she'd never have to hear that voice again? She racked her brain. Mr. Qian thought that the Li Corporation was untouchable. Guifan, with all his ideals, thought the same. Mr. Qian had asked her because he knew the same truth that she did—Guifan was paralyzed and couldn't be trusted to act without a push from someone else.

And then it came to her: she imagined that the next time he called, she might record his voice—his polite, enunciated voice—saying those words. Their tone wouldn't matter any longer; all that the central committee would care about was the threat implied.

Why hadn't she thought of such a possibility earlier? She'd felt entirely stuck. With Yitian's visit, her mind had started working in a way it hadn't in years, like brushing off a storage box found after years of disuse, the dust and cobwebs floating into the air before the opening.

Nineteen

When Yitian picked up the phone to Hanwen's voice that morning, he expected another invitation to a zoo, or a park, or some other attraction in town. He hadn't slept well the night after. He'd allowed himself to stroll around animal exhibits as if they were what he'd come back to the country to see, to sit in easy enjoyment with a woman who wasn't his wife. When at last he climbed into bed, he pulled the hotel phone right next to his face as a kind of penance.

He didn't fall asleep until dawn, closing his eyes to the first lightening of the horizon. He'd just begun a dream when he was startled awake by the harsh ring of the telephone.

"Hello?" he said sleepily.

"Yitian?" Her voice was sharp and alert. He looked at the bedside table, surprised to see the clock already read ten twenty. There'd been no sun to wake him; the sky from the tiny window looked listless and cloud filled. "Could you be ready to go in the next hour? I got a call just now from the police office. They said there's a man fitting your father's description who checked in to a hospital on the outskirts of the city."

Already he'd flung off the comforter, slung his feet out of bed and into the hotel slippers. His father had made it to a hospital. His father was alive.

"Yes. Of course."

"I'll send a car to take you. I'll meet you there."

Not until he was in the front seat of the car rolling away on the wide boulevard out of the city did he wonder at her assumption that she would come with him, whether he should have said he could go alone. She'd already helped how she could by contacting the police station; the rest, seeing his father, was his responsibility as a son. And yet, he felt reassured by her presence. Each time they'd met, he'd quietly noted how confident she was in this city. She did not second-guess every interaction, looking for the hidden catch, as he did. He could not say how he would feel when he saw his father again, but he could imagine that he would not want to experience it alone.

Her husband was there, standing with her in front of the hospital's awning. Their two figures were dwarfed by the building and the rush of patients around, but Yitian spotted them immediately. He'd allowed himself to think of her husband only a handful of times, imagining a lean, tall, sartorially appropriate figure. This man, however, was entirely unremarkable, dressed in the standard uniform of the cadres, plain black pants belted so high that they almost reached his waist. His thickening middle and lumpy cheeks showed the accrued business dinners. Yitian wondered why Hanwen would have married such a man. He could understand the set of calculations that would lead someone to choose for reasons other than love, knew such compromises were, in fact, common. Yet they suggested someone shrewder than he'd known, a person who'd had, somehow, to face up to the reality of life in a way he hadn't.

He thought wildly for a moment that he could stay in the car and delay meeting her forever. He didn't want to see his father, didn't want to face the naked truth of this moment, didn't want to experience it with her husband.

The man opened the door for Yitian, reaching out a hand.

"I'm Pan Jing. I work for Wang Guifan," he said. Yitian was surprised by the pressure flitting off his chest. Pan Jing was explaining something else, about how he'd been sent to make sure everything ran smoothly at the hospital, but Yitian was too relieved by the fact that this dull man wasn't Hanwen's husband. When she stepped out from behind Pan Jing, Yitian noted she wore less makeup today, a sign, he thought, that something had shifted and eased between them.

They walked underneath the punched-out bulbs of an electrical sign announcing the HEFEI CITY NO. 3 PEOPLE'S HOSPITAL, into a lobby absolutely crowded with patients queuing up for numbers. People sat directly on the floors, openly crying and, even then, still ignored. He tried not to scrunch up his nose to the smell that hung everywhere, of sour clothes worn for too long, of illness and the cover of bland antiseptic insufficient to the task.

The last time he'd gone to a hospital was with Mali in America, for an appointment with her gynecologist to discuss her difficulty conceiving. The doctor had asked Yitian to step out of the room. *It's just procedure*, the doctor said, *to interview the female patients alone. To ensure their privacy, you understand.*

There were no illusions of privacy in this hospital, four beds squeezed into each room, the visitors around each bleeding into the space around another, doctors discussing loudly the patient's ailments without any fear of being overheard.

"Well, let's hurry," Pan Jing said. "All kinds of people come in here, you know? You could enter this place healthy and leave sick." His laugh was an exaggerated affair, curling the skin of his forehead and jowls like an elephant's.

"Imagine, being sick and having to navigate such a place," Hanwen sighed.

He heard a reproach in her words, that he'd left his father to stumble into a place so unsuited for any type of care. He knew he should have felt fortunate, being with the two of them, striding purposefully toward doctors who could help. He'd once been anonymous, like one of the hundreds waiting anxiously in line, desperate to have someone, anyone, pay attention to him.

Weaving between the visitors, Pan Jing led them to a room on the hospital's top floor. Yitian had assumed they'd meet a doctor immediately, but instead they entered a sterile conference room. In the center, a table was covered with red cloth, dainty teacups, and name cards as if for an official meeting. His eyes darted immediately to the tented cream cardstock that read THE AMERICAN REPRESENTATIVE.

"I apologize, sir, that they weren't able to get your name card properly printed on time. I'll speak to them about it," Pan Jing said.

Yitian leaned over to Hanwen, whose assigned seat was next to his.

"What's all this?" he whispered. He caught Pan Jing's eyes lingering on them from the room's opposite corner.

"I'm not sure," she murmured. "They always care so much about formality. I'll try to get them to hurry."

Two doctors entered, flanked on both sides by young nurses. The doctors' coats showed remnants of stains, yellow and brown spots faded by washing, but all the nurses' clothes were so perfectly white and pressed that they had the impression of actresses playing nurses, Yitian a movie character awaiting salvation.

The older of the doctors introduced himself as the hospital director and apologized for the lateness. As they went around the table, he kept pushing his eyeglasses up, as if paying rapt attention. He had the face of a beleaguered public servant, the kind of face Yitian imagined Hanwen's husband would have.

When they reached Hanwen's position at the table, everyone looked at Yitian instead. He coughed and said, "My name is Tang Yitian. I'm from Tang Family Village. Not too far from here. I live in America now, where I'm a graduate student—excuse me, an assistant professor of mathematics." When he mentioned the name of his university, the others looked impressed and nodded their heads in recognition. "I've come here today because my father has gone missing, and I've heard there's a man here who matches his description."

"Someone from our hometown, who has gone so far and done such great things, of course we're eager to help you," the director said. "Rest assured, you're in good hands. First, let me tell you a little about our hospital." Again the eyeglasses went up and down his face.

The director signaled to the man next to him, who extracted a packet of papers from a white envelope and began to narrate the hospital's history.

Founded in 1912 by a medical missionary from America . . . as a hospital during the war . . . when Hefei City was not yet the provincial capital . . . eight departments . . .

The voice reading the detailed notes droned on. Yitian couldn't concentrate over the anxiety that began to grip him, a sensation like electricity tingling everywhere through his limbs. He'd left for so long that he'd allowed his father to stray into such a hospital, run by these men for whom concern for status preceded healing and care. When he heard, as if from some distant place, the story of the general whose handwriting was on the hospital's sign, he became aware of his foot, beating an anxious tap on the floor, faster than the cadence of the director's speech. What would happen if he simply ran out of this room and then went, one by one, through all the open rooms he'd seen earlier, checking each bed for his father? He could have looked into every part of this building during the time that this presentation continued on. The only thing keeping him seated was his fear that he would not be able to recognize his father in the sterile white of a hospital bed without these guides. In the early days of the summer season, when the first tomatoes ripened, he used to go with Yishou to harvest. They squatted amongst the thick foliage of vines, lifting the heavy leaves until they saw the first ripe tomatoes. Perhaps the feeling would be like that now, the jolt of recognition at his father's face the same as when he would spot a splash of bright red amidst all the green raw.

"Excuse me, but we're very short on time," he heard Hanwen say. "Our guest is worried, as you can see."

He hadn't known the signs of his impatience were so obvious.

The director looked nervously at him. "Right, so." He cleared his throat and picked up a second envelope in front of him. "An elderly man, age unknown, looks to be about age seventy, walked up to our hospital two mornings ago, alone. No one was with him, and when he was asked if he had a wife or family, he said that he had been traveling alone on the way to Beijing."

The Beijing detail was strange to Yitian, but the rest of the description was promising.

"You let him in?" Hanwen asked.

The director scanned the report. "It says here that he produced a large wad of bills—he'd brought quite a lot of money with him. Anyway, later we were notified of the message that was passed on from the local police bureau. Your father matches this man's appearance."

"How tall is he?"

"One and six three meters." Shorter than what Yitian remembered, but perhaps his father had begun the shrinking of older age.

"And we thought the weight and build seemed to be correct, too. But the reason we called about this particular man—because it's not so unusual, you know, that a homeless older man would try to gain admittance to our hospital—is because of the amount of money he had with him. That was very strange. Also, he said he was from the direction of the Tang villages—"

"Did he say which one?" Yitian interrupted.

The director frowned. "No, it's not here. My apologies. I wasn't the one who took these notes. But we can ask him when we go to his room."

Yitian jumped to his feet. The fact of the Tang villages was enough for him. There were eighteen total, but they formed only a small fraction of the large countryside surrounding Hefei—it couldn't be possible that there was another single, elderly man coming from exactly that direction on the day he was looking for his father.

"Just one moment, sir. The thing is . . . Please sit down."

The director gestured to Yitian's chair, but he didn't take it.

"We'll take you to see him, rest assured," the director hastily added. "We just want to make sure you're prepared with all the information about the situation before you go. You see, the man was already in very bad condition when we found him. He could hardly speak, and he was almost hypothermic. As you know, there was a record cold a few days ago. We think he might have been outside during the blizzard. Actually, if what you say about the date he left is true, it's quite a surprise he's even still alive. A man of that age, outside in that kind of cold . . . In any case, his condition is very bad. He's had a high fever for a few days and he's barely conscious."

Yitian felt a flash of lightness in his knees and realized his legs were shaking. He was suddenly returned to another time, staring at a different unconscious face on a hospital bed. He tried to shake away the image.

"Very fortunately, his condition stabilized this morning. I checked on him right before you came. He's still sleeping, not fully conscious, but his fever has subsided."

Relief spread over him like a warm blanket. "Can we go see him?"

"Of course. We'll take you now. We just—we don't want you to think that his condition is—could be—a result of our hospital's treatment of him. We've done our best, given how he came to us."

They all rose. They walked in a line through the hospital, the director in front, the nurses in back, he sandwiched in the middle between Hanwen and Pan Jing.

He legs retained a rubbery feeling, as if they would give if he tried to step too firmly. When he was sure Pan Jing wasn't paying attention, Yitian reached out his hand to steady himself on Hanwen, touching his fingers lightly to her forearm. For a second, she placed her hand on top of his, then drew it away, all without looking at him.

What would he say when he saw his father? Not today, when he would still be too sick to listen, but in a few days, perhaps, when his comprehension was restored. Yitian would explain everything that he'd accomplished in America. He would make concessions—he could understand now why his father had been worried about his plan to go to college. But everything had turned out all right. He wouldn't ask for forgiveness outright, but his father would surely see the case once all this evidence was presented.

The doctors and nurses in front of him were slowing down, nearing the room.

"Thank you, for doing all of this," he managed to say to Hanwen.

"What are you saying thank you for?" she said hazily. He turned to look at her, but saw that her gaze was directed at something in front of her, her brow furrowed in a line of concentration. The doctors had moved into a huddled circle in the middle of the hallway, unaware of the fact that they were blocking the passage. Another nurse, one Yitian hadn't seen before, was whispering urgently to them.

The nurses and doctors glanced at him, each seeming to will the others to go to him. Their gazes flickered back and forth, like guilty children trying to hide wrongdoing from an accusing adult. Finally, the director approached Yitian.

His chin shook as he said, "Your father has passed away."

The room numbers rushed past. The clack of high heels beat a frenzied rhythm behind him, then Hanwen's fingers were pressing into his arm, holding him back. She was saying something—*Just wait one moment.*

He threw off her hand and kept running.

He realized he had no idea what room he was looking for. He reached the end of the hall and doubled over, panting.

"Which room is he in?" he shouted, but when he was told the number, even the simple math of calculating in which direction to walk seemed impossibly hard, his brain performing the subtraction as if moving through sludge.

Then he was there, in front of the right room, as if by accident, as if guided by God. Three nurses gathered around a bed in the corner. The one with his father. The patient monitor pushed to the side, the air of defeat and an ending, another stretcher, bare and utilitarian, already prepared for the departure.

The nurses pulled the curtain.

"I'm sorry, sir, you can't come in here. We're still preparing—"

He pushed her aside and threw the curtain back. Not until later did he wonder if he might have hurt the nurse, but by that time her face had disappeared from his memory, indistinguishable from all the others he'd passed.

The paper curtain, sliding on its rusted rings, ripped in his hands. Then he looked—

It was the posture of his jaw that gave him away, even before Yitian had time to hesitate. The man's jaw was held slack. The pose was languid, belonging to someone who had lived his life in contentment. Though death could suddenly change the shape of a body, surely there had to be some melding to the soul that preserved the truth of the lived person.

He did not need to get any closer to tell: the man was not his father.

Twenty

DECEMBER 1977

They rode the final stretch back from Hefei on a tractor wagon, its only two passengers. As soon as they'd hopped over the barrier, Yishou tucked his body against a corner of the siding, squatted down, and slouched his head into the angular pillow he created out of his arms. As they passed under trees, the shadows of branches flitted birdlike, over his hands, crosshatching and webbing dark over his fingers.

Yitian, crouching against the opposite siding, watched his brother as the tractor ambled on along the dusty roads. He was amazed that Yishou could sleep against the bumpy jerking of the vehicle. He himself had too much on his mind to rest. Driving away from the city, he'd felt an unexpected wave of sadness and loss at the thought of returning home. The gaokao was done, its end arriving so much quicker than he'd expected, and he felt already the absence of purpose in its wake. And if he dared to imagine that he'd passed the exam, how would he tell his father? He wasn't afraid of a beating as punishment, as he'd been when he was younger. There were consequences much worse than that.

He reached his foot across the length of the wagon and nudged Yishou's thigh. His brother didn't even register the movement.

"Yishou! We're almost there!" He dug the toe of his shoe into Yishou's pants, harder this time.

Yishou lifted his head and squinted against the sunlight.

"What will Ba say?" Yitian asked. He had to yell in order to make himself heard over the tractor's loud rumbles, and he felt self-conscious and melodramatic at the volume.

"I was just in the middle of a dream! We're nowhere near home yet."

"Never mind that. Do you think Ba is going to be angry?"

Yishou rubbed his eyes, then wiped his forehead. "Not if you stick to the story we made up. Remember, Uncle hurt his arm in the harvest, so he doesn't want Ba to visit for a little while—"

"That's not what I mean. I'm talking about after, if I get to go to college. How will I explain to Ba?"

"Easy. I'll sneak off with you again to get you there. We'll make up another story, another uncle in another village where I have a girl I need to see."

"I'm serious! Can't you see why this is a big issue?"

"There are still months until you have to think about that, Yitian. Don't worry about it now."

It was useless to ask his brother for help with a problem like this. Yishou was adept at finding solutions to concrete questions, but it wasn't in his nature to worry about a future that had not yet arrived.

"Fine." He squinted. "Are you all right?"

Yishou had leaned forward and was holding his stomach with both hands. "God, I hate riding these tractors. The drivers are awful. It's like they drive badly just to annoy us."

Yitian didn't feel anything himself, but when the tractor slowed down, he yelled, "Can you slow down? My brother is feeling sick."

"It must have been the food we ate at the stall last night," Yishou said. "That proprietress, who was staring at us the whole time, she didn't seem clean at all. I knew that food wasn't to be trusted. This is why you can't eat on the street. And I have a headache, too."

Yitian supposed the real cause was all the alcohol Yishou had drunk the night before. Now that Yishou had shifted his face out of the sun, Yitian could see that what he'd thought was simply yellow cast by the light was actually his brother's sallow skin. The sheen of sweat on his forehead had reappeared.

They traveled on for another twenty minutes, during which Yishou had to demand the driver stop so he could get out and vomit. He dashed out to the side of the road, the sound so loud that Yitian could hear it from the truck. After he returned, he looked better for a while, but soon the nausea worsened again. When they finally arrived back at their village, he ran off the tractor with his belongings so that he could go to the outhouse. Yitian hurriedly thanked the driver, who was grumbling about young passengers like them who had no respect for those who offered them a favor.

Yitian walked slowly back to his home. He'd lost sight of Yishou's sprinting figure long ago. As he walked, an unexpected melancholy settled in on him. He saw the white-tailed eagles flying above and noticed the frost that lingered in the dirt until early spring, longer than anyone would have expected. The next winter he spent could be away from this, he realized.

"What happened to your brother?" his mother asked, when he arrived home. "He hardly greeted us."

"He's been shitting in the outhouse ever since he got home," his father grunted.

"I think it was some food we had"—Yitian caught himself—"at Aunt's house. She's not a very good cook, you remember?"

"This is why it's better to stay in one's own home. You never know what will happen outside of it," his father said. "So, how are they?"

"They're—they're good," Yitian stuttered. "Very good."

His mother looked up at him, confused. He'd never been a good liar; Yishou was much better—his light and humorous nature made lying a simple act, like an extension of playacting.

Luckily, Yishou entered at that moment, and they were all distracted by how poorly he looked. His head was still sweaty and his very outline seemed to be trembling.

"You look sick!" his mother said, alarmed.

"I'm fine," Yishou said, sitting down on the bench. When he lifted rice to his mouth, his throat bobbed, struggling to swallow.

"You should go rest," his mother said. "You've had a long journey. I'll bring some food to your bed."

"Nonsense!" his father said. "He'll be fine. He just needs some baijiu to clear up his system. I know this look. You drank too much last night, didn't you?"

Yishou nodded weakly. His father poured him a shot, muttering, "Hair of the dog . . . this will definitely make you feel better."

"So you had a lot of fun with Uncle and his son, it seems," their father said.

Yishou nodded. He began to tell the story they'd recited earlier, of how well their uncle was doing. His son had grown up a lot since they'd last seen him, Yishou explained slowly, and they got along perfectly. Uncle had said there was no need for their father to go visit him and inquire about his health, because he'd likely come to Tang Family Village that very summer.

Yitian didn't have to speak at all, and he felt relieved and amazed.

Yishou might not be able to plan into the future, but he was reliable in a situation like this.

That night was a village movie screening. When they'd parted in Hefei, Yitian, Hanwen, and Yishou had made a plan to attend together. They were screening an Albanian war film called *Rain and Thunder on the Seashore*, one of everyone's favorites. Yishou was always amongst the most eager attendees for the rare screenings, arriving early with his bench under his arm so he would be able to sit in the front row, sometimes even willing to walk dozens of li to another village to catch a showing. When Yitian went to call him to leave, however, Yishou was still in bed, which he hadn't left since lunchtime. He complained that his head hurt and snapped at Yitian to move the lamp away from his face.

Yitian felt his forehead and found it burning. His brother's face was flushed.

"I'll get Ma." He stood up, but Yishou grabbed his wrist. Yitian dropped his hand, alarmed. His brother's hand was limp, his grasp not at all like the firm grip he usually had when they wrestled.

"I don't want to bother her."

"Fine, then I'll stay here with you."

"And miss a movie screening? No way. I'm fine. I shouldn't have let Ba make me drink at lunch, that's all it is," Yishou said. "Just bring me some water."

When he explained his brother's absence to Hanwen, she said, "How strange. I hope he's all right." She smiled. "But I'm happy we get to spend some time alone."

She was in a joyous mood. They placed their benches at the very back of the field so that no one would see them and huddled together against the cold air. They'd both seen this movie twice before and only had to look up to pay attention during their favorite scenes. The last time this movie had been screened, the villagers had spent days afterward repeating the lines and imitating the actors until every scene was solidified in their memory.

"What city do you want to go to most?" she whispered.

"Shanghai, because of all the stories you've told me about it."

"All right. I'll take you to the movies when we go back. Before the Cultural Revolution, we used to be able to go to movies whenever we wanted. I used to make fun of people who wanted to watch movies all the time. I thought they weren't going to make anything of themselves, not like me. I was going to be different from them, because I spent my time studying, not at the theater. I never realized how lucky we were."

She looked expectantly at him, but the mention of people who only wanted to watch movies made him suddenly think of Yishou lying in bed alone. Once, when Yishou was younger and had fallen asleep during a movie, he'd cried for hours upon awakening and realizing what had happened. Something didn't seem right about how ill his brother was, when they'd done all the same things together the day before.

". . . we'll go to the Forbidden City in Beijing . . . ," Hanwen was saying, but he stood up instead of answering her.

"I need to go check on Yishou," he said. He hardly said goodbye, and ran all the way home.

Twenty-one

By the time they arrived at the county hospital, Yishou was an unconscious shape draped between their arms.

Yitian had never been to a hospital this large before—they'd visited the commune hospital once, when his grandfather was ill, but that had been a sparse and neat place compared to this. This hospital was relentless, uncaring, the smell of antiseptic and sugary vomit assailing his nose, and everywhere the sounds of desperation bouncing off the cement walls. Nurses and doctors ran through the lobby on their way to rooms, no one pausing to look at Yitian and his father. There seemed to be no order to the way that patients were approaching the doctors and when they were acknowledged, but when Yitian dared to question a nurse, she didn't even turn her head to listen.

Yishou had moaned intermittently on the ride here, but now his eyes were closed and he made no sounds at all. The only sign for Yitian that his brother was alive was the soft breeze of breath he felt when he held his hand directly under Yishou's nose, but even that was becoming more and more frail.

Four days had passed since they'd returned home from Hefei. The second morning, Yishou had decided that the best way to fight off the illness would be to work. He'd tried to shake the stiffness out of his body in the fields, but as the day progressed, he'd become so tired that he couldn't even lift his hoe off the ground. In the afternoon, a villager came to summon Yitian and his father, telling them Yishou had collapsed in the fields. When rest didn't help, they sent for the barefoot doctor. He'd checked Yishou's tongue for the color and prescribed him a medicinal soup made with ground perilla leaves, to be taken three times a day until the fever subsided. "It may get worse before he gets better. He needs to expel toxins in his system," he'd said as he packed up his traveling bag and left, telling them he had to return to his own farmwork. That morning, when Yishou shuddered in pain every time he so much as opened his eyes, they'd decided to go to the county hospital.

Now, in the hospital lobby, Yitian's arms were buckling under his brother's weight. His father noticed and shifted his body to take Yishou alone. He draped Yishou's body over his shoulder, a pose normally belonging to parents and their small children, strange to see with two grown men. Yitian stepped aside, embarrassed at his weakness.

Behind him, his mother was wringing her hands. "Look at how many people are here," she said. Panic made her voice high and frail. "How long will it be until we can see a doctor?"

Yitian went around the lobby, asking people how they could get help. He felt light-headed himself from the smells. "My brother is very sick. He needs treatment immediately," he said. He pointed to the wall where his parents had gone to wait, sitting directly on the cement floor and holding Yishou between their two laps.

People shrugged; many did not even turn to look at him when he spoke. "Everyone is sick. Everyone here is about to die. Do you think you're special?" one woman snapped at him. She had the sour-eyed look of one for whom hope had proved itself wingless, and she stared hungrily at Yitian, waiting for his disappointment to join her own.

No one would come to a place like this unless their situation was at a dire tenor. Near his parents, a prone woman was vomiting into a bucket in the middle of the lobby. Her husband, standing beside her, announced to the room that she'd drunk an entire bottle of pesticide, but everyone was ignoring her. "They're going to let her die," he cried, but people either didn't care or were too afraid to look.

The shared feeling of hopelessness in the room didn't make Yitian worry about Yishou any less. In fact, he found that, at this time, he cared remarkably little about everyone else. Perhaps he would be called selfish, but that did not concern him now. Disregarding their needs for his brother's was also a form of love.

How long has he been showing symptoms?"
Two hours later, they finally saw a doctor, a middle-aged man whose head was mostly obscured by the yellowing cap he wore over his hair and a surgical mask tied over his nose and mouth. They'd laid Yishou on a cot in the corner of the room.

"Excuse me," his father said, pushing with his forearm against another woman hovering near the doctor.

"How long has he been showing symptoms?" the doctor repeated.

Yitian looked at his father, ready to defer, as he usually would, in such a circumstance. But when his father opened his mouth, his bottom lip hanging heavy, no words came out.

"Four," Yitian scrambled to say, because he could see that the doctor, drumming his fingers on an empty clipboard, was impatient.

"Since the vomiting? Or the fever?"

"Both. But he started vomiting before he had a headache. We had a barefoot doctor who came. He said the wind in his chest was off—"

The doctor held up a hand to silence Yitian. He first took Yishou's temperature, then called for a nurse to help flip Yishou over. He pressed a stethoscope to Yishou's back.

"What's that for? Isn't that only for his heartbeat?"

"I'm checking the lungs," the doctor grunted. Yitian edged around, looking desperately into his face for a sign of what he was finding, but he could not read any emotion from behind the deep-set, hooded eyelids.

When the doctor pulled up Yishou's shirt, they saw small bumps, red and bulbous, which formed a rash that sprawled from his armpits to his upper back.

The doctor inhaled sharply. "How long have these been here for?"

"I—we don't know, sir," Yitian said. In all these days, he'd never once thought to examine his brother's skin.

The doctor moved to Yishou's neck and pressed two fingers against each side. Yitian winced at the sight of the pressure on the swollen flesh, bleaching the red white, but Yishou still did not react.

"Fever, headache, what else? Did his neck seem stiff?"

"He did mention that, a few days ago. But our family all does farmwork, so it's normal." Yitian remembered another thing. "And the light. He says it hurts him whenever he opens his eyes."

The doctor sighed and turned to address them. He hadn't even flipped Yishou back over. His cheek was pressed against the pillow and his matted hair spread, messy and grasslike, around his head. The harsh rash on his back seemed to glare at and accuse them.

"Almost certainly meningitis," the doctor said. "If I had to guess, it seems like it was the bacterial kind, based on how quickly the symptoms started and developed."

"That doesn't make sense," Yitian's mother said. "Are you sure, sir?"

"I'll see if they can run a test." He looked wearily at a nurse who'd just run into the room and then immediately shuffled back out. "But I'm almost certain."

"But, sir, isn't meningitis very rare in people my brother's age? I've heard of it before, but only for children," Yitian said. As kids, they'd worn amulets of mugwort around their necks to protect them from the disease. In their village, there'd been a plump baby who caught meningitis from another infant during a trip to the county hospital. She lived afterward, but suffered from severe epilepsy and died in a drowning accident when she was thirteen. She'd been overcome by an epileptic episode and the shallow water of the ditch she slipped into had been enough to cause her death.

"It's true that it's more common amongst children, but adults can also contract it. Especially if they're in some sort of crowded, dirty place in the city. Schools, universities, and hospitals are all the sorts of places that are quite fertile for the meningitis bacteria to spread. There was a small outbreak in Hefei recently."

Yitian could hardly think through his fogged mind as his mother shook her head and said, "No, he hasn't been anywhere like that. And no one else in our village has it. It can't be possible."

Yitian's father cleared his throat. He stopped his pacing to stare directly at the doctor. "What will happen to him?"

"Your family brought him in late. Very late. Usually, for meningitis, if we can start treatment within the first few days, adults could make a full recovery. But you waited four days to come."

"I know—I'm sorry, sir," Yitian said. He stumbled over his words. The feeling of blame was already accumulating in him, and he wanted to do anything to rid himself of it. Hadn't he done everything he could, based on the knowledge they had? "We'd called a barefoot doctor to our home, and he said that my brother would be fine if we just waited it out."

"Of course. How many times have I heard this story? The doctors going from home to home, giving the wrong advice. Do those people even have any kind of training? Our hospital wouldn't be half as full without all their mistakes."

Finally, the woman who'd been lingering around them managed to pull the doctor away with a question about her vomiting infant son. The doctor muttered that he would send someone to do a meningitis test, but Yitian was sure they'd seen the last of him. It wouldn't matter, in any case, whether he returned and gave a test or not. It would only confirm what Yitian already knew now, that he'd taken his brother into the city where he'd caught this disease.

A nurse came into the room and began to shoo them out, saying they needed the space for another patient.

"Can you help me flip him over?" Yitian asked. He looked around the room, but he could not find his parents. He could not leave Yishou like that, lying on his stomach, as a person abandoned and uncared for. The nurse, for a moment, had turned her attention to an equipment cabinet. He had to act quickly before they noticed he was still there. He spread his arms wide against Yishou's back, wincing at the heat of the skin, before heaving his brother's body up. Yishou grunted, but his arms and head stayed limp and powerless. Yitian was only a fraction of his brother, no match against the weight of Yishou's body. As he tried to lay Yishou down on his back, his older brother's torso flipped but the legs did not, and his face landed on its side, contorting and twisting his neck, making it floppy like a fish. Yitian rearranged the legs so they were straight, and then gently held the sides of Yishou's face to lay the back of his head against the pillow. He smoothed down his hair. At least he could give his brother this posture of dignity. Before leaving the room, he grasped Yishou's hand and held it, putting his rough hand against his brother's rougher one.

"*Meningitis?*"

His mother came to him and clutched his arms in the hallway. The phrase came out of her mouth, uncertain and halting with great pauses between the characters. "What does that mean? How could he have gotten that?"

He didn't even think of lying to her. There wasn't any other way to explain what had happened to Yishou. His mother was right—no one in their village had caught meningitis in years. There was only one place where Yishou could have contracted the disease.

He told his parents everything. Yishou sneaking away with the hukou booklet, registering him for the exam. How they'd lied about where they were going that week.

His father slapped him across the face. A sudden, stinging pain flowered in Yitian's left cheek. He was five again—his father's hand rising in a hot blur to bring a stick down onto him.

"It all makes sense now," his father said. "Why you two suddenly wanted to go visit your uncle. Ever since he came back from that trip with you, I thought he *looked* different."

He blinked at his father's face, expecting another hit.

"Ba—" he began, but stopped. Anything he could say would only be an excuse. The warmth on his cheek was fading now, but he wanted to be hit again, to take the pain inside him and place it in the external world where he deserved to feel punishment.

"It wasn't enough for you to try to ruin your own life. You had to ruin your brother's, too."

His father began cursing him, using words so violent that even others in the hallway, occupied with their own sick, stopped to stare. Yitian tilted his face upward and received them all. For months he'd been studying math and logic and now all the paths in his mind narrowed to the one certain conclusion that his father named.

His mother came between them, begging for his father to stop, her hands on his chest.

"Don't, don't," she pleaded. "Maybe what the doctor said wasn't right."

His father pushed her away.

"Ask *him* if it's right. Since he's so smart. Since he has all the education. *He'll* know what the truth is."

His mother raised her elbows around her face as if she were defending blows. She sank to the floor. *Please*, she said again, but her words were no longer directed at any object. The favor she asked was from the entire world.

Yitian grasped weakly at her arms to pull her up, then sank down beside her. All the strength in her body had given out. She fell against his chest, bringing him to the floor with her. He looked up to see that his father was walking away down the hallway. Yitian tried to stand up to run after him, but his mother's grip on him was too strong, pulling him back down. She pressed her face against his as she sobbed, and he allowed his body to go limp. Her voice joined the sounds of the hospital, roaring around him. The only feeling he was aware of was the wet dampness falling and pooling down his face, his mother's body around his as her chest clenched and unclenched again and again.

Twenty-two

They buried him in the plot of land behind their fields, where the people in their family had always been buried. The day was sunny, one of those strange winter days when the light was blindingly bright and baked itself into the ground, slowly warming the surface of the dirt after all the cooler days that had come before. The light reflected off the white mourning clothes the guests wore, so that Yitian could hardly look at them without his eyes burning. He was also wearing the clothes that his mother had sewed for the day. Earlier that morning, she'd tied a long, narrow piece of mourning fabric around his waist, and then another band that draped down from his forehead. For a moment, when her hands had been around him, he'd felt swaddled and protected. Then her hands had dropped and the reality of the day descended upon him. His brother was dead.

The mourners laid coins and baskets of food in front of the burial site as offerings to the deceased. At the burial mounds, there was a gap, a space prominent and forsaken, between the last buried and the next. One was the mound of Yitian's grandfather, where they'd all gathered months ago. Next to it was the space left for Yitian's father (behind that one was a place for his mother; tradition dictated she was not deemed worthy to be a part of the primary line). That open gap between their two places was shameful, representing a disruption in the natural pattern. A son was not meant to be buried before his own father.

His mother wailed, standing beside Yitian. They had not had money to hire any funeral criers. Between the hospital and the two sudden deaths, they hadn't been able, even, to pay the gravestone maker to add Yishou's name to the headstone.

His mother's loud cries caught and echoed through the air, rising above all the others, distinguishing her as the person most hurt.

"Too early, too early," a guest, someone Yitian did not recognize, said.

On the other side of his mother his father stood, stoic and quiet. He'd hardly made a sound all day, and had refused to speak much to anyone since returning from the hospital.

In a year, both Yitian's grandfather and brother had died. His father was the only one in the world who might have experienced the losses in the same way Yitian had, but instead their lonelinesses hummed quietly and apart. Yitian still couldn't believe Yishou was gone. He still half expected his brother to appear, his figure glimmering in the fields. This was how Yitian had known him: as a figure in motion, with the tightness of a body ready to spring into action. When Yitian was young, he would gaze out at the fields and see his brother. In the blurring waves of the early morning heat, Yishou's perfect body looked like a mirage. Muscles in a taut line, slack and then drawn, each next step assured as a machine's. Bringing the hoe up in a high arc, then down again, summoning up rainbows of dirt into the air.

Yitian stood and watched, amazed. There was still so much more he wanted to ask that person. He wished he could go back to his child-hood, to wait on that threshold and stand in disbelief at his brother, just one more time. His grandfather's death had operated by the logic and aging, but his brother was the healthiest person he'd ever known. Yitian owed so much of the person he was to these two people. It seemed to him that he had been accumulating debts all these years, and now he would never be able to repay them. This was the worst part of a death: that the dead could not collect on the balance they were owed, that they left all their burden to the living.

They returned to their home for a meal with the guests af-ter the ceremony. Yitian sat in a corner without greeting or speaking to anyone. He did not want to go through these ritual mo-tions with his relatives in order to prove they cared for Yishou and were saddened by his death. He saw his mother glance at him, and then at his father, who sat alone at the table, drinking. The baijiu was meant as an offering and for the guests, but instead his father had grabbed a bottle and begun serving himself without any regard for others.

Second Uncle, who'd been fidgety the entire day, tried to comfort him. "Now, it doesn't do to act in such a way," he said. The required solemnity had made his behavior jittery, and he left soon after, with a few customary words to Yitian's mother.

Most of the guests departed as the afternoon went on. Only a few stragglers stayed past sunset. They had a certain giddiness to them, happiness at the fact that others had a misfortune for them to comfort.

In late afternoon, his father wandered out into the backyard, ignoring the remaining guests. He wobbled as he walked, his drunkenness exaggerating his limp leg. After he'd gone, the room seemed emptied of the central figure. The final guests rose to leave.

Yitian checked on his father in the backyard, his outline shaky as he fiddled with the stacks of kindling. Yishou had collected the last round of wood before they left for Hefei City, and there was hardly anything left now—only the meager twigs that had broken off larger branches. Drunk, his father began to arrange them in a pile on top of the brazier. He ignored Yitian and built the twigs up in a circle, using one hand to keep them together and the other to jab more inside the cylindrical shape he'd built, working methodically in a seeming reverie.

Yitian returned inside, changed his clothes, and helped his mother clean up. He swept the floor and she boiled water so they could wash. He wanted the day to be over, to collect and then dispose of its remnants so that all its evidence was gone.

As he was stripping his clothes to wash, Yitian smelled the beginnings of smoke drifting in from outside. At first, he was confused as to the source of the smell, but then the thought struck him that his father must have lit the kindling on the brazier. The sun had set by now, and all that was left was cold winter air. He could not imagine what his father intended to do outside in the courtyard, alone and drunk.

In a hurry, he shoved his clothes back on and scrambled outside.

Small plumes of smoke were already collecting in the air of the courtyard and uncoiling themselves into the dusky night. On the doorstep, his father stood and watched the fire.

"Ba—what are you doing?" They were the first words that Yitian had spoken to his father since they'd left the hospital.

His father was hugging a large stack of papers to his chest, hunching over them the way a bird might hunch over something just captured. As Yitian approached, his father brought the bundle closer to the flames, so the contents were illuminated. Yitian startled to recognize his own handwriting, jutting and blocky, on notes that must have been written in elementary school. Farther behind in the stack, there were the tightly scrawled characters of his gaokao notes.

He lunged out at his father, trying to grab the papers.

His father, moving with a quickness that Yitian would not have expected him capable of after all he'd drunk that day, shuffled back quickly out of Yitian's reach.

"Take the rest of your clothes and possessions. You," he said, turning to Yitian, "are not my son." In the dusk, his father's shadow lengthened and merged with the dark shapes of the courtyard, rendering his outline bulky and terrifying in a way that Yitian had not felt since he was a child.

His mother had run out of the home at the sounds from the courtyard. "Don't do this to him," she cried. "He's the only son we have left."

"Because of him, our son died. If he hadn't had all these ideas and insisted on going to university, Yishou wouldn't have contracted that illness."

"How could we have known what would happen? It's not his fault. No one can predict what Heaven has in store for us."

His father turned to Yitian. "Always the same mistakes. You and my father, making the same mistakes. Giving up life for those books," he slurred. "Do you know what it's like, to be ten years old and responsible for the entire family? Because your own father doesn't know how to lift even a finger to work."

"Please, Ba," Yitian begged. "I don't want it anymore. I don't need to go to college." He was willing to say anything to stop his father's words from unspooling further.

The fire, feeding off a sudden gust of wind, released more plumes into the air. His father coughed deeply. "Go. It doesn't matter to me where you are anymore. You killed your brother."

"It's no use to talk about the past this way," his mother wailed.

He had the sensation that his parents were speaking about him as if he were a stranger visiting their home, already rendered the person his father had abandoned him to be. His father still clutched his papers, sandwiching them now between his arm and his torso as he waved his free hand around in accusation.

The sky was almost completely dark, and the red glow of the flames cast his father's wrinkles into a deeper etching than Yitian had ever seen before. He thought for a moment that he would be hit. The beatings of his youth had come in his father's fits of uncontrolled temper—Yitian cowering as the dirty edges of a wooden stake were brought onto his thighs—compounded by drunkenness, but his father's voice wasn't like that now. He spoke slowly, controlling his fury.

"He needs to know the debt his life is based on. He owes us a son."

"You cannot say that to your own son," his mother said.

His father ignored her and turned toward the fire with the pile of papers.

Yitian didn't have a plan as he lunged toward his father. There was already a finality to everything else he'd lost, but these were the few objects of meaning that he could still preserve. He reached around his father and clenched his hands around the pile, sheets ripping in his hands as he grasped.

His kick landed on his father's limp leg. His father spun around, his face pruned, first in surprise, then anger. His mother screamed. He brought his closed fist backward and then onto Yitian's face. This time, Yitian fell over, bracing himself against the dirt floor. He tried to scramble up just as he saw his father throw the first thick section of paper into the fire.

Yitian knew, then, that it was too late. He ran forward, but the papers, so thin to begin with, were already being eaten by the flames. Like a flower tightening in darkness, they closed up, then disappeared entirely. His father continued, throwing the notes into the fire in fat sections, until none remained in his arms.

Yitian was shocked at how quickly the papers burned and left nothing to remember them by, as if taunting him for how long he had taken to write each sheet. The flame's tongue darted quickly out over the pieces of paper and drew them into the hot center, curling each one black over the edges and making all the contents insignificant in an instant. He could see now how his father would assign cheapness to these words because of how easily they could be destroyed. They held nothing of that weighty and grounded world that his father valued, the one that Yishou had lived by.

Yitian was vaguely aware of shadows leaving the courtyard, of his father's shape, shuffling back inside. He lay on the floor and let the night air whip him. The wind was howling now, rising up and blowing the bare winter branches as if making up for the earlier stillness of the day. When he and Yishou had been young, they'd made up tales about the nights when the wind was like this, saying ghosts were particularly angry and wanted to make their presence known. Only the dead who had unfinished business on earth stayed to haunt the night, they said. If that was true, Yishou would be screaming in the wind for a very long time.

Twenty-three

FEBRUARY 1978

Hanwen squatted by the embankment and sank her undershirt into the river, allowing the icy surface to clutch at her hands and numb them. They'd just passed the fifth term of winter, and the next few weeks would be the coldest of the year.

She hadn't washed her clothes in four days, not since the announcement of the gaokao results. She hadn't seen Yitian in all that time, either. By now, the news had spread through the whole village—and even the surrounding ones—that he was going to that famous university in Beijing. Though they didn't know each student's particular scores, the meaning was obvious. He would have had to be within the top fifty scorers in the entire province to go to a school like that. Villagers and sent-down youth who didn't even know him were talking about him—they'd announced his name on the radio and printed it in the newspaper, along with the reports that only five percent of students had passed nationally.

When they began to hear rumors that students were receiving admissions letters, both Hanwen and Wu Mei had been too afraid to go to the commune, where the notices were sent. They'd begged Pan Niannian to go for them.

"It's so cold," Niannian said. "I don't want to bike all the way to the commune. Besides, I didn't even take that silly exam."

Niannian didn't agree until Hanwen offered to take one of her kitchen shifts. She borrowed a bicycle from a villager—the sent-down youth were not permitted to have their own—and set off on the fifteen li journey to the commune. Hanwen lent Niannian her warmest gloves, and she and Wu Mei huddled under the eaves of the dormitory as they watched her bike away. Her feet moved furiously against the pedals, trying to fight off the cold.

Hanwen and Wu Mei attempted to occupy themselves with all kinds of activities while they waited. They played tic-tac-toe, marbles, digging out things they hadn't touched since they were schoolchildren. As soon as they saw Niannian's shape on the bicycle coming back up the road, they sprinted outside.

She was moving more slowly this time. Hanwen had her first premonition, then, that there was bad news. She turned away from the road, afraid even to watch Niannian approach. She wanted to run back into the dormitory and shove her head under the covers, to feign deafness at the news.

But before Hanwen could do anything to stop her, Wu Mei was already shouting out to Niannian, "So? What's the news?"

Niannian spoke to the ground as she said, *There weren't any letters for you.* Hanwen felt too stunned to speak, but Wu Mei was already bombarding Niannian with questions.

"How can that be? Did you double-check? Maybe you just missed our names."

"I did double-check," Niannian said. "I asked three people at the commune office. That's why it took me so long."

Hanwen felt powerless, as if she were younger again, leaving her mother crying on the street as she rode the bus that took her away from Shanghai to this village. In her years here, she'd gone from a girl who tripped over the hoes and rakes to one who could do nearly as much work as any of the village women. She had her own life in the village, she'd thought, one for which she could feel a small tinge of pride. It didn't seem to matter anymore.

Wu Mei began to wail loudly. "What are you going to do?" she asked, during a brief break from her sobbing.

Hanwen did not know the answer to that question. For some reason, she couldn't bring herself to cry as Wu Mei did. Her entire body was still in shock, stuck in some purgatory of feeling. She went into her dorm room and sat on her bed, staring blankly at the wall in front of her. She didn't know how long she'd been there when Niannian sat down beside her.

"Is it possible there was a mistake on the test?" Niannian said.

Niannian's cadence had become gentle again. Hanwen suddenly felt a chasm opening in her chest and swallowing her. She wasn't going to college. She looked at the wall in front of her, papered with tattered posters of sent-down youth working alongside the villagers in the fields, cartoon people, smiles huge and false in a sun brighter than any she'd ever seen in real life.

"They don't make mistakes like that," Hanwen said. The very fact that they were considering reality as a mistake only meant that she didn't want to accept what fate asked her to confront.

"You can take it again next year," Niannian said. "You're so smart! Even the villagers talk about you. This year must have just been a fluke. You'll have no problem the next time around."

The villagers did often say she was too smart for this place, but she knew that their words had no meaning. They had no education themselves, and their compliments weren't any real measure of her. The test had revealed who she truly was.

She looked up at Niannian's face. Her older friend had a scar, nipple colored and rippled, under her right cheekbone, the remnants of an accident from years ago, when a villager had swung a hoe backward onto her face. When Hanwen had first arrived in the village, she could not believe how long Niannian had spent here, but now she understood. The years could easily accumulate when there was no change on the horizon, their numbers only becoming pronounced when you looked back and they surprised you. Niannian was evidence, in fact, that time could change a person so much that they would no longer even notice the scar that marked them.

Sunday came. She couldn't hold off meeting Yitian any longer. She'd been avoiding him all this time, though she knew he'd come to the dormitories asking for her. Each time, she'd told Niannian to pass on the message that she wasn't feeling well. Yitian would have heard that she hadn't passed by now, but she was still too embarrassed for the moment when she would have to acknowledge that fact out loud to him.

Before the results were released, he'd been coming to the dormitories to avoid spending time in his home, where his father wouldn't speak to him or even acknowledge his presence. Hanwen had struggled to comfort him. She hadn't known Yishou well, although he was one of the few people in the village who knew of their relationship. She'd never spoken with him much, because he seemed like one of those people for whom a simple acknowledgment was enough to establish feelings of warmth.

Her excuses in refusing to see Yitian became more and more

implausible, until she knew there was no point in continuing to delay the inevitable. She arrived at the embankment earlier than he did that day and tried to compose her features as she would have to make them when he told her his good news. She smiled and squinted her eyes upward in a look that she hoped would appear bright, but she found it was difficult to remember what happiness looked like.

When she could make out his shape coming toward her, she had to blink away the mistiness in her eyes. The wind was blowing his hair around, and she waited for his face to come into focus. As another strong gust pushed his hair back, she was surprised to see that his eyes appeared puffy and downcast. She couldn't keep that false look any longer. Her own face flattened as she watched him near.

They didn't embrace as they usually did. He was close to her, so close that their thighs could touch, but even this diminished contact felt heavier than before. He looked fatigued, dark circles rimming his eyes, the tip of his nose swollen bulbous. He'd obviously been crying.

"What's wrong? Aren't you happy?" Her words came out choked, surprising even her. She'd dreaded having to confront Yitian's joy at his accomplishment, but she hadn't realized how much she'd depended upon seeing his happiness. He looked the same as he had every day since Yishou's death.

"Stop looking so sad!" she cried, her voice high and desperate.

"I don't mean to."

"You have to be happy. You're going to college! So many people would give anything—"

"It's not that simple."

Her face burned as if she'd been slapped. "What do you mean? You're going, aren't you?"

"Of course I'll go. It's not that."

"Then what is it?"

"Yishou—and my father still angry at me. And you won't be going with me."

She was relieved he'd acknowledged what they both already knew.

He turned his face away—to hide his tears, she supposed. When he turned back to her, he said, "I thought it would be much simpler, but everything has changed. The acceptance letter I got was for the mathematics department. I didn't know Yi—" His voice still could not make it beyond his brother's name. "He must have chosen it for me when he registered me. I didn't know what would happen to him, when I took the test."

"Yishou would have wanted you to be happy," she said. "He went all the way with you, just so you could take that test. He wouldn't like to see you like this now."

She meant what she said, but she also couldn't deny that she would have felt the same way if she were in his position. This sense of responsibility for what you did to others, both intentional and not, was what bound their world.

Her words didn't appear to have any effect on him. He'd taken a twig and was using it to carve angry patterns into the dirt, sending specks of dust floating into the sky and onto their legs.

"Stop that," she said. She felt suddenly furious with him, though she knew it was unfair. In the absence of any other object, all her anger fell onto him.

"I thought you would pass, too. That would have made it better," he said.

Her heart stumbled into her stomach. "Well, I didn't," she said flatly.

He didn't appear to notice the disappointment in her voice. She realized he hadn't tried to comfort her a single time since he'd come. She'd thought that he had consolation in mind when he'd been trying to find her, but now she saw he only wanted to mourn his own situation.

"I would give anything to be in your position," she said. "To have passed the test." She'd never felt this angry with him before. She thought of her mother's face when they'd first gotten the news that Hanwen would be sent down. At the time, Hanwen had witnessed her mother's rage with her own, duller, sadness. Now as she watched Yitian, she finally knew the sense of futility that could give rise to such a feeling.

"You only say that because you don't know what it feels like," he said, and the fire in her heart raged further.

"And you don't know what it feels like to be sent down to a village where you have no one, and now you have no way of getting out."

She wanted to tell him how she'd been ready to hurt herself for an opportunity like the one he had. Hanwen was sure Hongxing, in Shanghai and with all that time to study, had passed. She remembered, suddenly, how she'd gone through such effort to help him, making him a study schedule, before she tried to hurt herself. She'd thought so carefully of him, but when he'd disappeared for a week, he'd offered no explanation. He hadn't worried about her at all.

"If it had been me, I wouldn't be sad and moping like you are." When she saw the hurt in his face, a small rush ran through her. She'd finally made him feel something. "I wouldn't spend any time thinking about leaving you."

She looked fiercely at him, daring him to respond, to tell her she didn't mean it. But instead he hung his head and refused to look at her.

The sad droop of his neck and his resignation muffled her. Unable to look at him a moment longer, she rose, gathering her jacket at her neck against the cold. As she trudged back toward the village, she felt a force tugging her gaze back at him, but she refused its pull. She held her chin high and let the winter wind slap her face.

Twenty-four

She hardly slept that night thinking about how his face looked when she'd left him at the embankment. When she was a girl and the shouts of the arguing couples echoed all down the longtangs, she'd learned that betrayal and hurt were always possible in an instant when it came to love, and vowed to protect herself. Now she saw that she, too, had the same capacity to cause pain.

Throughout the night, she heard Wu Mei waking at intervals and crying, her sobs muffled into her pillow. The next morning, the production team was off, their work more erratic during the slack season. After breakfast, she hurried toward Yitian's home. He'd described the location to her in the past, but she'd never visited before. At the corner of the village's main road, she found the roof with the cracked pattern in its tiles.

The door to the courtyard was tightly shut. At this time of year, most other families had begun to put up couplets and decorations for the New Year, but the doors of their home were bare. There was only a single, thin piece of white cloth hanging over their doorway, alluding to the recent death.

She paused with her hand upon the door. The villagers traveled easily between homes in the afternoons, stopping by for a bit of chit-chat, but she wasn't sure what was proper for her. Tentatively, she called out, "Yitian?"

No response. She pressed her ear to the door.

"Yitian?" she called again, louder this time.

There was the sound of shuffling behind the door. Only a few steps—he'd come halfway to the door and then decided better of it.

She called his name, a final time.

The door opened, and a woman's face appeared. Hanwen gasped. She was shocked by the resemblance. She'd seen this woman around the village before, but never this close, where she could notice how her eyebrows looked as they knitted together, the way her jaw narrowed as she bit in the sides of her mouth. Hanwen saw, in an instant, Yitian's face that first day on the hilltop, when she'd surprised him with her arrival.

But then in the next, this woman's eyes had an alertness, a quickness to evaluate her that Yitian never had.

"I'm sorry to bother you, Aunt," Hanwen grasped for words. "I made a mistake."

What would his mother think? Hanwen worried, as she rushed back down the alleyway, drawing up dust in her hurry. Hanwen's only consolation was that she'd seen in the woman's eyes a resigned sorrow, the sadness of one who had more things occupying her than a single strange encounter.

The production team was cleaning and fixing the old pesticide sprayers in the barn when she returned from Yitian's. During the slack season, the team leader was always finding tasks like this for them, anything so that the sent-down youth wouldn't spend the days playing cards in their dormitories, mucking through the empty time of the winter days. Normally, she enjoyed this kind of work—she would get to examine the old equipment carefully, learning how all the pieces slid and fit perfectly together to make a well-greased whole; she loved, especially, the miraculous moment when something broken would begin to whir again, after which she would see her own hands as if they were made of magic.

Today, she didn't have any of her old enthusiasm. She hadn't been back to the barn since she and Yitian had studied there. She saw someone had dragged their old desk into the corner, already layered with cobwebs.

Niannian, squatting by the doorway of the barn over her machine, gave her a searching look as she entered. Hanwen dragged a sprayer into the corner so that she wouldn't have to speak with her. She sat down on an old brick and examined the machine. When she pressed the lever, the nozzle emitted a defeated sputter. No liquid came out, though the tank was more than half full with the milky pesticide. The issue had to be in the pressure chamber. She had to work to unscrew the cap, breaking the places where liquid had congealed along the ridges of the lid. When it finally came loose suddenly, her nose was assaulted with a sharp smell that burned her nostrils. She quickly moved to cover her mouth with her hand, but the smell had already diffused through the air and up to her head, making her feel woozy at once. She searched for the handkerchief she usually carried with her, but she couldn't find it.

"Come out of there and work in the open air, Hanwen, what are you thinking?" Niannian shouted. "It's dangerous."

Hanwen ignored her, but took the handkerchief that Niannian threw across the barn. When she tied the cloth around the back of her head, the world suddenly became fuzzy and far away.

For the past few days, she'd craved a sense of separation just like this, to close herself off from the world. Everyone around her had wanted to ask *How are you doing? Are you all right?*, as if they did not already know the answer to that question, as if they could create a false reality from their concern. She'd started and thrown away piles of letters to her mother, making trivial waste out of the paper that she'd once been so careful to preserve. Her mother would certainly have guessed at the outcome by now.

She peered down the dark hole of the air chamber. She felt the beginnings of a headache in her right temple and stopped momentarily to apply pressure there with her fingers. There was the brief relief of nothing, but when she removed her hand, the dull ache returned, this time with an increased pounding that threatened to bloom outward and spread.

Her breath went out the fabric and she inhaled it back in, so that she felt like a person on a loop. Her head was pounding now. When she reached up to scratch her scalp, she accidentally undid the bandana in the process. The smell of the pesticide rose up to meet her, as if lying in wait all this time. She counted deep gulps of air, hoping to clear her head, but she only coughed and inhaled more pesticide.

One . . . two . . .

Her hand loosened upon the nozzle and she was dimly aware of it falling to the ground.

Three . . . four . . .

Her body gave out. She heard the sounds of the world from far away. There was shouting—had the sound come from her, or from someone else? *Hanwen . . . I've been trying to find you . . .* a voice was saying. She reached out to grasp the source with both arms but found only air. In the corner, at the desk where they'd studied, she saw Yitian sitting with his head bent. Was she asleep or awake, or something else entirely? She saw things that had happened in her life as if through the window of a speeding bus. There was so much she wanted to hold on to: the day she tested into the best high school in Shanghai, her mother's fortieth birthday, the first time she'd spoken with Yitian. She rushed toward the bus door. *Wait, wait!* she said to the bus operator, *please let me off here!* She couldn't breathe. Somewhere beyond her sight, magpies shrieked a crying alarm. *Are they calling for me?* And then he was on the hilltop with her, the spiky shells of a chestnut splayed open across his pale hand.

She didn't speak for days, neither in the truck to the county hospital nor on the train back to Shanghai. Words caught, large and looming, in her throat. She slouched against the window all throughout the daylong train journey, without the strength to lift her body up. Other passengers took pity on her and fed her hot water through their own thermoses. She moved from sleep to wakefulness and back, her neck in the same, cramped position. Each time she awoke, she saw the passing countryside outside the window as if she were traveling in reverse through the long, monotonous fields, erasing all the life of the past few years. She imagined herself arriving back at the platform at Shanghai station, sixteen again, skin still untanned, mind a blank.

Then she fell back asleep. She felt someone's hand on her forehead, a calloused palm, gently rubbing her. She wanted to call out his name, but knew the touch belonged to someone else. Someone who shuffled quietly to her bed, laid more blankets on her, then removed them, layering down her care.

Her mouth finally parted. She was back in her mother's apartment.

The room was lit by a single cloudy bulb hanging on a wire in the center of the room. Someone was holding a spoonful of warm soup to her lips.

Hanwen smelled and felt her mother before she saw her—the sharp scent of vinegar on her hands, and the feeling she associated with it, of cleanness.

"Ma," she said.

Her mother, seated on a wooden stool beside the bed, shushed her. "Drink," she said, prodding the ceramic spoon at Hanwen's lips.

Hanwen recoiled. The liquid was hot and bitter.

"It's medicine. You need to build your blood back up. Drink."

Hanwen opened her mouth reluctantly.

"You were so sick. They kept sending me telegrams from the county hospital."

"How many days have I been home? They let me take leave?"

"You're much too weak to work."

"But when will I have to go back?"

"Have I raised you to be so diligent?" her mother murmured. She pressed a hand against Hanwen's forehead and smoothed the wisps of hair that had drifted from her temples, just as she had during all her childhood illnesses and fevers.

"You won't have to go back for a long time. Maybe never."

Hanwen slouched back under the covers and burrowed her arms underneath the lumpy cotton. She was in her mother's bed, she realized. She looked around to see her mother had made a makeshift pallet near her feet. Past that, Hanwen saw the square dining table in the corner where she'd eaten and copied all the characters she now knew; the jugs and rice buckets neatly stacked beneath its legs; in another corner, the single wooden dresser with the trousseau chest on top, containing all the valuable items her mother had ever owned. A white cloth doily covered their chipped ceramic bowls, stacked upon a wooden shelf above the dresser. The portrait of her father under the shiny glass. It was so strange, after spending years in the countryside, to be surrounded by this quaint architecture of domesticity in the city once again. Just a few months ago, she would have given next to anything to be back here. Now it seemed a place as ordinary as any other.

Pinned onto the wall was a faded portrait of Chairman Mao, next to a calendar that appeared much newer. She squinted to make out the text. It was 1978. Her mother had crossed off all the passing days with a pattern of Xs. She counted all of them, and looked at the current date, surprised to find that the next day would be the New Year.

Twenty-five

Yitian's mother tied one last string around his nylon duffel bag. In the course of his packing, a small split had formed along one side of the checkered plastic, so old that the material had stiffened and cracked. Unable to get anything else to store his things in at this last minute, she'd resorted to tying meters of string around the bag in case it broke during the long journey to Beijing.

"When you get on the train, make sure to put this right above you so you can see it at all times. If you fall asleep, tie it to your arm so you'll feel if anyone tries to steal it."

He couldn't imagine that anyone would try to steal his sad, small bag, but he didn't say this aloud to his mother for fear his words would embarrass her. She'd already apologized so many times because she hadn't been able to get him new clothes or shoes or any extra spending money for when he arrived in the city. As it was, she'd only just been able to scrape together money for his journey to Beijing, passing the slight bills to him secretly in small increments whenever his father was out of the house. His father had let him stay the past few weeks only at his mother's pleading. In that time, he didn't speak to Yitian once, and refused even to sit at the table if Yitian was there. On the New Year, Second Uncle had taken Yitian in so that he didn't have to spend the holiday alone.

His father's anger at him made the departure easier in one way— Yitian did not have to worry anymore about disappointing him.

His mother was the only person to send him off. Hanwen was gone. After he'd learned of what happened to her, he'd written letters and letters to her house in Shanghai, telling her to respond in care of his university in Beijing. It occurred to him now that he'd never once tried to console her after her gaokao score, and he apologized for this in every letter he sent. After all Yishou had done for him, he slipped into his selfish habits again. He half hoped that she would have forgiven him by the time he arrived in Beijing, and there would already be a stack of letters from her waiting.

He and his mother walked to the village entrance, where he'd arranged for a truck to pick him up on its route into the township. He was so nervous that, for the first time in his life, he'd risen before his mother and was already dressed before she awoke.

There was a single red pine tree at the village entrance, next to the dirt road. The villagers had nicknamed it the welcoming pine for its crooked branches, curving to the left as if bowing in welcome. Could the tree also bow in goodbye? He looked at his feet, unsure of what more there was to be said. There, imprinted in the road, were his and his mother's feet, swaddled in their plain black cloth shoes. For the first time in his life, he noticed how they stood the same way: both with their feet pointing outward and weight shifted against the right hip.

"Don't speak to any strangers. If anyone asks you for money, just ignore them." His mother reached her two arms up to his neck, but only managed to get up to the fleshy part below his shoulders. "If you lose anything, I won't be able to send more to you. You can't be absentminded out there, like you are at home. People will take advantage of you." The heat of his mother's breath formed in plumes against the early dawn cold.

The tractor ambled up the road to them, sending dust up into the air as it approached. He wanted to take notes and remember everything in the village, to sit in the front row of the classroom again and furiously scribble all the details that were only now becoming visible to him as they were about to be lost. The smell of coal smoke coming up the chimney in the mornings, darker gray against the gray sky, his mother biting her cheeks when she worried, how the air hung tentatively before the day began.

Then the tractor was in front of them, its groaning engine loud and omnipresent, and the driver was instructing Yitian to squeeze himself and his bag against the sacks of grain in the back.

The driver shifted into gear. Yitian swiveled his body backward, bracing himself against the railing to say goodbye. He waved furiously. It had all happened so fast.

"Go home, Ma! Don't worry about me. I'll be safe. You don't need to send me off any longer!"

He clenched his jaw, grateful for the dust that was coming up from behind the rolling truck that would obscure his mother's vision of him.

He didn't know when he would see her again. Other than her, there was nothing left for him here. He wondered what he would be like the next time he saw this place. Was it possible to live a life, moving from place to place, yourself unfiltered? And yet, as Yitian thought of himself, he was sure that nothing could possibly change. He would remain exactly the same as he'd always been.

"Go home!" he called out again. He could not turn his head away. Suddenly his mother picked up her feet and began running toward him, her jacket flying open with the wind. Dust flew into her mouth and eyes, and she rubbed at her face to wipe it away.

She spoke, her words an echo of his own, fading . . . calling out . . .

"Go! Don't worry about us! 去吧, 去吧! Go, go . . . go . . ."

Part 4

迷途指南

A MAP FOR
THE MISSING

Twenty-six

1993

He couldn't explain his sudden need to call his mother, except to locate it in the same place as the need to have Hanwen near him. He felt like a child, grabbing anything he could hold. His body was still shaking from the hospital visit when they'd arrived back at his hotel, and it was she who'd spoken with the lobby clerk as he looked blankly forward from the edge of the lobby sofa, whose cushions were ragged with use. Dimly he heard her asking for them to bring a cup of hot water for him. When he saw his fingers reach out to accept it, his hands seemed to belong to someone else's body.

"I want to call my mother," he'd said, at the shock of the sensation.

The secretary at the village office answered and said he would send someone to get her from her home.

"What should I tell her?" the secretary asked.

"Tell her that we went to the hospital this morning," Yitian said. The words for the rest of the day escaped him. He gave the number for the hotel and retreated to the seating area.

Hanwen sat on the couch opposite as he waited. They didn't speak. At times when he looked up at her, the fine outline of her face hovered as if belonging to a dream world.

The realization that had seized him in the moment he backed away from the hospital bed was how little he knew about his father. He was grasping about for an object in the dark.

He thought about the last lesson he'd taught his topology class. It felt impossible now that only a week ago he'd stood in front of rows of students in a modern classroom and it had seemed imperative to him, despite their indifference, that he explain the subject clearly.

"Imagine a sphere and a cube," he'd said. "You'd think they were very different shapes, but not in topology. We don't think about shapes by how they look to the human eye, but rather in terms of unchanging properties, called their invariant properties. Let's take, for example, the number of holes. This property is called the genus of a shape."

He chalked a coffee cup and a donut on the board.

"Why might these things be the same?" he asked.

A student joked both were things policemen got at donut shops. He didn't understand, but others had laughed, so he joined in. He'd learned over the years in America that this simple act of mimicry could deceive others, and over time he could predict, like a sixth sense, when the laughter would begin, if it would require his brief chuckle or full-throated chortle—all from the way a person looked as they were telling a joke.

"That's a good guess," he continued, after the laughter had died down. "In mathematical terms, they both have the same invariant property of genus one. They each have only one hole. For a donut, it's the center. For a coffee cup, it's the handle. So we could topologically transform the donut into the coffee cup, like this." He drew more shapes:

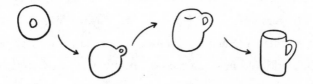

He expected the class to be amazed, but when he looked up, they only seemed to be as bored as they always were, not at all like he'd been when he heard about the idea of the genus. He could always tell when the end of their class was approaching by the early sounds of students closing notebooks and zipping up their backpacks. When he thought back to his years in university, he saw he'd maintained a certain innocence about life and learning these students hadn't. They were jaded about intellectual matters and couldn't summon up any awe about these ideas. It was amazing, he'd thought back then, that an unchanging property of an object wasn't only what was there, but also what wasn't. It meant that if you could define what was absent, create a map for the missing, that was also a way of knowing a thing.

He wished such a simple principle was true in his father's case—that the facts he didn't know could be as important as the ones he did. The objects of truths he knew about his father were small and uncertain, without shape. What year his father was born, the year he married, that he'd served in the army. That he hated his own father. The list of unknown things was much more numerous. Why his father could become so quiet, why he liked to drink, why he and Yitian's grandfather never spoke. In topology, cataloging the holes was a way of forming shape from the absences. The world of mathematics made this diminished way of knowing useful. Here, in the real world, Yitian couldn't even name how much he didn't know.

Yitian? Yitian?" he heard her saying. He looked down to see that her fingers were on his elbow, lightly pushing him. "They're saying your mother called back." Hanwen gestured with her chin toward the lobby clerk holding out a receiver, an invitation awaiting him.

He leaned against the counter and brought the cool plastic to his ear. He breathed deeply, bracing himself.

"Ma?" he began to tell the story about that morning, but he couldn't get his words out over his mother's sudden crying.

"Sorry. I'm so sorry," she was saying, over and over.

"What are you apologizing about?"

"I should have told you so much earlier, but I just didn't want you to worry, all the way out there in America. You couldn't have done anything, and I knew you were working so hard."

"What? Worry about what, Ma?"

He tried to interrupt her, but her continued apologies refused him any room for interjection. He wanted to reach through the phone and shake her so that she would explain.

He hung up the phone, unable to listen to the repetitive wailing any longer. He pressed his open palm to his chest, waiting for the rapid beat to slow. Then he watched the clock behind the counter until the long hand ticked itself over two minutes before calling her back.

She answered the phone midway through the first ring. "Where did you go? What happened?"

"I can't understand anything you're saying, Ma. What are you talking about? What didn't you tell me?"

"People start to forget things, you know, in their old age. I'm forgetting things, too, now, all the time. So I thought everything with your Ba was normal aging. It didn't seem a reason to tell you. I didn't want to worry you over something that happened to everybody." She took several deep breaths, heavy as if poured directly into the phone's receiver.

"Ma? Are you still there?"

"Yes." She inhaled deeply before continuing. "Your father . . . he was starting to forget things. But not normal things. Well, at first they were normal. Where we kept the pickled mustard greens or the winter blankets. And I didn't want to think too much of it, because it wasn't hard for me to help him find these things. Here's the cupboard, you know—that was easy enough to tell him whenever he needed help."

Yitian had the sensation that he was about to learn something awful. He turned his head, searching out Hanwen, who had remained on the couch. She raised her eyebrows slightly at him, a question in her eyes. She rose and hurried over to him.

"Nothing was that bad until one day when I returned home late," his mother said.

His hand shook on the receiver. He reached out and grasped Hanwen's fingers. He was aware of how much cooler her hand was than his. A feeling began to gnaw at him as his mother explained. He saw, vaguely then undeniably, what his mother's words pointed to—a disease that, unlike her, he was able to give a name to.

His feeling settled into certainty as she described returning home at dusk that day, calling out to his father to apologize for returning so late.

When I was standing in the courtyard, even before I entered the home, I had a feeling that something was wrong. It felt like there was a ghost who had entered the house. I can't explain where my feeling came from. From the outside, everything looked exactly the same as it always did, but I knew even before I went in.

Because she hadn't prepared dinner, she expected him to be

irritated, but when she went inside, she felt a deep silence like the kind in the middle of the night. He wasn't in the main room, where he usually would have been at that hour. She checked the two bedrooms, but both were empty. Still, she could sense there was some other presence in the air, that the space was not wholly hers. She walked through the house again. Main room, main bedroom, second bedroom, where Yitian and his grandfather used to sleep. This time she looked more closely. The room was so dark—in her fear, she'd forgotten to light a lamp—that she would not have noticed him if it hadn't been for the sharp cry, the noise of a desperate child who'd lost his parents in a crowd. A shadow emerged from the corner of the second bedroom, becoming larger and larger. She gasped—it was her husband. What was strange was that his back faced her, rather than the wall. All this time, he'd been standing in the corner and looking into the sharp edge where the walls met, as if that was where the real world was to be found. She hadn't noticed him earlier because his featureless back had blended into the shadows.

She would deny it to herself later, telling herself that what she saw was only a trick of the darkness, but at the moment she found him, when she looked into his eyes, she saw a bottomless fear. It was an expression she'd never seen him wear before. *Where am I?* he yelled. As she clutched him to her, telling him that he was in his home, safe, she was surprised to feel a dampness between them. She looked down. He'd soiled his pants.

Yitian could already picture it all as his mother spoke. There'd been villagers who behaved the way she described. Some of their families claimed these people were over a hundred years old. They rarely left their beds and could only eat porridge, fed to them by the younger members of their families, something thin enough that the soupy mixture could easily slip through their toothless gums. He'd seen them before, resting in storage sheds, skin like dried fruit peels hanging from their arms and legs, faces that were only a topography of jutting bones and the sunken spaces between. They couldn't speak, could only make choking noises that sounded like wind being forced through an old pipe. Mouths as bottomless as black holes, puckered at the edges.

These old people had no memory. They couldn't remember the names of their family members who fed them, couldn't even remember the names of their own fathers and sons. Their existences were worse even than a ghost's, who at least could know why it was haunting a place. Yitian sometimes saw them wandering around the village with a glassy look in their eyes, shuffling directionless on their weak feet. Back then, everyone knew where others belonged, so the job of whoever encountered them was to lead the lost old person back home.

The disease was one of old age, doomed to happen to anyone who lived long enough, but there were some for whom the symptoms appeared much earlier. As with so many other things, he'd been in college when he'd first heard it named formally, and then in America he learned the English name for the disease. *Alzheimer's*. In those years, many of the illnesses they'd once found mystical turned out to be curable once they were named. The infections, the fevers, sometimes even the cancers—all these needed were an identification, and then *poof*, the miracle of medicine could do its work. This disease was one of the few that had resisted the solution of categorization. The mystery of memory, still irreparable by any type of science.

All along, Yitian had the sense of circling around some deep hole of non-knowing. Now, with his mother's story, these fragmented pieces connected into an explanation he could make sense of.

"If—if we know what memory he had when he left this time, then we'd know what he was thinking, and we can figure out where he went."

"Yitian—he ran into someone on the way out of the village. He told them he was going to Hefei to look for you."

Yitian's throat closed in upon him. So this was the thing she'd been most afraid to tell him.

"I know I should have told you earlier, but I didn't want you to think he was still angry at you."

"But was he? Is that why he left?"

Beside him, Hanwen looked sharply up at the sudden change in his tone.

"I don't know," his mother said.

"Weren't you with him all this time? How could you not know?" He'd never spoken to his mother this way before, rarely spoke to anyone like this at all. His mother had kept the truth from him. For years, he had no evidence that his father even thought of him.

"This person who saw him in the village, why didn't they stop him from leaving?"

"She was one of the teenagers who grew up in the township, so she wasn't familiar with everyone. She didn't know who you or your father were—she just thought he was telling the truth about where he was going."

After a pause, his mother added, "I wanted to tell you sooner, but I didn't know how. I didn't know if it would be right. Please don't be mad at me."

But he did feel mad. The lies she'd told weren't harmless. She'd allowed him to spend all these days after the disappearance, the most crucial ones, looking for his father without telling him the full story. Because of her lie. For the past three days, he'd been in the exact place that his father said he was going. He could have been scouring the city, instead of sitting in his hotel room or going to the zoo or sleeplessly reviewing old math problems. All the while, his father has been out there, lost and helpless.

He felt a fantasy unraveling itself. He'd imagined finding his father, telling him about the life he'd made in America. He would show him that Yishou's death had not been useless. Nothing his father warned him about had come to pass, after all. But his father had gone to Hefei, where Yishou had gotten sick that year. The things that'd happened in this city were still the essential and defining event of his father's memory, even in its reduced state.

After he hung up the phone, he became aware of Hanwen's hand upon his. The cold marble of the counter. The clerk's alarmed stare. He wondered how loud his voice had become on the phone.

"Do you want to go somewhere else?" she asked. "Your room?" When she took her hand away from his, the very outline of him shook.

He said yes because momentum carried him, because his heart still rang from his mother's news, and he couldn't imagine going back to that empty and shabby room alone. Because he couldn't call his mother back, couldn't call Mali. Hanwen was the only person from his past life whom he could speak to, the only one who would understand.

Twenty-seven

He was sure he could read what the clerk was thinking as they headed together to the back of the lobby. Another couple, surreptitiously using a hotel together this late in the evening, displacing their needs onto a place not their home.

He entered the elevator first and pressed himself against the back wall. Turning his head, he was shocked to see his doubled reflection in the mirrors. How tired he looked, how depleted. He shifted his glance forward toward her. The unwavering outline of her face brought a calm over him. He could see in that outline her solidity and practicality; she was someone who could help him stand.

In his own room, he allowed her to lead him. She passed the bed looming in the center and sat at the low table in front of the window, through which they could see the streets below. He'd tried falling asleep on the chair there the first night, hoping that the darkness of the streets outside would lull his body into comfort.

"What did your mother say?" she asked.

He startled at the sound of her voice in the room. The table between them was much lower than their chairs, and he was forced to look directly at her when they spoke.

"She told me my father has a condition." He repeated his mother's story. It felt starker, somehow, to call what had become of his father a *condition*, rather than a misunderstanding or a trip out of the village—words that implied he still had some choice in the matter. Yitian craved another language, one that didn't already damn his father to an outcome.

"He came to Hefei to look for me. All this time, he could have been here in this city. Do you know what that means? His mind has been deteriorating, but I had no idea. The symptoms must have been building up for years now, if they were so bad he'd think I was here. It's been so long since I've even lived in this country. It's the last thing he would have done if he was lucid."

"But you don't know how your father feels about you now."

"I keep thinking I'd feel something if he wasn't alive." When his grandfather died, he'd felt a sigh leaving his body. "I keep searching for something, some intuition, I guess. I don't need it to tell me where he is, exactly. Just whether he's dead or alive. Whether he's still angry at me."

"Yitian—"

He looked up from the table. The glass was streaked with the oily residue of his fingerprints. He'd been mindlessly tracing as he spoke.

"It might not be my place to say this, but"—she took a deep breath, then continued—"there's nothing you could have done. I've heard of others' parents who've gotten this disease. There was nothing they could do about it, either. Once it starts, it eats away all the person's memories."

"But he went after *me*. In *Hefei*. I can't think of anything else it would mean."

"He didn't go after you, not in his real mind. Coming to Hefei might not mean what you think it means. People with that disease mix up past in present and come up with a different reality. They confuse things that are fantasy with things that are real, and it all becomes one true story in their heads."

"My mother waited so long to tell me. I could have done something." He surely would have noticed his father's illness earlier and taken him to the doctor at the first signs of forgetfulness. That was the point of all his education, to distinguish between nuances that the uneducated could not. What if his mother had deliberately kept the knowledge from him, as some unconscious punishment? He was the one who'd chosen not to visit for so long. He'd created the cleavages that allowed for secrets to be kept.

"If I hadn't left," he said slowly, "I'm sure this wouldn't have happened. I would have been able to help him."

She shook her head. "How could you have known what would happen? And what would you have been able to do, even if you'd known? There's no treatment."

He didn't want to agree. If he believed what she said, that the threads of memory simply unraveled and then became reknotted in a new order, then there was no repairing to be done. Memory was simply one of many things that could be lost in the course of a life, just like a father could be.

When he looked up at her this time, he caught her staring at him, searching his face. Throughout the time they'd been together these past few days, he'd examined her while her gaze was elsewhere, trying to see what had changed in her features. Now he sensed she was trying to do the same to him.

"I've realized"—she swallowed before continuing—"that there's only so much you can predict. When I look around at my life now, I think about how I never would have guessed I'd be here. When I first met Guifan, how could I have known what it would lead to?"

"But life surprised you pleasantly," he said.

"I don't know." She was silent for a moment. "It's so much different than what we wanted for ourselves, back then."

"I always wondered what happened to you that year." He chose his words carefully. "I was surprised when you didn't pass the gaokao. Did you try again?"

"No." She cast her eyes downward. "No, I didn't."

He sensed a hesitancy in her words and he wasn't sure she was telling the truth. It was so unlike her, to have given up so easily after a single failure. But he could see she didn't want to say more. "That's a shame," he said. "You would have passed if you kept trying."

"Do you really think so?"

Hope glimmered in her eyes, a feeling that he wanted to keep for her and preserve. "You were as smart as anyone I met later in Beijing. I couldn't have passed without your help."

"Don't be so modest." She waved her hand in the air. "But it's true that after I fainted from the pesticide exposure that year, I never felt quite the same. My mind didn't work like it used to. It moved so much more slowly. I couldn't make connections anymore." She paused. "Did you know, once I tried to hurt myself? So that I could be sent back to Shanghai to study? After the gaokao announcement."

"When?"

"Right after your grandfather died."

"You never told me."

Even now, she spoke slowly, as if reconsidering with each word whether to take it back. "We had that dream of going to college together, and I didn't want to hurt you. And then afterward, I thought, well, maybe it's good I didn't succeed, so I could study with him. Maybe this is what I need to pass. But it didn't work."

Walking around her beautiful home, he'd thought her the happy one, the one for whom life had played out as a series of fortunate surprises.

She said, "Do you remember Hongxing? One of the other girls there with me?"

He nodded.

"She's become a professor, too. Just like you. In English. It's a small teaching university in Jiangsu, nothing like the school you're at, of course. She got to go back to study in Shanghai, right before the gaokao. Do you know why? She hurt herself on purpose so they'd have to send her back. I tried it first, but she was the one who succeeded."

"I'm glad it didn't work." He remembered Hongxing's accident. The villagers had spoken about it with pity for the girl.

"Yes, well. I showed how far I was willing to go." She laughed and shook her head, as if clearing the dream away. "No, it doesn't do to think of what might have happened. I feel like Yuanyuan. Making up stories in my head to keep myself happy."

She looked so resigned, and this made him sadder than all the other revelations. He wanted to turn back time for both of them, to return her to a moment before. He moved suddenly across the table. When he interlaced his fingers with hers, he was shocked by the coldness.

Her body twitched slightly at the contact, but she spread her hand wider to allow his fingers into hers. Outside, he heard the long and drawn-out shout of a peddler, announcing himself.

They were both still, hands together.

Then the sound was gone. The room was silent for a single

moment, and in the next, her lips were on his. His hand was still reaching across the table, touching her knee. He had no other thoughts except to break that boundary on the way over to her.

He was surprised at how hard and determined their first kiss was. Their teeth knocked lightly against one another, the meeting of two people both pushing the limits of their momentum.

He pulled away, remembering suddenly how afraid she'd once been of even a kiss. "Is this all right?"

Instead of responding, she leaned in for a second time. He was amazed at this person she'd become in an instant, so willful and certain, allowing no fear to enter into her body. He pressed back against her this time. He had the feeling they were walking out on a tightrope together, farther and farther, that to look down would send them tumbling to the ground. He kissed her as he wished he had when he was a teenager, before everything else came, when there were no other facts in the world besides the simple desperation and joy of an embrace.

It was she who stood up first, holding her hand out to him and leading him to the dark bed. He felt shy, seventeen again, waiting to be led by her confidence, trying to catch a glimpse of her to know the next step. He hadn't felt like this in years. He and Mali made love with knowing, sex a dance they'd performed the choreography of hundreds of times. They cycled through the same positions, reached out to stroke the same part of one another. It was familiar, comfortable, easy. The ritual accumulation still revealed a glimpse of newness each time.

But this feeling now with Hanwen was made completely of raw spark, making up for everything they were once afraid to do. Every touch was new and unexpected and held two different kinds of feeling: the touch itself and his own surprise at how his body responded.

The thought of Mali gnawed at him, but he tried to shake away the knot of her. Then Hanwen leaned into the tiny section of her skin that made contact with his stomach. She pressed into him hard, as if wanting to sink into his body. When she removed her hand, Mali's face appeared. In the next, her soft hair fell onto his cheek, and Mali was gone again.

He was not sure what caused him to open his eyes at that moment. Later, he would tell himself that he felt a chill suddenly entering the room, a secret language whispering to him to look more closely.

He was kissing a stranger. In that instant, he saw her face, naked and pale, just as she was about to bring it to his. The expression there startled him. Her eyes were still closed, and her face was utterly vulnerable in this moment when she thought she wasn't under any gaze, how he imagined she must have viewed herself when she sat in the back of a car alone or closed the door of her home against outsiders. There was no desire on her features, none of the simple surrender he experienced as he kissed her. What he read there, instead, was determination. Her jaw, hard and set. Her eyes, a sternness in the way they crinkled harshly at the corners. She was willing herself toward him.

Her face looked nothing like it had on evenings when they snuck out together. He'd called it pale like the moon, then. Now she'd shed so much, her cheekbones becoming so angular that any round image for them was inapt. He'd held her memory in amber, a tool for his use, to believe there was a part of the world that hadn't moved on.

She opened her eyes as his touch drew away. There was surprise on her face, but for only a moment. Then she released a small sigh.

"Right," she said.

They both looked at the scene around them. The dark hotel room, the sheets rumpled by that burst of desire. He wanted to cover up his body, though he'd hardly shed any clothes. Already, the past few moments felt like they belonged to a different life, or one they'd never have the chance to live.

From the window he looked down at the taxi stand. He saw her exit from the revolving doors, the surprise of the attendant as he shook himself from his doze and rose from his chair. She stood just to the side of the overhang. Yitian watched her silhouette as the attendant waved down a taxi. She was as poised as he'd ever seen her, but he could read in the tap of her fingers against her purse strap that she was eager to leave.

The attendant returned, followed by a cab. He opened the door for her. She pulled her long, black coat against her neck, disappearing it from the world. She already had one foot into the car when she suddenly looked up. He was not sure what the hotel glass might have obscured, but he nodded, and she nodded back. The shadow of her chin dipped against the pale skin of her neck. Then the attendant closed the car door, and he felt, finally, the weight of her absence in the room.

Twenty-eight

FEBRUARY 1978,
BEIJING

Forget everything you knew before. Calculus, trigonometry, whatever . . ." Professor Leng said. "The purpose of this class is to rebuild your knowledge from the ground up. We will work to provide the *foundation* of all the rules you have learned. Your previous task was to memorize. Now, your job is to understand."

Out of all his classes, Yitian had been dreading Real Analysis most. The older students had told him it would be the most difficult of the first-year core, but so far, the class hadn't been nearly as hard as he'd anticipated. In math classes in high school, they had been instructed to simply memorize all the properties and axioms without any context or reasoning behind them. Each of those properties had drifted around Yitian's mind, unconnected to the others, vanishing quickly from his memory. He had always found himself asking *why*. *Why is this formula true, where did it come from?* "There is no *why* to fundamental things like this," his teacher in primary school had said, and then rapped his palm for being so insolent.

Professor Leng's Real Analysis class was teaching him that his old teacher had been wrong. Each property required a proof, which, in turn, was based on certain fundamental principles. All of these could be traced all the way back to a single starting point. This process was the same way he'd learned history from his grandfather, from the origin point of the Yellow Emperor to all the branches that derived from it. This way of learning math allowed him to watch how each law or property grew from a previous one, a lineage created from the first axioms, much easier for him to behold and remember than the equations he'd learned in any math class before. He surprised himself with how easily the thinking came to him. He wondered if his grandfather would feel the same if he were still alive, sitting in this lecture. Even now that he was at the best university in the country, he still thought his grandfather was the smartest person he'd ever know.

Still, he couldn't say he felt the same immediate yearning and interest for mathematics that he did for topics of history. In class, he had to force himself to focus and deliberately guide his mind back to attention each time he drifted off, as he did now when Professor Leng announced, "Today, we'll be learning the triangle inequality—the most important of all of mathematics." He wrote on the board:

If a and b are any two real numbers, then

$$|a + b| \leq |a| + |b|.$$

"In other words," Professor Leng said, "the absolute value of the sum of two real numbers is always less than or equal to the sum of their absolute values."

The inequality seemed simple enough, so basic that Yitian couldn't understand why they were spending so much time on the proof. But as Professor Leng wrote out the lines, his certainty lessened. For example, if he let $a = Hanwen$ and $b = Yitian$, was it true that:

$$|Hanwen + Yitian| \leq |Hanwen| + Yitian|?$$

On the left-hand side of the equation was the sum of Hanwen and Yitian, the way they were in the village. On the right was each of them individually, walled in their different worlds, as they were now. It didn't seem obvious to Yitian that the sums of their separatenesses was greater than what they were together.

He tried another case. Let $a = Yishou$ and $b = Yitian$:

$$|Yishou + Yitian| \leq |Yishou| + |Yitian|.$$

He didn't even add a question mark after the inequality, because it seemed so patently true to him; Yishou would have been better off alone.

The bell rang, signaling the end of the class period. Professor Leng, still in the middle of writing a line, dropped the piece of chalk. The unfinished equation hung uncertainly on the board, the equal sign rendered into a subtraction by the loss of its second underline. Yitian fought the urge to rise and correct it.

He allowed his focus to relax, his attention returning to the dull bleakness of the classroom, the gray light hardly filtering through dirty windows, and the rows and rows of his classmates, many of them who'd been secretly sleeping. He packed his bag quickly and deliberately. He had a particular task that he needed to complete now, one he'd been considering the entire morning.

The other students rushed out of class to fight for the most popular dishes at the canteen. He walked in another direction, toward the history department. He'd been going there every afternoon after mathematics classes ended in the morning. While the rest of his roommates napped, he snuck into the history classes, so often that some students had already asked him what year of the major he was in.

The building was at a far corner of campus, at the edge of a scenic, man-made lake. It was an old Qing dynasty–style construction, made of gray brick and flanked with red columns, windows covered in shades with intricate cutout patterns. Upturned eaves revealed the sapphire blue painted with gold on the fascia. This was what he'd thought of when he imagined a university, not the imposing cement of the Soviet-style buildings later added, one of which housed the math department. *This* was the kind of building used by the old scholars who'd passed the imperial exam and came to Beijing. The only sign that the building had gone through the tumult of the past few decades was the red paint chipping in places, revealing wood underneath, and the years when the maintenance of beauty had been considered a bourgeois endeavor.

It was the kind of building he was meant to study in, too. As he entered, he thought of his grandfather and reminded himself to be brave. He might have been finding the math classes better than expected, but it was obvious that this was the department where he truly belonged. He'd made up his mind to ask the history dean for a transfer. Though his banzhuren had already told him such a thing would be impossible, Yitian hoped that if he appealed directly to the dean, no one could override him.

He hopped up the stairs to the top floor two at a time, all the while muttering to himself the speech he'd prepared. He would start by telling the dean his grandfather's story. Then he would repeat everything he knew about the country's history, showing the dean he was as prepared for the major as any other student. If that didn't work, he would get on his knees and beg.

With his hand on the doorknob to the office, he took a deep breath, ready to burst in and interrupt the dean with his speech.

The room he almost fell into looked nothing like what he'd expected. There was no dean sitting behind a heavy oak desk. Instead, three women sat at shabby desks in three corners of the room, carefully carving characters onto wax paper. They all looked up, alarmed at the sight of him.

"Excuse me," came the voice of the woman sitting in the far-right corner. Her hair was drawn into a tight, gleaming bun, which pulled all her features severely upward. "Who are you here to see?"

Behind her, there was a wooden door that he supposed must lead to the dean's office.

"I'm here to see the dean." His voice, which he'd practiced making confident and strong, came out so frail that he winced at the sound.

"What do you want to see the dean about?"

"I—I prefer not to say."

"I can't let you go see the dean unless I know the reason you're here," she said.

"Okay, then." He swallowed, looking down at his feet as he spoke, so that he wouldn't have to see the judgment on her face. "I'm here to see the dean about changing into your department."

"So you're not in our major."

"No. I want to transfer in."

When he looked back up, the secretary's face was smug as she said, "The dean only meets with people in the history department. So I'm afraid that means he can't meet with you."

"But that's exactly it. I *want* to be in your department."

"As a student here, you should know that transfers are strictly forbidden."

"I know that, but I was hoping you could make an exception for me. I have a special case."

"There are no special cases with this policy." She narrowed her eyes. "Are you even a student at this university, anyway?"

He hurried to show her his student identification card.

"Fine, then. But the policy is the policy. Do you have any other business here?"

"Please, I have a special case. If I could just explain to the dean—" he said, but she'd already begun to ignore him. One other secretary had returned to her engraving, the sound of the stylus cutting against the steel grating in his ears. The woman at the desk directly in front of him was staring at him with naked surprise. He must have shocked her with the extent of his desperation.

He looked down at himself, at his plain rubber shoes against the clean green carpet, and felt suddenly embarrassed. He backed quickly out of the door and ran down the hallway. Turning the corner, he took a deep breath and pressed his back against the wall, allowing its cement surface to cool his scalp.

From the direction of the hallway behind him, he heard the sound of hard-heeled shoes clacking upon the linoleum. He hurriedly began walking away.

"Wait," the voice came from behind him. It was gentle, certainly not the voice of the severe woman. He turned around to see the secretary who'd been sitting closest to him.

She walked up to him and said to him in a low voice, "If you come back in twenty minutes, the dean will be back in the office." She spoke to the floor, so quietly that he had to lean in to hear her. "Everyone else will be at lunch. If you come by then, I can let you in."

"Really? Will I get into trouble?" He looked at her face to see if it was some trick, but her eyes appeared kind. She had a small mole in the cupid's bow above her mouth, which was held tightly in worry. She seemed even more nervous than he about breaking the rules.

She shook her head. "The dean's not like them."

"I can't thank you enough—"

She shushed him and was already walking away, gaze still directed at the floor.

From her description, he expected the dean to be some sort of kind older man, and so Yitian was surprised when he stood in front of the dean's desk for three minutes and the dean did not even look up once. He was scribbling something furiously.

As Yitian stood, his body felt heavier and heavier, a weight that was sinking down to the bottom of a river. He looked around the room to distract himself, eyes drawn to the two large wooden bookcases behind the desk, encased behind clean glass. Except for a single shelf that only held a framed picture of the Chairman, all the rows were filled so tightly with books that they seemed about to burst. The spines were almost breaking off the covers. He squinted—the *Twenty-Four Histories*! He'd never seen that book in printed form—

The dean cleared his throat. "So, you'd like to change your department."

Yitian was surprised by the dean's voice, which was not in the guttural Beijing dialect he'd heard since his arrival in this city, but was rather nasal and defined, somewhere from the south.

"Yes, sir."

"I'm sure your banzhuren must have told you about the likely outcome? So, I'm not sure why you've still come. Of course we cannot make such an exception for you." The dean had moved on from his writing. He was flipping quickly through a sheaf of papers on his desk now, leaving thin stamps, rectangular and red, in each corner.

It was not in Yitian's nature to argue against those in positions of authority, and the dean was probably the most important figure he'd ever stood in front of. But he could not believe he'd gone through everything to get into the dean's office, only to be delivered two sentences that his banzhuren had already told him.

There was a knock on the door. The dean looked up, seeming genuinely surprised to find that Yitian was still there.

"Look, boy—" The secretary opened the door, but the dean waved her off. He took off his thick, black-framed glasses. Without them, he looked quite like an ordinary middle-aged man. He was looking at Yitian curiously now, as if he were some interesting specimen. Self-conscious, Yitian immediately moved his hand up to cover his face.

The dean finally sighed and said, "You're from the countryside, am I correct?"

"Yes, sir."

"I can tell from your accent. And what province?"

"Anhui, sir."

"We're neighbors. I'm from Jiangxi myself."

"Yes, sir." It was a good sign that the dean was asking so many questions. If the dean cared to know of his past, perhaps the special details of his case were being considered.

"And what major are you in now?" the dean asked.

"Mathematics."

The dean rubbed his eyes. "It's curious . . . that a boy from the countryside like you would be brave enough to come to my office."

"It's because my brother and my grandfather—" Yitian started, but the dean ignored him and continued speaking. "From one southerner to another, mathematics is a very good major. You shouldn't be upset. Your score must have been very high in order to get into that major—higher than the scores our students had, even. Many students in your department have made stable lives for themselves. You're courageous, it's clear. You can go far in mathematics. It's much more difficult in our department. Here"—he lowered his voice—"all of our professors are very specific, very careful, very *correct*. The students must be, too."

The dean's sudden garrulousness gave Yitian hope. "I won't have any problem with that, sir. I'm also a very careful thinker, very deliberate—"

"That's not what I mean. You haven't understood me. It wasn't the same in the countryside during the worst years of the Cultural Revolution. You don't know what it felt like to see the people singled out to be denounced every day, how hard it was to escape it . . . you had to watch every word you uttered, anything you said about yourself. You're too young to know."

The dean sighed and put his glasses back on. "Even if I could help you change your major, I wouldn't. This is better for you. Just believe me."

"There's been a mistake, Professor," Yitian tried, desperate.

The dean was looking back down at his papers.

"I didn't mean to apply in math, all I ever wanted was to come to college so I could learn history more systematically, but my brother accidentally—"

"If that's really true, go to the library and check out some books. There's nothing in this building you couldn't just read about in your free time." He looked up. "It's time for my lunch now. You should eat, too, if you haven't yet. Goodbye."

The sun outside the building shone so brightly that Yitian had to squint against the glare. Everything was thrown into a harsher and clearer white light. Dirty streaks dripped down the cement surfaces of the buildings, remnants of each accumulated rain. A construction truck sauntered by, wobbling with a heavy load of rocks, throwing dust into his throat.

He felt completely powerless. That conversation couldn't have been all there was. There had to be more—some other chance, some other way he could convince the dean. Could the rules be so inflexible? The history dean would not take another meeting with him; his banzhuren would only feel satisfied to see the outcome he'd already predicted. The only person who could override the history dean was the president of the entire school himself, and Yitian had no idea how to contact him. He was just one part of a large university, as insignificant as an ant. At least at home, there were people who'd depended on him, whom he could help with his work points.

He didn't sneak into the history lectures that afternoon. There wasn't any point. Neither was there any reason to go to the library and read those history books any longer, as the dean suggested.

He went back to the dormitory room he shared with seven other boys. To his relief, none of them were there. He climbed up onto his bunk and pulled the blankets up over him, though their small room was dry and stuffy. The ceiling hovered only centimeters above his nose. He reached up and drew his thumbnail against the plaster, leaving a slash, angry and sharp. He did this again and again, clawing until the surface above him was covered in hashes, as if he were a person with a goal to count toward. How stupid he had been to think he could still change his major, to believe he could reverse the path he'd already traveled. The thoughts of his failures mounted. Hanwen, his brother's death, his grandfather; now, the loss of history. This surely was a punishment for the pain he'd caused Hanwen, Yishou, and his parents. He deserved this suffering, the balancing of the scale that would tip it away from his brother's sacrifice.

He stayed like this in bed for days, skipping classes and meals. In between, he slept more than he ever had in his life, awaking each time with a feeling of dark walls closing in on him. In the seconds after he awoke, he smelled wild ginger in his nostrils, but had no idea from where it might have come.

Twenty-nine

1980, SHANGHAI

Hanwen checked over the place settings a final time, adjusting the bowls so they were in proper alignment. That night there was a party of municipal officials hosting a delegation from out of town, and she would work their room. She knew it would be a VIP table by the amount of food they'd preordered, which the kitchen was already busy preparing.

Normally, she could have placed the chopsticks and cups in her sleep, but today she'd made such a mess of the settings on her first try that she'd had to redo them all. She'd been nervous ever since hearing from a neighbor that the gaokao scores would be posted that day at the district education bureau office. She'd taken the gaokao for the third time more than two months ago. Her supervisor, Auntie Bao, who liked to be wherever the gossip was, had offered to go check the postings during her lunch break.

After she finished the place settings, Hanwen reviewed with the chefs the sequence in which the dishes were to be brought out. At last, she went to the break room. The space reserved for the hotel employees was amongst the shabbiest in the building, barely large enough to fit a metal-framed twin bed that Hanwen had never seen anyone use. The once-whitewashed walls were covered with gray streaks. She picked up a small hand mirror that the waitresses kept in a utility cabinet and examined her hair in the reflection. She smoothed the flyaways that had risen from her scalp in the heat of the kitchen.

From the corner of the mirror, she saw Auntie Bao entering the room.

"Was my name there?" Hanwen said.

Auntie Bao leaned against the doorway and stared hard at her. "Heaven's lot is unfair for women," she finally said. "Look at you, waiting every day for the news, working so hard."

"So my name wasn't on there?" Hanwen swallowed. She refused to cry in front of her supervisor.

Auntie Bao shook her head. She lit a cigarette and took a drag. She raised her eyebrows whenever she inhaled, giving her the look of one generally unbothered and bemused by the world. "This is just the way things are. You studied more than the others, but it doesn't mean you're the one to get the reward."

Hanwen coughed at the smoke filling the small room. Auntie Bao was the first woman she knew who smoked. She herself might as well take up the habit now, too. If she was going to spend the rest of her life working in this hotel, she'd probably be promoted to a position like Auntie Bao's one day. She pictured herself, older, giving advice to another generation of young girls who arrived at the hotel, all while she puffed on a cigarette. Auntie Bao was about the same age as Hanwen's mother but seemed much older in appearance and demeanor. Though Hanwen's mother had led a difficult life, Auntie Bao's constant dissatisfaction gave off an even more pervasive air of fatigue.

"If you want to go home, I can make up some excuse for you, say you're sick," Auntie Bao said.

"No, I'll stay." It would be worse if she went home early. At least if Hanwen stayed through her shift, her mother would be asleep by the time she got home, and they wouldn't have to speak about the news. She dreaded her mother's reaction. For two years they'd settled into a rhythm, her mother usually in bed by the time Hanwen finished her shift. Her mother's class status had been rehabilitated after the fall of the Gang of Four, and she'd found a job as a cleaning woman in a factory cafeteria. She rose late at night to check whether Hanwen was studying—"If you don't pass the gaokao, we have no other hope," she'd say—before falling asleep again. Hanwen would warm up the rice and pickled vegetables her mother left for her—just that past year, they'd purchased an icebox—and then study until dawn. She got into bed just as her mother was leaving it, fitting her body into the place where her mother had slept.

There would never be another night or morning like that again, Hanwen realized.

"How do you stand it here, Auntie?" she asked suddenly. "You hate it so much. How can you come into work day after day like this? Don't you ever want to leave?"

Auntie Bao's laugh was almost indistinguishable from a cough. "Leave! Where would I go? When I first got this job, people were lucky to have any work at all. I don't have any other skills."

As if she'd seen the look on Hanwen's face, she added immediately, "It won't be like that for you, you hear? You're young, not like me. You still have time. Even if the gaokao didn't work out, so what? There are other things. People are opening up their own shops now, or you could go to trade school. Going to college isn't the only option. Don't get stuck here."

Hanwen couldn't imagine herself doing any of those things. Jobs like that were for people like the other girls who worked at the hotel, who were strong and sure of themselves in the world. She wasn't like them. The only thing she'd once had were her books and her smarts.

Huihong glanced into the room and huffed loudly at them. The other waitress had taken an almost immediate dislike to Hanwen when she'd begun working at the hotel.

"Yes? Do you have something to say to us?" Auntie Bao shouted at Huihong's back. "We've already set everything up for dinner." Auntie Bao was the only one who could get away with talking this way. Because of her seniority, no one dared to defy her when she smoked in the kitchen or left tasks to the younger women. Hanwen liked Auntie Bao for the older woman's no-nonsense attitude, but many of the other girls refused even to speak with her.

"The disrespect! That's what I mean," Auntie Bao said. "I'm just whiling my time away here, where they've left me like trash. You don't want to have to spend the rest of your life with people like them." She stamped out her cigarette and they rose to do one last check before the guests arrived. Hanwen looked down at her feet. In her rush, she hadn't put the mirror down carefully. Hairline fractures sprouted, branch-like, out of the base, splaying her reflection into pieces.

If she was being truthful with herself, she wasn't surprised that she'd failed the test for the third year in a row.

For the first year after her return to Shanghai, she stayed at home and didn't work. After she recovered, she began studying for the gao-kao in earnest. She had the free time she'd always dreamed of in the village, but studying was much more difficult now. Ever since she'd fainted, she had found it almost impossible to concentrate on words on paper for more than an hour at a time. When she tried to focus, a light feeling overtook her, just like the one she'd felt in the moments before she'd collapsed in the fields. She fought to keep the black only at the edges of her vision. Reading words was like looking at a point in the distance that would not stop shimmering from the heat rising all around it.

She withheld all this from her mother. When her score was lower the second year than the first, she told her mother the test had become harder, which wasn't untrue.

Earlier in 1980, they finally heard that the central government had sent out the directive that the sent-down youth policy, in place for almost two decades, would be terminated. By that time, the rules were only loosely enforced, in any case. She was never ordered to return to the village after she'd recovered.

At least when she'd been in the village, she received her work points, some of which she could redeem as money by the end of the year and send home. And her mother hadn't had to worry about buying food for her then. Hanwen had reached the age when she should have begun taking care of her mother, but she was still allowing her mother to sacrifice for her. The first thing Hanwen had noticed upon returning to Shanghai was how much older her mother appeared, her posture beginning to droop in the permanent half-frozen position of someone sweeping.

So after she failed the second year, she'd gone to her neighborhood subcommittee to see what jobs were recruiting. She'd been assigned a job as a restaurant worker in the Xinhua Hotel, a famous old building on the Bund. "You might as well be a cleaning woman like me," her mother protested, but Hanwen knew she wouldn't be able to do any better. She had no technical skills. She promised her mother she'd continue to study for the gaokao while she worked. They rode the same bus route to their respective jobs, her mother boarding at dawn, Hanwen squeezing in three hours later.

She was diligent. At the Xinhua Hotel, she retreated to the employee break room to read whenever she had a free moment. She felt strange, studying in the bare room, all alone. Whenever she remembered the first year of studying, reading by lamplight with the girls in her dormitory or with Yitian in the barn, she thought they hadn't known how fortunate they'd been. The exam had felt like a welcome surprise that year, a gift dropped in their laps at a time when there were no such things as gifts and had not been for a very long time.

Yitian had sent her letters occasionally. *Life in Beijing is both the same as and different from how we imagined it,* he wrote in one of his last ones to her. *History is all around me, but I feel far from it. The bus ride from the university to the Forbidden City is long, but I took it last weekend. I wonder what you would have thought of it, as I wonder often what you would think of this university campus.*

What was she to say to that? It was selfish of him, she thought, to imagine her in places she could never go. She missed his voice at the same time that she felt angry at him for telling her of a life she'd never get to access. Sometimes she went so far as to fill a pen with ink and sit at the kitchen table, but when she stared at the blank piece of paper, she found it impossible even to write a simple greeting, and instead the pen lingered heavily in her hand, empty of words.

Hanwen was to stand alert in case the table needed service, while Huihong and another waitress delivered food to the room. She hated this position, because the diners could go on for hours, and if you were stationed there, you could do nothing but wait.

When she saw the group of men gathering in the room, she wished she'd taken up Auntie Bao's offer to go home early. The host shoved a bottle of baijiu at her. She must have allowed her face to blanch, because the host shouted, "Come on, we need you to open it. We're here to eat and *drink*. We want to show our guests from Wuhan a good time."

"Yes, sir. Just one moment." She tried to make the voice sweet and elevated, but she could hear its thinness.

During her two years at the hotel, she'd learned there were two kinds of obnoxious guests: the first were rude to you without your input, but the second kind was worse for how they thought themselves charismatic and insisted on the waitresses' participation.

She tried to throw glances at the other girls when they brought dishes in, but they didn't meet her eyes. None of them liked her, which was why Auntie Bao had taken pity upon her. When Hanwen worked with them, she was often left to complete tasks by herself while they slunk to the hotel's garden, perching on the lips of the fountains to gossip.

They were so much more sophisticated than her, although they were all about her age. They did their makeup easily and talked openly about men and love and going out to bars on dates to drink. They'd stayed in the city when she was sent down, and it seemed to her that in those years, the village had softened her, while the girls who'd stayed in Shanghai had become harder around the edges, ready to bite. Their rudeness had started when they first commented on the fact that she studied every day. She wondered if their behavior was because there was so little to be had in their world, and her studying marked her as someone dissatisfied, who might one day have more. She felt like telling Huihong that she hadn't passed the gaokao after all, that, despite all her dreams, she would end up the same as all of them.

She was grateful when the food came. The men were occupied gnashing on the glistening parts of roast chicken and fried fish. Technically, the local governments were to operate on principles of austerity, but she'd seen enough dinners hosted here to know there were always workarounds. Night after night, she watched the diners devour dishes she and her mother would have died to try. Her mother wanted a life like this for her, she knew, like those of the men at the table and the well-coiffed women who were by their sides—not their drunkenness, but the ease of it all. What did they have that she didn't? Luck, that was all.

"We always appreciate the hospitality shown to us in the cities we visit," one of the guests was saying. She supposed that he was the leader of the visiting delegation, given the number of toasts that had been made to him. He had two snaggleteeth that caught on his lower lip when he closed his mouth, giving him the look of one perpetually on the verge of interrupting someone else.

"Of course. How could we let you come to Shanghai and not show you a proper reception?"

"If we didn't have you to guide us, I would never be able to understand the way you Shanghainese people speak."

There was laughter all around the table.

"Tell me," the man continued. "Is it true what they say about Shanghainese women? That they have the men here wrapped around their fingers? I heard they make the men cook, do the dishes, everything!"

"Our women are known for a certain *fiery* spirit," the host chuckled.

"Should we ask this young Shanghai lady what she thinks?" the visitor with the protruding teeth said. "She won't be afraid to give us her real opinion. Girl, what do you do for your husband? Or do you just order him around like all the other women of this city do to theirs?"

Her face was burning as she tried to think of something clever to say. "I'm—I'm not married, so I wouldn't know," she stammered. The words had sounded much better in her head. She resented the other waitresses, stationed in the safety of the kitchen. They were witty.

"How come you're not married?"

"I'm engaged," she said to the floor.

"Speak up. We can't hear you."

"I'm engaged."

"Oh, really?" He laughed again, as if her words had been some great joke. "Why do I have a feeling that's not true?"

"It is the truth," she mumbled, but he seemed to have grown bored of the conversation.

"Our teapot is empty. You haven't refilled it in a while."

The other men turned to each other and began another topic. No one watched her as she approached the table and refilled the teapot from a hot water thermos.

"You haven't filled my cup," the man said.

She was standing between him and another guest, leaning forward to reach the teapot. "What?" she said blankly.

"You filled the teapot, but you haven't poured our cups yet."

"Normally we don't—" She looked around, but none of the others were paying her attention any longer. Only a single man, seated directly across from where she stood, seemed to have heard. His eyes looked apologetic, but he didn't open his mouth or offer her any help.

She picked up the teapot and her hand buckled at its heaviness. Hot water spilled out of its spout, making puddles on the glass of the lazy Susan.

"Ouch," the man said. "Look what you've done." He gestured to his lap. Water was spreading down the sides of the tablecloth and onto his knee.

"I'm so sorry—I didn't mean to do that. I'll go—I'll go get some napkins for you."

She ran out of the room, so quickly that her heel snagged at the doorway and caught on a ripple in the carpet. Her body lurched forward. She hurried to straighten herself without looking back.

"What are you doing here?" Huihong said, in the kitchen. She was slouched against the metal counter, plucking her eyebrows while gazing at a compact mirror. "You're supposed to be back in the room."

"I spilled on the host. I can't go back in there." Her voice shook as she spoke. That old light-headed feeling was slowly creeping in on her.

"You *spilled*?"

"They kept leering at me, saying rude things. It was an accident. Could one of you switch with me?"

"You want us to switch with you? You were the one assigned there. It wouldn't be fair."

"Please."

"You need to go back. We'll all get in trouble if they need someone and no one is in there. Come on, *go*," Huihong hissed.

Hanwen was certain she heard the laughter of the two girls when the kitchen door swung closed behind her. She hated them at that moment. She hated everyone she worked with, and she hated the men in the room, who saw her as a nobody and thought they could do whatever they pleased with her. She hated even Auntie Bao, who only told her of the hopelessness of this place without showing her a single means of getting out. It seemed everyone had some idea for or of her, and no one wanted to ask what *she* thought. And now there was no place that she could ascend to, no test she could pass to show them that they were wrong.

She wiped hot tears from her eyes, her head swirling with anger and dizziness. She would have to go back. Counting to ten, she marched forward.

Her body banged against a hard shape in front of her. She jumped immediately at the impact. She looked up. It was the leader of the delegation.

"We were just calling for you. We want you to bring our last bottle of baijiu." When he smiled, his two teeth jutted out from the others like knives.

"I'm coming. I apologize," she managed, her nose and forehead still stinging. Dark spots were swirling in upon her vision, creating blots on the image of his face. Up close, she could see bits of crusted sauce at the corners of his mouth.

"Have you been crying? You look upset." His voice didn't sound sympathetic at all.

She turned her face to the floor so he couldn't look at her any longer, but he shoved his face underneath her chin.

"I'll be back in your room in just a moment," she said. She balled her hands into fists as she tried to fight off the darkness that was encroaching. She could not faint now, not here alone with this stranger.

She turned her head away again, but he put a finger underneath her chin, applying pressure and forcing her to look up. She winced immediately at the contact. No man had touched her face since Yitian.

"There's nothing to be afraid of," he said. "I just want to hold you."

She could feel that his hands on her forearms were much stronger than her own. She closed her eyes and squeezed as hard as she could, but the strength was draining from her arms. His hand slithered in between her elbows. His mouth was at her neck, hot breath on it. Then his hand was on her breast, squeezing it painfully, fingers kneading as if it were dough. She had never felt someone's fingers on that place on her body before and the pain of it was worse than she would have imagined, as if someone had dropped a pointed weight on her chest. She cried out, but her voice caught in her throat and came out jagged.

The man's head jerked up. Her body felt immediately breathless, free. She looked up: Huihong was standing at the entrance to the kitchen, staring at them.

"What are you doing?" Huihong said.

Hanwen looked back at the man. He met her eyes for a moment, the last she appeared to him as a person. When he looked back at her, his eyes had become a blank. She was nothing more than an object in his vision. She'd never felt more grateful to be invisible.

A voice came from the hallway, calling, "Boss? Boss?" The dim sound became louder as the person came closer.

The next time she turned to look at him, the man was gone. All she saw was the outline of a shoulder, turning the corner back into the main hallway. She felt immediate relief flowing through her. From the hallway, she could hear the other man's voice saying, "You were gone for such a long time, we thought you were throwing up in the bathroom."

She looked back to Huihong, wanting to explain.

"I—I," she stuttered. She looked down. Her dress was half un-zipped. There were bright red scratch marks along her arm.

Huihong looked her up and down, and then went back into the kitchen. Hanwen could hear the other girls talking, their voices leak-ing out of the door's seams. She heard her name repeated. "What the *fuck*," one of the girls said.

She leaned against the wall, catching her breath. Her hands had been clenched into fists all this time and when she released them, her palms were white and dotted with angry impressions where her nails had dug into them.

She wiped her face and walked, down the hallway, down three flights of stairs, and outside the hotel. It seemed that she had used all her energy on preventing herself from fainting earlier, and now her body moved behind her like an object being dragged. On the street, as she walked the five kilometers home, she brought her exposed arms limply to cover her chest. Shame pawed at her heart as she walked. She replayed the moments before the encounter in the hallway, imagining scenes in which she'd prevented the outcome. If she'd said no to pouring the tea, if she'd just gone home earlier like Auntie Bao had told her to do. With Yitian, whom she'd loved, she hadn't even dared to allow a kiss because she knew this certain danger had been lying in wait.

In Hanwen's neighborhood, she'd known an older girl named Peipei who lived in the upper-front unit of their building. She called Peipei "upstairs sister" and sometimes Hanwen went down to the shared kitchen to chat about school and the other neighborhood girls while Peipei cooked. They had to speak loudly to be heard over the sizzling wok. Hanwen liked her because she had a kind authenticity to her face and showed none of the haughty superiority of the other older girls.

Hanwen was twelve or thirteen on a winter evening when shouts from the outside alleyway had interrupted her quiet washing of her feet before bed.

"How could I have raised a daughter like you! Capable of such depraved acts!"

Hanwen and her mother rushed to the window to see what was going on. On the street, Peipei's father was screaming at his daughter, who cowered against the building wall. Before her mother shooed her away, Hanwen saw Peipei's father reach down to take off his shoe and throw it at his daughter. The next day, Hanwen found out through the neighborhood gossip that Peipei had been discovered having an affair with Uncle Cai, an older married man down the street.

At the neighborhood criticism session that followed, Peipei was forced to walk through the streets with worn shoes dangling from her neck, while the neighbors yelled after her, *Whore! Fox spirit! Loose woman!* Hanwen only vaguely knew what these words referred to, but she seized onto another one—after the parade, Peipei stood on a platform in front of the neighborhood and confessed aloud to her "error," which was the same kind of remark that Hanwen would receive when she answered a question wrong on her homework. What happened to Peipei terrified Hanwen, but that word meant consequences to behavior could be just as clear as a question on an exam. But what was the cause and effect of what that man had done to her tonight? All she'd done was stand quietly in the corner and do her job. There were rules governing behavior with men, how her actions would be read by them, ones that she'd been completely oblivious to.

She walked slowly home. Ever since she'd come back to Shanghai, she'd felt unaccustomed to the city air, heavy and artificial compared with that of the countryside. Now it seemed to reach like a snake, uncoiling and stuffing itself deep inside her.

Only when she arrived home did she realize she'd never zipped up her dress.

Thirty

The next day, when the time came for her to rise from bed and go
to work, she instead made the covers into a cave that swallowed
her. What she wanted was never to feel her own body again. She
hadn't washed since the night before, and though she wanted to scrub
herself away, she couldn't bear to look at herself naked. She wished
she could cry. At moments there was a welling in her chest and she
prayed for a release, but when she opened her mouth, she felt as if
she'd swallowed a stone.

Her mother returned at five thirty with a basket of vegetables in
her arm. She dropped them at the sight of Hanwen in bed. Potatoes
rolled down the floor.

"What's wrong? Are you feeling sick?"

"I failed the gaokao again, Ma." The words tumbled out of her
mouth. There wasn't any point in delaying the revelation any longer.

"What?"

Hanwen expected her mother to come and embrace her and her

body already shrank in anticipation of the contact. Instead, her mother broke into tears.

"It's not fair," she said. She flung one of the fallen potatoes against the wall. Dirt from the skin streaked the surface brown.

"I disappointed you," Hanwen said.

Her mother looked at her squarely—too objectively, Hanwen thought, not as someone's mother at all—and said, "It's not about you. How could this happen, after all I did?"

Hanwen was speechless as she watched her mother cry, then flip the sink's water on and off, then slam the cabinets. Resentment rose in her, a feeling that she'd never had toward her mother before. It was one thing to know her mother's wishes for her, another to hear about them day and night, to feel her entire life was an obligation to the sacrifices that had made it.

That night, Hanwen lay awake in bed while her mother flapped a fan in the air. Neither of them spoke. Her body felt too stiff even to turn. This, although it was one of the hottest days of the year and her skin stuck damp against the sheets. She didn't know when she fell asleep, but when she awoke the hot sun was already falling in shafts upon her and her mother was gone. She'd never before failed to feel the spring from the bed when her mother rose in the morning. It was as if her body's senses were all scrambled and she could no longer touch, smell, taste. Her mother left out breakfast for her, but she barely nibbled at it. Her mother didn't comment on the waste when she returned home. In the apartment alone, Hanwen experienced, alternately, the space as a sucking hole, borderless with its reach for her, or a pathetic remnant that encompassed the small limits of her past and future. She felt like a character in the background of her own life.

W hen her mother came home on the sixth day, Hanwen was still in bed. She turned her head to the wall and expected that they would again pass the evening in silence.

She felt her mother's calloused hands on her face. "My girl," she said. Her voice was warm, like the first sunny day after winter. "My poor girl."

Hanwen wasn't sure what had caused the sudden change, but this sympathy shocked her body into awareness. She felt the overflowing welling in her chest again, and this time when she scrunched her face the tears came and wouldn't stop.

"It's okay, my dear girl," her mother said. "We'll figure things out."

Hanwen buried her face in her mother's shoulder.

"I didn't want to disappoint you, Ma," she said.

"You haven't disappointed me."

She collapsed into her mother's arms then, sobbing until her eyes felt sore from the tears and her mother gently let go and rose to prepare dinner.

I n the storage room, there are some old plates and cutlery that need sorting," Auntie Bao said to her on her first day back to work. "Anything that's chipped or looks worn, the bosses want us to get rid of." She rolled her eyes. "We can take home anything we want."

Hanwen was never clear how much, or what, Auntie Bao knew. She was relieved she never had to use the lie she'd prepared, about being called to the suburbs to visit a sick relative. When she looked at Auntie Bao's aged face, her cigarette smoke curling around it, Hanwen wondered at this secret generosity it contained.

Even though the work was quiet and lonely, Hanwen was relieved that some power was being returned to her body. It once again became an object of use, rather than a heavy, clumsy appendage that she couldn't control.

The other waitresses sneered at her and ignored her each time she ran into them. One day, Huihong was waiting outside the dish room when she came out.

"Everyone knows what you did, Tian Hanwen," she said.

"I don't know what you think happened." She felt tired, like her tongue was heavy cotton in her mouth.

"You did something with the men that night, and now because you're Auntie Bao's favorite, she's letting you get away without doing any work, instead of punishing you like you deserve. We've all had to work even harder since you left, all because you were acting like a slut."

The last word, almost spat out, landed on Hanwen like a slap in the face. Her body burned as if she'd been encircled by the man again.

"Don't think you'll be able to rest like this forever," Huihong finished before walking away. The next day, Auntie Bao told Hanwen that she couldn't stay in the sorting room any longer. Huihong had complained higher up, reporting that there were people on the team who weren't pulling their weight.

She was assigned back to the dinner floor rather than the banquet rooms, a decision that she entirely understood. Under the bright, open space of the main dining room, so many tables and diners to service, nothing bad could happen. The work was less prestigious in the hotel's hierarchy and required more concentration to keep attuned to multiple tables at once, but she preferred the vastness of this space to the darker enclosures of the private dining rooms. She liked that, in the early hours of the dinner shift, sun still streamed through the skylights and the tall arched windows that covered almost an entire wall. She wove through the tables and the imported palm plants, delivering food for this table, taking an order for that.

She occasionally passed Huihong in the hallway, rushing into a banquet room. The other girl would make a big show of hurrying away. Otherwise, there were no remnants of what had happened to Hanwen.

It was many months later, in winter, the night a single diner came toward the end of her shift. Single tables were rare, the hotel's prices justified largely by their ability to impress guests. The waitresses moved more languidly by this late hour in the dinner service, taking more time to clean off the used plates and dinner tables on their tired feet. When the lone man waved her over in the middle of his meal, she wondered if she'd been too inattentive. The plates had hardly been touched.

"Is something wrong with the dish, sir?"

"You don't remember me, do you?" he said. "I've been coming the past two nights hoping I would see you."

"Sorry, you must be confusing me for someone else. There are many waitresses here."

"No, I'm sure it was you. I came here a few months ago with some others. Maybe you can hear it from my accent. I was with the group that came from Wuhan."

She peered at his face. He was wearing round black glasses with thick frames, making it difficult to see much of his features. But the glasses themselves struck a chord of recognition in her. Now she remembered. He was the man who'd been seated across from the visitor from Wuhan that night, who'd looked up at her from behind his frames. She'd wanted to discern that evening whether he was sympathetic to her, she recalled.

"Oh. Yes, I remember you."

"I wanted to find you that night. To apologize for the way he was behaving." He took off his glasses and rubbed his eyes, as if unsure what to say to her. With his glasses off, she could see him more clearly. He looked much younger without them, younger than anyone else at the table would have been. His chin sloped slightly upward at one side, giving him a look of constant contemplation. Every word he spoke gave the impression of being held in and carefully considered before being released.

"He's often—look, I've had to travel with him a lot, and he always gets drunk and acts that way. He's a good man when he's sober. It makes us—what should I say—uncomfortable, when he acts like that."

"Never mind," she said. "It doesn't matter now."

"It does matter. I'm sorry I didn't stop him from bothering you."

"Really, it's fine. We don't need to talk about it." She turned to leave the table.

"Wait, excuse me, waitress. Please come back."

She winced at this name being used for her, the same the man had used that evening.

"I just wanted to know—by the time I called him back to the dining room that night, he'd been gone for so long. I should have gone earlier. When he got back, his hair was messed up and I was afraid— did anything happen?"

His voice was low. Even the way he talked around the implication was too much for her. She hadn't told anyone what happened that evening.

"Nothing that bad," she said. "So you don't need anything else, right?"

"No—I suppose not." He put his glasses back on, and he looked older again, even wearier than before.

She left the table. She only looked back at him again when he stood to leave, sneaking a glance when his head was turned away. Standing against the high and gilded ceiling, he was short, barely taller than her. It was hard to imagine him in any sort of stance that would protect her. Her irritation at him dissolved and she felt a certain kindredness with him, standing there, shrunken and too small for the world.

She shook the feeling away and returned to her work. Thinking of men was a luxury. If she ever caught herself looking too long at the way a handsome man crossed the street with his confident strides, she scolded herself, reminding herself of what her mother's life looked like, her daily routines having hardly changed since Hanwen left for the village. A sense of expectancy permeated the corners of the house, as if, all this time, she was only waiting for Hanwen's return for a container to pour her hopes into. She could not disappoint her mother's hopes for something so small as love.

Her lie didn't stop the man from coming to dinner for the next two days. She deliberately ignored plates to be sent to his table and refused to go to him until other waitresses had no choice but to step in. She never turned around to look at him, but she was sure she would have seen him staring if she had.

Near the end of the second evening, Auntie Bao was waiting for her in the kitchen when she walked in.

"There you are." She handed Hanwen a plate of marinated tofu skins. "Give this to the man who's eating alone in the eastern corner of the room. Tell him it's on the house."

"That's not my table."

She turned toward the kitchen exit, but Auntie Bao called her back.

"Hanwen, you aren't a stupid girl, are you? That man has been watching you for two nights. He clearly has some interest in you, anyone can see that. Even I've noticed it."

"Maybe he does. I don't know."

"I'm trying to help you here. He's a good man. I spoke to him earlier, and he seems dependable. Nothing at all like some of the other men who come through here. He has a very good position. It's rare to meet someone like this, Hanwen, I'm telling you. And he already likes you. Get over your shyness and go over there."

Hanwen could see how Auntie Bao would see this situation, perform the addition and weighing, calculate how much there was to be gained.

"It's not because I'm shy. I just don't want to."

"Oh, I know. You have some secret boyfriend you never told us about?"

"It's not that, either."

"Good. Because even if you did, he wouldn't be as good a match as this one." She thrust the plate at Hanwen again.

Hanwen took the dish from Auntie Bao's outstretched hands but didn't move.

Auntie Bao's voice softened. "There'll be more opportunities for a future. But you have to keep looking for them."

Perhaps that was true, but weren't there other options besides trawling for a husband amongst the diners in this hotel? Would all her books go to waste?

She walked out of the kitchen and to his table with a dull inertia pushing her steps. "The boss sent you this," she said.

He looked surprised, before quickly rearranging his face into a more neutral expression. Quietly, he said, "I thought you weren't going to speak to me again before I left."

"I'm speaking to you now," she said lamely.

"I hope you don't mind me saying this—"

"I really just don't want to talk about it anymore." She didn't want an apology, not from the man who'd touched her and not from this other man, either. All she wanted was for the episode to be lost to the past.

"No, it's not that. What I wanted to say was, even before what happened that night, I noticed you. You acted differently than the other women. Somehow."

The line was a cliché, and besides, there wasn't anything special about her. She'd worried earlier about what would arise from all her learning, but now she had her answer. It could help her attract a man, that was all.

"My name is Wang Guifan." He paused. "I'm leaving Shanghai tomorrow morning, but I was wondering—can I send you a letter? I come to this city sometimes for meetings, so I may see you again soon. But I'd like to write to you in between that. If you don't mind."

His hand was shaking as he took down her address. Now that she'd spent more time speaking with him, she could tell that his nervous manner wasn't due to the subject matter, but rather something more closely related to his disposition. Perhaps he wore glasses to protect himself from being examined too closely. She wondered how a man like this could work in the government, how he managed to make himself endure over and over dinners like the one she'd witnessed.

Guifan's first letter came a week and a half later, so she supposed he must have written it as soon as he arrived back home. It was long and assured in tone, in contrast with the apprehensive way he spoke. His penmanship flowed neat and precise.

She was surprised by how she felt by the time she received his third letter. She would not have called the feeling love, not even close, but she had affection for him and his uncertain demeanor. He wrote to her in that third letter about how he seldom met new people because of how much he worked. His mother was anxious—he would be thirty-two that year—and had tried to set him up with the daughters of other women she knew. *I have rejected all her requests. For some reason, I feel attached to finding a love of my own.* It was a romantic notion against everything else she learned of him from the letters, which suggested a person dedicated to rationality and efficiency.

Only once did he write something that irritated her. *I hope you know this isn't because I want something from you.* This was much later, in the tenth letter. Any earlier and she might have stopped corresponding with him altogether, but by then she thought well enough of him to overlook this silly statement. Of course he wanted something from her. He could be honest and sorry for what had happened while also hoping something would come from his gift. Reality apportioned itself somewhere between what he said and what he wanted. Unlike Huihong, she felt oblivious about the world of men, and yet she wondered at how transparent they could be, how little they even knew of themselves.

Her correspondence with Guifan made her think about Yitian often, more than she had in a long time. By this time, she hadn't received a letter from him in months. She wondered what kind of person he'd become, away in college all these years. If she wrote a letter to him now, she wouldn't even know how to speak to him—he would have learned so much by now that all their old discussions would have seemed childish to him.

Her feelings at Guifan's letters were different, somehow less than how she'd felt when a letter from Yitian came. That had been with a sharpness beating in her chest, but she expected something mildly pleasant when she read Guifan's letters, that was all. It was not a matter of loving one person more than the other, she told herself; only that some feelings became out of reach with age and knowing, just as some doors closed in a life.

"If you two are corresponding like this, I supposed it's time for me to meet this man," her mother said when Hanwen told her Guifan was coming to Shanghai. "We'll invite him for dinner at our house."

"Do you really think he is so important?" Hanwen asked.

It was nighttime and her mother was boiling water for them to wash their feet before bed. She didn't look at Hanwen as the steam rose around her face and she said, "That's up to you to decide."

It was the first time her mother hadn't told her not to worry about marriage. Like a photograph, Hanwen could see herself from the outside, could decipher what all the letters and the dinner at her house signaled in symbols. Feelings were worth only as much as the performances that demonstrated them, and Guifan's behavior clearly pointed one way.

As she lay in bed awake that evening, she thought about what she wanted. She reached out to caress the skin on her mother's fingertip. They slept close enough so that they would have each other's warmth, but not close enough to touch. The things she held in the basket of her life, the ones she needed to ferry from here to there, were more than just her own. She'd been living in a limbo for so long, acting as if she could take the test over and over, that one day the results would save her life, that she wouldn't have to make any other meaningful decisions. She could see more clearly now that some things were not about want, but rather about the sacrifices one had to make to survive in this place, in this time. What her mother had been trying to tell her was that her dreams could no longer hold.

Thirty-one

JANUARY 1982

By ten p.m., Yitian already regretted allowing himself to be dragged to the dance, and it was only the second waltz of the evening. He watched from a corner of the repurposed canteen, which still smelled hotly of that evening's dinner of sautéed pork and wheat buns. The signs advertising the day's special of tomatoes and eggs, hanging from the canteen windows, shook from the collective stamping of the students' feet against the floor. Though it was the coldest time of the year and outside the ground was hardened in frost, there were so many gathered in the small space that his collar stuck to his neck and his palms were damp in his pockets.

On the dance floor, boys wiped sweat from their foreheads in grim concentration on the steps. His roommates had been trying to get him to attend a dance for four years, but he'd always refused. "But how will you ever meet a girlfriend?" Li Jianguo asked. Yitian laughed at how earnestly Jianguo asked the question. Other than Yitian and Mingliang, who had a wife back in Shaanxi, the boys of their dormitory, and all of the dormitories, went to the Saturday night dances held by the mathematics department with a sense of duty approaching the filial. Still, it was rare they actually *danced*. Their department was known to be notoriously dominated by boys. There was fierce competition to dance with the few girls, requiring a certain disregard of face that none of his roommates could quite surrender to.

He'd only agreed tonight because it was the last Saturday before they'd graduate, and his roommates wanted to spend all their last days together. Even though most of them would stay in Beijing, having taken instructor positions at their university or at others around the city, life afterward wouldn't be same. In just another week, they would all move out of the cramped room where they'd known each other so intimately—more intimately than they would have desired—for almost four years. What would also end was this period of freedom. They'd had untrammeled reign of the beautiful campus, their only job to sit and ponder questions. Yitian had spent so many evenings by the lake on its small pagodas, having heated discussions about poetry or the future of the country late into the night. Such occurrences would soon be luxuries.

At the dance, there seemed to be an order by which the boys approached the girls who'd lined themselves up along the walls. Those who didn't dance sat in chairs or stood in circles with their friends, tapping their feet to the music playing over the loudspeakers. Yitian was confronted with a feeling he hadn't had in some time, of stepping into a world that had already formed rules by which everyone else knew how to behave. In their dormitory preparing, the other boys had joked with him to ask someone to dance. He knew how they saw him, as the studious boy who always stayed in their dorm room, never speaking to or showing any interest in girls, the topic constantly on everyone else's minds. His roommates talked of wanting to kiss girls or even taking them to the lake, where the students were known to have sex away from the exposed spaces of their packed dorms. With each story, some knot inside him had loosened. He wondered now why Hanwen had been reluctant against even a kiss that year.

He tapped a beat with his shoe against the cement as he searched for Jianguo amongst the dancers. The scene slowly charmed him. His classmates had donned bright white outfits that illuminated them amidst the dim dance floor. Jianguo—his closest friend and bunkmate—had spent the past hour talking himself up in the dorm, declaring that tonight was the night he'd finally ask a girl to dance. He'd pomaded his hair, struggled into a necktie, and spritzed himself with a cologne of unknown provenance. Yitian didn't understand why Jianguo was so scared. Jianguo was also from Anhui Province, but he was the son of a local cadre and had city habits. He walked with a bearing so regal that Yitian was sure no girl would reject him.

Yitian finally spotted him near the corner of the dance floor and grinned. Jianguo had a girl with him, who looked to be quite attractive. He was spinning her around in agile circles. Soon, however, his excitement got the better of him. When he pulled her deeply to his body, one of the janitors who'd been working at the university for decades stepped between them. Jianguo was caught completely unawares when the old man waved a flashlight between the two and barked at them to break apart.

Yitian brought his hand up to his mouth to stifle a laugh. Jianguo was always so concerned about maintaining proper behavior and Yitian was sure this would mortify him. Still laughing, Yitian went outside to spare Jianguo any further embarrassment.

The cold of the air shocked him pleasantly. He was still warm from inside and he left his coat unbuttoned. The chill of a northern city had been one of the things that most worried him, but he now found that he enjoyed the crisp air on nights like these and that it was useful for work. The frigid and lonely months of winter sharpened his mind and allowed him to think clearly in a way he couldn't any other time of the year.

A few other girls, who didn't look like students, gathered under the eaves of the building. These girls seemed more carefree than his classmates, who were always busy either explaining something they knew or trying to cover up things they didn't. Anyone could buy a ticket for the dances, so it wasn't uncommon for outsiders to come, wanting to watch what the students of a famed university looked like on the dance floor.

Out of the pocket of his blue jeans—one of the currently fashionable items all the city youth owned, which his mother would surely have laughed to see him wearing—he fished out a packet of Zhongnanhai cigarettes and lit the last one nestled within the crinkled paper. He'd guiltily spent a portion of his savings on the expensive items when his classmates told him smoking helped with their concentration. He portioned out the cigarettes slowly while he wrote his thesis to make sure they would last.

He inhaled and returned to the problem he'd been considering before the dance. He was working in the field of Complex Analysis, which had been his favorite course at the university. On the first day of class, the professor began by writing a quote from Leopold Kronecker on the blackboard:

God made the integers; all else is the work of man.

"Why am I writing this, you might ask? Is this a mathematics course, or philosophy?" the professor asked rhetorically. "Humans have created what we call an *imaginary number*, *i*, that is equivalent to the square root of negative one, an expression that has no solution in the real numbers. These imaginary numbers form the basis of complex numbers, which can be written in the following form . . .

$$a + bi,$$

. . . where a is the *real part* and b is the *imaginary part*. And we can also think of complex numbers as a two-dimensional vector in the plane $\mathbb{R}^2$ where the x-axis is the *real axis* and the y-axis is the *imaginary axis*."

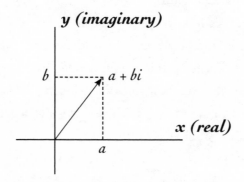

"But, Professor"—Yitian's hand had shot up—"does that mean real numbers are also part of the complex numbers, simply with imaginary part b equal to 0?"

"Yes. All real numbers are complex numbers."

It was an obvious insight that the rest of the class quickly moved on from, but Yitian had continued to ponder this model for the rest of the day. In it, he discovered a language to explain all the people he lived with, those who followed him and seemed cleaved off from his very self, invisible to the eye. As if another axis itself rose from him, extending far off into the past, and would continue to extend forever toward the future. He walked with their knowledge and weight, so that if he were to think of himself, it would be something like this:

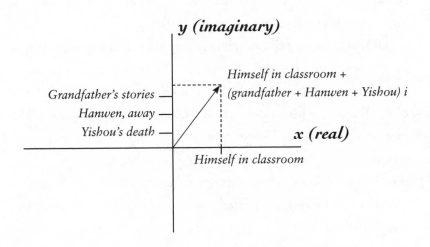

The model satisfied him. In the years since he'd come to Beijing, studying math had slowly cemented itself into his life and become an unchangeable truth of it, one he no longer fought against. At times he wondered who he would have become had he been allowed to continue studying history, but by now this fantasy seemed so far away that he couldn't imagine the details of how it would manifest. In his years at the university, he'd heard stories about the history department, of how certain events were left out of classes and professors dodged questions they didn't have the official language to answer. He understood what the dean had meant when he'd refused Yitian's request to join the department.

There had been no moment in which he discovered he loved math, not at all like the night in his youth when he became enraptured with his grandfather's stories. The steady accumulation of knowledge simply settled to become the factual sediment of his mind. He often caught himself thinking of everyday things within the mathematical frameworks he'd been taught, and then he would be surprised with how instinctual it had become to him.

He'd also found a certain relief in the numbers. Putting the pieces of these equations together was so different from anything he'd ever done before that it was as if he were entering into a new, fresh room of his life, one with its door closed against all the mistakes of the past. His math classes allowed him to create knowledge of his own—writing proofs, designing models—in a way that he'd never experienced in any other discipline, not even history. History had been his grandfather's knowledge, passed down to him, but mathematics felt like stumbling upon an ancient text in a library, one that no one else had ever seen before.

He reached the end of his cigarette. He stamped it out onto the ground and noticed that the group of girls was staring at him.

"Excuse me, comrade . . . ," he heard a voice call out. One of the girls from the circle was walking toward him. She marched with purpose, as if he'd taken something from her.

"You were leaving. Can I walk with you for a bit?" she asked. She had the rolling accent of a Beijinger, so he'd been right that they were locals. Her voice was loud, as if she were performing in a play. The two girls behind her laughed hysterically with their hands over their mouths, gripping each other's arms to manage their shaking bodies.

So her friends had sent her to make fun of him for their amusement. Normally, this would have embarrassed him—a reminder of his fundamental difference, that he was still an unmannered country boy teased by the city dwellers—but tonight the mood left by the dance made him too calm to care.

He was surprised when she continued to speak, her voice quieter this time as she turned toward him and said, "They dared me to come talk to you. But there's something I want to ask you about. Will you say yes?"

There was something different in the way she said this sentence, her voice stripped of the act, which made him agree.

"He's asked me to go on a walk with him," she announced, turning her head back to face her friends. He was wondering if he'd been tricked into some elaborate game, when she turned back to him and added, again in the low voice he was not sure why he trusted, "Sorry. I have to say something to explain to them." And then back to her friends. "Don't wait for me! We'll pass by my home."

This final statement made the girls' laughs ascend to their highest pitch yet. As they walked away, the sounds of their squeals reminded Yitian of the way cats screamed in heat.

"Should we go by the lake, then?" she said briskly, as if there were no question about it. He liked how Beijingers reminded him of the people from his village in how straightforward they were.

They walked quietly by the lake for a while. During the daytime, the paths and benches around the water were busy with people exercising and students studying, but this late on a weekend the only others were lonely wanderers and couples who'd snuck out together. It was the singular time of the week he could access quiet, so he looked forward to these evenings when everyone else went to the dances and he walked around the lake alone. In his dorm room, no word could be spoken without inhaling the thick air of so many young boys' bodies cramped together; no feeling, even loneliness, could be experienced in solitude.

The remnants of music from the dances, the drawn-out strings of the waltzes and dull thumping of the discos, floated to them, but the notes seemed like those of a faraway world. While they walked, they could hear, seated at the benches or tumbling from the bushes, the low, suggestive mumbling of boys and the flirtatious pitch that girls' voices took on in response. To sneak out on a cold night like this would have required a particular amount of determination.

"You don't remember me, do you?" the girl asked after they'd walked for some minutes. Her breath formed a cloud in the air.

He'd been staring ahead but turned now to examine her. He noticed she was clutching her arms with cold, but when she spoke, there was no sign of shiver in her voice.

"I always wondered if I would see you here," she said. "My friends and I often come to the dances, just to watch. I thought it might be you tonight, and then when you finally stepped into the streetlight, I was sure."

She looked at him and laughed aloud suddenly. "Forgive me, you must think me so strange! Sometimes I think that everyone can already understand the thoughts going through my head. I was the one who let you into the dean's office, in the history department that day."

He closed his eyes and pictured. Walls narrowing in on him, the speckled linoleum floor, footsteps, and then a low voice. A low voice.

He opened his eyes, looked into her face, searching for it—there. There it was, the large mole in her cupid's bow. He remembered it clearly now, the way his eyes had focused on it when she'd come up to him in the hallway.

The rest of her face was unique, and he was surprised he'd forgotten it. Striking in its own way. It was wide but tapered into an unlikely narrowness around the chin. Her mouth was large and expressive, the kind that made it easy to both smile and frown, and which would not be able to hide any emotion. In a way that was rare, her face seemed entirely suited to the person, at least as he knew her so far.

"You know," she said, "I've been wanting to find you because I've wondered all this time whether you were doing okay. For some reason it stuck with me, how badly you wanted to change your major."

He thought about his naked display of emotion that day with shame. Even now, the sight of her face made him remember the feeling of his heart dropping at the loss of a dream.

"Are you surprised that I remember after all this time?"

He nodded.

"That was my first week on this job. I was so nervous. My mother had to ask all sorts of people in order to get me this position. In this fancy university, you know."

So the memorable moments of their lives had intersected.

"But think—I let you into the dean's office, risked my job for you on my first week, and you don't even remember me!"

"Did you get in trouble?"

"No, even though I was very scared." She laughed. "I didn't know anything back then. Now I know all the tricks. If you ever want to go into the dean's office to see him now, I can help you."

"So you still work in the history department."

"I do."

"That's why I've never seen you. I never walk by there anymore."

They'd walked halfway around the lake. She pointed to a cluster of staff dormitories, low buildings with roofs of aluminum sheets. "Here's me. All the secretaries live here."

"Well, goodnight then," he said.

She peered at him expectantly. When he didn't say anything else, she looked disappointed. He was aware of this, and yet couldn't say any more. He knew there had to be some uncaging, a release of his heart to allow it to exist in the space outside of his chest. How easy that had been when there hadn't yet been a closing there.

She said goodbye and walked away.

"Wait, thank you—" he realized he did not know her name.

She turned back.

"What is your name?"

"Ren Mali," she said.

"Mali," he repeated. "Like this?" He drew the characters into the air.

She nodded.

"Ren Mali, I just wanted to say thank you. For letting me into that office three years ago. Even if it didn't work out. I'm fine, actually. Just so you know."

She smiled, and this time he returned it.

"It's a nice name," he said.

"My parents only wanted me to be a good worker. Nimble and fast. Isn't that funny? The students here all have better names, about writing, or scholarship, or the future of the country. Your parents knew what kinds of people you were going to be."

"Not me," he said. "My name isn't about any of those things. Tang Yitian."

"Yitian? Like this?" She drew in the air with her index finger, the wrong characters, meaning tranquility.

He shook his head. It was the kind of elegant name a scholar might have.

"Then show me." She stuck out her palm, motioning for him to write the correct characters on it. Just the thought of such an intimate gesture frightened him, but he didn't know how to refuse. He placed his index finger on her palm. Her skin was soft against the pad of his finger. He wrote 唐一田.

"Oh, a single field," she said.

He nodded. The yearning for something simpler.

She closed her hand around his name.

After she left him, he watched and waited until a light came on in a corner of the building, before continuing to walk, alone, around the lake.

The thought that crossed his mind, that she might like him, seemed almost impossible. She was an attractive girl from Beijing, and he was a boy from the countryside with strange habits. The only girl who'd ever liked him had been an aberration, only possible because it happened in a different place, a place that had fooled her. He'd hardly even talked to a girl with love in mind in the years since then. It was not that he never found girls, on campus or in the city, attractive, but rather that it was simpler to limit the ways he thought of them.

The sounds of snores already filled his dormitory when he returned an hour later. He climbed up into his bunk. Jianguo still wasn't back, and Yitian hoped that perhaps his bunkmate had taken the girl he danced with out on a walk.

His body still felt sweaty from the dance, and he lay awake for some time with the heavy sensation of the blanket pressing upon his sticky skin. He was surprised that when he thought again of Mali, he felt himself growing hard. He felt even more uncomfortable now than before, and kicked the blankets aside, despite the cold. He lay like this, ignoring the chill creeping up his bones, until the cool air softened him.

Thirty-two

DECEMBER 1984

Yitian was relieved when the bell rang to signal the end of class. He stopped speaking midsentence and dropped the piece of chalk, which had almost crumbled entirely in his fingers during the course of his lecture. The cloud of dust he clapped up hung in the air momentarily before dissolving.

No matter how many times he taught, he would always feel relieved when class ended. When he first began teaching, he'd stammered through lectures, which felt longer than the hour they actually were. The rows of open-faced students staring up at him looked completely puzzled. In the year that had passed, he'd learned that the speed at which his mind worked was not the same as others', so it was necessary to show all the intermediate steps that he could navigate through intuitive jumps. Slowly, the expressions on students' faces had eased.

"Professor Tang," a student called through the din of the others packing up their book bags. His head jerked up. He still wasn't accustomed to being referred to this way.

"When you derived the function of growth, I didn't understand why you had to take the inverse of the matrix . . ."

He was teaching the mathematics curriculum for economics majors this semester. The students were demanding and unafraid to challenge him when they thought he'd made an error. At nineteen, he'd been shy, preferring to spend hours in the library rather than ask a professor a single question.

He hurried through a response to the student. Normally, he would have taken more time, but today, his department chair had asked him to come to his office as soon as class got out. He liked the chair, Professor Wu, who'd supervised his thesis. Whenever Yitian went to his office with questions that he was sure were basic, Professor Wu acted as if they were in fact some deep principle about the complex numbers. But Professor Wu never called him into his office, and there could surely be no good reason it was happening now. The possibilities ran through his mind: some student had finally gone to complain about him for his bad teaching, there was no more funding for his position; perhaps this was the day he would be fired.

But he was admitted immediately into Professor Wu's office and met with a smile.

"I won't keep you with any small talk," Professor Wu said. Yitian sat hunched in the stuffed leather chair across from the desk, his hands already sweaty as they gripped the armrests. "I called you in here today to tell you some good news. The university will be able to send some students as visiting scholars to a university in the United States. They asked us for recommendations, and I've nominated you.

"It's only a yearlong visiting scholarship, at this point. But all the students we've sent in the past have managed to extend the term. Then you can get a foot in the door and apply for a doctoral degree at an American university."

Yitian struggled to reorient himself. His classmates, particularly those who'd grown up in big cities like Beijing or Shanghai, had spoken of going abroad as early as their first year in college. They talked of Japan, Australia, England—but America was considered the best of all. He kept quiet during these conversations, because already he felt like he was testing fate by making it to Beijing all the way from his small village. Only at night, when all the boys of his dormitory were asleep, would he sometimes allow himself to dream of what America might be like. He imagined cloudless skies that shone so much they would appear to be white and people who spoke kindly to one another at the store while waiting patiently in line. Tall buildings neat against the blue air. On college campuses, students would walk out of a history lecture discussing the topics with one another fearlessly and wouldn't sleep six to a room.

"Is there a test I need to take?"

Professor Wu's mouth opened in surprise, then closed. "Forgive me—sometimes I forget where you're from. There's no test. We've submitted your name. All you need to do is fill out a form with your personal information. One of the department secretaries will help you."

"But how will they know that I'm smart enough to go to their university?"

"The fact that we're endorsing you will be evidence enough. They'll put you through a review process, of course, but there shouldn't be any problem now that we've recommended you. They unofficially reserve a few spots for students from our university every year.

"You should be pleased," Professor Wu said after some time. "This is a good university, one of the best in the world." He repeated the name, but Yitian shook his head. He'd never heard of it.

"Is it as good as ours, professor?" Their university was the only one his parents knew existed, and one of the few that he'd known of himself before enrolling.

Professor Wu laughed. "Much better than ours. In fact, once you go abroad, I think you'll find that most people haven't even heard of our university. We don't stay here because it's a famous university. Many of us could go elsewhere in the world if we wanted. We stay here . . ." He sighed. "We stay here because we believe in this country."

"I don't mean to be rude, professor, but then why do you suggest that I leave?"

Professor Wu paused, then said, "Let me speak candidly. Of course, this stays between us. The situation here—it's not entirely open. It won't be for many years, decades perhaps. There's a limit to what you can reach here, right now. Better you go abroad, get credentials. Maybe you'll come back, and by that time, things will be different."

"But what will I do, after this degree? Here, or there?"

"Why, you'll be a professor, of course. It's what all of us here have done. We receive graduate degrees and then teach mathematics."

Yitian's chest filled with pride at this possibility. Ever since coming to university, he'd wondered at how incredible the lives of the professors seemed. He couldn't imagine any version of a life more perfect than a job in which he spent days reading books and living on a quiet university campus. "Do you really think I'd be able to do something like that? Be a professor?"

"Boy"—he'd never addressed Yitian so familiarly—"I've been teaching here for many years, and I know when I meet someone like you, who is so suited to academia in both skill and temperament. I can't imagine you doing anything else, and quite frankly, I don't think you'd be very good at it if you tried.

"I went to America last year with a visiting delegation," he continued. "Life there is different. You wouldn't believe it. You will enjoy it, I'm sure."

Yitian wished he could do this himself. Go abroad for just a few weeks as a tourist to try things out, wear that new country like a cheap shirt only meant to last a season. What Professor Wu was suggesting was entirely different—to commit to years, possibly a whole new life, in the country.

"Smile a little, boy. You should celebrate. Let loose, for once."

It didn't seem to matter what he thought. After he left the office, Yitian had the distinct sense he'd been bound to a future he hadn't decided for himself. Professor Wu had presented the nomination as an opportunity he could choose whether or not to take, but the more he spoke, the clearer it was that Yitian's future had already been determined. Yitian looked at his watch—he'd had the sensation of sitting in the office for hours, but in fact his fate had been announced to him in only thirty-five minutes.

So it will begin next year?" Mali asked that evening when Yitian told her and Jianguo of the meeting. She sat in a chair in the corner of the single room he shared with Jianguo. His roommate was lying on his back, lazily flipping through a book in bed. Since moving into the university's instructor dormitories two years ago, they'd grown accustomed to the freer space, and Yitian could not believe he'd once lived together with so many for so long.

"I suppose. If I get it, I mean."

"How many people did they choose?" Jianguo asked.

Yitian tried to remember if Professor Wu had mentioned such a detail. "I don't think he told me that."

Jianguo sighed and mumbled something.

"What did you say?"

"I said, I don't even know if I would want to go, anyway. Americans think they're better than everyone else. Who knows if it's even any good over there?"

Jianguo ignored them for the rest of the evening. He went through his book rapidly, flipping each page with such force that Yitian feared he would rip one of the thin pages in half. Yitian hurried with Mali out of the apartment to walk her home, not wanting to spend any more time in the tense room.

He and Mali had developed this routine over the year and a half that they'd now been dating. Three nights a week, she would come to their dorm room after dinner at the canteens and sit for a while. Afterward, he walked her across the lake to the dormitories where the university staff lived in triple bunks, eight to a room.

"I hope Jianguo will get over it," Yitian said.

"Doubtful," Mali said. "You can bet he and his family have been talking about going abroad for years. And now *you* get the chance? You, a country boy?"

"It's strange because, to be honest, I've spent a lot of time feeling jealous of *him*." His best friend's life in university had seemed much easier than his. Jianguo's father was so good at mathematics that Jianguo had been able to ask him for help, and his mother mailed him extravagant desserts every month whenever she feared Jianguo was becoming homesick.

"But I've done better than him on tests before," Yitian said. "He's always recovered eventually." Each time Yitian did better on a test, it was balanced out by Jianguo scoring higher on the next. He felt thrilled, though he was too embarrassed to say it aloud. He, a boy from a small town, who'd struggled all alone and had no wind at his back, had done the thing that Jianguo couldn't.

"It's all well and good when you do better than him on one test, but what do you think you all were working toward all this time? Going abroad, going to America—that was what all the tests and good grades were for. And now you've managed it, but he hasn't."

If Mali said this, it was probably true. She had an uncanny gift for understanding the moods of others. The strange thing was that Yitian never even noticed her watching other people. She said this ability of hers was a gift that came from growing up in Beijing, two kilometers from Zhongnanhai, during the worst years of the Cultural Revolution, when it was not uncommon for people who appeared to be friendly neighbors turning and reporting on others. She'd had to keep alert, monitor people's faces for any sign of guile, in order to protect herself and her family.

When they stopped to sit on a bench by the lake, he asked her, "You said everyone wanted to go to America. Including you?" He turned his head to seek out her face, but she was staring into the bushes beside them. They'd crawled into one of those crevices in the undergrowth two months ago and made love for the first time, joining the other students who came here for intimacy in a city where nothing else was private.

"I've never imagined going to America," she said.

"What about now? Can you imagine it?"

She scrunched up her eyes. "Palm trees. Skyscrapers. Something like that?" She laughed, "I don't know! I'm not a student in this great university, like you. You all dream about the future and all these places you'll go. I wouldn't even know how to think about something like that."

He suddenly could not imagine going to America alone. When they'd begun dating, he'd supposed that her family was well-off by virtue of the fact that they lived in Beijing. He'd visited her home many times now, taking the bus from campus, and had learned her family lived in just one section of a narrow hutong home, small and cramped, multiple beds stuffed in a single bedroom they all shared. They shared a public toilet and wash facility with all the other families in the alleyway. Neither she, nor any of her siblings, had even considered going to college. She'd fought for her independence by living away from her parents, even though they had a home in the city and she could have ridden the bus each day. The cramped secretaries' dormitory wasn't so different from their hutong, but she liked the small collection of her objects on the shelf above her bed, the sense that she owned a small piece of the world for herself.

He knew women who wouldn't have given him a second glance before would chase after him, now that he had this opportunity to go to America. He didn't blame them, but neither could he say he wanted to marry a person like that. He was relieved that Mali hadn't even brought up the possibility. He would think about it later, on his own. So much had happened in one day.

Thirty-three

AUGUST 1985

Mali invited her entire family to the wedding: her parents, two brothers, and three sisters.

"We'll have to get your parents here from Anhui. And your brother, too, right?" she asked him.

He'd only ever mentioned his brother in passing to her; she would have assumed that he was still alive.

When he told her that Yishou was dead, she gasped, "I never knew. When did he die? I'm so sorry."

He mumbled through the barest of details, that the death had happened long before he'd met her. Even though many years had passed, saying the words still made his voice shake. Perhaps because he'd barely spoken about Yishou in all this time, the death never had the chance to congeal into a truth he could hold steadily in his mouth.

She said, "So young! What a life he could have led. You must have been very sad."

"Not as sad as my father. He cared for my brother the most, more than anyone." He'd never said this aloud before, but now that he did, he was sure the words were true.

"What happened? How did he die?" She had so many questions. He was suddenly irritated. He didn't want to share this part of his life with her. He'd only ever known her in Beijing, long after Yishou's death and after he'd stowed the event away into the compartment of his life before. He wanted to keep these parts of his life separate, far enough away from each other so that they would never touch.

"An accident. A sudden sickness."

"What kind?" When he did not respond, she put a hand under his chin and brought his face to hers. "Tell me," she said, but he turned his face away. He pretended to go to his bookshelf to examine a spine. He could hear her crying. He felt sorry for her, but still he couldn't make himself tell her what had happened or even give her comfort. He left the room, letting the lock of the door click gently after him, walked down the hallway, and fled to the lake.

They rarely argued, and this was the first time he'd made her cry. If they ever disagreed, it was because she said he was closed off and secretive, a mystery to her. Her reaction scared him, the height of the emotion she'd felt when he refused to say more. He didn't want to lose her, but this was a threshold they could not cross together.

But when he returned to his room, she called his name. "Yitian, I managed to get us a discount on the banquet room," she said.

She never brought up his brother again, and he felt enormously grateful to her for pretending that the conversation never happened.

Yitian told his mother he'd asked a woman from the city to marry him. He assumed that she would be surprised, as she hadn't even known he had a girlfriend. He wasn't prepared for the letter she sent back, detailing the immediate preparations she'd make for the wedding in the village—the meeting space she would reserve, the extended family to invite, the fireworks they'd purchase for the wedding procession through the streets. Yitian wrote her back, explaining they'd already booked a small private room in a roast duck restaurant in Beijing and invited all the guests—although of course his mother could invite others, if she wished. Most of the guests were Beijingers Mali knew from childhood or his classmates from university. Weddings like this, in midgrade restaurants, were popular among young couples who married in the city, and they wanted to be like their peers. They'd set the date for three weeks before he was due to leave for America, so that when he arrived he would be able to quickly apply for a spousal visa for Mali.

"I suppose this is what your new wife, who is from a large city, must want," she wrote back to him. "Likely, she thinks that all our old traditions are beneath her. You are an adult, so I cannot tell you what to do. All I can do is warn you against marrying someone outside your own social class. Your wife will never understand you, and she will look down upon you for the rest of your life." He imagined his mother, furiously dictating the contents of the letter to a village child who could help turn her anger into written text.

He wanted to explain to her that Mali was not that kind of person, that her family, like the small party they would have on their wedding day, was extremely modest. But he knew his mother wouldn't be able to understand how city people could also be poor. At middle age, she couldn't rewrite her understanding of the world's contours and how money and poverty mapped onto city and country. She'd think he'd had the wool pulled over his eyes by the city's bright lights.

Still, she said she would attend. It was her only son's marriage, after all. Yitian sent her some money, just enough to cover the multiple train rides and transfers all the way from Anhui to Beijing. These days, he was carefully apportioning the money his American university had loaned him before his departure. He'd promised he would pay them back as soon as he could, but in reality he had no idea of when that future would be, or if he would ever reach it all.

On the day of his mother's scheduled arrival, he went to wait for her at the Yongdingmen Station. He stood amidst the crowds on the platform, jostling to get a good look at the lines of people exiting each train. He didn't know which one she'd be arriving on, so he had to pay very close attention.

It had been seven years since he'd last seen her. Afraid of his father, he'd never returned to the village. The only communication he had with his mother were the letters he sent to her before important holidays, each with a small amount of money enclosed, which he tutored students in math to save. He asked her to keep some for herself to use, and then to lay out the rest at Yishou's grave on his behalf. His mother only occasionally wrote back, but he was sure she read every single letter. Once, after he'd written to say that the buns they served in the canteens lumped up in his throat and slid down like gravel into his stomach, she'd mailed him a burlap bag filled with crusty rice, his favorite snack. When the rice arrived, he'd held a large clump in his mouth, letting his spit soften the hard edges until they were pure mush. He'd swallowed the rice, nearly weeping.

As he waited for his mother to arrive, he saw, over and over, women that he thought must be her. They had the same broad shoulders, firm calves, no-nonsense hairstyles. The terminal grew dark. When he finally found her, her eyes were the only part of her that hadn't changed. Even then, the flurry of wrinkles etched around them seemed to bring the whites out in brighter relief than before. She was looking anxiously around the terminal, frightened by the expansive space and the crowds of people who rolled around them in waves.

He ran to her, calling out, "Ma, Ma," echoing the sounds of so many other boys in the terminal.

When they finally stood in front of each other, he was speechless. She held his face between her hands and rubbed his cheeks over and over with her thumbs. He looked at her, trying to find his reflection in her eyes. He realized he must have changed even more than she had.

He was afraid of how she might react when she met Mali, whose hands had the softness of someone who'd never had to do hard labor. His mother might say something too direct, not even conscious of how rude she sounded. After arriving in Beijing, however, she became quiet and demure, as if the city had pulled a thin layer of gauze over her and dulled her body into stillness. Whenever she spoke she covered her mouth, hiding her dark teeth and afraid that her country accent wouldn't be understood.

"She is extremely beautiful" was all his mother said about Mali. He was sure she didn't mean this; it was never Mali's beauty that he'd found remarkable.

For the wedding, Mali lined her mouth with red rouge and warmed her eyelashes curly. He watched her getting ready that morning, holding twin matches, just blown out, to her eyes, opening them wide so that she wouldn't blink. They got dressed together. He wore a white button-down shirt and gray slacks that didn't quite fit his skinny frame, and she, a dress made of creamy silk taffeta with puffy half sleeves and a ruffled bib, borrowed a week ago from her older sister. The dress ended at midcalf, a fashionable cut from which the milky skin of her legs emerged.

Yitian resolved to be like her on this day, clinking her glasses with the guests heartily. She used her own chopsticks to force food onto their plates and made loud jokes about which of their friends would be the next in line to be married.

The gathering was small. They'd invited just two round tables of ten people each. Yitian and Mali sat at one together with her family and Yitian's mother. Seated around the other table were all their friends. Everyone was there except for Jianguo. Yitian was not surprised when Jianguo refused the wedding invitation, mumbling something about a prior engagement. He finally understood. He was a country boy, who, by being invited to America, had exceeded the cup allowed to him, the types of things that better-off people could condescend to admire.

As the lunch wore on and on and guest after guest approached them with toasts, what he wanted most was to slip outside. Now that he was surrounded by the raucous noises of so many people, he could only think of those who hadn't come. The tally of the missing weighed much heavier than those present. Jianguo, Yishou. His father and his grandfather. Hanwen. That morning, he'd briefly wondered how she'd act on such a day. She was not capable of Mali's blissful unawareness. Hanwen, getting ready in the morning, would have acknowledged the same weighted heaviness he'd felt all day, the intuition that one part of their lives had irrevocably finished to allow this new one to begin. As he looked back upon the past few years, he could see this fundamental principle guiding events through one another. Each opening had necessitated a closure enabling it, the hinge upon which the door had swung.

He put his hand around Mali's shoulders and took the hem of her sleeve between his fingertips, rubbing the outlines of the embroidered eyelets. "Let's go outside for a moment," he whispered in her ear. She turned to him and laughed without registering what he'd said, her breath, hot with alcohol, blowing upon his cheek.

"Ma, thank you!" she said, raising a toast to Yitian's mother.

Just then, Xie Han, Mali's cousin, shoved a camcorder in front of Yitian's face. He'd leased it with his own money and had been recording videos all day—his wedding gift to the couple, he said.

"What would you like to say on this momentous occasion?" Xie Han bellowed. The butt end of the bulky plastic device bumped Mali on her shoulder. Xie Han, who had already toasted the couple three times, was too drunk to notice. Yitian worried whether the expensive piece of equipment would make it through the night.

"Hello," he said, turning to the camera. "Thank you to everyone who has come to celebrate with us today."

"No, no, you have to say something more than that!" Xie Han said. "Don't be so formal."

"What would you like me to say?"

"Say something in ENGLISH! Since you're going to AMERICA!" Xie Han slurred, but Yitian demurred. The English words sounded misshapen in his mouth and he was embarrassed to have them recorded.

He tapped his foot to the beat of music that played over the speakers and counted the number of songs that were left until their reservation would expire.

Mali's father, a short and plump balding man, approached him for his second toast that day. He hadn't liked Yitian the first time Mali had brought him home, refusing to even acknowledge him across the dinner table piled with food that Mali's mother had prepared. When Yitian left that evening, he heard, through an opened window, her father refer to him as a peasant. But after Yitian announced he was going to America, her father's entire demeanor changed. Yitian was not sure if he would ever be able to see Mali's father as anyone other than the man who'd diminished him to a single word. He dutifully clinked his glass low against his father-in-law's and called him Ba. He assured her father he would take care of his daughter, because he knew that was what was expected of him as a husband. Money, stability, and safety were all his domain. But whenever he looked at Mali, he felt sure that she was the one more likely to offer him the protection.

As their wedding gift to the couple, Mali's parents paid for them to have a room in the hotel attached to the restaurant. Long after Yitian first wished they would, their friends rose from the tables and carried them to their hotel room. He was tossed haphazardly onto the bed, while Mali was placed gently onto the comforter, so that her styled and shiny hair would stay in perfect place. Their friends milled about in the hotel room for a few minutes, making jokes about how the guests would creep outside their door for the entire night to keep watch. In his village, the tradition was for the children to crouch under a windowsill to confirm the marriage was consummated, but in the city there was a hope for privacy. Their friends eventually filed out and left them in a silence that felt sudden after all the day's noise.

The hotel had scattered rose petals over the bedspread. Wondering where they'd come from, he picked one up and rubbed it between his fingers. It was only made of fabric and plastic, after all.

"I thought my cousin would never leave!" She laughed and kissed him firmly on the mouth. Her face still had the glow of excitement and alcohol. She washed her makeup off in the bathroom and returned to the bed, pressing her body to his. It was the first time they were able to lie next to one another without fear of a roommate walking in.

Like most other students, the only times they'd been able to be together intimately were late at night by the lake, where they went and moved their bodies with hurry and frenzy. Every time they pushed themselves against each other, Yitian was surprised at how much he could feel her want. It was an experience unlike any he'd ever known, to be desired by someone like this, allowing himself the rare moment of being taken out of the shadows of the past and of occupying his body wholly as it existed in the present. He'd felt desire like this on evenings with Hanwen—always at night, after the dark had set in and made her skin bright and almost see-through—but he could not have said if she reciprocated.

The first time he and Mali slept together, when they'd fumbled in the dirt while they took off their clothes, a warmth had spread through his face and limbs. Everything he wore had strange tightness and elastic that he'd never noticed before. He felt awkward lying outside there, and worried that he would not know where to go on her body. But then she'd covered his body with hers, and all the embarrassment of a moment earlier had disappeared. When the time came, the heat of her told him like a route on a map.

He did not grow hard now as she hugged him.

"I'm a little tired tonight," he said.

"All right."

He could hear the disappointment in her voice, but she loosened her arms. He turned his back to her and gently moved her arms to drape them across his shoulders. In this way, her body acted like a larger parentheses to his. He fell asleep quickly and dreamed he was in an earlier time, when he could feel the body of his grandfather's next to his, as small as Mali's. He placed his palm against the sheets and could swear that he felt the cotton poking out. How many times his mother had kept patching over those holes, how each stitch always required another by the next season.

They didn't see the video from their wedding day until their second month in America. The tape arrived in a bulky brown envelope bearing stamps suggesting a long journey. Inside, there was a letter from Xie Han explaining that he'd waited to send the tape so that it could welcome them to their new country.

They watched. Her cousin's hand, shaky and drunk, scanned the smoky banquet room with the video camera, focusing on details that Yitian only now remembered. Piles of sunflower seeds picked over by the guests, duck bones licked so clean they shone, asymmetric spills of Coca-Cola on the white tablecloth. One by one, images came into the frame, at first out of focus and then sharp and defined. Then, suddenly, Xie Han dropped the camera. It landed loudly on the table. Xie Han cursed, but the camera was still filming. The lens settled on the crumpled napkins piled upon the lazy Susan, and then on Yitian's mother in vignette on the old tape. While the shouted glee around her continued, she looked directly at the lens, curious at its glossy eye, her own expression unreadable. She was completely alone. Her face looked smaller than Yitian had ever remembered it.

Those days after they first moved to America were the darkest and most difficult. Sometimes he felt so lonely that he purposefully bought groceries in increments, buying a shaker of salt one day and then waiting the next to go back for the matching pepper, just so that he could have an excuse to go to the store once more and feel people walking around him in the aisles. When they watched the video and he saw his mother's solitary figure, Yitian imagined her on her own wedding day, an event he'd only ever been told about through stories. She'd just turned eighteen when she married. He wondered if, entering the home-to-be with her husband for the first time, she'd felt as lonely as he did in this new country.

Part 5

二十四史

THE
TWENTY-FOUR
HISTORIES

———

Thirty-four

1993

When he was a child and knew he'd done something wrong, he would run through the fields to hide from his mother. His feet pounded through the furrows and deepened them. He ran until he couldn't hear her voice any longer and the crops gave way to the hillside and the only sound remaining was of the wind whispering through grass.

Now he wanted nothing more than to run, to put as much distance as he could between himself and Hanwen. Kissing her earlier that evening, he'd felt light, that he could close himself off from every other thing tying him to the world and see only her face. What a lopsided bargain that had been, exchanging the ease of a few moments for this aftermath.

That night he didn't sleep. He paced his hotel room, glad only for the movement. When the worn tread of his footsteps in the carpet no longer seemed like enough, he went downstairs. He roused the night clerk, asleep at the desk, and asked to make a call.

The phone rang for so long he became sure she already sensed what he'd done and was refusing to answer.

"Hello?"

Mali's voice, at last.

He could hear the loud sizzling of a pan in the background. It would have been around lunchtime, she cooking a meal to eat alone.

"It's me," he said.

The line suddenly gave over to a sudden burst of cracking, making it impossible to hear her response.

"What?" he repeated the question, louder this time. The lobby clerk glared at him through bleary eyes. He understood now why his mother had always yelled across the phone, because of how uncertain the connection sounded. He could read so many things into that silence.

"I turned off the stove. Is that better?"

"A little."

"I asked why you were calling so late."

"I couldn't sleep. Listen, I want to come home." As soon as the words tumbled from his mouth, he was sure that they were his deepest, most primal urge, the one that he would whisper to a stranger in the dark if he could.

"What about your father?"

He grasped for any excuse.

"I feel bad for leaving you for so long."

"Oh, you know that I can take care of myself. This thing with your father is important."

"I don't know anymore if I'll be able to find him here." He was startled to feel a sting behind his eyes.

"You're sure? Well, of course I miss you," she said.

"Then I'll come back," he answered immediately. He was awash with relief. Earlier in the week, he'd been irritated by her eternal optimism, but now there was nothing he wanted more than to return to that more brightly tinted version of life.

"Can you help me book a ticket back? In three days? I need to go say goodbye to my mother." He felt grateful for the disguise the distance of the phone enabled. He could turn his head as he said these words, would not be forced to subject every sentence to her gaze.

After he hung up, he returned to his room and packed his bag as daylight slowly warmed the sky. He had hardly taken anything out, and found himself to be a person easily cleaned up and stowed.

At the lobby, as he returned his room key, he wondered briefly if he should call Hanwen to tell her. No, he wouldn't want to wake her this early. Their last departure from one another had been marked by silence, she slipping out the door. This was simply their way.

The bus station was crowded with men whom he imagined to be laborers in the city, polystyrene bags strapped crooked to their slouching backs. They counted out money for their tickets slowly and using the smallest denominations of coins. Filled with passengers, the bus ambled slowly and heavily out of town. He was squished against a window as he watched the tall constructions of the city once again give way to the low fields and vastness of the countryside surrounding them, the terrain that he would always see as the real truth of this place.

His mother dropped and shattered a clay plate when he stepped back into the home.

"I had no idea you were coming back," she exclaimed. "I would have prepared something for you, I'm sorry . . ."

Her face was even more weary than it had been when he'd left her, and he could see her struggling to rearrange her expression from the unwitnessed state of a person alone.

Again she hurried to make breakfast, just as she had a few days ago on the morning of his first return. It was almost as if he'd re-wound the videotape, except this time all his ideas of what would happen on the trip had already shown themselves to be delusions. He looked back on his self of only a few days past and couldn't believe how childish he'd been to believe he'd find his father or prove his worth. All he could hope for now was that the time he'd spent back in the country wouldn't entirely undo the life he'd made.

Thirty-five

Is it because you're angry at me?" his mother asked, when he told her about his plans for departure.

"No," he said truthfully. He found it easier to speak to her after she'd revealed the secret she'd hid. He'd always been ashamed over Yishou, the ledger of her wrongs so empty in comparison. The unconditional weight of her forgiveness finally seemed more measured, light enough for him to accept.

Now that there was nothing else to do for his father, Yitian fidgeted in the home. The breakfast of noodles had already been cleared away and there were still hours to go until lunch. He didn't know how he'd spent so many hours in this blank space when he'd been young. Time was a different feeling back then, stretching and endless, a truth of the world rather than something to work against and make efficient, as it was in America. Suddenly and absurdly, he wished for the television he'd seen in the villager's house earlier that week. He was sure that the village's sense of time would change now that they had the TV programs.

He felt overcome by the restlessness in his limbs as he watched her, sweeping the same spot over and over in the corner. One moment he thought he'd done the right thing by making plans to return to his wife, and in the next he saw his mother there and how alone she would be once he left without fulfilling his obligation to his father. If she were to directly admonish him, even that would be more manageable.

"I'm going to go for a walk, Ma," he said. This was how he'd relieved himself of his mother's watchful eye when he'd been younger. She didn't ask to accompany him. The gulf beyond accusation from which she stared at him reminded him of how little claim she had on his life now.

He'd done what he could, he told himself as he walked down the small alleyway behind their home, past the embankment, and then onto the wider dirt road leading to the fields. In another season there would have been lines of rice seedlings jutting from the wet paddies, but at this time of year the trenches were dry, and the only remnants of the harvest were weeds, overgrown and yellow.

He walked down the slope into the depression of the paddy and deliberately stepped on the blunted stalks, savoring the sounds of their crunch under his feet. He allowed the toes of his sneakers to dig into the frost collecting in the dirt. He went through one column of the paddy this way and then turned around to continue onto the next, as an ox might during plowing.

Soon, he heard the crunch of another's footsteps moving through the fields. He looked up to see Second Uncle walking slowly toward him.

"What are you doing here?" Second Uncle asked.

"I just wanted a walk," Yitian said lamely.

"So, I hear you're leaving us again, huh?"

News traveled so quickly here. He scuffed the toe of his shoe into a stem of dead grass to avoid looking at Second Uncle. He dreaded another conversation about his life in America and his return.

"I figured you would. Some of the other villagers were saying, maybe he's come back to stay, but I told them of course not! Why would he come back to stay here forever when he could live in America instead?"

The thought of remaining in the village had never crossed Yitian's mind. He hadn't known that the other villagers thought that a possibility. In all his time in America, he'd never heard even a single story of someone returning to live in their village after they'd made it so far out.

"Just be sure to take care of your mother even after you leave," Second Uncle said. "Don't forget about her, alone here. She's a strong woman, but she still needs your help."

"I will." Yitian didn't even have it in him to find a curt response. He turned his head back toward the ground, hoping Second Uncle would leave of his own accord.

Instead, he stretched his arms before squatting down into the grass. He cleared his throat. "Listen, Yitian. You understand why we didn't tell you about your father—"

"Don't worry about it." Of course none of the villagers would have gone against his mother's wishes. He hadn't realized until now that his mother would have had to ask everyone in the village to be complicit in keeping a secret of his father's illness. Sometimes, her desires seemed so simple that he forgot about her ability to play the fool. She'd been the one who'd shepherded their family through the years of famine and the Cultural Revolution, flattening paper money in crannies that wouldn't be suspected, singing the Chairman's praises loudly in public so that there would be no doubt cast over the family's allegiances.

"Weren't you worried, though?" he asked abruptly. "The first day I came back, when you visited. If you'd told me then, I could have spent the rest of the days looking for him. If any of you had just told me earlier that he was in Hefei, maybe I could have found him."

Second Uncle looked at Yitian, bewildered. "It was your father!" He shook his head to cast off the idea. "None of us were really worried about him. He was so strong, so capable. Nobody thought anything really bad had happened. We thought he'd come back at any moment."

"But that's not how it works. The disease worsens over time."

"I didn't really understand how bad things could get." Second Uncle sighed. "But how could we? I couldn't have ever imagined anything happening to your father that he couldn't get out of himself. When that thing happened with his leg, he started moving more slowly. Even that was a big shock to me. I just always thought he was invincible, I suppose. Even when we were kids, he was our leader."

"He'd gotten older, though. He wasn't the same anymore."

"You wouldn't understand, because you didn't know your father when he was younger."

"Maybe."

"And I'm sure your father never told you about his past."

He continued on, oblivious to Yitian's impatience. "There was a little gang of five of us. Big Mosquito and Tang Yuan—they both died before you were born, so you wouldn't have known them. One in a truck accident and the other drowned. And then Fourth Brother Tang, he was always a little smarter than the rest of us, so he moved to the township. But yes, even though he wasn't the largest, your father was our leader." He chuckled. "He was a bit of a bully, to be honest. He'd decide what to do and the rest of us would just follow his plans. It was so funny to see him threatening Big Mosquito. But he always won. If he wanted to go steal watermelons, we did that. If he wanted to go throw sticks at some of the girls, we'd go do that. Everyone was a little scared of us."

"Then why did you all stay with him, if he was such a bully?" The child Second Uncle described sounded just like the father Yitian knew as an adult.

"Well, everything he did was something that we other kids wanted to do, but we would have been too afraid to try if it wasn't for him. So it wasn't hard to be convinced. Anyway, your father wasn't all bad. You know that. He took care of your family and did all the things that mattered. You have to be grateful for that."

"I am."

"Good. Because your father didn't have it easy, you know. What with your grandfather not helping at all. Your father led that family from a young age, and we all admired him for that. Perhaps that's why it was easy to listen to him."

"What do you mean?"

"I already told you. He was our leader—"

"Not about that. I mean, what you said about my father not having it easy."

"Oh, he must have told you about that before. After your grandfather was denounced, it was your father who had to do everything for the family."

"No, that can't be true."

Second Uncle laughed loudly, then quieted. "What do you mean? Of course it's true! You think I'm lying to you?"

"But my grandfather—"

"You must have noticed that your grandfather couldn't really do work, all these years."

"That can't be right."

"When did you see your grandfather doing farmwork?"

Yitian had scattered memories of his grandfather's back bent with a hoe, but that was all. And if he was truthful to himself, there was a rigidity to the movement he saw in his mind, unlike the way his father or Yishou held their tools.

"We thought he would have learned, but he just couldn't pick it up. Always would end up hurting himself if he so much as tried to pick up one of the tools. Of course, we weren't able to help him, you understand. We could have gotten in trouble, because he'd been labeled a counterrevolutionary early on . . . and your grandfather—I know you were close with him, Yitian, but he was different when he got older, so forgive me—he always seemed as if he wasn't really trying to learn, either. As if he thought he was above it all."

All throughout Yitian's childhood, the villagers who came to speak to his grandfather lavished praise upon him. At times the words of awe sounded exaggerated—his grandfather doing such an ordinary thing as holding a book in his hand enough for them to say he belonged in the imperial court—but Yitian had always assumed that their behavior was out of respect for him as an elder and the holder of a kind of book learning uncommon in the village. Now, he saw a different interpretation—perhaps what he'd always seen as reverence for his grandfather was the remnant of people who were ashamed for how they'd once refused to help him.

"So your father went and learned himself, did almost all the farming for his family, when he was just a young teenager. He left for the army but couldn't ascend far because of your grandfather's background. And your grandfather didn't help things by how he treated your father. Even after all your father did for your family, your grandfather was always calling him stupid, because he wasn't good at school." Second Uncle glanced quickly at Yitian. "He couldn't help it, we all knew. Some people just don't have a mind for practical things."

"So my father hated him because of all that work he had to do."

"Well, not at first. But as time went on, he became resentful. Your grandfather used to really hurt your father, saying he didn't know how your father could be his son because he was so stupid, stuff like that. Your father even cried to me about it once," Second Uncle laughed. "Before he became the tough guy. '*The characters just swim in front of me, I can't help it!*' Of course, later he made me swear never to tell anyone about that single instance when he cried. Even made me draw blood to promise. He was so embarrassed! And I never did tell anyone, but I'm not sure if it matters now.

"I'm always talking too much when I'm around you. Never mind. I'll leave you be," Second Uncle said, rising. "Who knows what year it will be when we see each other again? Have a safe journey, all right?"

Yitian nodded and stood, too shocked to give Second Uncle a proper greeting. He wanted to go to his father, to ask him if it was all true. He would only ever be able to hear about his father through the stories of others, he now realized.

"Wait," he said suddenly to Second Uncle. He'd forgotten something.

Second Uncle turned back, surprised.

What was left to say?

"Thank you."

———

Yitian walked mechanically back to the village. His memory overtook his steps, so that he was startled by how quickly he was faced with the door to their home.

His mother came out of the courtyard immediately at the sound of his approach.

"I was just thinking about going out to look for you. I didn't know what you wanted to eat for lunch."

"Oh, anything," he mumbled.

He sat at the center table while she prepared food in the kitchen. If he was honest with himself, he'd noticed before that there was something in how his grandfather accepted his father's rudeness, never protesting as Yitian did, as if it were deserved. Yitian hadn't ever wanted to follow the thought fully through. He'd admired his grandfather too much. His grandfather had always been patient with him, never sharp or dismissive. Even if he took a long time to grasp an idea on occasion, his grandfather would never have called him stupid. But between Yishou and his grandfather there was always a shallow silence, as if Yishou was hardly a being worth attention or care. Perhaps this was the form that his grandfather's earlier dismissal of his own son had taken by the time he had grandchildren, scorn slackening into its more benign form of indifference. Was it possible that, without this earliest wound, his father would have been someone else entirely?

Something else struck him about Second Uncle's description of his father. *The characters just swim in front of me*, he'd repeated. Yitian had once heard his older brother saying this exact phrase. *How do you do this? The characters just swim in front of my eyes,*

Yishou had said, picking up Yitian's papers and marveling at the sentences.

At the time, Yitian hadn't thought much of it. But now, hearing that his father had once said something similar, he was reminded of another memory.

In his first year teaching in America, one of his students had approached him with an official university document. Yitian, occupied enough at that point with other worries about teaching American students for the first time, placed the paper somewhere on his office desk, where it quickly disappeared under the piles of grading to be done. Not until after the midterm did he think about that document again, when the student came to his office hours to protest the poor grade she received, saying that he hadn't given her the appropriate testing accommodations.

That evening, when he returned home, he'd complained about the student to Mali.

"She doesn't grasp the material, and so she comes whining to me? It's so American, to have a made-up reason like this for not understanding something so basic."

"Let me see the note," Mali said. She read the words slowly aloud. "Well, it looks very official, from the university. It says you're supposed to give her extra time on tests and ignore minor mistakes in how numbers are written."

"Of course I read it. But it's a mathematics course. The numbers being written the right way is the whole point." Her response annoyed him. By this time, Mali's English ability was already outpacing his, despite the fact that she'd known little of the language when they both left China. He knew he was only imagining that she was questioning his ability to understand the words, and yet he felt embarrassed by her. "Anyway, you can't really believe what she's saying on there, can you?"

"It says she has a diagnosed medical condition. *Dyslexia*," she'd read slowly.

That first time, she'd pronounced the word *DIES-lex-ia*, but the next night when he returned home, she read the *y* with a lighter sound, as it had been described in the book she'd found at the library about the condition. "And the doctors say it's a real disorder. They say as many as fifteen percent of the population has it," she said, handing him the sheaves of paper she'd photocopied.

"No one in China ever had it." He'd tried to look up the word in his Chinese-English dictionary but hadn't found anything.

"What if people had it but we just didn't have the words for it? Look, there's all these studies done by scientists. Some of them are even at Harvard."

"All right." He felt embarrassed by the amount of research she'd done. Next to it, his own defense sounded unscientific and stubborn. It challenged his idea of their roles—he was supposed to be the analytic one, not her. He brushed her off, but that evening after she went to bed, he'd looked at the photocopied papers, filled with testimonials from young children describing how they felt when they tried to read.

Other children say that words on papers sit still, but for me they sort of swim around the page and it's hard for me to follow them to read, Kris, 5, said.

Second Uncle's phrasing was strange and specific enough that the words had to be exactly the ones Yitian's father used.

He had an idea. He called to his mother, who immediately came to him, letting the stove go out.

"What is it?" He could hear in her voice how eager she was to help.

"I was just thinking . . . Did Ba ever keep any papers or notes?"

"What do you mean?"

"Anything that he would have written on."

She twisted the washcloth in her hands. "No, your father never had any reason to write things, you know that . . ."

"Not even any forms? Anything he had to fill out?"

"Oh! He had to fill out these forms awhile ago to get his pension. Let's see."

And then they were both hurrying to the wardrobe in her bedroom, which had, since his childhood, held all the items she was afraid might one day come of use. He supposed she'd accumulated more things in the years that he'd been gone, but still the crash of objects tumbling out of the closet startled him. The four dusty shelves were entirely piled with scraps of fabric, empty picture frames, the jagged and rusted bits of metal that had fallen out of little mechanical objects, even old toothpaste tubes. In their home in California, Mali was always cleaning and rearranging, deciding what needed to be kept and what was to be discarded. She would never allow a cabinet to become so disorganized as this. Her ideas of neatness and efficiency, of not keeping more than what was needed, didn't make sense in a world where they were once so afraid that everything would be taken away, where even the smallest of items might one day come to show their value.

He held up a knotted green yo-yo.

"Some child left it outside when they were playing." His mother shrugged.

He saw the corners of paper poking out from underneath the detritus, and he and his mother slowly removed the other items until they reached them. The topmost sheet was so old that it cracked in his hands. He flipped through the others. He'd never even seen his father's handwriting and was unsure of what he was looking for. Most of the papers were in typed text—forms distributed from the government—or otherwise notices and receipts written by the smooth hand of another.

By the time he found the folded piece of notebook paper, he almost ripped the thin sheet in his haste.

The notes appeared to be an accounting of various plots of land and crops in his family's possession and their locations. The writer had listed the number of mu dedicated to each crop, until halfway down the paper, where they'd stopped in the middle of the word *peanuts*. The characters floated at different heights around the page, unfettered by the lines that were meant to organize hand-writing.

There were mistakes, too, within the characters. They were of the kind a young schoolchild would make, confusing the radicals within characters. Instead of 稻子 the writer had scrawled

resulting in a character that didn't exist. Farther down, they'd mistaken 山芋 for

Yitian thought of Yishou, of his older brother's wide shoulders hunched over a table as he did homework. But from the date scrawled in the top corner, a day six years ago, this document would have been written long after Yishou's death.

"Did Ba write this?"

His mother took the paper and squinted. She wouldn't be able to make any sense of the characters. He tried to remember what that girl's, his student's, writing had looked like, but the writing in Chinese characters was too different from her English letters to be helpful.

"Is it there? What you were looking for?" his mother asked.

He knew what she meant by the question. No, there wasn't anything that gave him another clue as to where his father might be, yet as he looked at the childish mistakes, he felt the sense of discovery burning within him.

For the second time that day, he was overwhelmed with the urge to turn to his father and ask what had gone through his mind when he mistook these characters. Or to reverse the question onto Yishou and ask, "How do *you* do this?"

But he'd never bothered to understand the ways they might have been different from him. The explanation wasn't complex—a disorder, an illness of the mind—categorized, even common. Here was this reason, so beyond their control, that had written their lives. Intelligence had been such a mysterious gift in his youth, a concept as unknowable as whether the weather would be favorable for that season's harvest. In many ways, the life of his adulthood was so much simpler than he could have imagined, processes made legible and circumscribed by rationality and science. How would his father and Yishou have existed in this more nameable world?

He continued to go through the items in the wardrobe for the rest of the afternoon. There were objects inside that he hadn't thought about in years—marbles he and Yishou used to roll with the other village boys, angular toys carved from splintered wood. He only found one more item in that same shaky handwriting, on a government form for subsidies for veterans in the countryside. By this time, Yitian was sure of what he'd discovered. His father had filled out his name as the main claimant of the subsidies. Even those three characters, the ones that should have been most familiar to a person, were angular and blocky with uncertainty.

Thirty-six

Hanwen was lying in bed with Yuanyuan when Ayi came to the door. When she had returned home the night before and gone to check on him, she'd found his forehead burning hot. The heat of his soft skin against her palm read to her as a rebuke against what she'd done with Yitian that evening. Normally, she wasn't superstitious like this, but ever since Yitian's return, events seemed to arrange themselves in front of her like pieces on a chessboard daring her to make the connections between them.

She stayed in bed with him the next day, spooning him simple soups and soft mixtures of rock sugar and water while they both drifted in and out of sleep. She felt grateful for the illness, for the opportunity of tangible work, which kept her from thinking too much about Guifan and Yitian. She liked that when her mother had come to check on them, she'd been able to say, *No, Ma, I can take care of this.*

It was through this suspended sense of time that she heard Ayi's voice, so dimly at first that she wasn't sure whether it belonged to reality.

"Miss? Miss?"

"What is it?"

"There's a phone call for you," Ayi said.

Hanwen blinked rapidly to shake herself back to the room. She'd known she would have to speak with Yitian again eventually, but she'd thought there would have been more time to think over what she would say.

She slid out of bed and into her slippers. She tucked the blankets carefully around Yuanyuan's body before getting up. She wanted to find any excuse to extend the time.

She inhaled and gathered her courage as she picked up the phone receiver.

"Yitian?"

"What?" The voice belonged to a woman, and Hanwen imagined absurdly for a moment that Yitian's wife had called to berate her.

"I'm calling for Mrs. Wang?" the woman continued. "From the police chief? There was some news he asked to transmit to you."

"Oh. Yes."

"Is this Mrs. Wang?"

"Yes, this is she."

"Is now a good time? Should I call back?"

"No, no. Please."

"Okay. We've heard something about the case you asked about."

Hanwen reached for the first piece of paper she could find, a gridded sheet that Yuanyuan used to copy his characters for school. Her hand moved mechanically over the paper as the woman told her of the report they'd received of a man, likely about seventy, who'd been reported wandering around Five Groves Township. He'd said he needed to go to Hefei City. A shopkeeper—who'd later gone to the police—had given him some directions, but when she asked where he'd come from, he couldn't remember the name of his home. He seemed lost and said he hadn't eaten all day. The shopkeeper had offered him a meal and the man said he would come back the next morning to buy something from them, but never returned. Something about the old man's manner didn't sit right with the shopkeeper. When he didn't show up the next morning as he said he would, she'd gone to the local police bureau to ask if they'd heard anything, and from there the story had traveled up.

Hanwen took down the address of the shop, thanked the woman, and hung up the phone. She flipped her address book until she found the number to Yitian's hotel. She had no excuse to dawdle any longer. At least they would be able to talk about the disappearance. Maybe he would be so overtaken by the news that they wouldn't have to speak about the previous night at all.

"Thank you for calling the Overseas' Trading Hotel." The woman's voice was cloying and melodic.

"Hi, I'd like to speak with Tang Yitian? He's staying in your hotel. In—" She scanned her notes. "Room six-oh-nine, I believe."

"Room six-oh-nine? One moment."

Hanwen waited.

"Hi, ma'am? The guest in room six-oh-nine already checked out this morning."

"What? Are you sure?"

"Yes, ma'am."

"Can you double-check? Maybe I got the room number wrong. Is there anyone named that in another room?"

"We do have a record of someone named Tang Yitian staying in that room, but he already checked out. This morning."

"Did he say where he was going?"

"No."

Hanwen hung up the phone. There was that old dizzy feeling in her head again. She couldn't believe that he'd left like that, without even telling her. They'd made a mistake the night before, yes, but was she not worth, at least, a goodbye?

Her mother entered the living room.

"What's wrong? Are you all right?"

"Yes, Ma. Just one moment."

She picked up the phone again and dialed the number for the village office. Yitian had given it to her the first day in case the police needed information.

"Wei?" The voice of the man who picked up was gruff and irritated.

"I'm looking to speak with Tang Yitian."

"Who's calling? Are you his wife?"

She slammed the phone back into its cradle. If Guifan left her without any notice, would she feel a shock like this?

Her mother was staring at her, brows furrowed, lips frowning. "Hanwen, I spoke with you about this, didn't I? You can't keep—"

Hanwen held up her palm to her mother. Not with anger. She was only tired, so tired, of the assumptions and the advice, and then she, expected to absorb it all like a sponge. She pressed her other hand to her eyes.

"I know, Ma. I know."

And then he called back. Late that afternoon, the sun setting, when she was already imagining him on a train ride, his head propped against the window, watching the light dim over his old country and glad to be riding away from her forever.

"Hanwen?"

"Where are you?"

"I'm back at my village. Listen, I'm sorry I didn't tell you—"

She could hear the tremor in his voice, that he didn't know what to say.

"I heard some news. From the police chief."

It was a relief, however temporary, to read the words from the paper to him, to hear him say, "I know Five Groves! That's only two townships away from here. Do you think he might have been on his way home?" His voice fell. "But this happened eight days ago."

"At least there might be some news, right?" she said as gently as she could. "Perhaps it will give you some other clue."

"I'll go first thing tomorrow. It's amazing that the shopkeeper helped my father. It reminds me of how people used to be in our village. Willing to help a stranger."

"Yes, they were."

"Hanwen?"

"Yes?"

"I was going to call you earlier today when I left. I'm sorry I didn't. I should tell you. I made plans to return to America in two days. I'm supposed to leave Anhui tomorrow."

So she'd shaken him so much the previous night that he'd decided even to give up his search. "But what about your father?"

"Am I really helping, by staying here longer? I didn't realize how much bigger everything had become. I don't know anything about this place anymore, Hanwen. The last thing I am is helpful."

"I see," she said. "Then I hope this shopkeeper has some news for you. If she does, will you stay longer?"

He paused. "I really don't know." Those words again, unfamiliar in his voice. She could picture him with his hands spread over his eyes and forehead, trying to puzzle this question out. When she'd sat on the embankment with him and he paused over a question, she knew it would only be moments before the breaking of understanding on his face. Once when it hadn't come, he'd risen from his spot on the embankment, collected the cold river water in his hands, and thrown it onto his face.

"You'll figure it out, Yitian. Whatever it is. I know you will," she said now. As soon as she said this, she believed it utterly for him. He'd always come to some solution.

He didn't reply.

"Well. Goodbye then," she said. She didn't know how to state the logical implication that they wouldn't see each other before he left. Perhaps never again.

"Hanwen," he spoke abruptly, just as she was about to drop the receiver, "thank you for everything. Really. Even if I don't learn anything new from the shopkeeper. You've been a big help to me." He inhaled. "You've always been a big help to me."

"Of course, it was nothing. It's what friends do for one another."

"Thank you," he said. "Goodbye."

She closed her eyes. She wanted to remember the sound of his voice as he said these last simple words.

"Goodbye."

After she put down the phone, she sat there for a long while. Her mother and Ayi both came and spoke to her, words that came to her like a low hum in the background. She didn't respond, and they both left. Her feet and hands grew cold and her back ached as she sat perched on the sofa arm.

The night before, after they'd risen from the bed, they'd dressed, her discomfort made stark by the gangly motions of limbs being stuffed back into clothes. They sat across from one another, she on the edge of the bed, he on the edge of the table. Neither of them had been ready to leave the room but she wasn't sure of what else there was to say.

At last, he said, "I thought we'd never speak to each other again. Why didn't you ever reply to any of my letters?"

"It was too hard," she said. "It had all been so easy for you. I didn't want to hear about your life in college with all the freedom that we'd dreamed about together. You'd gotten everything we wanted and I had nothing."

"I thought that you didn't want to talk to me all those years. I was scared to write you."

"I'm sorry," she said. And then, because there was no longer anything to lose in being completely honest with him, "Did you know that I think of you as a hero? We used to read all those old stories, remember? The hero has a dream, and he goes on a quest for it. He has some obstacles, sure, but in the end, he always makes it. You know the whole time he's going to make it. I remember how nervous we were in those days, studying, but when I think back, I ask myself, why were *you* nervous? I knew you'd be fine. That wasn't what it was like for me. I had a feeling that I wouldn't make it, and I was right. You got what you wanted, but for me—in the end, I had to find a different way."

Sitting in her home now, the image that appeared in her mind wasn't of Yitian's face the night before, but of how hopeful he'd been when he was seventeen, when they'd returned from taking the test. She saw how sure he was of himself then—how sure he still was now. She wanted that sureness for herself. She'd thought that by kissing him she could have taken some of that feeling, but she'd been wrong. What had surprised her most about the night before was that she hadn't been able to will even more into existence. She'd closed her eyes and tried to disappear this world, to enter into the old one with him, but they hadn't been able to make it there. There was a distance between their lives that meant she would never have what he did. What she felt wasn't desire for him, but rather a yearning for his very life.

But did she not have a life of her own, too? Her eyes darted around the room, trying to tally up its objects as evidence of her solidity. The jade vase with fake orchids set inside, the ceramic carved ashtray on the coffee table, the television with the gleaming, polished screen—she'd learned in the last month how precarious these accumulations were.

She rose and went toward Yuanyuan's bedroom, feeling the urgent need to see him, even if he was still asleep.

At the threshold she paused, overcome with calm at the image of his small shape, barely registering as a bump beneath the comforter.

She got into bed next to him, sitting cross-legged beside his head. Yuanyuan's eyes blinked open at the sensation.

"Are you feeling better?" she asked. His hair stuck up from the back of his head after being squished against the bed all day.

"I'm still so tired." He rubbed at his face with his fist, and then crawled into her lap in a way that he hadn't in many months now. He was heavier than she'd remembered him to be, his weight pinning down her arms. She was sure her own mother had never held her like this, at least not in any memory she had. Perhaps when she'd been a very young infant, when cradling was a matter of necessity. Her mother loved her, of that Hanwen was sure, but not like this. Her mother's tenderness had been shown through all she'd wanted for Hanwen, all that she'd dreamed for Hanwen to accomplish, so that now she lived in that want, too, and had created her life to fill it. Perhaps that was why Yitian got the chance she never did. He'd learned for its own sake, but she'd always kept this secret reason behind the reason.

Her son's life would not be like that. When his fever subsided, she would read him a story, she decided, and then she'd start telling him about math and science, and later on he could tell her he didn't care about any of it at all. He would make choices about the person he wanted to be. Perhaps the country had finished its wars, was done with sending people away without notice and changing in an instant the course of one's life. Or maybe it was not—how would she know? Guifan's mistake had shown her that even the world of tall towers being built was not so reliable as it seemed. And so she would keep building this life and her son's, so that they were strong enough to withstand the people around them trying to make history.

Yuanyuan's small breaths blew and lingered in ripples across her chest, and she thought of how she knew she wouldn't go to Yitian again, because of this. Because she knew she'd feel this way when her son came to her. Her life had unfolded in a way entirely unexpected to her; how could she have predicted the path it would take? But she would have to face it. She inhaled deeply, trying to gather the courage for what she knew she would have to do next.

Thirty-seven

She'd spent more time on the phone these past few days, she marveled, than ever before in her life. In time, she might miss this period, her home and family transformed by the flurry of activity. But for now, all she wanted was to return to the quiet of before.

She tucked Yuanyuan in bed and went to the telephone. She dialed the number and held her breath.

"Mr. Qian? This is Tian Hanwen. Vice Mayor Wang's wife?"

"Yes, yes. To what do I owe the pleasure, Mrs. Wang?"

She paused. She had to be particularly careful with the words she chose. "I'm calling because I've been talking to Guifan about—about what we were discussing."

"Oh, and what did he say?"

She rolled her finger inside the phone cord. For each sentence she spoke, she flattened a coil. She only needed a few, and then she'd be done. "Well, I was saying, there's no need to make this so difficult. We met Mr. Li at dinner, and he seemed to want to help the city. The shopping center will be good for Hefei. Those old homes, you know, what's the use of having them there? They'd have to get demolished eventually anyway, right?"

"That's what we've been saying all along. What did your husband say?"

"I had some difficulty convincing him, but he agreed with me in the end."

"Good. Very good. I can tell your husband is one of those very technical men. They like to analyze. Sometimes analysis doesn't make things easier. It makes the situation more complicated, in fact. It's better to trust your gut."

"So, since he's agreed—then you won't come and talk to us anymore, is that right?"

"Have I been bothering you, Mrs. Wang?"

"No, no, of course not. I just wanted to . . . understand."

"Well, if you don't want to see me anymore, then I suppose I'll be gone forever," he said.

She took a deep breath. "Nothing will happen to our family now that Guifan's agreed, right? That's a deal?"

He laughed, a truly joyous laugh. "Just like a Shanghai woman, the way you speak. Yes, it's a deal. I always knew you were the right person to talk to. You knew what was at stake."

"I did."

"And why shouldn't you have some nice things, some help? We'd like to give you some gifts to thank you."

"All right."

"Let's call it all sorted, then? Just tell him to send one of his secretaries over to our office, when he gets a chance."

She hung up the phone.

Her hand was trembling as she pressed the button on the machine that would stop the recording. But she hadn't faltered or become light-headed. She rewound the tape and played it. The sounds of her voice and Mr. Qian's were a little scratchy, but the important parts were there—his acknowledgment of the deal, the offer of other gifts. She was startled to find her voice didn't sound shaky at all. Was that how she seemed to others, out there in the world? It was she who'd given Yitian the information he needed. How different would her life have been, in America and with Yitian? She did not know. She could only say this: on the tape, she sounded confident and natural, sure of her statements, her voice never breaking, arriving in the world assured and steady.

She'd surprised Guifan on many occasions over the course of their marriage. When she'd been able to cook a dish from his hometown of Wuhan—she'd simply followed the directions she found in a newspaper column—or when she recognized some obscure character he couldn't. But she'd never seen him so surprised as when she handed over the tape and explained what it was. He was sitting at the kitchen table over the bowl of rice they'd saved for him.

His spoon clattered to the floor. "You didn't tell me you were doing this."

"I was worried you weren't going to do anything. So I had to."

"I didn't ask you to—"

"What was I supposed to do? Just wait and watch you?"

He ran his fingers around the edges of the tape and sighed heavily.

"The mayor is going to get in trouble if I turn this in," he said. "Others, too." He spoke slowly, as if each word handed out a sentence.

Even now, given such a gift, he wasn't capable of decisiveness. She'd learned something new about her husband in these past weeks, long after she would have believed the time for learning new things about each other had passed. If she were to reach down inside him, she would find his core to be soft and pliable. There was nothing inside him she could truly stand up against, and perhaps this is why she didn't feel remorse about kissing Yitian, as she'd supposed she would. She felt free and released, seeing her husband as he truly was.

"You have to decide what to do with the tape," she said. "I can't turn it in. But just think, if you gave it to the Party. Or even if you told the Li Corporation you had it. That would be enough."

He looked at her and nodded. She could see, slowly, sharpness returning to his expression. He could do the weighing and the analysis of the relative consequences.

He ran his finger over the edge of the cassette. "You're right. Thank you. I'll figure out what to do."

She left him there at the table, alone.

She found her mother in her room, preparing for bed.

"Ma, I'm sorry for ignoring you earlier. There was something going on with Guifan."

"I could guess that." Her mother was sitting on the edge of her bed, soaking her feet before sleeping. Hanwen kneeled beside her and dipped her fingers into the plastic tub, the same baby-blue one that they'd used to bathe Yuanyuan when he was just born. The water had gone cold.

"I can't tell you everything that happens in our lives."

"I know, I know. This is your family now. I don't mean to intrude. Sometimes I just get worried."

"You don't need to worry about it. I've taken care of it." And Hanwen could hear her voice as it had sounded on that recording as she said this, decisive and certain.

Her mother squinted at her, as if trying to make sense of a person she hadn't seen in years.

"What is it, Ma?"

For a moment, her mother's eyes seemed to sharpen into that old expression. Then in the next, all the tension was gone from them. Her eyes relaxed back into her face.

"Nothing. It's just that this stable life, with no worries for you, is all I've ever wanted you to have. My job as a mother is done."

What was there to say to that? Hanwen had spent all these days carefully treading around her mother, worried about telling her the truth, when all along her mother had been like a child who just wanted to be told that everything would be all right.

Except her face was not like a child's at all. She was old, older than she'd ever looked. It struck Hanwen that the same thing would happen to her, in time—she could drift along vaguely with Guifan and her mother would grow old and die and Yuanyuan would grow up and leave. What else was there to expect?

Ever since Yitian had come back, she'd been thinking about her days in the village, wanting to return to that hopeful time. But what if she could go back to even earlier, to Shanghai? That was what she'd missed so much when she'd been sent down, wasn't it? And she'd never really gotten to *live* in the city after the country had transformed. She wondered if it would be like the place she'd always heard stories of, the lights on the Bund shimmering at night, women made up beautifully in bars with dreams animating their dance steps— that sense of living as something that deserved to be enjoyed on its own. The wives of the other cadres went on long vacations, even international trips, and no one blinked an eye. This wouldn't be any different.

"Ma—" She edged toward her question at last. "What do you think about going away for a while? Just you, Yuanyuan, and me?"

Thirty-eight

W hat will you do, after this visit?" Yitian's mother asked.
"Let's see what the shopkeeper says, first. Then I'll decide, all right?"

They were sitting in the back of a wagon pedaled by the villager
he'd hired to take them to Five Groves Township. These were the first
words that she'd said this entire ride, jammed against him in the tight
space and with her scarf pulled over her face to protect herself from
the cold of the winter wind.

Unlike her, he left his face uncovered. He knew his cheeks would
soon turn red, as if they'd been slapped, but now that he was about
to leave, everything, even discomfort, had already transformed into
the pleasant softness of a memory.

He thought about his mother's question as the wagon's wheels
hummed steadily beneath them. After Hanwen's call, he had asked
Mali to delay his plane ticket two more days so he could visit the
township. But what if the shopkeeper had some information that

would lead further to his father? He'd heard from the village office that Mali had already called for him twice in the day since then—to verify some detail of his plane ticket, he supposed. He knew he should have been more concerned about the logistics of his departure. He hadn't returned any of her calls.

The last time he'd been to Five Groves Township was when he was thirteen and Yishou had led him on an expedition here to steal books from the library, the only one within miles. At this hour of the day, the town was still sleepily awakening from the midday nap. A few shopkeepers were rolling up their steel doors, but most of the storefronts were either closed or empty.

He followed the directions Hanwen had given him to a building tucked behind the town's three-road crossing. The sign above the storefront bore no name, only the word *bookstore*.

He double-checked to make sure he was in the right place, but there was no mistake. From Hanwen's description of the shop, he was sure it would be some noodle stand, a dry-goods shop, perhaps. It made sense that his father would need to stop and eat.

He worried the store would still be closed, but when he pushed on the door, it swung open easily. Upon entering, he coughed immediately. Dust lay in a feathery layer upon every surface and floated in the air wherever it caught the sunlight. Unbelievably, the room was filled with books, stuffed from the top to bottom of every wall, soaking up every inch of space. The room couldn't be larger than the courtyard of their home, but Yitian was sure there must have been thousands of books crowded into its four corners. They overflowed into the aisles and made the passageways so narrow that he had to sidestep them to avoid the jutting sharp corners. He'd never seen a place like this before. His gaze darted from book to book, unsure of the point where his eyes could finally settle.

They maneuvered around the narrow aisles. "Hello?" his mother shouted out. The sound was absorbed by the stacks of old pages.

Yitian examined the spines as they passed through the aisle. Some he recognized, the famous histories everyone knew. Many more bewildered him. Obscure family or county chronicles of places he'd never heard of, instructional manuals for agricultural tools, treatises on methods for planting tea. He couldn't imagine who would come here to read all these books; some could not have more than a single reader in a lifetime. Behind the bookcases, pressed directly against the walls, were thousands of unbound sheets of paper piled one upon another.

They reached an empty cashier stand in the back of the shop. He looked over the counter to see a small notebook with columns recording sales numbers and dates. There hadn't been an entry in four days.

A sudden rustling sound startled him. Surprised, his mother threw her arm back and toppled a stack of books that had been haphazardly placed directly on the floor. She rushed to fix them. The source of the noise seemed to have come from near his feet. Behind the wooden stand he noticed, for the first time, a shape—an old woman's body, huddled there on a cotton pallet spread onto the floor. When Yitian's gaze fell upon her, her eyes fluttered open.

Curiously, she didn't seem to be frightened by their sudden appearance, despite the fact that he sensed visitors to this store were rare. She jumped up.

"Hello! Do you want to buy something? We have many books, yes!" she squeaked, brushing off her legs. Her voice was vigorous and as high-pitched as a baby's. Standing up, she barely came up to his chin. Her arms appeared glued to her sides, frozen and curling into her torso. She moved with surprising speed for her size and age. The countryside could be deceptive about appearances, but she must surely have been older than his mother.

"Hi, ma'am. We're here because we heard from the police that a man came in here?"

"What?" she cupped her ear at them.

"I said, we heard from the police that a man came in here. I think I might know him."

"Oh! Yes, yes, Officer Ju said someone might be coming. We were wondering what was taking you so long."

"We just got the news—"

"We were worried about him! We thought someone should have come and helped him immediately. In fact, I wanted to, but then he never came back! And now, how many days have passed?" She opened her hand and counted off the days on her fingertips, marking each one with a mutter. "Eight! Eight!"

"I would have come sooner. I didn't hear about this until yesterday."

"What took them so long to tell you? Sometimes I really wonder about what the police are doing."

"Tell us about this man," Yitian's mother interrupted. He could see she'd grown impatient.

"I'm getting there, I'm getting there," the old woman said. She leaned her elbows against the cashier stand, appearing to settle in. "Well, eight days ago he came in, and he seemed to be very confused, obviously. I thought, someone needs to help him! I wondered if he was one of the old people who'd lost their minds, to be honest with you. You know the kind?"

"What puts you in a position to judge that? Are you a doctor?" his mother snapped. She pulled on Yitian's hand, ready to leave.

"Just hold on one second," he said to his mother. And then, to the shopkeeper, "Auntie, was this the man?" He passed her the photograph of his father.

She squinted into the picture. Then her face broke into recognition. "Yes, yes, this is definitely him!" She tapped furiously at his father's face.

"Are you sure?" He winced at the deep creases her wrinkled hand were already pressing into the photograph. "It's an old picture, but it's all we have."

"Even I can hardly recognize your father in that picture," his mother whispered.

"Do you remember anything else? His height?" Yitian asked.

The old woman bit her lip, then said, "It wasn't notable. Probably about average." After Yitian's mother sighed in exasperation, she added, "But there was something—he had a limp, I think."

"A limp? You're positive?"

"Well, I don't know if it was a limp, but he was walking strangely. At first I couldn't tell why I thought something was off. He was pretty good at hiding it. But when he turned around to leave, I noticed. It would have been pretty hard for him to walk any farther by himself. That's why I was worried for him, you see?"

"Do you remember which leg it was on?"

"I think . . . left? No, left, I'm sure. Because when he walked away from the counter, he bumped into that pile." She pointed. "We had to rearrange the stack after he'd gone."

"It was him."

"Who?"

"My father." He felt his mother's hand clench around his. It made no sense. Why would his father come this way, and for a bookstore, of all places? But a second thought toward logic fought this first—everything about the description was too close to his father's.

"Oh, this man you're looking for, it was your *father*! Well, I see now why you came, although, honestly—you should have come sooner. Now that you mention it, he did speak of a son."

"Really? What did he say?"

She chewed at the insides of her mouth, sinking her cheeks even deeper. "He said his son was very strong, very capable. He said you were the most powerful person in the village, the one who worked the most during every harvest. But even then I thought, this man is bragging—you know how the old men like to brag about their children? No offense, but look at you. You can't be the strongest man in the village, right?"

Then it was Yishou his father had tried to search out. Yishou who it had always been. Even in that final haze of the corridors into which his father's memory had been transformed, there his older brother was, at the end of each one. When he'd learned of his father's disappearance, Yitian had been so shocked that there'd been no room left in his heart for sadness or any other emotion. The feeling at this new understanding was nothing like that. He'd never be able to write a new story that would replace the one his father told about him.

"Are you all right?" the shopkeeper said. She peered at him with genuine concern, and Yitian felt a stab of affection for this old woman he'd only just met. "I didn't mean to offend you. Your father must have really cared for you, to go out there and look for you. He said he was walking from your village all the way to Hefei City, just to go talk to his son! That's a long walk, I told him. Why don't you take a bus? That's how I knew something wasn't right in his head. And also, if his son was farming like he said, what was he doing out in Hefei? I could tell you guys had gotten into some fight, is that right?"

"Was he asking you for directions? Is that why he came in here?" His head still swam with unanswered questions.

"No, no! Haven't you been listening to what I've been saying? You haven't understood me. He *knew* he was going to Hefei. *That* wasn't what he was confused about. No, he came in here because he said he was looking for a book, and he knew our town was known for its old library. He wanted to give a gift to his son when he saw him, your father said. That's when he started talking about you. How you loved to read, but he never bought you any books when you were younger. How interesting, I thought. He has this son who's so good at farming but also loves to read. No offense, but that seems like a wasted talent to me. Take my advice," she leaned closer to Yitian. "If you're farming, stop! Why would you do that if you could get an education? Move to the city, get an urban hukou. That's where all the real money is."

"Yishou didn't like to read," his mother said.

"Yishou! What a nice name you have," the shopkeeper said.

"No, that's my brother's name." He couldn't make any sense of it. "What book did he buy?"

"No idea. I can't read any of the titles. Isn't that funny? An old lady who owns a bookshop can't read anything! Ha. Let me call my husband."

She shouted, and a man—also elderly, but less stooped than her—emerged from behind a curtain in the back of the store. The opening it covered was barely wider than his body.

"What is it?" the man grumbled. He rubbed his bald head. Like his wife, he was impossibly thin. "When are you going to start making lunch?"

"Remember that strange old man that was here, about a week ago?"

"The only people who come in here are strange old men," he muttered.

"No, no, the one who you wouldn't let stay. Remember he was going to go see his son? Look, he's arrived." She nodded her chin toward Yitian. "I told you something was wrong with him! We should have helped him. Now his son is here and said his father never turned up."

"That was *your* father?" The old man squinted at Yitian. "You don't look anything like him."

"Of course they look alike!" Yitian's mother cut in. Yitian waved his hand at her impatiently.

"Look, look—I wasn't sure whether he was some riffraff, you have to understand. There have been people like that in the past. My wife wants to help everyone. But I can't let just anyone who comes in stay with my family."

"I don't care about any of that. Can you just tell me what book he wanted to buy?" Yitian said.

The man's mouth closed just as he was about to reply. He turned around brusquely to the glass-enclosed bookcase behind the counter. The layer of dust covering it was so thick that it was impossible for Yitian to see what was inside.

The old man slid aside the glass and placed a volume onto the counter. A particle cloud flew up into their faces.

"What is it?" Yitian's mother asked between coughs.

The volume was one of the old books that had been bound without hard covers, raw signatures exposed along with the thick thread that knotted each group of pages together. Yitian ran his fingers down the front page gently so he wouldn't disturb the ancient paper. One small catch and it could snag and rip.

He inhaled deeply when he found the title. The first volume of the *Twenty-Four Histories*.

"Your father wanted to buy all of them," the man gestured to the opened bookcase, which Yitian could now see was filled with rows of identical volumes. "But obviously he didn't realize how much it would cost. I told him to go home and get some more money."

Yitian trembled as he flipped the pages of the book. The type inside was minuscule, vertically printed and further obscured in places where the printer's hand must have pressed unevenly upon the ink blocks. Even now, he couldn't help the smile tugging at his lips at the names that jumped out at him, ones he'd first learned when his grandfather told him stories and that he hadn't heard in years. The brothers Boyi and Shuqi. Confucius's disciples. Han Fei, the scholar with whom the emperor was so desperate to have an audience that he'd been willing to go to war. That was the first time Yitian had stood in awe of the value of sustained thought—it could make even an emperor feel helpless.

Would any such memories have surfaced for his father, looking at this page? Yitian was convinced of one thing. This book couldn't possibly have been for Yishou.

"They could have helped him," his mother whispered. But Yitian was filled with gratitude; he couldn't summon up any anger toward the old couple at all.

The bell over the shop door clanged, startling him. He looked over to see a young boy and girl skipping in, their bodies deftly moving through the narrow aisleways. At once, the old woman was upon them, using her finger to clean some speck of dirt off the boy's face, needling the girl to button her coat properly. The old man's face broke into the first smile Yitian had seen all this time. "Slow down, slow down," he shouted at his grandson. He turned to Yitian. "I've told you everything I know. I'll need to go prepare lunch for my grandchildren now."

"Sorry, I just have one more question. What is this place?"

"Ha! You're not from here, I can tell. Everyone around here knows this town. We used to be famous for our library."

"No, no, I know that place. I've been before. With my brother."

"Are you sure? If you'd been here, you'd know people from as far as five townships over used to come here to borrow books. We were known everywhere around here for that. Whenever I could tell people that I was from Five Groves, I felt very proud."

"But how did all the books get in *here*?"

"Well, you know, people started going to the cities to live after the Chairman died. The librarian couldn't earn any money from what he was doing, so finally his daughter told him they had to go to Shanghai. I was tired of farming, looking for a business opportunity. I used some savings to buy the collection. I've always liked books, since I was a kid. That's the only reason I did this stupid thing. Everyone else now is rich! Opening their chicken farms, their factories to manufacture candy. Every time I heard about something like that, I had to say no because I was running this store." He sighed. "Well, anyway. It's enough to live."

The tinkling sound of glass rang through the shop, and Yitian looked back to see the grandchildren rolling marbles, squatting in the corner of the room they'd staked out for themselves. From the back room, where the old woman had disappeared, Yitian heard the sounds of a knife slicing neatly through vegetables. Soon the smell of cooking garlic drifted through the store.

"Time for lunch, time for lunch," the man said. "So, do you want to buy anything?"

Yitian pointed to the *Twenty-Four Histories*.

"Just this? Or the whole set?"

"Just the one, please."

"Suit yourself."

The old woman returned to say goodbye. In between batting at the grandchildren, who were now swarming her knees, she wrapped the book in thin tissue paper.

"A book like this deserves to be protected, yes?"

She handed the book to him.

"If you find your father, will you let us know?"

Yitian nodded.

"Ask him if he remembers us."

He felt weak in the knees as they exited the shop. He leaned against his mother and she circled her arm around his waist to steady him.

When he put his own arm around her shoulders, the book fell to the ground. They stood there, two people interlocked and bound. He felt the certainty, and he was sure she did, too, that his father had stood in this place. Wobbling, like them. There was no making sense of this moment; all his equations and models had fled him. He wanted only a single thing. Not the miracle of finding his father now, but only that he'd been there to receive his father's gift.

Part 6

回归

RETURN

———

Thirty-nine

1993

Before he placed it in his suitcase, he carefully wrapped the book inside a square of cotton padding that his mother had cut for him from an old blanket. She'd also given him an arm-length section of twine, which he bound tightly around the package and knotted around the top. He'd been in a rush for these last few hours, but this very last thing he did slowly.

"You can use that as a blanket for the child, too," his mother said to him, when he'd protested against her taking scissors to the quilt. "Much more than I need," she said, gesturing to the piles of blankets folded in the corner. He could recall the year to which each one belonged just by looking at the designs. The peonies against green bushes—those came from when he was five. His mother couldn't watch him while she worked in the fields, so she sent him to school early and he was the youngest of all the students there. The blue and yellow cranes with their necks intertwined were from the year Yishou had stopped going to school. His older brother had bunched the blankets under his fists in anger when their mother mentioned to him that he might return.

The square his mother cut for him to bring back to America was of blue morning glories against a white background, the simplest of them all, from the year of his grandfather's illness. The yellow that dribbled out of his grandfather's mouth had stained the white background. Though his mother scrubbed and scrubbed at it, the remnants of color remained, the spots as pale as sunlight now.

Earlier that day, after they returned from Five Groves, Yitian made up his mind to delay his ticket back. Another week—that was all he would give himself—for his father who remembered him in his last moments. Then, finally, he told himself he had to call Mali. He found a ride into the city and went to the telecommunications building.

"Yitian? Yitian? Is that you? I've been trying to reach you all day."

Her sound was so urgent and unknown to him that he almost admitted everything to her, right there. For a brief, desperate moment, he imagined what it would be like if she simply told him not to come back, if he remained in this village forever.

"I was busy saying goodbye to everyone here—" he began to grasp at some excuse, until she interrupted him to say she was pregnant.

And then he understood what he read as urgency in her voice was not that at all; instead, it was excitement at the unknown, an emotion that she almost never showed. It was not because she was an unhappy person, but because there was so little, even within that vast new world, that was truly indecipherable to her. An event had finally caught her off guard.

"Yitian? Yitian?" He heard Mali's voice through the drumming of blood in his ears. "Are you all right?"

"Yes, I'm very happy." He realized, as soon as he said the words, that they were, quite simply, the truth. As if his body had separated, he had the sudden awareness that he had a face and was smiling so much that he could feel the stretch of his cheeks.

"Finally," she said.

"Finally."

"We shouldn't give ourselves bad luck right now by telling everyone," she said. He agreed. "But," she added, "it's good you're with your mother now. You can tell her. Maybe the news will finally make her like me."

They both laughed. It was true, that all of these years his mother had never stopped holding Mali apart. The two of them rarely spoke with one another after the wedding.

He realized, on his way home, that he still didn't have any more clarity about what was worrying him before. He still did not know if he would tell Mali about Hanwen. He'd thought about Hanwen since they kissed, but not as much as he would have supposed. When he imagined the scene in the hotel room, he saw her face as if she were still seventeen, rather than as the woman she was now. And he saw, too, that he loved that girl because she came from a time before the worst thing that ever happened to him, and that loving her as she was then was an impossibility, a way of wishing for the past back. Living in that past, he could still believe the future was a perfect place where he would one day arrive. How easy they'd believed it would be! The gaokao, university, their life as scholars together. They'd thought their hope and ambition was enough.

When he first started dating Mali, he'd seen her one summer afternoon on campus, wearing a poplin dress that the breeze stirred around her calves. How she'd walked with the balance of her body on the balls of her feet, paused to speak to a friend she saw, unafraid to move her arms around and take up space, so different from all the other girls he knew back then. Already at that moment he had a presage of what her gesture meant. Sometimes the sadness came over him like a sudden summer rainstorm in those early days. But each time he thought too much of the past life, she closed the lid of the box containing his memory and instead took him into her arms: her embrace an antidote against the missing. She gently pushed the memories away into negative space and held him apart from the absence. Still, when he first met her, he thought he would never love her like he'd loved Hanwen; that the best he could do was come close. But now, he thought: I do not know what the difference between love and not-love is. When had I crossed that threshold, when had I relinquished?

And what of the future? Now he knew that, one day, he would bring his child here. He imagined hoisting a chubby toddler onto his shoulders while they walked through the village, pointing to the fields and saying, *This, here, is where your father used to work.* He would take the child through his old home, bring them around to show off to neighbors, and together they would walk deep into the fields until the grass made their legs itch. He wondered how his child might see this place, dirty and dusty, how they might cry because of the mosquitoes biting into the soft flesh under their skin; how, if that happened, he would pretend to fuss and coo but really in his heart he would be too happy to worry.

It wasn't without a pang that the dream ended. The child would always see this place not as their own home, but someone else's.

His mother cried for a long time when he told her the news, then went immediately to the grave mounds to offer thanks to the ancestors. After all the doctor's visits and what he'd learned of how the body could become an object ordered and solved, a single event like this could still remain as mysterious and sudden as it would have been in the past.

Perhaps she could come to America to help them take care of the grandchild, he said. Now that he had a green card, he would be able to sponsor a visa for her. To his surprise, she replied, yes, perhaps I will do that.

That night, he washed his mother's feet. When she went to boil the water as she did every night before bedtime, he said, "Sit, Ma, I'll do it."

She acquiesced, placing her stool against the wall and leaning back.

He mixed the boiled water with cold water from the well and dipped his fingers in to check the temperature. Then he brought the wooden tub over to where his mother sat. Gently, he lifted her feet and placed them into the water. The skin around her bones there was thinner than paper and seemed to hover apart from her frame like an insufficient blanket.

When her feet were submerged, she sighed. He washed her in silence for some minutes, rubbing soap and then gliding water over the skin now made slippery. At moments she wiggled her toes and flexed her heels.

He looked up at her and asked, "You don't think he'll ever make it back, do you?"

She didn't reply for a long while. When she finally spoke, her voice came to him from above, as if from another world, a world of certainty and acceptance.

"I knew he wasn't going to make it back since the day he left. I had a feeling."

His mother used to drop everything and rush to the door whenever his father announced *I'm home* from the courtyard entrance. During those weeks when his father came back from the barracks every year, she beamed doing even the most ordinary of chores.

"There were many years when you weren't here," she said, as if she knew what he was imagining.

"I know that, Ma. I'll never be able to make them up to you."

"No, that's not what I mean. I know why you stayed over there. You have your own family to take care of now."

"Still, I could have come—"

She interrupted him. "After he became sick, your father talked about you a lot. He called you Yishou, but he was always talking about you. I realized that when we were talking to the shopkeeper. I thought that it was just because of the disease, that he was suddenly misremembering Yishou's name. But now I know he was talking about you, all that time."

He cried silently as he pushed hot water into the webbing between her toes. He imagined the night before his father left, his mother washing his feet to prepare him for a journey she didn't know he would take. He imagined this, and all the nights that would have come before. His mother, boiling water and filling the tub. How she would have taken his wrinkled feet in her wrinkled hands. The feeling of one foot always stronger than the other, leading to the limp leg his father hated. There was someone his father must have become in that accumulation of nights and days. His father's story would have a beginning and an ending for which he couldn't stitch together a middle. And yet, Yitian had chosen his life. *He* made the blanks by leaving and refusing to come back, this final silence the agreement he signed with his act of departure. Forever, he would hope to retrieve the very things he'd decided to let go.

He looked back up at his mother and was struck by her sense of peace. It was a feeling he often thought about in America. Where to find it? Sometimes he woke up and rose in the darkest part of the night so that he could pace the empty streets by himself and discover that feeling. What he accessed would never be like her private emotion. Her peace wasn't self-aware; it was one derived from the simple fact of her living.

He lifted her feet out of the old wooden tub. The water's warmth returned some firmness to them, so they felt heavier and more powerful in his hands now, more like her strong feet that he remembered from before. He dried them in a towel, and then she rose and they both prepared for bed.

Forty

He wanted to ask for only one thing, and that was forgiveness. This was his single clear thought as he walked the road that led out of his village.

The night before had been sleepless, as many had become. Beside him his wife breathed softly as she slept. Sleeping here was never easy since he returned from the army barracks—it was too silent. He was accustomed to the collective sounds of all the men snoring or taking up space with their demented sleeptalk, the constant noise leaving little room for his own thoughts.

That night, lying in bed, the faces of his sons kept coming to him, as they did often now. One of his sons, Yitian, had gone to Beijing, but where was the other one? Last he could remember, Yishou had gone to Hefei City to help his younger brother take a college entrance exam. But what had happened after that? He had not heard from Yishou for a very long time.

Because he could not sleep, he rose from bed and paced the room while thinking about this question, not noticing when dawn came and his wife rose. She made breakfast while he sat at the kitchen table, and when she asked, *What are you thinking about*, he answered, *Nothing*. All the while, in his mind, he tried to remember where Yishou was. He followed the path of his son through the places he always went: the fields, the other village where he had a woman he would marry, and then there was always a sudden wall, hard as brick, that he came to and couldn't think past.

They had gone to Hefei together, and then what?

All throughout breakfast he muttered this question to himself. Only afterward, when his wife had gone out, did the answer occur to him. *He* had done something wrong. To both of his sons. That was why they never spoke to him anymore.

He did not know what his mistake was, or why they had ignored him for so long. It did not matter anymore; the only thing that mattered was that he needed to fix it. This was what he thought of as he pulled on his cloth shoes and packed a small plastic knapsack and tied it over his wrist. Whatever he'd done, he would go make it right. He just needed to find his sons first.

原谅我, he would say to them, as he dropped to his knees.

He walked for a few hours until he passed through a village he'd never seen before. Here, he saw Yitian for the first time, in the corner stand of a marketplace on a busy selling morning. There was dust all around the stalls from the movement of people and live animals, but there was the clear face of his son, looking as serious as he always did, handing a seller some money. When he tried to follow his son, however, Yitian had already disappeared.

No matter, he would see him again, later on his journey. The appearance meant he was on the right track.

He rested that night, and the next, under the thatched roof of an old abandoned cowshed that he passed. He remembered a time when there were those who lived in these sheds, always the poorest people in a village, but he hadn't seen something like that in a very long time. What had happened to all of them?

He did not sleep long that first night, or the next. The cold kept awakening him, even despite his jacket, and he was determined to get to his destination quickly.

W here is forgiveness? How far is it, and how long must I walk until I reach there? On the third day, he arrived at Five Groves Township. He remembered the place from the stories that his own father used to tell about the library there. His father, whom he missed all the time, too. He had not been kind to his father, but now he couldn't think of anything so important that it could be worth the silence.

He stopped a woman to ask where the library was, and she walked with him to a shop to which she said all the books had been moved.

"My father would have loved this place," he thought. "And so would have Yishou." Inside, there were two children running around among the stacks of books, and an old woman, slow on her feet, chasing after them.

"Are you looking for any book in particular?" she asked.

"The *Twenty-Four Histories*." Unlike everything else, the memory of this book's name came to him easily.

"I'll call my husband to look," she said.

While her husband came and opened a cabinet, he chatted with the two shopkeepers.

"This book is for my son. I'm going to Hefei to see him. He loves to read. Always has his head buried in some book."

"Then he must be doing well. Did he go to college?"

"Oh, yes. Well, he was accepted. But he stayed in the village instead."

"He stayed in the village? That was a mistake! All the rich people now, they went to college," the old lady said.

He was offended, but did not tell her so. "You wouldn't say that if you knew him. He's the best farmer in the whole village. We never go hungry with him working for us."

"Say what you want," the old woman said. "No farmer will ever be able to earn as much money as a college graduate. Not in these times we live in."

He opened his mouth to retort, but decided against it. He had the sensation that he'd had this conversation before, in a different place and time, but could not say with whom or when it had happened.

"How many would you like to buy?" The male shopkeeper motioned to the set of books he'd revealed in the cabinet, all without binding, their paper signatures showing.

"All of them."

The shopkeeper laughed. "I don't think you have enough money for all of them. Besides, how will you carry them home?"

They told him the price.

"I'll go get the money together, and then come back," he said.

"All right. Would you like to stay for dinner before you go?" the woman said to him, but her husband shushed her.

"He can't stay. He needs to go collect the money to buy the set, right?"

Right, right, he said. Even though he could sense the other man's rudeness to him, he didn't retort. There wasn't a point to wasting any more time.

How strangely they spoke to me, as if they did not believe me, he thought, after he'd left the shop. People spoke to him slowly and strangely all the time now, as if he were too stupid to understand what they said. He never could find the words to make them believe his mind worked.

As he walked on, he spoke to his father, to Yishou, and to Yitian. He tried to explain to them how much there was still left to say. I will go get money and buy the entire set of books, so we can finish our conversation, he told them.

The shopkeepers did not believe me because Yitian chose to leave forever. He realized this with a shock. He did not know where the sudden thought came from, but he knew immediately that it was the truth. He stopped walking, somewhere on this empty street in a town he'd never seen before. It took him every bit of concentration he had to follow the memory to its origin. Dimly, he saw Yishou lying on his stomach on a hospital bed. The awful red rash that had appeared, as if conjured by magic, on his back.

The sunset had begun while he was thinking and staring at his feet. He did not know what to do next. Beside him, there was a stoop leading to a closed store and he decided to sit there while he pondered his dilemma. What was he doing here? What had he been thinking, to believe he could make it all the way out here alone? He could no longer feel his hands, he noticed suddenly. He wanted, surely and desperately, to go home. His son was gone. Another was dead. How many days had it been since he left? Two, he thought. He could make it back. He had some money left. He rose, but instead of walking out of Five Groves Township toward Hefei, he turned around and tried to retrace his steps to the ones he'd taken out of the village.

As he walked, something amazing began to happen, something he could hardly believe. It was snowing! So rapidly, fat white flakes falling on his nose and eyelashes and exposed hands and then melting. Like he'd done when he was a child, he stuck out his tongue to catch the snowflakes and taste the bursts of coolness in his mouth. He was cold, colder than he ever remembered feeling before, but seeing the snowflakes made him happy.

His entire body was shivering, he realized. He needed to hurry. There was a woman waiting for him back home, and he did not know who she was, but she would be angry if he did not return in time for dinner. It was cold, so cold. How had the years accumulated and counted themselves, leaving him here? He could not remember.

原谅我, he thought. He repeated the words out loud, and dropped to his knees in the snow. He brought his forehead to the ground. Please forgive me. This one time, I ask for your pardon.

What does he look like as he falls? Yitian used to watch the men in the fields, their hoes arcing up and down as the farmers drove them again and again into the dirt. Or the men leading plows, rope drawn taut behind their backs, all the tension pulled there in an unbroken line.

He always thought they seemed as if they were just about to fall. How would that look—clumsy and hard, face-first into the yellow soil? No, it would be like this: the knees catching upon the ground before the fall, a moment of pleading in the snow before the body gave out.

Acknowledgments

When I first began harboring the secret dream of writing, I could not have imagined that I'd really one day get to have a published book, and I would really never have, if not for the kindness shown to me by friends, family, and teachers in the years since then.

Maria Hummel, my first writing professor, was so warm and insightful that a confused economics major began to consider the possibilities of writing. Since then, I've been lucky to have the kindest teachers and mentors to guide me: Garth Greenwell, Liam Callanan, Rachel Smith, Christopher Tilghman, Jeffery Renard Allen, Micheline Aharonian Marcom, Tracie Morris, Ethan Canin, Jamel Brinkley, and Charles D'Ambrosio. Thank you, especially, to Lan Samantha Chang, for letting me come to Iowa twice, and for the hours of life and writing advice. I look up to you very much.

Thank you to the members of Garth Greenwell's 2020 Tin House Summer Workshop and Liam Callanan's 2019 Bread Loaf Summer Workshop for their comments on this book. Particular gratitude goes to the 2019 Novel Workshop at Iowa, for reading 150+ pages and helping me to figure out where it was going. Several early readers provided much-needed feedback: Samantha Xu, Alonzo Vereen,

Gemma Sieff, Ada Zhang, Niuniu Teo, and Amir Tarsha. Xochitl Gonzalez and IfeOluwa Nihinlola read almost as many drafts of this book as I did myself.

I am indebted to my team of Juli(e)'s. I could not have dreamed I'd get such a supportive team. To my agent Julie Barer, thank you for believing in this book and for generously providing helpful comments through so many rounds of edits. I feel unbelievably lucky to work with you. To my editor, Juliana Kiyan, thank you for your vision of this book and helping me to see my own more clearly. I'm so glad we get to do our first books together. Thanks also to Nicole Cunningham for her smart comments, and the entire team at the Book Group. At Penguin Press, I'd like to thank Victoria Lopez and Lavina Lee for all their help with production, and Grace Han for the beautiful cover design. Sam Mitchell and Lauren Lauzon have been amazing and enthusiastic shepherds of this book into the world.

In Iowa City and Charlottesville, I expected small-town dreariness and instead found community and friendship. In Iowa City, thanks to Matthew B. Kelley, Santiago Sanchez, Jeffery Boyd, Abigail Carney, Jing Jian, Kirsten Johnson, and David McDevitt. My gratitude to Sasha Khlemnik for keeping the workshop alive and helping me with all my many, many logistical struggles, to Deb West and Jan Zenisek for all the kindness, and to Jane Van Voorhis for her championing of emerging writers. I'd also like to thank the Truman Capote Foundation for financial support while I worked on this book. Thanks to all my friends in Charlottesville: Khaddafina Mbabazi, Suzie Eckl, Miriam Grossman, Jessica Walker, Juan E. Suarez, Helena Chung, Barbara Moriarty, Jeb Livingood, and Lisa Russ Sparr. And a special shout-out to Diana C. Brawley, whose therapy changed my entire life.

I'm so grateful to the work of many scholars whose research and writing helped me tremendously in writing this book: Yunxiang Yan,

Chen Huiqin, Chen Shehong, Anita Chan, Wang He Sheng, Zuo Jiafu for research on customs, life, and the environment of rural China; Anne McLaren, Thomas B. Gold, Jonathan Unger, Thomas P. Bernstein, and Liyan Qin for their work on the sent-down youth; Jie Li for insight on the Shanghai longtang ecosystem; Gao Yue for the same in the Beijing hutongs; Emily Honig, Lisa Rofel, and Li Yu-ning for work on Chinese women in the 1960s through 1980s, and sexual mores; and Joseph Esherick, Andrew Walder, Yang Su, Jiangsui He, Kang Zhengguo, for their writing on life during the Cultural Revolution. The collection *Some of Us*, edited by Xueping Zhong, Wang Zheng, and Bai Di, was particularly helpful in writing about sent-down girls and Chinese women's lives in the 1970s and 1980s, especially the essays by Naihua Zhang, Zhang Zhen, and Jiang Jin. I also relied on blogs from Wang Li, Ding Ning, Wang Xiaoni, Luo Yaqi, Cheng Yan, Li Ting, Li Yunshen, Qian Chang, Chen Xianqing, and countless other anonymous memoir bloggers for personal accounts of being sent down and taking the 1977 gaokao. Finally, thanks to He Xiaoxi and Ning Ayi for generously speaking with me in person about your experiences during this time. The gaokao exam and study questions came from 1977 archives from various provinces, but the Lu Xun quote did not appear on any test that year. Any and all remaining historical errors in this book are solely my own.

Thank you to all my friends who have provided support, both in writing and in life, in the years while I worked on this book: Daniel Agness, Paul Toribio, Amanuel Abebe, King Adjei-Frimpong, Sudarshana Chanda, Christopher Murphy, Alexandria S. Williams, Liu Ruoxi, Zhou Tianyao, Jing Hao Liong, Caitlin Spring, Alexandra Gray, Tianlang Shan, James Honsa, Allison Otis, Robert Burns, Austin Deyan, Brandon Liu, Ian Chan, Jodie Ha, Matthew Colford, and A. J. Sugarman. Special thanks to Will Toaspern, the first person who

I confessed a writing aspiration to on a drunken and frigid Boston evening and who didn't let me forget it on the hungover morning. Meredith Wheeler, there is no one I would rather travel the world with more. Lexie Frosh, I'm so glad you talked to me across the bathroom stalls that evening when we were eighteen.

My biggest resource in writing this book was my own family. I spent two magical years in China, made so by the hospitality of everyone there. Thank you for making me feel more at home than I ever thought possible, and for answering countless questions about the world of this book. Thanks to 念念姐姐, 宇阳哥哥, 涵涵弟弟, 辰辰姐姐, 晓军舅舅, 郭敏舅母, 小姥, 小姑爷, 大佬, 大姑爷, 三姨奶奶, 涂平, 美方舅母, and 俊明舅舅. And my 阿奶.

This book is for my grandma, who loved me very much and who I wish had lived to see it.

Thanks, last and first, goes to my family: my brother, Isaac, for the sweetness and advice beyond your years. And to my parents, for everything. I wrote this book thinking about all we couldn't say.